Interzone

Edited by James Grauerholz

PICADOR
published by **Pan Books**

Interzone

William S.
Burroughs

First published in the United States 1989 by
Viking Penguin Inc

First published in Great Britain 1989 in Picador by
Pan Books Ltd

This Picador paperback edition published 1990 by
Pan Books Ltd Cavaye Place London SW10 9PG

9 8 7 6 5 4 3 2

ISBN 0 330 31659 1

Passages from *Naked Lunch* used by permission of
Grove Press, a division of Wheatland Corporation.

"The Finger," "Lee's Journals,"
"An Advertising Short for TV," "Antonio the Portuguese
Mooch," "Displaced Fuzz," "Spare Ass Annie,"
and "The Dream Cops" first appeared in
Early Routines, Cadmus Editions.

"The Conspiracy" was previously published in *Kulchur*.

Printed in England by Clays Ltd, St Ives plc

Contents

Introduction

William Burroughs has always presented interesting challenges to his editors. Throughout his career he has often rejected the concept of linear composition or narrative. Moreover, much of his significant work was written in times of great personal disarray and tossed off in various directions, especially to friends in correspondence. He is also one of the great recyclers in literary history, a programmatic one—in the creation of his powerful language mosaics, Burroughs will use whatever materials are at hand. The scattered circumstances of his literary efforts are reflected in the scattered provenance of much of Burroughs' archival material. In the long run, there will be plenty of work for the critics and the textual scholars of Burroughs' work to perform as they begin to unravel the tangled history of Burroughs' works: published, unpublished, and perhaps yet to be discovered.

This volume, however, may be described as a product of the medium run. This book was conceived as a response to the news in 1984 that the original manuscript of *Interzone*, the working title of the book that, in somewhat different form, was to become *Naked Lunch*, was rediscovered among Allen Ginsberg's papers at Columbia University. It was soon apparent that the *Interzone* manuscript did contain unpublished material of great value and interest. The Burroughs of the *Interzone* period was a man breaking through into unexplored literary territory.

The same is true of writings leading up to that breakthrough. Many of Burroughs' texts from the period between the completion of his novel *Queer* and the beginning of *Interzone/Naked Lunch* (roughly 1953–58) have seen publication only in fugitive ways: included, sometimes in fragmentary form, in larger works or in various collections of uncertain duration and availability. Much else of value has remained in manuscript form until this time. Until now, the reader or critic wishing to understand how the precise, laconic and deadpan writer of *Junky* and *Queer* transformed himself into the uncompromising prophet and seer of *Naked Lunch* has had to piece the puzzle together from multiple sources, with several crucial pieces missing. *Interzone* has been compiled with the intention that readers may now be able to see that transformation take place in the course of one volume.

William Burroughs was almost thirty-nine years old when he departed Mexico City for the last time, in January of 1953. He left behind him the shambles of his life until that age: a St. Louis childhood and Harvard education, followed by a miscellany of odd jobs in Chicago and New York. In 1944 he had first become addicted to heroin; in that same year he met Allen Ginsberg at Columbia. These two circumstances would have a profound effect on his development as a writer.

As Burroughs' legal difficulties from his addiction mounted, he was obliged to move on from New York: to East Texas, New Orleans, and finally Mexico City, while Ginsberg and Jack Kerouac remained in New York, giving rise to an ample correspondence, which in turn led directly to Burroughs' discovery of his writing talents. Ginsberg enjoyed the intelligence and humor of Burroughs' letters from the far-flung precincts of Louisiana and Mexico, and he continually encouraged Burroughs to consider himself a writer.

A forged-prescription arrest had precipitated the departure from New York, in 1946; in New Orleans a 1949 marijuana arrest had put him through the rigors of heroin withdrawal in a jail cell; and although at first blush he found the liberal mores of Mexico much to his liking, in time the abuse of drugs and alcohol led to the careless, accidental death of his wife, Joan Vollmer, on September 6, 1951. A drunken pistol game of William Tell in an apartment above the Bounty Bar ended in tragedy for both.

In the spring of 1950, after about six months in Mexico City, Burroughs had begun writing a first-person account of his experiences in the junk world, which he entitled *Junk*. Ginsberg's friend Carl Solomon had interested his uncle in publishing such an account as an Ace Books paperback, and a contract was signed in July 1952. The book appeared as *Junkie: Confessions of an Unredeemed Drug Addict* a year later. Not included in this text was the second part of the original book, entitled *Queer*, which was begun in the spring of 1951. (*Junkie* was re-edited, with censored passages restored, and republished as *Junky* by Viking Penguin in 1977; *Queer* was finally published by Viking in 1985.)

As *Queer* relates, Burroughs was infatuated with a young American boy called Allerton and took him along on a trip to Ecuador in a fruitless search for *yagé*, a reputedly telepathic drug. He returned to Mexico City only days before the fatal incident. During the course of the novel, the protagonist, Lee, develops and elaborates an absurdist form of soliloquy known as the "routine," in his constant attempts to capture and hold Allerton's attention under increasingly difficult circumstances. This "Tom Sawyer handstand meant to impress the work's *blaue Blume*, Eugene Allerton," as Alan Ansen* describes it, takes on a life of its own, even as Allerton is drifting away from Lee.

As Burroughs recounts in "Lee's Journals" (page 63), he was often "possessed by a wild routine. . . . These routines will reduce me to a cinder." Such intensity naturally sought a human outlet, and as Allerton became emotionally distanced, and with Joan gone, Burroughs' friendship with Allen Ginsberg took on greater significance. After giving up on Allerton and Mexico City in late 1952, he made a visit to his parents' home in Palm Beach, Florida, and from there departed for Panama and the headwaters of the Río Putumayo in Colombia. Not two weeks after reaching Panama City, he wrote the first of what would be many "letters from the road" to Ginsberg, retailing his travels and adventures in a hilarious mixture of amorous anecdotes and anthropological essays.

Burroughs returned to the U.S. in August 1953, and after a month in Palm Beach, he returned to New York for the first time in six years. *Junkie* had now been published, and although it was hardly considered a literary event at the time, this encouraged him to go on with his writing. He stayed on East Seventh Street with Ginsberg, whose constant interest and warm responses to the stream of *"yagé* letters" had endeared him to Burroughs, far beyond anything he had felt for Ginsberg before. They worked together on a revised transcription of Burroughs' letters from the *yagé* trip, but Burroughs' dream of finding in Ginsberg the "perfectly sponta-

---

* Alan Ansen, *William Burroughs* (Sudbury, Mass.: Water Row Press, 1986).

neous, perfectly responsive companion" (Ansen, *ibid.*) was frustrated by Allen's lack of interest in a sexual relationship.

In early 1954 Burroughs sailed for Rome, Athens and eventually Tangier. He continued to woo Ginsberg during the middle fifties, entirely by correspondence, except for a memorable visit that Ginsberg and his new lover, Peter Orlovsky, made to Tangier in 1957. In his letters from the time of the visit, Ginsberg writes that he scarcely recognized "the new Bill Burroughs." By then Burroughs had almost completed the transition from suitor-correspondent to literary creator, which resulted in a profusion of manuscripts that he referred to in toto as *Interzone*. In these four crucial years, 1954–57, Burroughs had been transformed into a writer.

As he had done with *Junky* and the handful of more or less finished stories that Burroughs sent from Tangier to him in New York, Ginsberg assisted in the editing of the early drafts of *Interzone*. While visiting in 1957, he retyped portions of the raw manuscripts, as did Jack Kerouac and Alan Ansen, and they each proposed different chapter sequences. The best account of their attitudes toward the work at that time can be gleaned from Alan Ansen's pioneering and perceptive essay in *Big Table* in 1959, "Anyone Who Can Pick Up a Frying Pan Owns Death," collected in his 1986 Water Row Press booklet.

In April 1958, on Ginsberg's referral, Burroughs submitted a draft of *Interzone* to Lawrence Ferlinghetti's City Lights Books (by now the publishers of Ginsberg's *Howl*), but it was not accepted. Maurice Girodias of the Olympia Press in Paris also turned down the book. Ginsberg sent eighty pages of Burroughs' work to Irving Rosenthal, editor of the *Chicago Review*, but when University of Chicago authorities objected, Rosenthal published an issue privately as *Big Table, No. 1* in the spring of 1959. Included were ten episodes from *Interzone*, which was by then called *Naked Lunch*, at Kerouac's suggestion. Within a few months, Girodias had published the novel in France. The rest is literary history.

What remains of these early writings, between the period of composition of *Junky* and *Queer* and the publication of *Naked Lunch*? The letters from South America during 1953 were finally edited, with letters added from Ginsberg's own 1960 trip to Peru in search of *yagé*, and responses from Burroughs, and this book was published as *The Yagé Letters* by City Lights in 1963. A short collection of stories, journals and letter fragments was edited for publication in 1982 by Jeffrey Miller's Cadmus Editions in Santa Barbara, in a small edition now out of print, under the title *Early Routines*. A large surviving group of letters to Ginsberg was also published in 1982, under the eponymous title *Letters to Allen Ginsberg, 1953–1957*, by Full Court Press; this volume, also now out of print, is a valuable companion to the present *Interzone*.

Many of these 1950s writings are fragmentary in nature; in many cases, pages that began as letters to Ginsberg were not sent but condensed and retyped together with other material; the letters that *were* sent included long patches of work in progress. Therefore the lines between "letters," "journals" and "writings" are blurred, at least as regards the manuscript material that remains available from the period. And Burroughs' papers have had a harrowing voyage to the hands of today's scholars: what exists from the period (mostly at Columbia University, Arizona State University and the Humanities Research Center of the University of Texas at Austin, as well as the author's own collection) is jumbled and incomplete, and many other manuscripts remain in uncooperative private hands at this writing. So what is included in this volume has been determined, in part, and fittingly enough, by random factors.

One of the hallmarks of Burroughs' style is the reappearance of many phrases and images throughout his work. This is partly the result of Burroughs' multifarious memory, partly due to the chaos of his manuscript drafts, and partly inherent in the nature of the "cut-up" technique. This "repetition," or self-appropriation, may even at times be unintentional, but overall it unites the whole of

Burroughs' work and lends a kaleidoscopic quality to the writing—and what is a kaleidoscope but a device to reassemble endlessly the same particles? As if anticipating modern atomic physics, his world model is that of an indeterminate universe of endless permutation and recombination. Finding the conventional novel form inadequate to this task, he deconstructs and ransacks it, so that his form is as reflective of twentieth-century life as his content is predictive of it.

"Twilight's Last Gleamings" is often cited as Burroughs' first attempt at writing; it was written in Cambridge, Massachusetts, in 1938, with the collaboration of his childhood friend Kells Elvins. The thirteen-page manuscript at Arizona does not appear to be the original but a reconstruction from memory at some later point, when Burroughs was using a typewriter with the Spanish inverted exclamation point, hence probably in Tangier. The author has written that the piece was inspired by the sinking of a ship, the *Morro Castle*, in 1935, and this rollicking, exploding fantasy pointed the way toward his eventual literary destination. Much shorter versions of it have appeared throughout his writings, most notably in *Nova Express* (Grove, 1964); this is the fullest version yet published.

"The Finger" is an account of how Burroughs deliberately cut off the last joint of his left little finger, in New York during 1939, partly in an attempt to impress Jack Anderson, a young man with whom he was preoccupied. This chilling episode gives a rare glimpse of Burroughs' emotional state at that time. In a letter to Ginsberg from Tangier, apparently written in 1954, he mentions having sent the story to Allen to see if it could be sold for publication; so it was probably written soon after his arrival in Tangier.

"Driving Lesson" is a quasi-autobiographical account of an incident from 1940, during Jack Anderson's visit to Burroughs in

St. Louis. It seems to have been written during Burroughs' Mexico stay but was in any case rewritten and sent to Ginsberg sometime in 1954. In a letter of August 18, 1954, Burroughs wrote: "As regards that story, you might try placing it, I don't know just where"; and again, August 26: "I rewrote the story about the car wreck with Jack A." In *The Wild Boys* (Grove, 1971) and *Port of Saints* (Am Here, 1974; Blue Wind, 1980), the car has become a Duesenberg, and Jack is "the new boy, John Hamlin," "a mysterious figure from a parallel dimension"; the crash itself takes on the magical power of time travel.

"The Junky's Christmas" dates from Mexico or early Tangier days, and is set in New York in the 1940s. Danny the Car Wiper is a young junky trying desperately to score on Christmas Day. His experiences are written in a straightforward third-person narrative style, somewhat reminiscent of Truman Capote's. This sentimental story was the basis of a later, and much different, story: "The Priest, They Called Him," published in the London *Weekend Telegraph* in 1967 and collected in *Exterminator!* (Viking, 1973). Burroughs has written several "Christmas stories" over the years, but never again in this style.

"Lee and the Boys" appears to have been written in the Tangier period. The untitled story begins in manuscript on a page with paragraphs also found in an April 1954 letter to Ginsberg. Although it has an indeterminate ending, it is worth reproducing here for its remarkably straightforward and detailed self-portrait of Burroughs' daily life in Tangier at that time. We see him scoring his drugs, shooting up and sitting down to work on a "letter to Ginsberg," and then receiving his boyfriend KiKi for an evening's diversion. His emotions about the boys of Tangier are heartbreakingly felt, and his bravado has a tremulous edge.

"In the Café Central," also from this time, is a very funny sketch of the social scene in the Socco Chico, written without much of Burroughs' trademark exaggeration. The claustrophobia of Tangier's small-town feel, at least among the expatriate queer set, comes across vividly.

"Dream of the Penal Colony" is labeled in manuscript "Fall of 1953," which suggests it was written in New York at the beginning of Burroughs' stay with Ginsberg. Its point of departure is the first paragraph of the passage in *Queer* where Lee and Allerton are staying in a chilly hotel room in Quito, Ecuador: "That night Lee dreamed he was in a penal colony. All around were high, bare mountains. . . . He tightened the belt of his leather jacket and felt the chill of final despair." In the novel, Lee gets up and crawls into Allerton's bed, shaking with cold and junk sickness. The parallel suggested is between Allerton and Ginsberg, objects of Burroughs' affection and desire, and if this fragment was actually not written until after work on *Queer* stopped, in late 1952, the compositional intention toward Ginsberg is even clearer. But the boy in the story is modeled on Allerton, and the author paints a harsh picture of his own manipulative, changing moods and importuning routines.

"International Zone" was written in a deliberate attempt to achieve a magazine sale, via Ginsberg. The name of the piece refers, of course, to the quadripartite administration of Tangier, divided between the U.S., French, Spanish and English sectors. On January 12, 1955, Burroughs wrote to Ginsberg: "When I don't have inspiration for the novel [*Interzone*, then in progress], I busy myself with hack work. I am writing an article on Tangier. Perhaps *New Yorker:* 'Letter from Tangier.' " Again, on January 21: "I wrote an article on Tangier but it depresses me to see it even. It is so flatly an article like anybody could have written." On this point the author was mistaken; the language and style are distinctively his own. Here, between sociological information and analysis, are several incisive portraits of the habitués of the Socco Chico, and a snapshot of Burroughs' own image of himself on that set.

"International Zone" was apparently sent to Ginsberg in the

summer of 1955, perhaps nine months after it was first composed. In the original manuscript there is a postscript (not included in the piece as presented here), which exemplifies a typically Burroughsian shift of viewpoint on a new locale:

"Since I wrote this article, conditions in Tangier have changed. There is a strong feeling of tension and hostility. Children shout insults as you walk by. The streets are no longer safe. A Canadian acquaintance of mine, coming home at 3 A.M., was stabbed in the back. . . . The Nationalists have already demanded the integration of Tangier into an independent Morocco. They may resort to terrorism if the occupying powers refuse to relinquish the International Zone. . . . Business has hit a new low. The tourist trade is falling off. Many of the residents are talking about leaving." This shift echoes the transformation of Mexico City, from being "one of the few places left where a man can really live like a Prince," in Burroughs' 1949 letters to Ginsberg, to "this cold ass town," in a letter from late 1952, again to Ginsberg: "I am so fed up with these chiseling bastards I don't ever want to see Mexico again."

In late 1954, when "International Zone" was composed, Burroughs was changing his view of Tangier as a superlatively liberal culture where boys and drugs were concerned, to a vision of the City as a great world crossroads for losers and lamsters, an "interzone" between failed and abandoned old lives (like Burroughs' own) and the dream of a new life ahead—the sort of "waiting room" that is a recurrent image in Burroughs' fiction. In the article, he writes that "Tangier is a vast penal colony," which again recalls the dream he had in Quito in 1951. Especially interesting is Burroughs' self-portrait as "Brinton, who writes unpublishably obscene novels and exists on a small income. He undoubtedly has talent, but his work is hopelessly unsalable."

This same passage is echoed in the first pages of "Lee's Journals," which were assembled from sections of letters to Ginsberg and pages written in Burroughs' attempt to find his own voice and to record his experiences in Tangier. Also included here are several short untitled fictional and autobiographical sketches, many written during his series of heroin "cures" at Benchimal Hospital. The fag scene of Tangier is bitingly depicted, and it is interesting to observe that Burroughs' first encounters with the late Brion Gysin ("Algren") were ambivalent, giving no hint of the almost symbiotic friendship the two men would later evolve.

The sketch (in "Lee's Journals") of "Martin" revisiting the Römanischer Baden in postwar Vienna surely draws on Burroughs' own experiences in that city in 1937. And "Mark Bradford," the playwright visiting Tangier who snubs Lee, may well be Tennessee Williams, with whom Burroughs did not become friends until the 1970s. Similarly, at his 1954 meeting with Paul Bowles, the latter "evinced no cordiality," but within two years not only was their friendship forged but Bowles had also brought Burroughs back together with Brion Gysin.

Increasingly, the journals record Burroughs' attempts to define himself as a writer, and the frantic routines continue to pour out of him. His extended sketch of Antonio, the Portuguese mooch mentioned in "International Zone," is hilarious and ghastly. The vision of Antonio's mother's kidney-dialysis machine being unhooked leads to a wise-guy cops routine about the "displaced fuzz" paying a disconnection visit. There follows an account of a bust by "dream cops," which is the forerunner of the "Hauser and O'Brien" section of *Naked Lunch*: two imaginary cops burst in on "the Agent" and demand to inspect first his arm, then his penis. After a surreal dialogue, they depart, but one of them laughs and leaves behind a gold filling, which the Agent finds next morning, calling the irreality of the dream into question.

Some filling in is necessary for the next section, "The Conspiracy," to make narrative sense. In the "Hauser and O'Brien" episode, the Agent or "Lee" shoots the two cops dead and escapes from the hotel. He finds his pusher, Nick, and explains that he is leaving town and must stock up on junk. Nick makes small talk about the connection's frequent delays, and then shrugs: "What can I say to him? He knows I'll wait." At this point "The Conspiracy" picks up: "Yes, they know we'll wait," and Lee muses over the identity of the stoolie who has fingered him. The pages that follow were taken from the original 1958 *Interzone* manuscript.

"Iron Wrack Dream," so named by Ginsberg, records a vision of "the City" as "a vast network of levels . . . connected by gangways and cars that run on wires and single tracks." This futuristic dream was to be seminal to Burroughs' image of the City in *Interzone*. The nightclubs that are "built on perilous balconies a thousand feet over the rubbish and rusty metal of the City" are reminiscent of Lee's experiences in the "Mexico City Return" section of *Queer*: "I walked around with my camera and saw a wood and corrugated-iron shack on a limestone cliff in Old Panama, like a penthouse." They also call to mind the collapsing Mexican balconies of "Tío Mate Smiles" in *The Wild Boys*. Here we can see how Burroughs refines and poetically cross-associates his observations and dream images.

Incomplete fragments of unpublished letters to Ginsberg around 1955, or retyped versions of them, are found in the Arizona State collection and fittingly conclude "Lee's Journals," since they furnish an explicit statement of the literary direction Burroughs was moving in. As he wrote to Ginsberg on October 21, 1955: "The selection chapters [of *Interzone*] form a sort of mosaic, with the cryptic significance of juxtaposition, like objects abandoned in a hotel drawer, a form of still life." It is clear from these early thematic propositions that Burroughs' first encounter in 1959 with the "cut-up" method of writing, as developed by Brion Gysin from the Dada movement's existing aleatory and collage techniques, would exert an inescapable attraction for him and revolutionize his work.

The original *Interzone* manuscript is located in the Ginsberg collection at Butler Library, Columbia University, and consists of 175 pages, comprising twelve sections: "WORD"; "Panorama (Andrew Kief and the K.Y. Scandal)"; "Voices"; "County Clerk"; "Interzone University"; "Islam, Inc."; "Hassan's Rumpus Room"; "Benway"; "A.J.'s Annual Ball"; "Hospital" (including the "detective story" later divided into "Hauser and O'Brien" and "The Conspiracy"); "The Technical Psychiatry Conference"; and "The Market." This first sequence was decided upon with the help of Ginsberg and Ansen in Paris, in early 1958.

In the course of assembling the final *Naked Lunch* manuscript, the majority of these pages were used—but the longest and most unusual section, "WORD," was the source of only a few short lines and paragraphs, which were sprinkled mostly into the novel's final chapter, "An Atrophied Preface . . . Wouldn't You?" Wherever possible, these passages have been deleted from the otherwise intact "WORD" section, but the acute reader will find a handful of them retained, for the sake of the sense of surrounding lines. And a few short sections that remained unused from "Voices," "Interzone University," "Benway" and "A.J.'s Annual Ball" have been inserted at an appropriate place toward the end of "WORD," so that the text may end as it was originally written.

This manuscript lay forgotten for twenty-five years, until Barry Miles, Ginsberg's biographer, who was doing research at Columbia, came across it in 1984. At Miles' suggestion, a copy was sent to Burroughs in Kansas, where he was able to oversee the editing of the thematically and historically linked materials gathered together in this volume, which represents the first publication of "WORD," essentially in its entirety. This chapter was apparently typed by Kerouac, and in certain instances words that were clearly misread have been changed, but it is otherwise faithful to the 1958 text.

What is the significance of "WORD" to Burroughs' career as a writer? It shows the complete transformation of the straightforward style of the two early novels into a manic, surreal, willfully disgusting and violently purgative regurgitation of seemingly random images. "WORD" is a text written at the white heat of Burroughs' first command of this later style. Although it is the direct precursor of *Naked Lunch*, very little of this text was used in that novel, and as far as can be readily determined, none of it was utilized in the composition of his next three books: *The Soft Machine*, *The Ticket That Exploded* and *Nova Express* (Olympia Press, 1961, 1962 and 1964). Ansen described it as: "WORD, in which the author, all masks thrown aside, delivers a long tirade, a blend of confession, routine and fantasy, ending in 'a vast Moslem muttering.' "

In his letters to Ginsberg throughout 1955–57, Burroughs wrote often of his progress with the writing of *Interzone*. December 20, 1956: "I will send along about 100 pages of *Interzone*, it is coming so fast I can hardly get it down, and shakes me like a great black wind through the bones." January 23, 1957: "*Interzone* is coming like dictation, I can't keep up with it. I will send along what is done so far. Read in any order. It makes no difference." There exist many other references in these letters; clearly, he was conscious of a climactic moment in his life, a turning point past which he would never be the same. But curiously, the tone and style of "WORD" are unique in Burroughs' work; he never returned to the same kind of profane, first-person sibylline word salad, although it marked the breakthrough into his own characteristic voice.

This book is meant to portray the development of Burroughs' mature writing style, and to present a selection of vintage Burroughs from the mid-1950s—a kind of writing he can no more repeat than he can once again be forty-four years old in Tangier. The willfully outrageous tone of voice represents the exorcism of his four decades of oppressive sexual and social conditioning, and his closely-observed experience of mankind's inexhaustible ugliness and ignorance. Only by dispensing with any concept of "bad taste" or self-repression could he liberate his writing instrument to explore the landscapes of Earth and Space in his work written over the following thirty years. Reading *Interzone*, you are present at the beginning.

—*James Grauerholz*

I. STORIES

TWILIGHT'S LAST GLEAMINGS

PLEASE IMAGINE AN EXPLOSION ON A SHIP

A paretic named Perkins sat askew on his broken wheelchair. He arranged his lips.

"You pithyathed thon of a bidth!" he shouted.

Barbara Cannon, a second-class passenger, lay naked in a first-class bridal suite with Stewart Lindy Adams. Lindy got out of bed and walked over to a window and looked out.

"Put on your clothes, honey," he said. "There's been an accident."

A first-class passenger named Mrs. Norris was thrown out of bed by the explosion. She lay there shrieking until her maid came and helped her up.

"Bring me my wig and my kimono," she told the maid. "I'm going to see the captain."

Dr. Benway, ship's doctor, drunkenly added two inches to a four-inch incision with one stroke of his scalpel.

"There was a little scar, Doctor," said the nurse, who was peering over his shoulder. "Perhaps the appendix is already out."

"The appendix *out!*" the doctor shouted. "*I'm* taking the appendix out! What do you think I'm doing here?"

"Perhaps the appendix is on the left side," said the nurse. "That happens sometimes, you know."

"Can't you be quiet?" said the doctor. "I'm coming to that!" He threw back his elbows in a movement of exasperation. "Stop breathing down my neck!" he yelled. He thrust a red fist at her. "And get me another scalpel. This one has no edge to it."

He lifted the abdominal wall and searched along the incision. "I know where an appendix is. I studied appendectomy in 1904 at Harvard."

The floor tilted from the force of the explosion. The doctor reeled back and hit the wall.

"Sew her up!" he said, peeling off his gloves. "I can't be expected to work under such conditions!"

At a table in the bar sat Christopher Hitch, a rich liberal; Colonel Merrick, retired; Billy Hines of Newport; and Joe Bane, writer.

"In all my experience as a traveler," the Colonel was saying, "I have never encountered such service."

Billy Hines twisted his glass, watching the ice cubes. "Frightful service," he said, his face contorted by a suppressed yawn.

"Do you think the captain controls this ship?" said the Colonel, fixing Christopher Hitch with a bloodshot blue eye. "Unions!" shouted the Colonel. "Unions control this ship!"

Hitch gave out with a laugh that was supposed to be placating but ended up oily. "Things aren't so bad, really," he said, patting at the Colonel's arm. He didn't land the pat, because the Colonel drew his arm out of reach. "Things will adjust themselves."

Joe Bane looked up from his drink of straight rye. "It's like I say, Colonel," he said. "A man—"

The table left the floor and the glasses crashed. Billy Hines remained seated, looking blankly at the spot where his glass had been. Christopher Hitch rose uncertainly. Joe Bane jumped up and ran away.

"By God!" said the Colonel. "I'm not surprised!"

Also at a table in the bar sat Philip Bradshinkel, investment banker; his wife, Joan Bradshinkel; Branch Morton, a St. Louis politician; and Morton's wife, Mary Morton. The explosion knocked their table over.

Joan raised her eyebrows in an expression of sour annoyance. She looked at her husband and sighed.

"I'm sorry this happened, dear," said her husband. "Whatever it is, I mean."

Mary Morton said, "Well, I declare!"

Branch Morton stood up, pushing back his chair with a large red hand. "Wait here," he said. "I'll find out."

Mrs. Norris pushed through a crowd on C Deck. She rang the elevator bell and waited. She rang again and waited. After five minutes she walked up to A Deck.

The Negro orchestra, high on marijuana, remained seated after the explosion. Branch Morton walked over to the orchestra leader.

"Play 'The Star-Spangled Banner,' " he ordered.

The orchestra leader looked at him.

"What you say?" he asked.

"You black baboon, play 'The Star-Spangled Banner' on your horn!"

"Contract don't say nothing 'bout no Star-Spangled Banner," said a thin Negro in spectacles.

"This old boat am swinging on down!" someone in the orchestra yelled, and the musicians jumped down off the platform and scattered among the passengers.

Branch Morton walked over to a jukebox in a corner of the saloon. He saw "The Star-Spangled Banner" by Fats Waller. He put in a handful of quarters. The machine clicked and buzzed and began to play:

"OH SAY CAN YOU? YES YES"

Joe Bane fell against the door of his stateroom and plunged in. He threw himself on the bed and drew his knees up to his chin. He began to sob.

His wife sat on the bed and talked to him in a gentle hypnotic voice. "You can't stay here, Joey. This bed is going underwater. You can't stay here."

Gradually the sobbing stopped and Bane sat up. She helped him put on a life belt. "Come along," she said.

"Yes, honey face," he said, and followed her out the door.

"AND THE HOME OF THE BRAVE"

Mrs. Norris found the door to the captain's cabin ajar. She pushed it open and stepped in, knocking on the open door. A tall, thin, red-haired man with horn-rimmed glasses was sitting at a desk littered with maps. He glanced up without speaking.

"Oh Captain, is the ship sinking? Someone set off a bomb, they said. I'm Mrs. Norris—you know, Mr. Norris, shipping business. Oh the ship *is* sinking! I know, or you'd say something. Captain, you will take care of us? My maid and me?" She put out a hand to touch the captain's arm. The ship listed suddenly, throwing her heavily against the desk. Her wig slipped.

The captain stood up. He snatched the wig off her head and put it on.

"Give me that kimono!" he ordered.

Mrs. Norris screamed. She started for the door. The captain took three long, springy strides and blocked her way. Mrs. Norris rushed for a window, screaming. The captain took a revolver from his side pocket. He aimed at her bald pate outlined in the window, and fired.

"You Goddamned old fool," he said. "Give me that kimono!"

Philip Bradshinkel walked up to a sailor with his affable smile.

"Room for the ladies on this one?" he asked, indicating a lifeboat.

The sailor looked at him sourly.

"No!" said the sailor. He turned away and went on working on the launching davit.

"Now wait a minute," said Bradshinkel. "You can't mean that. Women and children first, you know."

"Nobody goes on this lifeboat but the crew," said the sailor.

"Oh, I understand," said Bradshinkel, pulling out a wad of bills. The sailor snatched the money.

"I thought so," said Bradshinkel. He took his wife by the arm and started to help her into the lifeboat.

"Get that old meat outa here!" screamed the sailor.

"But you made a bargain! You took my money!"

"Oh for Chrissakes," said the sailor. "I just took your dough so it wouldn't get wet!"

"But my wife is a woman!"

Suddenly the sailor became very gentle.

"All my life," he said, "all my life I been a sucker for a classy dame. I seen 'em in the Sunday papers laying on the beach. Soft messy tits. They just lay there and smile dirty. Jesus they heat my pants!"

Bradshinkel nudged his wife. "Smile at him." He winked at the sailor. "What do you say?"

"Naw," said the sailor, "I ain't got time to lay her now."

"Later," said Bradshinkel.

"Later's no good. Besides she's special built for you. She can't give me no kids and she drinks alla time. Like I say, I just seen her in the Sunday papers and wanted her like a dog wants rotten meat."

"Let me talk to this man," said Branch Morton. He worked his fingers over the fleshy shoulder of his wife and pulled her under his armpit.

"This little woman is a mother," he said. The sailor blew his nose on the deck. Morton grabbed the sailor by the biceps.

"In Clayton, Missouri, seven kids whisper her name through their thumbs before they go to sleep."

The sailor pulled his arm free. Morton dropped both hands to his sides, palms facing forward.

"As man to man," he was pleading. "As man to man."

Two Negro musicians, their eyes gleaming, came up behind the two wives. One took Mrs. Morton by the arm, the other took Mrs. Bradshinkel.

"Can us have dis dance witchu?"

"THAT OUR FLAG WAS STILL THERE"

Captain Kramer, wearing Mrs. Norris' kimono and wig, his face heavily smeared with cold cream, and carrying a small suitcase, walked down to C Deck, the kimono billowing out behind him. He opened the side door to the purser's office with a pass key. A thin-shouldered man in a purser's uniform was stuffing currency and jewels into a suitcase in front of an open safe.

The captain's revolver swung free of his brassiere and he fired twice.

"SO GALLANTLY STREAMING"

Finch, the radio operator, washed down bicarbonate of soda and belched into his hand. He put the glass down and went on tapping out S.O.S.

"S.O.S. . . . S.S. *America* . . . S.O.S. . . . off Jersey coast . . . S.O.S. . . . son-of-a-bitching set . . . S.O.S. . . . might smell us . . . S.O.S. . . . son-of-a-bitching crew . . . S.O.S. . . . *Comrade* Finch . . . comrade in a pig's ass . . . S.O.S. . . . Goddamned captain's a brown artist . . . S.O.S. . . . S.S. *America* . . . S.O.S. . . . S.S. Crapbox . . ."

Lifting his kimono with his left hand, the captain stepped in behind the radio operator. He fired one shot into the back of Finch's head. He shoved the small body aside and smashed the radio with a chair.

"O'ER THE RAMPARTS WE WATCH"

Dr. Benway, carrying his satchel, pushed through the passengers crowded around Lifeboat No. 1.

"Are you all all right?" he shouted, seating himself among the women. "I'm the doctor."

"BY THE ROCKETS' RED GLARE"

When the captain reached Lifeboat No. 1 there were two seats left. Some of the passengers were blocking each other as they tried to force their way in, others were pushing forward a wife, a mother, or a child. The captain shoved them all out of his way, leapt into the boat and sat down. A boy pushed through the crowd in the captain's wake.

"Please," he said. "I'm only thirteen."

"Yes yes," said the captain, "you can sit by me."

The boat started jerkily toward the water, lowered by four male passengers. A woman handed her baby to the captain.

"Take care of my baby, for God's sake!"

Joe Bane landed in the boat and slithered noisily under a thwart. Dr. Benway cast off the ropes. The doctor and the boy started to row. The captain looked back at the ship.

"OH SAY CAN YOU SEE"

A third-year divinity student named Titman heard Perkins in his stateroom, yelling for his attendant. He opened the door and looked in.

"What do you want, thicken thit?" said Perkins.

"I want to help you," said Titman.

"Thtick it up and thwitht it!" said Perkins.

"Easy does it," said Titman, walking over toward the broken wheelchair. "Everything is going to be okey-dokey."

"Thneaked off!" Perkins put a hand on one hip and jerked the elbow forward in a grotesque indication of dancing. "Danthing with floothies!"

"We'll find him," said Titman, lifting Perkins out of the wheelchair. He carried the withered body in his arms like a child. As Titman walked out of the stateroom, Perkins snatched up a butcher knife used by his attendant to make sandwiches.

"Danthing with floothies!"

"BY THE DAWN'S EARLY LIGHT"

A crowd of passengers was fighting around Lifeboat No. 7. It was the last boat that could be launched. They were using bottles, broken deck chairs and fire axes. Titman, carrying Perkins in his arms, made his way through the fighting unnoticed. He placed Perkins in a seat at the stern.

"There you are," said Titman. "All set."

Perkins said nothing. He sat there, chin drawn back, eyes shining, the butcher knife clutched rigidly in one hand.

A hysterical crowd from second class began pushing from behind. A big-faced shoe clerk with long yellow teeth grabbed Mrs. Bane and shoved her forward. "Ladies first!" he yelled.

A wedge of men formed behind him and pushed. A shot sounded and Mrs. Bane fell forward, hitting the lifeboat. The wedge broke, rolling and scrambling. A man in an ROTC uniform with a .45 automatic in his hand stood by the lifeboat. He covered the sailor at the launching davit.

"Let this thing down!" he ordered.

As the lifeboat slid down toward the water, a cry went up from the passengers on deck. Some of them jumped into the water, others were pushed by the people behind.

"Let 'er go, God damn it, let 'er go!" yelled Perkins.

"Throw him out!"

A hand rose out of the water and closed on the side of the boat. Springlike, Perkins brought the knife down. The fingers fell into the boat and the bloody stump of hand slipped back into the water.

The man with the gun was standing in the stern. "Get going!" he ordered. The sailors pulled hard on the oars.

Perkins worked feverishly, chopping on all sides. "Bathtardth, thonthabitheth!" The swimmers screamed and fell away from the boat.

"That a boy."

"Don't let 'em swamp us."

"Atta boy, Comrade."

"Bathtardth, thonthabitheth! Bathtardth, thonthabitheth!"

"OH SAY DO DAT STAR-SPANGLED BANNER YET WAVE"

The Evening News

Barbara Cannon showed your reporter her souvenirs of the disaster: a life belt autographed by the crew, and a severed human finger.

"I don't know," said Miss Cannon. "I feel sorta bad about this old finger."

"O'ER THE LAND OF THE FREE"

THE FINGER

Lee walked slowly up Sixth Avenue from 42nd Street, looking in pawnshop windows.

"I must do it," he repeated to himself.

Here it was. A cutlery store. He stood there shivering, with the collar of his shabby chesterfield turned up. One button had fallen off the front of his overcoat, and the loose threads twisted in a cold wind. He moved slowly around the shopwindow and into the entrance, looking at knives and scissors and pocket microscopes and air pistols and take-down tool kits with the tools snapping or screwing into a metal handle, the whole kit folding into a small leather packet. Lee remembered getting one of these kits for Christmas when he was a child.

Finally he saw what he was looking for: poultry shears like the ones his father used to cut through the joints when he carved the turkey at Grandmother's Thanksgiving dinners. There they were, glittering and stainless, one blade smooth and sharp, the other with teeth like a saw to hold the meat in place for cutting.

Lee went in and asked to see the shears. He opened and closed the blades, tested the edge with his thumb.

"That's stainless steel, sir. Never rusts or tarnishes."

"How much?"

"Two dollars and seventy-nine cents plus tax."

"Okay."

The clerk wrapped the shears in brown paper and taped the package neatly. It seemed to Lee that the crackling paper made a deafening noise in the empty store. He paid with his last five dollars, and walked out with the shears heavy in his overcoat pocket.

He walked up Sixth Avenue, repeating: "I must do it. I've got to do it now that I've bought the shears." He saw a sign: *Hotel Aristo*.

There was no lobby. He walked up a flight of stairs. An old man, dingy and indistinct like a faded photograph, was standing behind a desk. Lee registered, paid one dollar in advance, and picked up a key with a heavy bronze tag.

His room opened onto a dark shaft. He turned on the light. Black stained furniture, a double bed with a thin mattress and sagging springs. Lee unwrapped the shears and held them in his hand. He put the shears down on the dresser in front of an oval mirror that turned on a pivot.

Lee walked around the room. He picked up the shears again and placed the end joint of his left little finger against the saw teeth, lower blade exactly at the knuckle. Slowly he lowered the cutting blade until it rested against the flesh of his finger. He looked in the mirror, composing his face into the supercilious mask of an eighteenth-century dandy. He took a deep breath, pressed the handle quick and hard. He felt no pain. The finger joint fell on the dresser. Lee turned his hand over and looked at the stub. Blood spurted up and hit him in the face. He felt a sudden deep pity for the finger joint that lay there on the dresser, a few drops of blood gathering around the white bone. Tears came to his eyes.

"It didn't do anything," he said in a broken child's voice. He adjusted his face again, cleaned the blood off it with a towel, and bandaged his finger crudely, adding more gauze as the blood soaked through. In a few minutes the bleeding had stopped. Lee picked up the finger joint and put it in his vest pocket. He walked out of the hotel, tossing his key on the desk.

"I've done it," he said to himself. Waves of euphoria swept through him as he walked down the street. He stopped in a bar and ordered a double brandy, meeting all eyes with a level, friendly stare. Goodwill flowed out of him for everyone he saw, for the whole world. A lifetime of defensive hostility had fallen from him.

Half an hour later he was sitting with his analyst on a park bench in Central Park. The analyst was trying to persuade him to go to Bellevue, and had suggested they "go outside to talk it over."

"Really, Bill, you're doing yourself a great disservice. When you realize what you've done you'll need psychiatric care. Your ego will be overwhelmed."

"All I need is to have this finger sewed up. I've got a date tonight."

"Really, Bill, I don't see how I can continue as your psychiatrist if you don't follow my advice in this matter." The analyst's voice had become whiny, shrill, almost hysterical. Lee wasn't listening; he felt a deep trust in the doctor. The doctor would take care of him. He turned to the doctor with a little-boy smile.

"Why don't you fix it yourself?"

"I haven't practiced since my internship, and I don't have the necessary materials in any case. This has to be sewed up right, or it could get infected right on up the arm."

Lee finally agreed to go to Bellevue, for medical treatment only.

At Bellevue, Lee sat on a bench, waiting while the doctor talked to somebody. The doctor came back and led Lee to another room, where an intern sewed up the finger and put on a dressing. The doctor kept urging him to allow himself to be committed; Lee was overcome by a sudden faintness. A nurse told him to put his head back. Lee felt that he must put himself entirely in the care of the doctor.

"All right," he said. "I'll do what you say."

The doctor patted his arm. "Ah, you're doing the right thing, Bill." The doctor led him past several desks, where he signed papers.

"I'm cutting red tape by the yard," the doctor said.

Finally Lee found himself in a dressing gown in a bare ward.

"Where is my room?" he asked a nurse.

"Your room! I don't know what bed you've been assigned to. Anyway you can't go there before eight unless you have a special order from the doctor."

"Where is my doctor?"

"Doctor Bromfield? He isn't here now. He'll be in tomorrow morning around ten."

"I mean Doctor Horowitz."

"Doctor Horowitz? I don't think he's on the staff here."

He looked around him at the bare corridors, the men walking around in bathrobes, muttering under the cold, indifferent eyes of an attendant.

Why, this is the psychopathic ward, he thought. *He put me in here and went away!*

Years later, Lee would tell the story: "Did I ever tell you about the time I got on a Van Gogh kick and cut off the end joint of my little finger?" At this point he would hold up his left hand. "This girl, see? She lives in the next room to me in a rooming house on Jane Street. That's in the Village. I love her and she's so stupid I can't make any impression. Night after night I lay there hearing her carry on with some man in the next room. It's tearing me all apart. . . . So I hit on this finger joint gimmick. I'll present it to her: 'A trifling memento of my undying affection. I suggest you wear it around your neck in a pendant filled with formaldehyde.'

"But my analyst, the lousy bastard, shanghaied me into the nuthouse, and the finger joint was sent to Potter's Field with a death certificate, because someone might find the finger joint and the police go around looking for the rest of the body.

"If you ever have occasion to cut off a finger joint, my dear, don't consider any instrument but poultry shears. That way you're sure of cutting *through* at the joint."

"And what about the girl?"

"Oh, by the time I got out of the nuthouse she'd gone to Chicago. I never saw her again."

DRIVING LESSON

The red-light district of East St. Louis is a string of wood houses along the railroad tracks: a marginal district of vacant lots, decaying billboards and cracked sidewalks where weeds grow through the cracks. Here and there you see rows of corn.

Bill and Jack were drinking in a bar on one corner of the district. They had been drinking since early afternoon, and were past the point of showing signs of drunkenness. Through the door, Bill could hear frogs croaking from pools of stagnant water in the vacant lots. Above the bar was a picture of Custer's Last Stand, distributed by courtesy of Anheuser-Busch. Bill knew the picture was valuable, like a wooden Indian. He was trying to explain this to the bartender, how an object gets rare and then valuable, the value increasing geometrically as collectors buy it up.

"Yeah," the bartender said, "you already told me that ten times. Anything else?" He walked to the other end of the bar and studied a *Racing Form*, writing on a slip of paper with a short indelible pencil.

Jack picked up a dollar of Bill's money off the bar. "I want to go in one of these houses," he said.

"All right . . . enjoy yourself." Bill watched Jack as he walked through the swinging door.

On the way back to St. Louis, Bill stopped the car.

"Want to try driving a bit?" he asked. "After all, you'll never get anywhere sitting on your ass. I remember when I was a reporter on the *St. Louis News*, my city editor sent me out to get a picture of some character committed suicide or something. . . . I forget. . . . Anyway, I couldn't get the picture. Some female relative came to the door and said, 'It would be a mockery,' and they wouldn't give me the picture.

"And next morning I went in the john and there is the city editor taking his morning crap. So he asks me: 'You got that picture, Morton?' And I said, 'No, I couldn't get it—at least not yet.'

" 'Well,' he says, 'you'll never get anywhere sitting on your ass.'

"So I start laughing, because that's exactly what he is doing, sitting on his ass, shitting. And I'll stack that up against any biographical anecdote for tasteless stupidity."

Jack looked at Bill blankly, and then laughed. *The plain truth is, he's bone stupid,* Bill thought. He opened the door and got out and walked around the car, through the headlights, and got in the other side. Jack slid in under the wheel, looking dubiously at the gadgets in front of him. He had only driven twice before in his life, both times in Bill's car.

"Oh, it's quite simple," Bill said. "You learn by doing. Could you learn to play piano by reading a book about it? Certainly not." He suddenly took Jack's chin in his hand and, turning Jack's face, kissed him lightly on the mouth. Jack laughed, showing sharp little eyeteeth.

"I always say people have more fun than anybody," Jack said.

Bill shuddered in the summer night. "I suppose they do," he said. "Well, let's get this show on the road."

Jack started the car with a grinding of gears. The car bucked, almost stopped, shot forward. Finally he got it in high and moving at an even speed.

"You'll never learn this way," Bill said. "Let's see a little speed."

It was three o'clock in the morning. Not a car on the street, not a sound. A pocket of immobile silence.

"A little speed, Jackie." Bill's voice was the eerie, disembodied voice of a young child. "That thing under your foot—push it on into the floor, Jackie."

The car gathered speed, tires humming on asphalt. There was no other sound from outside.

"We have the city all to ourselves, Jackie . . . not a car on the street. Push it all the way down . . . all the way in . . . all the way, Jackie."

Jack's face was blank, oblivious, the beautiful mouth a little open. Bill lit a cigarette from the dashboard lighter, muttering a denunciation of car lighters and car clocks. A piece of burning tobacco fell on his thigh, and he brushed it away petulantly. He looked at Jack's face and put the cigarettes away.

The car had moved into a dream beyond contact with the lives, forces and objects of the city. They were alone, safe, floating in the summer night, a moon spinning around the world. The dashboard shone like a fireplace, lighting the two young faces: one weak and beautiful, with a beauty that would show every day that much older; the other thin, intense, reflecting unmistakably the qualities loosely covered by the word "intellectual," at the same time with the look of a tormented, trapped animal. The speedometer crept up . . . 50 . . . 60 . . .

"You're learning fast, Jackie. Just keep your right foot on the floor. It's quite simple, really."

Jack swerved to avoid the metal mounds of a safety zone. The car hit a wet spot where the street had been watered and went into a long skid. There was a squealing crash of metal. Bill flew out of the car door and slid across the asphalt. He got up and ran his hands over his thin body—nothing broken. Somebody was holding his arm.

"Are you hurt, kid?"

"I don't think so."

He remembered seeing his car hauled away by a wrecker, the front wheels off the ground. He kept asking, "Where is Jack?" Finally he saw Jack with two cops. Jack looked dazed. There was a bruise on his forehead, standing out sharply on the white skin.

They rode in a police car to the hospital, where the doctor put a patch on Jack's forehead. He found a cut on Bill's leg, and swabbed it with Mercurochrome.

At the police station, Bill asked to call his father. It seemed to Bill literally no time before his father appeared, conjured by an alcoholic time trick. Suddenly there he was, cool and distant as always, talking to the cops. They had hit a parked car. The owner of the other car was there.

"So I met my wife at the train and took her to see the new car, and there wasn't any car. All four wheels knocked off."

"That will all be taken care of," Mr. Morton told him.

"Well, I should think so. That car can't be fixed. There's nothing left of it."

"In that case you will get a new car."

"Well, I should think so! People driving like that should be in jail. Endangering people's lives!" He glared at Bill and Jack.

One of the cops looked at him coldly. "We'll decide who to put in jail, mister. The gentleman is getting you a new car. What are you kicking about?"

"Well, so long as I get a new car."

There was an exchange of cards and arrangements. The desk sergeant accepted one of Mr. Morton's cigars and shook hands with him. No one paid any attention to the owner of the other car.

Bill and Jack walked out of the station with Mr. Morton.

"Where do you want to be dropped off?" Mr. Morton asked Jack. Jack told him. He got out at his street, and Bill said, "Good night, Jack. I'll give you a ring."

Jack said, "Thank you, Mr. Morton." Mr. Morton shifted his cigar without answering. He put the car in gear and drove away.

It was a long ride to the Mortons' house in the suburbs. Father and son rode in silence. Finally Bill said, "I'm sorry, Dad . . . I—"

"So am I," his father cut in.

When they reached the garage door, Bill got out and opened it, closing it again behind the car after Mr. Morton got out. Mr. Morton opened the door with a key in a leather folder. They entered the house in silence.

"It's all right, Mother," Mr. Morton called upstairs. "Nobody hurt." He started toward the pantry. "Want some milk, Bill?"

"No, thanks, Dad."

Bill went upstairs to bed.

THE JUNKY'S
CHRISTMAS

It was Christmas Day and Danny the Car Wiper hit the street junk-sick and broke after seventy-two hours in the precinct jail. It was a clear bright day, but there was no warmth in the sun. Danny shivered with an inner cold. He turned up the collar of his worn, greasy black overcoat.

This beat benny wouldn't pawn for a deuce, he thought.

He was in the West Nineties. A long block of brownstone rooming houses. Here and there a holy wreath in a clean black window. Danny's senses registered everything sharp and clear, with the painful intensity of junk sickness. The light hurt his dilated eyes.

He walked past a car, darting his pale blue eyes sideways in quick appraisal. There was a package on the seat and one of the ventilator windows was unlocked. Danny walked on ten feet. No one in sight. He snapped his fingers and went through a pantomime of remembering something, and wheeled around. No one.

A bad setup, he decided. *The street being empty like this, I stand out conspicuous. Gotta make it fast.*

He reached for the ventilator window. A door opened behind him. Danny whipped out a rag and began polishing the car windows. He could feel the man standing behind him.

"What're yuh doin'?"

Danny turned as if surprised. "Just thought your car windows needed polishing, mister."

The man had a frog face and a Deep South accent. He was wearing a camel's-hair overcoat.

"My caah don't need polishin' or nothing stole out of it neither."

Danny slid sideways as the man grabbed for him. "I wasn't lookin' to steal nothing, mister. I'm from the South too. Florida—"

"Goddamned sneakin' thief!"

Danny walked away fast and turned a corner.

Better get out of the neighborhood. That hick is likely to call the law.

He walked fifteen blocks. Sweat ran down his body. There was a raw ache in his lungs. His lips drew back off his yellow teeth in a snarl of desperation.

I gotta score somehow. If I had some decent clothes . . .

Danny saw a suitcase standing in a doorway. Good leather. He stopped and pretended to look for a cigarette.

Funny, he thought. *No one around. Inside maybe, phoning for a cab.*

The corner was only a few houses away. Danny took a deep

breath and picked up the suitcase. He made the corner. Another block, another corner. The case was heavy.

I got a score here all right, he thought. *Maybe enough for a sixteenth and a room.* Danny shivered and twitched, feeling a warm room and heroin emptying into his vein. *Let's have a quick look.*

He stepped into Morningside Park. No one around.

Jesus, I never see the town this empty.

He opened the suitcase. Two long packages in brown wrapping paper. He took one out. It felt like meat. He tore the package open at one end, revealing a woman's naked foot. The toenails were painted with purple-red polish. He dropped the leg with a sneer of disgust.

"Holy Jesus!" he exclaimed. "The routines people put down these days. Legs! Well, I got a case anyway." He dumped the other leg out. No bloodstains. He snapped the case shut and walked away.

"Legs!" he muttered.

He found the Buyer sitting at a table in Jarrow's Cafeteria.

"Thought you might be taking the day off," Danny said, putting the case down.

The Buyer shook his head sadly. "I got nobody. So what's Christmas to me?" His eyes traveled over the case, poking, testing, looking for flaws. "What was in it?"

"Nothing."

"What's the matter? I don't pay enough?"

"I tell you there wasn't nothing in it."

"Okay. So somebody travels with an empty suitcase. Okay." He held up three fingers.

"For Christ's sake, Gimpy, give me a nickel."

"You got somebody else. Why don't he give you a nickel?"

"It's like I say, the case was empty."

Gimpy kicked at the case disparagingly. "It's all nicked up and kinda dirty-looking." He sniffed suspiciously. "How come it stink like that? Mexican leather?"

"So am I in the leather business?"

Gimpy shrugged. "Could be." He pulled out a roll of bills and peeled off three ones, dropping them on the table behind the napkin dispenser. "You want?"

"Okay." Danny picked up the money. "You see George the Greek?" he asked.

"Where you been? He got busted two days ago."

"Oh . . . That's bad."

Danny walked out. *Now where can I score?* he thought. George the Greek had lasted so long, Danny thought of him as permanent. *It was good H too, and no short counts.*

Danny went up to 103rd and Broadway. Nobody in Jarrow's. Nobody in the Automat.

"Yeah," he snarled. "All the pushers off on the nod someplace. What they care about anybody else? So long as they get it in the vein. What they care about a sick junky?"

He wiped his nose with one finger, looking around furtively.

No use hitting those jigs in Harlem. Like as not get beat for my money or they slip me rat poison. Might find Pantopon Rose at Eighth and 23rd.

There was no one he knew in the 23rd Street Thompson's.

Jesus, he thought. *Where is everybody?*

He clutched his coat collar together with one hand, looking up and down the street. *There's Joey from Brooklyn. I'd know that hat anywhere.*

"Joey. Hey, Joey!"

Joey was walking away, with his back to Danny. He turned around. His face was sunken, skull-like. The gray eyes glittered under a greasy gray felt hat. Joey was sniffing at regular intervals and his eyes were watering.

No use asking him, Danny thought. They looked at each other with the hatred of disappointment.

"Guess you heard about George the Greek," Danny said.

"Yeah. I heard. You been up to 103rd?"

"Yeah. Just came from there. Nobody around."

"Nobody around anyplace," Joey said. "I can't even score for goofballs."

"Well, Merry Christmas, Joey. See you."

"Yeah. See you."

Danny was walking fast. He had remembered a croaker on 18th Street. Of course the croaker had told him not to come back. Still, it was worth trying.

A brownstone house with a card in the window: *P.H. Zunniga, M.D.* Danny rang the bell. He heard slow steps. The door opened, and the doctor looked at Danny with bloodshot brown eyes. He was weaving slightly and supported his plump body against the doorjamb. His face was smooth, Latin, the little red mouth slack. He said nothing. He just leaned there, looking at Danny.

Goddamned alcoholic, Danny thought. He smiled.

"Merry Christmas, Doctor."

The doctor did not reply.

"You remember me, Doctor." Danny tried to edge past the doctor, into the house. "I'm sorry to trouble you on Christmas Day, but I've suffered another attack."

"Attack?"

"Yes. Facial neuralgia." Danny twisted one side of his face into a horrible grimace. The doctor recoiled slightly, and Danny pushed into the dark hallway.

"Better shut the door or you'll be catching cold," he said jovially, shoving the door shut.

The doctor looked at him, his eyes focusing visibly. "I can't give you a prescription," he said.

"But Doctor, this is a legitimate condition. An emergency, you understand."

"No prescription. Impossible. It's against the law."

"You took an oath, Doctor. I'm in agony." Danny's voice shot up to a hysterical grating whine.

The doctor winced and passed a hand over his forehead.

"Let me think. I can give you one quarter-grain tablet. That's all I have in the house."

"But, Doctor—a quarter G . . ."

The doctor stopped him. "If your condition is legitimate, you will not need more. If it isn't, I don't want anything to do with you. Wait right here."

The doctor weaved down the hall, leaving a wake of alcoholic breath. He came back and dropped a tablet into Danny's hand. Danny wrapped the tablet in a piece of paper and tucked it away.

"There is no charge." The doctor put his hand on the doorknob. "And now, my dear . . ."

"But, Doctor—can't you inject the medication?"

"No. You will obtain longer relief in using orally. Please not to return." The doctor opened the door.

Well, this will take the edge off, and I still have money to put down on a room, Danny thought.

He knew a drugstore that sold needles without question. He bought a 26-gauge insulin needle and an eyedropper, which he selected carefully, rejecting models with a curved dropper or a thick end. Finally he bought a baby pacifier, to use instead of the bulb. He stopped in the Automat and stole a teaspoon.

Danny put down two dollars on a six-dollar-a-week room in the West Forties, where he knew the landlord. He bolted the door and put his spoon, needle and dropper on a table by the bed. He dropped the tablet in the spoon and covered it with a dropperful of water. He held a match under the spoon until the tablet dissolved. He tore a strip of paper, wet it and wrapped it around the end of the dropper, fitting the needle over the wet paper to make an airtight connection. He dropped a piece of lint from his pocket into the spoon and sucked the liquid into the dropper through the needle, holding the needle in the lint to take up the last drop.

Danny's hands trembled with excitement and his breath was quick. With a shot in front of him, his defenses gave way, and junk sickness flooded his body. His legs began to twitch and ache. A cramp stirred in his stomach. Tears ran down his face from his smarting, burning eyes. He wrapped a handkerchief around his right arm, holding the end in his teeth. He tucked the handkerchief in, and began rubbing his arm to bring out a vein.

Guess I can hit that one, he thought, running one finger along a vein. He picked up the dropper in his left hand.

Danny heard a groan from the next room. He frowned with annoyance. Another groan. He could not help listening. He walked across the room, the dropper in his hand, and inclined his ear to the wall. The groans were coming at regular intervals, a horrible inhuman sound pushed out from the stomach.

Danny listened for a full minute. He returned to the bed and sat down. *Why don't someone call a doctor?* he thought indignantly. *It's a bringdown*. He straightened his arm and poised the needle. He tilted his head, listening again.

Oh, for Christ's sake! He tore off the handkerchief and placed the dropper in a water glass, which he hid behind the wastebasket. He stepped into the hall and knocked on the door of the next room. There was no answer. The groans continued. Danny tried the door. It was open.

The shade was up and the room was full of light. He had expected an old person somehow, but the man on the bed was very young, eighteen or twenty, fully clothed and doubled up, with his hands clasped across his stomach.

"What's wrong, kid?" Danny asked.

The boy looked at him, his eyes blank with pain. Finally he got out one word: "Kidneys."

"Kidney stones?" Danny smiled. "I don't mean it's funny, kid. It's just . . . I've faked it so many times. Never saw the real thing before. I'll call an ambulance."

The boy bit his lip. "Won't come. Doctors won't come." The boy hid his face in the pillow.

Danny nodded. "They figure it's just another junky throwing a wingding for a shot. But your case is legit. Maybe if I went to the hospital and explained things . . . No, I guess that wouldn't be so good."

"Don't live here," the boy said, his voice muffled. "They say I'm not entitled."

"Yeah, I know how they are, the bureaucrat bastards. I had a friend once, died of snakebite right in the waiting room. They wouldn't even listen when he tried to explain a snake bit him. He never had enough moxie. That was fifteen years ago, down in Jacksonville. . . ."

Danny trailed off. Suddenly he put out his thin, dirty hand and touched the boy's shoulder.

"I—I'm sorry, kid. You wait. I'll fix you up."

He went back to his room and got the dropper, and returned to the boy's room.

"Roll up your sleeve, kid." The boy fumbled his coat sleeve with a weak hand.

"That's okay. I'll get it." Danny undid the shirt button at the wrist and pushed the shirt and coat up, baring a thin brown forearm. Danny hesitated, looking at the dropper. Sweat ran down his nose. The boy was looking up at him. Danny shoved the needle in the boy's forearm and watched the liquid drain into the flesh. He straightened up.

The boy's face began to relax. He sat up and smiled.

"Say, that stuff really works," he said. "You a doctor, mister?"

"No, kid."

The boy lay down, stretching. "I feel real sleepy. Didn't sleep all last night." His eyes were closing.

Danny walked across the room and pulled the shade down. He went back to his room and closed the door without locking it. He sat on the bed, looking at the empty dropper. It was getting dark outside. Danny's body ached for junk, but it was a dull ache now, dull and hopeless. Numbly, he took the needle off the dropper and wrapped it in a piece of paper. Then he wrapped the needle and dropper together. He sat there with the package in his hand. *Gotta stash this someplace*, he thought.

Suddenly a warm flood pulsed through his veins and broke in his head like a thousand golden speedballs.

For Christ's sake, Danny thought. *I must have scored for the immaculate fix!*

The vegetable serenity of junk settled in his tissues. His face went slack and peaceful, and his head fell forward.

Danny the Car Wiper was on the nod.

LEE AND THE BOYS

The sun spotlights the inner thigh of a boy sitting in shorts on a doorstep, his legs swinging open, and you fall in spasms—sperm spurting in orgasm after orgasm, grinding against the stone street, neck and back break . . . now lying dead, eyes rolled back, showing slits of white that redden slowly, as blood tears form and run down the face—

Or the sudden clean smell of salt air, piano down a city street, a dusty poplar tree shaking in the hot afternoon wind, pictures explode in the brain like skyrockets, smells, tastes, sounds shake the body, nostalgia becomes unendurable, aching pain, the brain is an overloaded switchboard sending insane messages and counter-messages to the viscera. Finally the body gives up, cowering like a neurotic cat, blood pressure drops, body fluids leak through stretched, flaccid veins, shock passes to coma and death.

Somebody rapped on the outside shutter. Lee opened the shutter and looked out. An Arab boy of fourteen or so—they always look younger than they are—was standing there, smiling in a way that could only mean one thing. He said something in Spanish that Lee did not catch. Lee shook his head and started to close the shutter. The boy, still smiling, held the shutter open. Lee gave a jerk and slammed the shutter closed. He could feel the rough wood catch and tear the boy's hand. The boy turned without a word and walked away, his shoulders drooping, holding his hand. At the corner the small figure caught a patch of light.

I didn't mean to hurt him, Lee thought. He wished he had given the boy some money, a smile at least. He felt crude and detestable.

Years ago he had been riding in a hotel station wagon in the West Indies. The station wagon slowed down for a series of bumps, and a little black girl ran up smiling and threw a bouquet of flowers into the car through the rear window. A round-faced, heavyset American in a brown gabardine suit gathered up the flowers and said, "No want," and tossed them at the little girl. The flowers fell in the dusty road, and the little girl turned around crying and ran away.

Lee closed the shutter slowly.

In the Rio Grande valley of South Texas, he had killed a rattlesnake with a golf club. The impact of metal on the live flesh of the snake sent an electric shiver through him.

In New York, when he was rolling lushes on the subway with Roy, at the end of the line in Brooklyn a drunk grabbed Roy and started yelling for the law. Lee hit the drunk in the face and knocked him to his knees, then kicked him in the side. A rib snapped. Lee felt a shudder of nausea.

Next day he told Roy he was through as a lush worker. Roy looked at him with his impersonal brown eyes that caught points of light, like an opal. There was a masculine gentleness in Roy's voice, a gentleness that only the strong have: "You feel bad about kicking that mooch, don't you? You're not cut out for this sort of thing, Bill. I'll find someone else to work with." Roy put on his hat and started to leave. He stopped with the doorknob in his hand and turned around.

"It's none of my business, Bill. But you have enough money to get by. Why don't you just quit?" He walked out without waiting for Lee to answer.

Lee did not feel like finishing the letter. He put on his coat and stepped out into the narrow, sunless street.

The druggist saw Lee standing in the doorway of the store. The store was about eight feet wide, with bottles and packages packed around three walls. The druggist smiled and held up a finger.

"One?" he said in English.

Lee nodded, looking around at the bottles and packages. The clerk handed the box of ampules to Lee without wrapping it. Lee said, "Thank you."

He walked away through a street lined on both sides with bazaars. Merchandise overflowed into the street, and he dodged crockery and washtubs and trays of combs and pencils and soap dishes. A train of burros loaded with charcoal blocked his way. He passed a woman with no nose, a black slit in her face, her body wrapped in grimy, padded pink cotton. Lee walked fast, twisting his body sideways, squeezing past people. He reached the sunny alleys of the outer Medina.

Walking in Tangier was like falling, plunging down dark shafts of streets, catching at corners, doorways. He passed a blind man sitting in the sun in a doorway. The man was young, with a fringe of blond beard. He sat there with one hand out, his shirt open, showing the smooth, patient flesh, the slight, immobile folds in the stomach. He sat there all day, every day.

Lee turned into his street, and a cool wind from the sea chilled the sweat on his thin body. He hooked the key into the lock and pushed the door open with his shoulder.

He tied up for the shot, and slid the needle in through a festered scab. Blood swirled up into the hypo—he was using a regular hypo these days. He pressed the plunger down with his forefinger. A passing caress of pleasure flushed through his veins. He glanced at the cheap alarm clock on the table by the bed: four o'clock. He was meeting his boy at eight. Time enough for the Eukodal to get out of his system.

Lee walked about the room. "I have to quit," he said over and over, feeling the gravity pull of junk in his cells. He experienced a moment of panic. A cry of despair wrenched his body: "I have to get *out* of here. I have to make a break."

As he said the words, he remembered whose words they were: the Mad Dog Esposito Brothers, arrested at the scene of a multiple-slaying holdup, separated from the electric chair by a little time and a few formalities, whispered these words into a police microphone planted by their beds in the detention ward.

He sat down at the typewriter, yawned, and made some notes on a separate piece of paper. Lee often spent hours on a letter. He dropped the pencil and stared at the wall, his face blank and dreamy, reflecting on the heartwarming picture of William Lee—

He was sure the reviewers in those queer magazines like *One* would greet Willy Lee as heartwarming, except when he gets— squirming uneasily—well, you know, a bit out of line, somehow.

"Oh, that's just boyishness—after all, you know a boy's will is the wind's will, and the thoughts of youth are long, long thoughts."

"Yes I know, but . . . the purple-assed baboons . . ."

"That's gangrened innocence."

"Why didn't I think of *that* myself. And the piles?"

"All kids are like hung up on something."

"So they are . . . and the prolapsed assholes feeling around, looking for a peter, like blind worms?"

"Schoolboy smut."

"Understand, I'm not trying to *belittle* Lee—"

"You'd better not. He's a one-hundred-percent wistful boy, listening to train whistles across the winter stubble and frozen red clay of Georgia."

—yes, there was something a trifle disquieting in the fact that the heartwarming picture of William Lee should be drawn by William Lee himself. He thought of the ultimate development in stooges, a telepathic stooge who tunes in on your psyche and says just what you want to hear: "Boss, you is heartwarming. You is a latter-assed purple-day saint."

Lee put down the pencil and yawned. He looked at the bed.

I'm sleepy, he decided. He took off his pants and shoes and lay down on the bed, covering himself with a cotton blanket. *They don't scratch*. He closed his eyes. Pictures streamed by, the magic lantern of junk. There is a feeling of too much junk that corresponds to the bed spinning around when you are very drunk, a feeling of gray, dead horror. The pictures in the brain are out of control, black and white, without emotion, the deadness of junk lying in the body like a viscous, thick medium.

A child came up to Lee and held up to him a bleeding hand.

"Who did this?" Lee asked. "I'll kill him. Who did it?"

The child beckoned Lee into a dark room. He pointed at Lee with the bleeding stub of a finger. Lee woke up crying "No! No!"

Lee looked at the clock. It was almost eight. His boy was due anytime. Lee rummaged in a drawer of the bed table and found a stick of tea. He lit it and lay back to wait for KiKi. There was a bitter, green taste in his mouth from the weed. He could feel a warm tingle spread over his body. He put his hands behind his head, stretching his ribs and arching his stomach.

Lee was forty, but he had the lean body of an adolescent. He looked down at the stomach, which curved in flat from the chest. Junk had sculpted his body down to bone and muscle. He could feel the wall of his stomach right under the skin. His skin smooth and white, he looked almost transparent, like a tropical fish, with blue veins where the hipbones protruded.

KiKi stepped in. He switched on the light.

"Sleeping?" he asked.

"No, just resting." Lee got up and put his arms around KiKi, holding him in a long, tight embrace.

"What's the matter, Meester William?" KiKi said, laughing.

"Nothing."

They sat down on the edge of the bed. KiKi ran his hands absently over Lee's back. He turned and looked at Lee.

"Very thin," he said. "You should eat more."

Lee pulled in his stomach so it almost touched the backbone. KiKi laughed and ran his hands down Lee's ribs to the stomach. He put his thumbs on Lee's backbone and tried to encircle Lee's stomach with his hands. He got up and took off his clothes and sat down beside Lee, caressing him with casual affection.

Like many Spanish boys, KiKi did not feel love for women. To him a woman was only for sex. He had known Lee for some months, and felt a genuine fondness for him, in an offhand way. Lee was considerate and generous and did not ask KiKi to do things he didn't want to do, leaving the lovemaking on an adolescent basis. KiKi was well pleased with the arrangement.

And Lee was well pleased with KiKi. He did not like the process of looking for boys. He did not lose interest in a boy after a few contacts, not being subject to compulsive promiscuity. In Mexico he had slept with the same boy twice a week for over a year. The boy had looked enough like KiKi to be his brother. Both had very straight black hair, an Oriental look, and lean, slight bodies. Both exuded the same quality of sweet masculine innocence. Lee met the same people wherever he went.

IN THE CAFÉ CENTRAL

Johnny the Guide was sitting in front of the Café Central with Mrs. Merrims and her sixteen-year-old son. Mrs. Merrims was traveling on her husband's insurance. She was well-groomed and competent. She was making out a list of purchases and places to go. Johnny leaned forward, solicitous and deferential.

The other guides cruised by like frustrated sharks. Johnny savored their envy. His eyes slid sideways over the lean adolescent body of the boy, poised in gray flannels and a sport shirt open at the neck. Johnny licked his lips.

Hans sat several tables away. He was a German who procured

boys for English and American visitors. He had a house in the native quarter—bed and boy, two dollars per night. But most of his clients went in for "quickies." Hans had typical Nordic features, with heavy bone structure. There was something skull-like in his face.

Morton Christie was sitting with Hans. Morton was a pathetic name-dropper and table-hopper. Hans was the only one in Tangier who could stand his silly chatter, his interminable dull lies about wealth and social prominence. One story involved two aunts, living in a house together, who hadn't spoken to each other in twenty years.

"But you see, the house is so huge that it doesn't matter, really. They each have their own set of servants and maintain completely separate households."

Hans just sat there and smiled through all of these stories. "It is a little girl," he would say in defense of Morton. "You must not be hard with him."

Actually Morton had, through years of insecurity—sitting at tables where he wasn't wanted, desperately attempting to gain a moment's reprieve from dismissal—gained an acute sense for gossip and scandal. If someone was down with the clap, Morton always found out somehow. He had a sense for anything anyone was trying to conceal. The most perfect poker face was no protection against this telepathic penetration.

Besides, without being a good listener, sympathetic, or in any way someone you would want to confide in, he had a way of surprising confidences out of you. Sometimes you forgot he was there and said something to someone else at the table. Sometimes he would slip in a question, personal, impertinent, but you answered him before you knew it. His personality was so negative there was nothing to put you on guard. Hans found Morton's talent for collecting information useful. He could find out what was happening in town by spending half an hour listening to Morton in the Café Central.

Morton had literally no self-respect, so that his self-esteem went up or down in accordance with how others felt about him. At first he often made a good impression. He appeared naïve, boyish, friendly. Imperceptibly the naïveté degenerated into silly, mechanical chatter, his friendliness into compulsive, clinging hunger, and his boyishness faded before your eyes across a café table. You looked up and saw the deep lines about the mouth, a hard, stupid mouth like an old whore's, you saw the deep creases in the back of the neck when he craned around to look at somebody—he was always looking around restlessly, as if he were waiting for someone more important than whomever he was sitting with.

There were, to be sure, people who engaged his whole attention. He twisted in hideous convulsions of ingratiation, desperate as he saw every pitiful attempt fail flatly, often shitting in his pants with fear and excitement. Lee wondered if he went home and sobbed with despair.

Morton's attempts to please socially prominent residents and visiting celebrities, ending usually in flat failure, or a snub in the Café Central, attracted a special sort of scavenger who feeds on the humiliation and disintegration of others. These decayed queens never tired of retailing the endless saga of Morton's social failures.

"So he sat *right down* with Tennessee Williams on the beach, and Tennessee said to him: 'I'm not feeling well this morning, *Michael*. I'd rather not talk to anybody.' '*Michael!*' Doesn't even know his *name!* And he says, 'Oh yes, Tennessee is a good friend of mine!' " And they would laugh, and throw themselves around and flip their wrists, their eyes glowing with loathsome lust.

I imagine that's the way people look when they watch someone burned at the stake, Lee thought.

At another table was a beautiful woman, of mixed Negro and

Malay stock. She was delicately proportioned, with a dark, copper-colored complexion and small teeth set far apart, her nipples pointed a little upward. She was dressed in a yellow silk gown and carried herself with superb grace. At the same table sat a German woman with perfect features: golden hair curled in braids forming a tiara, a magnificent bust, and heroic proportions.

She was talking to the half-caste. When she opened her mouth to speak, she revealed horrible teeth, gray, carious, repaired rather than filled with pieces of steel—some actually rusty, others of copper covered with green verdigris. The teeth were abnormally large and crowded over each other. Broken, corroded braces stuck to them, like an old barbed-wire fence.

Ordinarily she attempted to keep her teeth covered as far as possible. However, her beautiful mouth was hardly adequate to perform this function, and the teeth peeked out here and there as she talked or ate. She never laughed if she could help it, but was subject to occasional laughing jags brought on by apparently random circumstances. The laughing jags were always followed by fits of crying, during which she would repeat over and over, "Everybody saw my teeth! My horrible teeth!"

She was constantly saving up money to have the teeth out, but somehow she always spent the money on something else. Either she got drunk on it, or she gave it to someone in an irrational fit of generosity. She was a mark for every con artist in Tangier, because she was known to have the money she was always saving up to have her teeth out. But putting the touch on her was not without danger. She would suddenly turn vicious and maul some mooch with all the strength of her Junoesque limbs, shouting, "You lousy bastard! Trying to con me out of my teeth money!"

Both the half-caste and the Nordic, who had taken on herself the name of Helga, were free-lance whores.

DREAM OF THE
PENAL COLONY

That night Lee dreamed he was in a penal colony. All around were
high, bare mountains. He lived in a boardinghouse that was never
warm. He went out for a walk. As he stepped off the street corner
onto a dirty cobblestone street, the cold mountain wind hit him.
He tightened the belt of a leather jacket and felt the chill of final
despair.

Nobody talks much after the first few years in the colony, because
they know the others are in identical conditions of misery. They
sit at table, eating the cold, greasy food, separate and silent as

stones. Only the whiny, penetrating voice of the landlady goes on and on.

The colonists mix with the townspeople, and it is difficult to pick them out. But sooner or later they betray themselves by a misplaced intensity, which derives from the exclusive preoccupation with escape. There is also the penal-colony look: control, without inner calm or balance; bitter knowledge, without maturity; intensity, without warmth or love.

The colonists know that any spontaneous expression of feeling brings the harshest punishment. Provocative agents continually mix with the prisoners, saying, "Relax. Be yourself. Express your real feelings." Lee was convinced that the means to escape lay through a relationship with one of the townspeople, and to that end he frequented the cafés.

One day he was sitting in the Metropole opposite a young man. The young man was talking about his childhood in a coastal town. Lee sat staring through the boy's head, seeing the salt marshes, the red-brick houses, the old rusty barge by the inlet where the boys took off their clothes to swim.

This may be it, Lee thought. *Easy now. Cool, cool. Don't scare him off*. Lee's stomach knotted with excitement.

During the following week, Lee tried every approach he knew, shamelessly throwing aside unsuccessful routines with a shrug: "I was only kidding," or, "*Son cosas de la vida*." He descended to the most abject emotional blackmail and panhandling. When this failed, he scaled a dangerous cliff (not quite so dangerous either, since he knew every inch of the ascent) to capture a species of beautiful green lizard found only on these ledges. He gave the boy the lizard, attached to a chain of jade.

"It took me seven years to carve that chain," Lee said. Actually he had won the chain from a traveling salesman in a game of Latah. The boy was touched, and consented to go to bed with Lee, but soon afterward broke off intimate relationships. Lee was in despair.

I love him and besides, I haven't discovered the Secret. Perhaps he is an Agent. Lee looked at the boy with hatred. His face was breaking up, as if melted from inside by a blowtorch.

"Why won't you help me?" he demanded. "Do you want another lizard? I will get you a black lizard with beautiful violet eyes, that lives on the west slope where the winds pick climbers from the cliff and suck them out of crevices. There is only one other purple-eyed lizard in town and that one—well, never mind. The purple-eyed lizard is more venomous than a cobra, but he never bites his master. He is the sweetest and gentlest animal on earth. Just let me show you how sweet and gentle a purple-eyed lizard can be."

"Never mind," said the boy, laughing. "Anyhoo, one lizard is enough."

"Don't say anyhoo. Well, I will cut off my foot and shrink it down by a process I learned from the Auca, and make you a watch fob."

"What I want with your ugly old foot?"

"I will get you money for a guide and a pack train. You can return to the coast."

"I'll go back there anytime I feel like it. My brother-in-law knows the route."

The thought of someone being able to leave at will so enraged Lee that he was in danger of losing control. His sweaty hand gripped the snap-knife in his pocket.

The boy looked at him with distaste. "You look very nasty. Your face has turned all sorta black, greenish-black. Are you deliberately trying to make me sick?"

Lee turned on all the control that years of confinement had taught him. His face faded from greenish-black to mahogany, and back to its normal suntanned brown color. The control was spreading through his body like a shot of M. Lee smiled smoothly, but a muscle in his cheek twitched.

"Just an old Shipibo trick. They turn themselves black for night hunting, you understand. . . . Did I ever tell you about the time I ran out of K-Y in the headwaters of the Effendi? That was the year of the rindpest, when everything died, even the hyenas."

Lee went into one of his routines. The boy was laughing now. Lee made a dinner appointment.

"All right," said the boy. "But no more of your Shipibo tricks."

Lee laughed with easy joviality. "Gave you a turn, eh, young man? Did me too, the first time I saw it. Puked up a tapeworm. Well, good night."

INTERNATIONAL ZONE

A miasma of suspicion and snobbery hangs over the European Quarter of Tangier. Everyone looks you over for the price tag, appraising you like merchandise in terms of immediate practical or prestige advantage. The Boulevard Pasteur is the Fifth Avenue of Tangier. The store clerks tend to be discourteous unless you buy something immediately. Inquiries without purchase are coldly and grudgingly answered.

My first night in town I went to a fashionable bar, one of the few places that continues prosperous in the present slump: dim light, well-dressed androgynous clientele, reminiscent of many bars on New York's Upper East Side.

I started conversation with a man on my right. He was wearing one of those brown sackcloth jackets, the inexpensive creation of an ultra-chic Worth Avenue shop. Evidently it is the final touch of smartness to appear in a twelve-dollar jacket, the costume jewelry pattern—I happened to know just where the jacket came from and how much it cost because I had one like it in my suitcase. (A few days later I gave it to a shoeshine boy.)

The man's face was gray, puffy, set in a mold of sour discontent, *rich* discontent. It's an expression you see more often on women, and if a woman sits there long enough with that expression of rich discontent and sourness, a Cadillac simply builds itself around her. A man would probably accrete a Jaguar. Come to think, I had seen a Jaguar parked outside the bar.

The man answered my questions in cautious, short sentences, carefully deleting any tinge of warmth or friendliness.

"Did you come here direct from the States?" I persisted.

"No. From Brazil."

He's warming up, I thought. I expected it would take two sentences to elicit that much information.

"So? And how did you come?"

"By yacht, *of course*."

I felt that anything would be an anticlimax after that, and allowed my shaky option on his notice to lapse.

The European Quarter of Tangier contains a surprising number of first-class French and international restaurants, where excellent food is served at very reasonable prices. Sample menu at The Alhambra, one of the best French restaurants: Snails *à la bourgogne*, one half partridge with peas and potatoes, a frozen chocolate mousse, a selection of French cheeses, and fruit. Price: one dollar. This price and menu can be duplicated in ten or twelve other restaurants.

Walking downhill from the European Quarter, we come, by inexorable process of suction, to the Socco Chico—Little Market—which is no longer a market at all but simply a paved rectangle about a block long, lined on both sides with shops and cafés. The Café Central, by reason of a location that allows the best view of the most people passing through the Socco, is the official meeting place of the Socco Chico set. Cars are barred from the Socco between 8 A.M. and 12 midnight. Often groups without money to order coffee will stand for hours in the Socco, talking. During the day they can sit in front of the cafés without ordering, but from 5 to 8 P.M. they must relinquish their seats to paying clients, unless they can strike up a conversation with a group of payers.

The Socco Chico is the meeting place, the nerve center, the switchboard of Tangier. Practically everyone in town shows there once a day at least. Many residents of Tangier spend most of their waking hours in the Socco. On all sides you see men washed up here in hopeless, dead-end situations, waiting for job offers, acceptance checks, visas, permits that will never come. All their lives they have drifted with an unlucky current, always taking the wrong turn. Here they are. This is it. Last stop: the Socco Chico of Tangier.

The market of psychic exchange is as glutted as the shops. A nightmare feeling of stasis permeates the Socco, like nothing can happen, nothing can change. Conversations disintegrate in cosmic inanity. People sit at café tables, silent and separate as stones. No other relation than physical closeness is possible. Economic laws, untouched by any human factor, evolve equations of ultimate stasis. Someday the young Spaniards in gabardine trench coats talking about soccer, the Arab guides and hustlers pitching pennies and smoking their *keif* pipes, the perverts sitting in front of the cafés looking over the boys, the boys parading past, the mooches and pimps and smugglers and money changers, will be frozen forever in a final, meaningless posture.

Futility seems to have gained a new dimension in the Socco. Sitting at a café table, listening to some "proposition," I would suddenly realize that the other was telling a fairy story to a child, the child inside himself: pathetic fantasies of smuggling, of trafficking in diamonds, drugs, guns, of starting nightclubs, bowling alleys, travel agencies. Or sometimes there was nothing wrong with the idea, except it would never be put into practice—the crisp, confident voice, the decisive gestures, in shocking contrast to the dead, hopeless eyes, drooping shoulders, clothes beyond mending, now allowed to disintegrate undisturbed.

Some of these men have ability and intelligence, like Brinton, who writes unpublishably obscene novels and exists on a small income. He undoubtedly has talent, but his work is hopelessly unsalable. He has intelligence, the rare ability to see relations between disparate factors, to coordinate data, but he moves through life like a phantom, never able to find the time, place and person to put anything into effect, to realize any project in terms of three-dimensional reality. He could have been a successful business executive, anthropologist, explorer, criminal, but the conjuncture of circumstances was never there. He is always too late or too early. His abilities remain larval, discarnate. He is the last of an archaic line, or the first here from another space-time way—in any case a man without context, of no place and no time.

Chris, the English Public School man, is the type who gets involved in fur farming, projects to raise ramie, frogs, cultured pearls. He had, in fact, lost all his savings in a bee-raising venture in the West Indies. He had observed that all the honey was imported and expensive. It looked like a sure thing, and he invested all he had. He did not know about a certain moth preying on the bees in that area, so that bee-raising is impossible.

"The sort of thing that could only happen to Chris," his friends say, for this is one chapter in a fantastic saga of misfortune. Who but Chris would be caught short at the beginning of the war, in a total shortage of drugs, and have a molar extracted without anesthetic? On another occasion he had collapsed with peritonitis and been shanghaied into a Syrian hospital, where they never heard of penicillin. He was rescued, on the verge of death, by the English consul. During the Spanish occupation of Tangier, he had been mistaken for a Spanish Communist and held for three weeks incommunicado in a detention camp.

Now he is broke and jobless in the Socco Chico, an intelligent man, willing to work, speaking several languages fluently, yet bearing the indelible brand of bad luck and failure. He is carefully shunned by the Jaguar-driving set, who fear contagion from the mysterious frequency that makes, of men like Chris, lifelong failures. He manages to stay alive teaching English and selling whiskey on commission.

Robbins is about fifty, with the face of a Cockney informer, the archetypal "Copper's Nark." He has a knack of pitching his whiny voice directly into your consciousness. No external noise drowns him out. Robbins looks like some unsuccessful species of *Homo non sapiens*, blackmailing the human race with his existence.

"Remember me? I'm the boy you left back there with the lemurs and the baboons. I'm not equipped for survival like *some* people." He holds out his deformed hands, hideously infantile, unfinished, his greedy blue eyes searching for a spot of guilt or uncertainty, on which he will fasten like a lamprey.

Robbins had all his money in his wife's name to evade income tax, and his wife ran away with a perfidious Australian. ("And I thought he was my friend.") This is one story. Robbins has a series, all involving his fall from wealth, betrayed and cheated by dishonest associates. He fixes his eyes on you probingly, accusingly: are you another betrayer who would refuse a man a few pesetas when he is down?

Robbins also comes on with the "I can't go home" routine, hinting at dark crimes committed in his native land. Many of the

Socco Chico regulars say they can't go home, trying to mitigate the dead gray of prosaic failure with a touch of borrowed color.

As a matter of fact, if anyone was wanted for a serious crime, the authorities could get him out of Tangier in ten minutes. As for these stories of disappearing into the Native Quarter, living there only makes a foreigner that much more conspicuous. Any guide or shoeshine boy would lead the cops to your door for five pesetas or a few cigarettes. So when someone gets confidential over the third drink you have bought him and tells you he can't go home, you are hearing the classic prelude to a touch.

A Danish boy is stranded here waiting for a friend to come with money and "the rest of his luggage." Every day he meets the ferry from Gibraltar and the ferry from Algeciras. A Spanish boy is waiting for a permit to enter the French Zone (for some reason persistently denied), where his uncle will give him a job. An English boy was robbed of all his money and valuables by a girlfriend.

I have never seen so many people in one place without money, or any prospects of money. This is partly due to the fact that anyone can enter Tangier. You don't have to prove solvency. So people come here hoping to get a job, or become smugglers. But there are no jobs in Tangier, and smuggling is as overcrowded as any other line. So they end up on the bum in the Socco Chico.

All of them curse Tangier, and hope for some miracle that will deliver them from the Socco Chico. They will get a job on a yacht, they will write a best-seller, they will smuggle a thousand cases of Scotch into Spain, they will find someone to finance their roulette system. It is typical of these people that they all believe in some gambling system, usually a variation on the old routine of doubling up when you lose, which is the pattern of their lives. They always back up their mistakes with more of themselves.

Some of the Socco Chico regulars, like Chris, make a real effort to support themselves. Others are full-time professional spongers.

Antonio the Portuguese is mooch to the bone. He won't work. In a sense, he can't work. He is a mutilated fragment of the human potential, specialized to the point where he cannot exist without a host. His mere presence is an irritation. Phantom tendrils reach out from him, feeling for a point of weakness on which to fasten.

Jimmy the Dane is another full-time mooch. He has a gift for showing precisely when you don't want to see him, and saying exactly what you don't want to hear. His technique is to make you dislike him more than his actual behavior, a bit obnoxious to be sure, warrants. This makes you feel guilty toward him, so you buy him off with a drink or a few pesetas.

Some mooches specialize in tourists and transients, making no attempt to establish themselves on terms of social equality with the long-term residents. They use some variation of the short con, strictly one-time touches.

There is a Jewish mooch who looks vaguely like a detective or some form of authority. He approaches a tourist in a somewhat peremptory manner. The tourist anticipates an inspection of his passport or some other annoyance. When he finds out it is merely a question of a small "loan," he often gives the money in relief.

A young Norwegian has a routine of approaching visitors without his glass eye, a really unnerving sight. He needs money to buy a glass eye, or he will lose a job he is going to apply for in the morning. "How can I work as a waiter looking so as this?" he says, turning his empty socket on the victim. "I would frighten the customers, is it not?"

Many of the Socco Chico regulars are left over from the Boom. A few years ago the town was full of operators and spenders. There was a boom of money changing and transfer, smuggling and borderline enterprise. Restaurants and hotels turned customers away. Bars served a full house around the clock.

What happened? What gave out? What corresponds to the gold, the oil, the construction projects? Largely, inequalities in prices and exchange rates. Tangier is a clearinghouse, from which currency and merchandise move in any direction toward higher prices. Under this constant flow of goods, shortages created by the war are supplied, prices and currency approach standard rates, and Tangier is running down like the dying universe, where no movement is possible because all energy is equally distributed.

Tangier is a vast overstocked market, everything for sale and no buyers. A glut of obscure brands of Scotch, inferior German cameras and Swiss watches, second-run factory-reject nylons, typewriters unknown anywhere else, is displayed in shop after shop. There is quite simply too much of everything, too much merchandise, housing, labor, too many guides, pimps, prostitutes and smugglers. A classic, archetypical depression.

The guides of Tangier are in a class by themselves, and I have never seen their equal for insolence, persistence and all-around obnoxiousness. It is not surprising that the very word "guide" carries, in Tangier, the strongest opprobrium.

The Navy issues a bulletin on what to do if you find yourself in shark-infested waters: "Above all, avoid making uncoordinated, flailing movements that might be interpreted by a shark as the struggles of a disabled fish." The same advice might apply to keeping off guides. They are infallibly attracted by the uncoordinated movements of the tourist in a strange medium. The least show of uncertainty, of not knowing exactly where you are going, and they rush on you from their lurking places in side streets and Arab cafés.

"Want nice girl, mister?"

"See Kasbah? Sultan's Palace?"

"Want *keif*? Watch me fuck my sister?"

"Caves of Hercules? Nice boy?"

Their persistence is amazing, their impertinence unlimited. They will follow one for blocks, finally demanding a tip for the time they have wasted.

Female prostitution is largely confined to licensed houses. On the other hand, male prostitutes are everywhere. They assume that all visitors are homosexual, and solicit openly in the streets. I have been approached by boys who could not have been over twelve.

A casino would certainly bring in more tourists, and do much to alleviate the economic condition of Tangier. But despite the concerted efforts of merchants and hotel owners, all attempts to build a casino have been blocked by the Spanish on religious grounds.

Tangier has a dubious climate. The winters are cold and wet. In summer the temperature is pleasant, neither too hot nor too cool, but a constant wind creates a sandstorm on the beach, and people who sit there all day get sand in their ears and hair and eyes. Owing to a current, the water is shock-cold in mid-August, so even the hardiest swimmers can only stay in a few minutes. The beach is not much of an attraction.

All in all, Tangier does not have much to offer the visitor except low prices and a buyer's market. I have mentioned the unusually large number of good restaurants (a restaurant guide put out by the American and Foreign Bank lists eighteen first-class eating places where the price for a complete meal ranges from eighty cents to two dollars and a half). You have your choice of apartments and houses. Sample price for one large room with bath and balcony overlooking the harbor, comfortably furnished, utilities and maid service included: $25 per month. And there are comfortable rooms for $10. A tailor-made suit of imported English material that would cost $150 in the U.S. is $50 in Tangier. Name brands of Scotch run $2 to $2.50 a fifth.

Americans are exempt from the usual annoyances of registering with the police, renewing visas and so forth, that one encounters in Europe and South America. No visa is required for Tangier. You can stay as long as you want, work, if you can find a job, or go into business, without any formalities or permits. And Americans have extraterritorial rights in Tangier. Cases civil or criminal involving an American citizen are tried in consular court, under District of Columbia law.

The legal system of Tangier is rather complex. Criminal cases are tried by a mixed tribunal of three judges. Sentences are comparatively mild. Two years is usual for burglary, even if the criminal has a long record. A sentence of more than five years is extremely rare. Tangier does have capital punishment. The method is a firing squad of ten gendarmes. I know of only one case in recent years in which a death sentence was carried out.

In the Native Quarter one feels definite currents of hostility, which, however, are generally confined to muttering in Arabic as you pass. Occasionally I have been openly insulted by drunken Arabs, but this is rare. You can walk in the Native Quarter of Tangier with less danger than on Third Avenue of New York City on a Saturday night.

Violent crime is rare. I have walked the streets at all hours, and never was any attempt made to rob me. The infrequency of armed robbery is due less, I think, to the pacific nature of the Arabs than to the certainty of detection in a town where everybody knows everybody else, and where the penalties for violent crime, especially if committed by a Moslem, are relatively severe.

The Native Quarter of Tangier is all you expect it to be: a maze of narrow, sunless streets, twisting and meandering like footpaths, many of them blind alleys. After four months, I still find my way in the Medina by a system of moving from one landmark to another. The smell is almost incredible, and it is difficult to identify all the ingredients. Hashish, seared meat and sewage are well represented. You see filth, poverty, disease, all endured with a curiously apathetic indifference.

People carry huge loads of charcoal down from the mountains on their backs—that is, the women carry loads of charcoal. The men ride on donkeys. No mistaking the position of women in this society. I noticed a large percentage of these charcoal carriers had their noses eaten away by disease, but was not able to determine whether there is any occupational correlation. It seems more likely that they all come from the same heavily infected district.

Hashish is the drug of Islam, as alcohol is ours, opium the drug of the Far East, and cocaine that of South America. No effort is made to control its sale or use in Tangier, and every native café reeks of the smoke. They chop up the leaves on a wooden block, mix it with tobacco, and smoke it in little clay pipes with a long wooden stem.

Europeans occasion no surprise or overt resentment in Arab cafés. The usual drink is mint tea served very hot in a tall glass. If you hold the glass by top and bottom, avoiding the sides, it doesn't burn the hand. You can buy hashish, or *keif*, as they call it here, in any native café. It can also be purchased in sweet, resinous cakes to eat with hot tea. This resinous substance, a gum extracted from the cannabis plant, is the real hashish, and much more powerful than the leaves and flowers of the plant. The gum is called *majoun*, and the leaves *keif*. Good *majoun* is hard to find in Tangier.

Keif is identical with our marijuana, and we have here an opportunity to observe the effects of constant use on a whole population. I asked a European physician if he had noted any definite ill effects. He said: "In general, no. Occasionally there is drug psychosis, but it rarely reaches an acute stage where hospitalization is necessary." I asked if Arabs suffering from this psychosis are dangerous. He said: "I have never heard of any violence directly and definitely traceable to *keif*. To answer your question, they are usually not dangerous."

The typical Arab café is one room, a few tables and chairs, a huge copper or brass samovar for making tea and coffee. A raised platform covered with mats extends across one end of the room. Here the patrons loll about with their shoes off, smoking *keif* and playing cards. The game is Redondo, played with a pack of forty-two cards—rather an elementary card game. Fights start, stop, people walk around, play cards, smoke *keif*, all in a vast, timeless dream.

There is usually a radio turned on full volume. Arab music has neither beginning nor end. It is timeless. Heard for the first time, it may appear meaningless to a Westerner, because he is listening for a time structure that isn't there.

I talked with an American psychoanalyst who is practicing in Casablanca. He says you can never complete analysis with an Arab. Their superego structure is basically different. Perhaps you can't complete analysis with an Arab because he has no sense of time. He never completes anything. It is interesting that the drug of Islam is hashish, which affects the sense of time so that events, instead of appearing in an orderly structure of past, present and future, take on a simultaneous quality, the past and future contained in the present moment.

Tangier seems to exist on several dimensions. You are always finding streets, squares, parks you never saw before. Here fact merges into dream, and dreams erupt into the real world. Unfinished buildings fall into ruin and decay, Arabs move in silently like weeds and vines. A catatonic youth moves through the marketplace, bumping into people and stalls like a sleepwalker. A man, barefooted, in rags, his face eaten and tumescent with a horrible skin disease, begs with his eyes alone. He does not have the will left to hold out his hand. An old Arab passionately kisses the sidewalk. People stop to watch for a few moments with bestial curiosity, then move on.

Nobody in Tangier is exactly what he seems to be. Along with the bogus fugitives of the Socco Chico are genuine political exiles from Europe: Jewish refugees from Nazi Germany, Republican Spaniards, a selection of Vichy French and other collaborators, fugitive Nazis. The town is full of vaguely disreputable Europeans who do not have adequate documents to go anywhere else. So many people are here who cannot leave, lacking funds or papers or both. Tangier is a vast penal colony.

The special attraction of Tangier can be put in one word: exemption. Exemption from interference, legal or otherwise. Your private life is your own, to act exactly as you please. You will be talked about, of course. Tangier is a gossipy town, and everyone in the foreign colony knows everyone else. But that is all. No legal pressure or pressure of public opinion will curtail your behavior. The cop stands here with his hands behind his back, reduced to his basic function of keeping order. That is all he does. He is the other extreme from the thought police of police states, or our own vice squad.

Tangier is one of the few places left in the world where, so long as you don't proceed to robbery, violence, or some form of crude, antisocial behavior, you can do exactly what you want. It is a sanctuary of noninterference.

II.
LEE'S
JOURNALS

LEE'S JOURNALS

Lee's face, his whole person, seemed at first glance completely anonymous. He looked like an FBI man, like anybody. But the absence of trappings, of anything remotely picturesque or baroque, distinguished and delineated Lee, so that seen twice you would not forget him. Sometimes his face looked blurred, then it would come suddenly into focus, etched sharp and naked by the flashbulb of urgency. An electric distinction poured out of him, impregnated his shabby clothes, his steel-rimmed glasses, his dirty gray felt hat. These objects could be recognized anywhere as belonging to Lee.

His face had the look of a superimposed photo, reflecting a

fractured spirit that could never love man or woman with complete wholeness. Yet he was driven by an intense need to make his love real, to change fact. Usually he selected someone who could not reciprocate, so that he was able—cautiously, like one who tests uncertain ice, though in this case the danger was not that the ice give way but that it might hold his weight—to shift the burden of not loving, of being unable to love, onto the partner.

The objects of his high-tension love felt compelled to declare neutrality, feeling themselves surrounded by a struggle of dark purposes, not in direct danger, only liable to be caught in the line of fire. Lee never came on with a kill-lover-and-self routine. Basically the loved one was always and forever an Outsider, a Bystander, an Audience.

Went to Brion Gysin's place in the Medina for lunch: Brion, Dave Morton, Leif and Marv, and a handsome New Zealander who is passing through the Zone. A ghastly, meaningless aggregate.

Morton said to me: "How long were you in medical school before they found out you weren't a corpse?"

The standard double entendres and coy references to test the stranger. Brion says: "I'm queer for shoes," and begins polishing his shoes during lunch.

Marv says: "I'm very sensitive to that word. I wish you wouldn't use it," rolling his round gray eyes, speckled with flaws and opaque spots like damaged marbles, at the young stranger. . . . Oh God!

But none of this is the real horror. Looking around the room, I suddenly saw that the other people were figures in a waking nightmare where no contact with anyone else is possible.

Somehow it was worse than a gathering of out-and-out squares, say the St. Louis country club set I was brought up with. There, a dreary formalism reigns. It is just dull. But this was horrible, pointing to some final impasse of communication. There was nothing said that needed to be said. The dry hum of negation and decay filled the room with its blighting frequency, a sound like insect wings rubbing together.

Dream: I am in Interzone some years ago. I meet a silly fairy who twists every remark into obscene, queer double entendre. Under this vacuous camping I see pure evil. We meet two lesbians, and they say, "Hello, boys," a dead, ritual greeting from which I turn away in disgust. The fairy follows me, moves into a house with me. I feel nauseated, as if a loathsome insect had attached itself to my body.

I am walking out along a dry, white road on the outskirts of town. There is danger here. A dry, brown, vibrating hum or frequency in the air, like insect wings rubbing together. I pass a village: mounds about two feet high, of black cloth over wire frames like a vast hive.

Back in the city. Everywhere is the dry hum. Not a sound, exactly, but a frequency, a wavelength. A Holy Man with a black face is causing the waves. He operates from a tower-like structure covered with cloth.

I contract to assassinate the Holy Man. An Arab gives me a pink slip to present at a gun store, where a rifle with a telescopic sight will be issued to me. A Friend walks with me. He says: "There is no use to oppose the Holy Man. The Holy Man is reality. The Holy Man is Right."

"You're wrong," I say. "Wrong! I don't want to see you again for all eternity."

I hide from the Friend in a florist's shop, under a case of flowers. He stands by the case as though at my coffin, crying and wringing his hands and begging me to give up the assassination of the Holy Man. I am crying too, my tears falling in yellow dust, but I won't give up.

It is frequently said that the Great Powers will never give up the Interzone because of its value as a listening post. It is in fact the listening post of the world, the slowing pulse of a decayed civilization, that only war can quicken. Here East meets West in a final debacle of misunderstanding, each seeking the Answer, the Secret, from the other and not finding it, because neither has the Answer to give.

I catch sluggish flies in the air with the curious pleasure one derives from taking an eyelash from an eye, or extracting a hair from a nostril, the moment when the hair gives way with a little snap and you turn the greasy black hair between finger and thumb, looking at the white root, reluctant to let it go. So I felt the cold fly moving between my fingers, and the soft crunch as I delicately crushed the head to avoid a hemorrhage of sticky juice or blood—Where does the blood come from? Do they bite and suck blood?—finally letting the dead fly drop to the floor, spinning like a dry leaf.

Failure is mystery. A man does not mesh somehow with time-place. He has savvy, the ability to interpret the data collected by technicians, but he moves through the world like a ghost, never able to find the time-place and person to put anything into effect, to give it flesh in a three-dimensional world.

I could have been a successful bank robber, gangster, business executive, psychoanalyst, drug trafficker, explorer, bullfighter, but the conjuncture of circumstances was never there. Over the years I begin to doubt if my time will ever come. It will come, or it will not come. There is no use trying to force it. Attempts to break through have led to curbs, near disasters, warnings. I cultivate an alert passivity, as though watching an opponent for the slightest sign of weakness.

Of course there is always the possibility of reckless break-through, carrying a pistol around and shooting anybody who annoys me, taking narcotic supplies at gunpoint, *amok* a form of active suicide. Even that would require some signal from outside, or from so deep inside that it comes to the same thing. I have always seen inside versus outside as a false dichotomy. There is no sharp line of separation. Perhaps:

"Give it to me straight, Doc."

"Very well . . . A year perhaps, following a regime . . ." He is reaching for a pad.

"Never mind the regime. That's all I wanted to know."

Or simply the explosion of knowing, finally: "This is your last chance to step free of the cautious, aging, frightened flesh. What are you waiting for? To die in an old men's home, draping your fragile buttocks on a bench in the dayroom?"

Just thought of the story about how cats sit on your chest and breathe your breath out of you so you suffocate. Just sit there, you dig, their nose one-quarter inch from yours, and whenever you take a breath you get the cat's exhaust carbon dioxide. This story is like the Protocols of the Elders of Zion. Invented by cat-haters. So I start an anti-cat movement, pointing out their sneaky, sensual, unmoral traits, and begin wholesale extermination, genocide of the feline concept. There is always money in hate.

Perhaps Hitler was right in a way. That is, perhaps certain subspecies of genus *Homo sapiens* are incompatible. Live and let live is impossible. If you let live, they will kill you by creating an environment in which you have no place and will die out. The present psychic environment is increasingly difficult for me to endure, but there is still leeway, slack that could be taken up at any time. Safety lies in exterminating the type that produces the environment in which you cannot live. So I will die soon—why bother? Some form of transmigration seems to me probable. I am now, therefore I always was and always will be.

Looking down at my shiny, dirty trousers that haven't been changed in months, the days gliding by, strung on a syringe with a long thread of blood . . . it is easy to forget sex and drink and all the sharp pleasures of the body in this Limbo of negative pleasure, this thick cocoon of comfort.

More and more trouble at the *farmacía*. Spent all day until 5 P.M. to score two boxes of Eukodal. I'm running out of everything now. Out of veins, out of money. I can sense the static at the drugstore, the mutterings of control like a telephone off the hook.

"*Muy difícil ahora*," the druggist tells me.

What is this creeping cancer of control? The suicided German is a plant, a pretext— Some days ago I was standing in a bar when a man touched my arm. I immediately made him for fuzz. In my pocket I had a box of methadone ampules I had just bought in the Plaza Farmacía. Could he be concerned about that? No, not in the Zone. He asked me if I was Max Gustav. I said, "No," naturally. The cop had a passport and showed me Gustav's picture, which he thought resembled me.

Next day I read in the paper that Max Gustav had been found dead in a ditch outside the town, apparently a suicide from overdose of Nembutal. It seems at the time the cop asked if I was Max they did not know he was dead. He had checked out of his hotel, leaving a suitcase. After two days the hotel called the law. They opened the suitcase, found the passport, and started looking for Max Gustav. . . . Well, the next time I went to the Plaza Farmacía they would not sell me methadone ampules without a script. A new regulation had gone into effect as a result of Max Gustav's suicide.

And that shows how things are related, or something. Bill Gains here would be the last straw. But everything has two faces. You need a paper now for everything. Why not apply for a permit to buy junk?

Such a sharp depression. I haven't felt like this since the day Joan died.

Spent the morning sick, waiting for Eukodal. Kept seeing familiar faces, people I had seen as store clerks, waiters, et cetera. In a small town these familiar faces accumulate and back up on you, so you are choked with familiarity on every side.

Sitting in front of the Interzone Café, sick, waiting for Eukodal. A boy walked by and I turned my head, following his loins the way a lizard turns its head, following the course of a fly.

Running short of money. Must kick habit.

What am I trying to do in writing? This novel is about transitions, larval forms, emergent telepathic faculty, attempts to control and stifle new forms.

I feel there is some hideous new force loose in the world like a creeping sickness, spreading, blighting. Remoter parts of the world seem better now, because they are less touched by it. Control, bureaucracy, regimentation, these are merely symptoms of a deeper sickness that no political or economic program can touch. What is the sickness itself?

Dream: Found a man with both hands cut off. I was pouring water on the stubs to stop the bleeding— Years ago in New York a young hoodlum borrowed a gun from me and never returned it. In a spasm of hate, I put a curse on him. A few days later both his hands were blown off when a gasoline drum exploded while he was working on it. He died. Are curses effective? Of course they are, to some extent.

More and more physical symptoms of depression. The latest is a burning sensation in the chest.

Until the age of thirty-five, when I wrote *Junky,* I had a special abhorrence for writing, for my thoughts and feelings put down on a piece of paper. Occasionally I would write a few sentences and then stop, overwhelmed with disgust and a sort of horror. At the present time, writing appears to me as an absolute necessity, and at the same time I have a feeling that my talent is lost and I can accomplish nothing, a feeling like the body's knowledge of disease, which the mind tries to evade and deny.

This feeling of horror is always with me now. I had the same feeling the day Joan died; and once when I was a child, I looked out into the hall, and such a feeling of fear and despair came over me, for no outward reason, that I burst into tears. I was looking into the future then. I recognize the feeling, and what I saw has not yet been realized. I can only wait for it to happen. Is it some ghastly occurrence like Joan's death, or simply deterioration and failure and final loneliness, a dead-end setup where there is no one I can contact? I am just a crazy old bore in a bar somewhere with my routines? I don't know, but I feel trapped and doomed.

Waiting for Eukodal, I was subject to a series of beggars. Two girls paralyzed from the waist down, swinging around on blocks. They bar the way, clutching at my pants legs. An English seaman on the beach. He gets his face very close to mine, and says, "You may be in the same position someday." I go into a café and sit at the counter drinking a cup of coffee. A child about seven years old, barefooted and dirty, touches my arm. These people are raised in beggary and buggery.

The nightmare feeling of my childhood is more and more my habitual condition. Is this a prevision of atomic debacle? Dream of a sixteenth-century Norwegian: He saw a black, mushroom-shaped cloud darkening the earth.

We have a new type of rule now. Not one-man rule, or rule of aristocracy or plutocracy, but of small groups elevated to positions of absolute power by random pressures, and subject to political and economic factors that leave little room for decision. They are representatives of abstract forces who have reached power through surrender of self. The iron-willed dictator is a thing of the past. There will be no more Stalins, no more Hitlers. The rulers of this most insecure of all worlds are rulers by accident, inept, frightened pilots at the controls of a vast machine they cannot understand, calling in experts to tell them which buttons to push.

Junk is a key, a prototype of life. If anyone fully understood junk, he would have some of the secrets of life, the final answers.

I have mentioned the increased sensitivity to dreamlike feelings of nostalgia that always accompany light junk sickness. This morning when I woke up without junk, I closed my eyes and saw cliffs on the outskirts of a town, with houses on top of them, and china-blue sky, and white linen snapping in a cold spring wind.

The pure pleasure of cold Whistle on a hot summer afternoon of my childhood. In the 1920s the United States, even the Midwest, was a place of glittering possibilities. You could be a gangster, a hard-drinking reporter, a jittery stockbroker, an expatriate, a successful writer. The possibilities spilled out in front of you like a rich display of merchandise. Sitting on the back steps drinking Whistle at twilight on a summer evening, hearing the streetcars clang past on Euclid Avenue, I felt the excitement and nostalgia of the twenties tingling in my groin.

Interesting that out of morphine has been made the perfect antidote for morphine, and that it creates its exact antidote in the body. And from junk sickness comes a heightened sensitivity to impressions and sensation on the level of dream, myth, symbol. On the penis there might be bits of flesh half-putrescent and half-larval, separating from the host and degenerating to less specific tissue, a sort of life jelly that will take root and grow anywhere.

Seemed to see West St. Louis, the moving headlights on Lindell Boulevard. Very vivid for a moment. I was in a study with soft lights, an apartment probably. Horrible feeling of desolation. Imagine being old, paralyzed or blind, and forced to accept the charity of some St. Louis relation. I continue writing, but publication is hopeless. The book market is saturated. It is all done now by staff writers and is as much a job as working in an advertising agency. Not even anyone I can read it to, so that when I know it is good I feel more sad because then the loneliness is sharper.

Would it be possible to write a novel based on the actual facts of Interzone or anyplace?

Marv and Mohamed—this "friendship," as Sam calls it:
"Once he brought me a dead sparrow."
Marv's grating, continual laugh, his angular, graceless movements. They could not be called clumsy. Quick, not fumbling, he moves in galvanized, pathic jerks, never sliding into fluid grace, or off the other edge into actual tic.
And Mohamed—sulky, stupid, whore to the bone. He is a favorite among the Arabs because of his chunky, fat ass. A fat ass is considered highly desirable by the Arabs. How Oriental and dull at the same time, like a carryover from camel trading.
So Marv says all the time: "I don't mind him going with Arabs,

you understand, but just don't let me catch him with another American or a European. Better not let me catch either of them. You have to fight for what you want in this world."

I wonder if Mohamed has any desires that are really his, that is, starting from inside out and seeking the projection of his desire? But they don't function that way. They are excited by situation, not by fantasy. This is partly due to the immediate availability of sex to the Arab, which is difficult for an American—accustomed to frustration, certainly to delay, expense, buildup—to realize. The Arab achieves immediate satisfaction because he is willing to accept homosexual contact.

As Marv puts it: "It's three in the morning, so Ali meets Ahmed and says to him: 'Do you want to?' That's the standard phrase. The whole deal takes five minutes." It's expected the one who makes the proposition should give something to the other. A few pesetas, some cigarettes. Anything. A matter of form. So perhaps an Arab has no type he is looking for, no specialized desires at all. Man or woman, it's all sex to him. Like eating. Something you do every day.

No one I really want to see here. So far as friendship goes, I can't live off the country. So few people I want to see anywhere. KiKi is ten minutes' perfunctory talk or sex, and I am completely unable most of the time on accounta the family jewels is in hock to the Chinaman. Must cut down or kick. The price is going up to where I can't pay. Since that fucking German had to come here and commit suicide, you have to buy a script every time. Why couldn't he have done it someplace else? Or some other way? Waited all day until eight at night for two boxes.

A novel that consists of the facts as I see and feel them. How can it have a beginning or an end? It just runs along for a while and then stops, like Arab music.

I can hear some Arabs singing in the next house. This music goes on and on, up and down. Why don't they get bored with it and shut up? It says nothing, goes nowhere. There is no lift in it, no emotion. Sounds like a chorus of boys singing out lottery numbers, or a tobacco auction. Apparently they are beating a tambourine, dancing and singing. Every now and then they reach a meaningless climax and everybody lets out shrill yipes. Then they stop for a while, presumably resting for another period of the same routine. Is it sad, happy, sinister, sweet? Does it express any deep human emotions? If so, I don't feel it.

I have wondered if it would be possible to find a note of music that would produce orgasm in the listener, that would reach into the spinal column and touch a long white nerve. Tension grows in the abdomen and breaks in long waves through the body, colonic undulations rising to a sudden crescendo. Arab music sounds like that. An orgasm produced mechanically without emotion, a twanging on the nerves, a beating on the viscera.

After a shot I went up to the Bagdad and met Leif and Marv. The manager is an unsuccessful artist named Algren. If he has a first name, I never heard it. Tall, broad-shouldered, handsome, with a cold, imperious manner. When I first came to Interzone he was exhibiting some of his paintings. Not distinguished work. Vistas of the Sahara, the best of them recalling the bare, haunted rock and desert of Dalí's dream landscapes. There is skill, he can draw but he has no real reason to do so. I found he was as niggardly in putting out in personal relation as in painting. I could make no contact with him. He lives with a young Arab painter, a phony primitive. As a fashionable restaurateur, Algren is superb, just the correct frequency of glacial geniality. He expects the joint to become world-famous.

"Last night the coatroom was stacked with mink. There's a lot of money in Interzone," he says. Maybe, but it is a bit out of the way. A rich old woman put up the loot. Algren doesn't have dime one, but he's a character who will get rich by acting like he is rich already. And Algren is crazy in a way that will help. He has a paranoid conceit. He is a man who never has one good word to say for anybody, and that's the way a man should be to run a fashionable night spot. Everyone will want to be the exception, the one person he really likes.

He has some Arab musicians from the Rif, a three-man combo, and a little boy who dances and sings. The kid is about fourteen and small for his age, like all Arabs. There is no stir of adolescence in his face, no ferment, nothing there to awaken. The face of an old child, doll-like with a monkey's acquisitiveness. He puts the money you give him in his turban so it hangs down on his forehead. What does he do with the money? His voice is very loud, the up and down of Arab music bellowed out by this grasping, whirling doll. He twitches his hips not only sideways but up and over in a peculiar, double-jointed movement. His sexual and acquisitive drives are completely merged. It would never occur to him to go to bed with anyone for a reason other than money. There is about him a complete lack of youngness, of all the sweetness and un-certainty and shyness of youth. He is hard and brassy as an old whore, and to me about as interesting as a sexual object.

There is a nightmare feeling in Interzone with its glut of nylon shirts, cameras, watches, sex and opiates sold across the counter. Something profoundly menacing in complete laissez-faire. And the new police chief up there on the Hill, accumulating dossiers—I suspect him of unspeakable fetishistic practices with his files.

When the druggist sells me my daily ration of Eukodal, he smirks like I have picked up the bait to a trap. The whole Zone is a trap, and someday it will close. Not snap shut, but close slowly. We will see it closing, but there will be no escape, no place to go.

Speaking of the new chief of police reminds me, when I first got here KiKi's mother beefed about me to the fuzz I was debauching her only child, or so the story went. I was living in Matty's place, and Matty swore it was true, and claimed there was a detective prowling around outside the door—it turned out he wasn't a detective at all but an old queen who had his eye on KiKi, and the whole story was just Interzone bullshit. At the same time Antonio, the mooching Portuguese, starts a rumor there is junk heat on me. He hopes I will lam out of the Zone.

Matty is a pimp who loves his work, a fat, middle-aged, queer Cupid. He kept casting reproachful glances at me in the hall: "*Ach,* fifteen years in the Zone, and never before do I have such a thing in my house. Now is here since two weeks an English gentleman. With him I could make good business except my house is so watched at."

Bedroom farce of police and terrible mother coming in the front door. I try to push KiKi into Marv's room and he says: "Dump your hot kids someplace else, Lee." A handkerchief with come on it is extremely damning evidence. The best thing is to swallow it.

I am writing this in a hospital where I am taking the cure again. A typical Interzone setup. Jewish hospital, Spanish-run, with Catholic sisters as nurses. Like everything Spanish it is run in a sloppy, lackadaisical manner, thank God! No nurse walking in at the crack of dawn to slop tepid water all over you. No good explaining to some Swedish nurse from North Dakota how a junky can't stand the feel of water on his skin. I been here ten days and haven't had a bath. It is 8 A.M. and the day shift comes on sometime in the next half hour. In the room next to me someone is groaning. A horrible, inhuman sound, pushed out from the stomach. Why don't they give him a shot and shut him up? It's a drag. I hate to hear people groan, not because of pity but because it is a very irritating sound.

That reminds me of a skit I once wrote about a junky whose mother was dying of cancer, and he takes her morphine, substituting codeine. To substitute codeine was worse than stealing the morphine outright and substituting milk-sugar placebo. A placebo, by the shock, the gap between the pain-torn tissues straining for the relief of morphine, and the sheer nothingness in the placebo, might galvanize the body into a miracle, an immaculate fix. But codeine would blunt the edge of pain so that it would liquefy and spread, filling the cells like a gray fog, solid, impossible to dislodge.

"Better now?" The groaning had stopped.

"Much better, thank you," she said dryly.

She knows, he thought. *I could never fool her.*

Perhaps one would feel better in an out-and-out police state like Russia or satellite countries. The worst has happened. The outer world realizes your deepest fears—or desires? You don't get bends of the spirit from sudden changes of pressure. Inner and outer pressure are equalized.

So I wrote a story about a man who gets the wrong passport in a Turkish bath in the Russian Zone of Vienna, and he can't get back through the Iron Curtain. Incomplete, of course. What you think I am, a hack?

The sky over Vienna was a light, hard, china blue, and a cold spring wind whipped Martin's loose gabardine topcoat around his thin body. He felt the ache of desire in his loins, like a toothache when the pain is light and different from any other pain. He turned a corner; the Danube stabbed his eyes with a thousand points of light, and he felt the full force of the wind and had to lean forward to maintain balance.

If there's no guard at the line there can't be too much danger, he thought. *They could hardly accuse me of spying in a Turkish bath*. He saw a café and went in. A huge room, almost empty. Green upholstered seats like old Pullman cars. A sullen waiter with a round pimply face and white eyelashes took his order for a double brandy. He swallowed the brandy straight. For a moment he gagged, then his stomach smoothed out in waves of warmth and euphoria. He ordered another brandy. The waiter was smiling now.

What the hell, he thought. *All they could do is kick me out of the Russian Zone.*

He sat back anticipating the warm embrace of steam, letting go, liquefying like an amoeba, dissolving in warmth and comfort and desire.

Why draw the line anywhere? What a man wants to do he will do sooner or later, in thought or in fact. . . . But nobody is giving you an argument. The third brandy was anesthetizing the centers of caution. *I'm hard up and I want a boy, and I'm going to the Roman Baths, Russian Zone or no. Too bad we didn't have a queer representative when they split up Vienna. We'd have gone to the barricades before Russia got the Roman Baths.*

He saw a legion of embattled queens behind a barricade of Swedish-modern furniture. They staggered and died with great histrionic gestures and pathic screams. They were all tall, thin, ungainly queens in Levi's and lumberjack shirts, with long yellow hair and insane blue eyes, all screaming, screaming. He shuddered. *Perhaps I'd better just go back to the hotel and . . . no, by God!*

The streetcar was crowded and he had to stand. The people looked gray, hostile, suspicious, avoiding his glance. They were passing the Prater. He was in the Russian Zone. He remembered the Prater before the war, a huge park always full of people and plenty of pickups. Now it was an expanse of rubble with one vast Ferris wheel, bleak and menacing against the cold blue sky. He got off the streetcar. The conductor stood leaning out of the back platform watching Martin until the streetcar turned the corner. Martin pretended to look for a cigarette.

Yes, there were the Roman Baths, looking much the same. The street was empty. Perhaps there would be no boys. But a youth sidled up to him and asked for a light. *Not too good*, he decided. *I'll find better inside*.

He paid for a room, leaving his wallet and passport in a deposit box.

(This is after he has got the wrong passport, been arrested and deported to Budapest, or somewhere far behind the Iron Curtain.)

He learned a new kind of freedom, the freedom of living in continual tension and fear to the limit of his inner fear and tension so the pressure was at least equalized, and for the first time in his adult life he knew the meaning of complete relaxation, complete pleasure in the moment. He felt alive with his whole being. The forces that were intended to crush his dignity and existence as an individual delineated him so that he had never felt surer of his own worth and dignity.

And he was not alone. Slowly he discovered a vast, dreamlike underground: a cop examining his papers would suddenly turn into a friend. And he learned the meaning of the hostile, averted faces on the streetcar in Vienna, learned to distrust the friendship too quickly offered.

Martin had lost fifteen pounds since leaving the West. His hand rested now on his stomach, feeling the muscle hard and alive with an animal alertness. Steps on the stairs. Two men, strangers. He knew the step of everyone in the One World pension. He slid off the bed. Moving with economy and precision, he shoved a heavy wardrobe in front of the door. He crossed the room, opened the window and stepped out onto the fire escape, closing the window behind him. He climbed a shaky iron ladder to the roof. He heard the wardrobe crash to the floor. Seven feet to the next roof. He looked around. No plank, nothing. He heard the window open.

I'll have to jump, he decided.

(To be continued)

Went to bed with KiKi. He said he couldn't come because he is all wore out from wet dreams about me the night before. That really takes the rag offen the bush.

Developed routine during dinner with Kells Elvins. We kidnap the Sacred Black Stone out of Mecca and hold it for ransom. We swoop down in a helicopter, throw the Stone in and take off with it like a great roc, the Arabs following the 'copter across the square, reaching up at it and shouting imprecations. (Maybe the Stone is too big to move?)

Lee sat with the syringe poised in his left hand, pondering the mystery of blood. Certain veins he could hit at two-thirty in the afternoon. Others were night veins, veins that appeared and disappeared at random. Lee found his hunches were seldom wrong. If he reached for the syringe with his right hand, it meant try the left arm. His body knew what vein could be hit. He let the body take over, as in automatic writing, when he was preparing to pick up.

There was a single candle burning in a brass stick on the bed table. KiKi and Lee lay side by side in bed, a sheet thrown across their bodies waist high. They passed a *keif* cigarette back and forth, inhaling deeply and holding the inhale. KiKi had a case of benign shingles, and there was a great hive on his back and swelling in the glands under his arms. Lee ran gentle fingers over the inflamed area, asked questions, nodded gravely from time to time. The candle light and smoke, the low voices, imparted a quality of ritual to the scene. . . .

Following is a story of a young man in Spain sentenced to be hanged by a council of war (the military handles capital cases in Spain):

Antonio sat down on the iron shelf covered with old newspapers that was his bed. He lay down on his side and pulled his knees up to his chest, hands pressed against his genitals.

A council of war! he thought. *That completes the picture of a barbarous, obscene ritual like an Indian tribe's. They've been trying to get me like this ever since they found out I'd been born alive. But I had an animal's feel for traps—until they found the right bait. It was a clumsy snare, and I could have seen the noose under the leaves that first night in Tío Pepe's. That is, I could have seen it if I hadn't been looking someplace else. . . .*

Fade out . . . Flash back . . . Music (obviously I have an eye on TV and Hollywood):

It was early for Tío Pepe's, which is a late place that gets going when the bars close down, after one o'clock. No one at the bar. I ordered a cognac. There was a boy standing in front of the jukebox. He had on one of those summer shirts with holes in it, a white shirt hanging outside his pants. Through the shirt, in a halo of hideous man-made colors, chlorophyll greens, reds and oranges of synthetic soft drinks, the purples of a fluorescent-lighted cocktail lounge, the ghastly light pinks and blues of religious objects, I could see the lean young body alive with an animal alertness. He was leaning against the jukebox, his hip thrown to one side, his face bent over, reading the song titles, all the awkwardness and grace and sweetness of adolescence in his stance, those terrible colors playing over him.

He looks like an advertisement for something, I thought, but that wasn't exactly what I meant. There was some significance in the young figure leaning over the jukebox that eluded me. Then he turned around, pivoting with a sudden movement. I could hear my own breath suck in with a sharp hiss of air. He didn't have any face. It was a mass of scar tissue. . . .

I see the way to solve contradictions, to unite fragmentary, unconnected projects: I will simply transcribe Lee's impressions of Interzone. The fragmentary quality of the work is inherent in the method and will resolve itself so far as necessary. That is, I include the author, Lee, in the novel, and by so doing separate myself from him so that he becomes another character, central to be sure, occupying a special position, but not myself at all. This could go on in an endless serial arrangement, but I would always be the observer and not the participant by the very act of writing about a figure who represents myself.

I feel guilty writing this when I should be up to my balls in work. But feller say: "Nothing is lost." . . . A horrible vision of suffocating under the accumulated piss and shit and nail clippings and eyelashes and snot excreted by my soul and body, backing up like atomic waste. "Go get lost for Chrissakes!" I already made a novel outa letters. I can always tuck one in somewhere, bung up a hole with it, you know. . . .

I hear that baneful, unfrocked Lt. Commander prowling about the halls. They took his buttons off and cut his stripes away, but unfortunately neglected to hang him in the morning or at any other time. The reference, in case you are fortunate enough not to know, is to "The Hanging of Danny Deever" by Kipling. For a real bum kick you should hear a decaying, corseted tenor singing "The Hanging of Danny Deever," followed by "Trees" as an unsolicited encore.

Like I say, this fucking ex-Commander is casting a spell of silliness over me so that I sometimes come up with these awful, queer double entendres myself. Last night I told him straight, by God I wasn't going to stand still for any more of his shit: "Don't you know about Joe Reeves? Why, I hear he likes boys! Did you ever hear of such a thing, Bill? Heh heh heh." Rolling his eyes at Kells.

So I really had all I could take. And the typewriter is fucked again. I'm a martyr to this fucking typewriter—a man as basically unmechanical as I am should never buy used machinery—but before I'll ask help from that Commander I'll write with blood and a hypodermic needle.

Loaded on methadone. I bought out Interzone and the south end of Spain on Eukodal. Like I say, loaded, impotent, convulsed with disembodied limitless desire. Appointment with KiKi *mañana*. I am supposed to be taking the cure again. KiKi has my clothes and money and is doling out ampules—

I pulled a sneak. Pants borrowed off a clothesline, *dégagé* in a dirty sweatshirt like returning from tennis or a hike on the mountain, finally managed to cash one of my special traveler's checks. Even my traveler's checks are wrong, vaguely disreputable and disturbing. No one thinks they are actually forged or counterfeit, you understand. They just feel something wrong with me.

A fat blond beast of a desk sergeant throwing himself at the feet of a thin, crippled, red-haired lush worker: sparse red hair, the junky gray felt hat which leaves a line on his forehead when he takes it off—it is that tight. So this cop comes down from the rostrum of his desk and grovels at the feet of this skinny little middle-aged lush worker known as Red from Brooklyn, to distinguish him from another Red, who has no such definite and particularizing place of residence. Red shrinks back, expecting to get worked over.

"Red!" A horrible sound of defeat, a sordid battle fought and lost in a psyche as bleak as a precinct cell. "Reddie Boy!" He makes a kissing bite for Red's shoe. Red retreats again.

"Now, Lieutenant! I didn't so much as put my hand out."

The sergeant jumps up like a great albino toad. He reaches out and grabs the trembling lush worker by the coat lapels.

"Lieutenant! Listen to me. I didn't."

"Reddie Boy!" He throws his fat but powerful arms around Red, pinioning both of Red's arms. He runs one hand up behind Red's neck, kisses him brutally, repeatedly.

"Reddie Boy! How I've wanted you all these years! I remember the first time you came in, with Dolan from the Fifteenth. Only it wasn't the Fifteenth then, it was the Ninth. . . ."

Red gives a horrible, sickly, cautious smile. *The fuzz has flipped. I gotta play it cool . . . cool. . . .*

"Many's the night I've cried for you like this, Reddie Boy."

"Jeez, not that way, Sarge. I got piles."

"You haven't been a naughty boy with someone else, have you? Wonder if we could use this floor wax?" This last sentence in his hard, practical cop voice.

Someone just died in the hospital downstairs. I can hear them chanting something, and women crying. It's the old Jew who was annoying me with his groans. . . . Well, get this stiff outa here. It's a bringdown for the other patients. This isn't a funeral parlor.

What levels and time shifts involved in transcribing these notes: reconstruction of the past, the immediate present—which conditions selection of the material—the emergent future, all hitting me at once, sitting here junk-sick because I got some cut ampules of methadone last night and this morning.

I just went down to the head and passed the dead man's room. Sheet pulled up over his face, two women sniffling. I saw him several times, in fact this morning an hour before he died. An ugly little man with a potbelly and scraggly, dirty beard, always groaning. How bleak and sordid and meaningless his death!

God grant I never die in a fucking hospital! Let me die in some *louche* bistro, a knife in my liver, my skull split with a beer bottle, a pistol bullet through the spine, my head in spit and blood and beer, or half in the urinal so the last thing I know is the sharp ammonia odor of piss— I recall in Peru a drunk passed out in the urinal. He lay there on the floor, his hair soaked with piss. The urinal leaked, like all South American pissoirs, and there was half an inch of piss on the floor— Or let me die in an Indian hut, on a sandbank, in jail, or alone in a furnished room, on the ground someplace or in an alley, on street or subway platform, in a wrecked car or plane, my steaming guts splattered over torn pieces of metal. . . . Anyplace, but not in a hospital, not in bed . . .

This is really a prayer. "If you have prayed, the thing may chance." Certainly I would be atypical of my generation if I didn't die with my boots on. Dave Kammerer stabbed by his boy with a scout knife, Tiger Terry killed by an African lion in a border-town nightclub, Joan Burroughs shot in the forehead by a drunken idiot—myself—doing a William Tell, trying to shoot a highball glass off her head, Cannastra killed climbing out of a moving subway for one more drink— His last words were "Pull me back!" His friends tried to pull him back inside, but his coat ripped in their hands and then he hit a post—Marvie dead from an overdose of horse—

I see Marvie in a cheap furnished room on Jane Street, where I used to serve him—sounds kinda dirty, don't it?—I mean sell him caps of H, figuring it was better to deliver to his room than meet him someplace, he is such a ratty-looking citizen, with his black shoes and no socks in December. Once I delivered him his cap, and he tied up. I was looking out the window—it is nerve-racking to watch someone look for a vein. When I turned around he had passed out, and the blood had run back into the dropper, it was hanging onto his arm full of blood, like a glass leech— So I see him there on the bed in a furnished room, slowly turning blue around the lips, the dropper full of blood clinging to his arm. Outside it is getting dark. A neon sign flashes off and on, off and on, each flash picking out his face in a hideous red-purple glow— "Use Gimpie's H. It's the greatest!" Marvie won't have to hustle tomorrow. He has scored for the Big Fix.

—Leif the Dane drowned with all hands in the North Sea—he was a drag anyhoo. Roy went wrong and hanged himself in the Tombs—he always used to say: "I don't see how a pigeon can live with himself." And P. Holt, the closest friend of my childhood, cut his jugular vein on a broken windshield . . . dead before they got him out of the car. A few of them died in hospitals or first-aid stations, but they had already had it someplace else. Foster, one of my anthropology friends in Mexico, died of bulbar polio. "He was dead when he walked in the door," the doctor at the hospital said later. "I felt like telling him, 'Why don't you check straight into a funeral parlor, pick your coffin and climb into it? You've got just about time.' "

I've had trouble with this Spanish methadone before. Often I have bought boxes with one or two empty ampules. Accident? Spanish sloppiness? Ixnay. These Spanish factories are flooding Southern Europe with methadone.

Is it safer to put an empty ampule in every ten boxes or so, or to fill all the ampules with adulterated mixture? Hard to say. People are more likely to beef about empties, but it is easier to alibi. Accidents can happen—though they shouldn't happen in a methadone factory. Not that kind of accident. A beef is less likely with an adulterated mixture, but more serious if it occurs, and somebody who hasn't been paid off, or who has a political angle, starts making spot analyses of the product. There is no alibi-ing that. And they are getting too greedy. Last night's shot was *plain water*. That's not smart.

The Man is getting edgy. His boy is squawking for a star sapphire: "Daddy, you wanna get the best for me." His blonde wants a custom-made Daimler so long it can't turn corners—only also-rans turn corners. If you got real class to you, you never look sideways. The bang-tails are running offbeat, some citizen unloaded a salted uranium mine on him. (The uranium mine is a new con. You plant a tube of atomic waste in the mine site so the Geiger counter goes wild over it. Or you can use a gimmicked Geiger counter with an electric motor concealed in it so you can speed it up or slow it down.)

My thoughts have been turning to crime lately. And of all crimes, blackmail seems to me the most artistically satisfying. I mean, the Moment of Truth when you see all his bluff and bluster and front collapse, when you know you've got him. His next words—when he can talk—will be: "How much do you want?" That must be real tasty. A man could get his rocks off on a deal like that.

Like a guy pushed his boy off a balcony and claimed it was an accident, the kid slipped on a gob of K-Y and catapulted over the rail. No witnesses. He seems to be in the clear. Then Willy Lee drops around.

Lee: "You see, Mr. Throckmorton, I'm broke."

Throckmorton: "Broke! I don't know why you come to me with this revolting disclosure. It's extremely distasteful. Have you no pride?"

Lee: "I thought you might want to help a fellow American, and buy this gadget off me." He shows a German spy camera attached to powerful field glasses for long-range pictures. "It's worth quite a bit."

Throckmorton: "Take it to a pawnshop. I have no interest in photography."

Lee: "But this is a very special gadget. Look from that balcony. . . . *Say*, isn't that the balcony that kid fell from?"

Throckmorton looks at him coldly. Lee stammers, pretends to be embarrassed.

Lee: "Now I hope I haven't gone and said the wrong thing. Must have been a terrible shock for you, losing a friend . . . and such a *good* friend. . . . What I wanted to say was from that balcony you can hardly see my trap over on the wrong side of the Medina, but if I took a picture from that balcony it would show my place and how dirty the windows are and how one has a broken pane mended with adhesive tape. . . ."

Throckmorton (looking at his watch): "I'm not interested. Now if you will excuse me, I have an appointment. . . ."

Lee: "I'm sorry to take up your time like this. . . . Like I was saying, you could take a picture that would show my place, or you could take a picture in the other direction—one that would show *your* place. I've taken some pictures of your place, Mr. Throckmorton. . . . I hope you won't think me presumptuous." He pulls out some photos. "I'm a pretty good photographer. Maybe you would want to buy some of these pictures I took of your house and that balcony. . . ."

Throckmorton: "Will you please leave my house."

Lee: "But, Mr. Throckmorton, one of these pictures is really interesting." He holds the picture three inches in front of Throckmorton's face. Throckmorton starts back. A cry of anger dies away to a gurgle in his throat. He reaches for a chair and collapses into it, like an old man having a stroke.

Lee: "Like the song say, *Mister* Throckmorton, you're beginning to see the light. . . . What's your first name, lover?" He sits on the arm of Throckmorton's chair and playfully ruffles his hair. "I got like a presentiment we're going to get to know each other real well . . . see quite a bit of each other."

—

I have a feeling that my real work I can't or, on a deep level, won't begin. What I do is only evasion, sidetrack, notes. I am walking around the shores of a lake, afraid to jump in, but pretending to study the flora and fauna—those two old bags. I must put myself, every fucking cell of me, at the disposal of this work.

Oh, God! Sounds like posthumous biographical material—Lee's letters to his beloved friend and agent, who writes back that the work must develop in its own way and reveal as much of itself to me as I am able to interpret and transcribe. I have but to act with straightaheadedness, without fear or holding back.

"At this time the creative energies of Lee were at lowest ebb. He was subject to acute depressions. 'At times,' he writes in a letter to his agent, 'my breath comes in gasps,' or again, 'I have to remember to breathe.' "

But the fragmentary, unconnected quality of my work is inherent in the method, and will resolve itself as far as is necessary. The Tangier novel will consist of Lee's impressions of Tangier, instead of the outworn novelistic pretense that he is dealing directly with his characters and situations. That is, *I include the author in the novel*.

Civilian casualties of those books on combat judo and guerrilla war. Country club cocktail party: A man who had been a great athlete in his youth, still powerful but fattish, a sullen-faced ash blond with droopy lips, stands in front of another man, looking at him with stupid belligerence.

"Bovard, I could kill you in thirty seconds. No, in ten seconds. I have a book on combat judo. . . . Like this—" He leaps on Bovard, planting a knee in his back. "I hook my left middle finger into your right eye, meanwhile my knee is in your kidney and I am crushing your Adam's apple with my right elbow and reaching around to stamp on your instep with . . ."

Sharp words with the *criada*. Half an hour past breakfast time, I ring and ask for breakfast and the silly little bitch comes on sulky and surprised, like I was out of line.

I say sharply: "Look, *señorita*" (there is no English equivalent for *señorita*, which means a young, well-brought-up, unbanged young lady, I mean a virgin; you even call sixty-year-old whores *señorita* as a politeness—especially if you want something from them, you dig, I shouldn't take it upon myself to imply she *isn't señorita*)—so I say, "Look, *señorita*, breakfast is at eight. It's now eight-thirty."

I am not one of those weak-spirited, sappy Americans who want to be liked by all the people around them. I don't care if people hate my guts; I assume most of them do. The important question is what are they in a position to do about it. My affections, being concentrated on a few people, are not spread all over Hell in a vile attempt to placate sulky, worthless shits.

Of course, they could cut off my junk. That happened once and I beefed loud, long and high up, straight to the head croaker of this crummy trap. (I'm about the only cash customer they got. If I'd claimed to be half-Jewish I would be here for free.) My purpose in beefing was just in case somebody on the premises lifted the ampule and give me a shot of water, though the stuff was probably cut at the factory like Jewish babies, like all babies now. There is a night nurse who looks like junk, but it's hard for me to be sure with women and Chinese. Anyhoo, she give me a shot of water one night and I don't want her ministering to me no more—

Actually I savor like old brandy, rolling it on my tongue, the impotent hate of people who cannot, dare not retaliate. *That is, you dig, if I am in the right putting them down,* if they really have come up lousy. My epitaph on Old Dave the Pusher who died last year in Mexico, D.F.: "He looks like junk as he would catch another user in his strong toils of grace."

This place is *mad*. There are six people in my room now, washing the floor, putting up a mirror, taking the bed out and putting another one in, hanging curtains, fixing the light switch, all falling over each other and yelling in Spanish and Arabic, and the piss-elegant electrician only deigns to speak French—in Interzone it is a sign of class to speak nothing but French. You ask a question in Spanish, they answer in French, which is supposed to put you in your place. Citizens who come on with the "I only speak French" routine are the sorriest shits in the Zone, all pretentious, genteel—with the ghastly English connotation of lower-middle-class phony elegance—and generally don't have franc one. This electrician looks like a walking character armor with nothing inside it. I can see some Reichian analyst who has succeeded in dislodging the electrician's character armor. The analyst staggers back, blasted, blighted, a trembling hand covers his eyes: "Put it back! For the love of Christ, put it back!"

I met Mark Bradford, the playwright. He says: "I didn't catch your name."

"William Lee."

"Oh!" He drops my hand. "Well . . . uh, excuse me." He left Interzone the following day.

To a person in the medium of success, Willy Lee is an ominous figure. You meet him on the way down. He never hits a place when it is booming. When Willy Lee shows, the desert wind is blowing dust into empty bars and hotels, jungle vines are covering the oil derricks. A mad realtor sits in a spectral office, a famished jackal gnaws his numb, gangrenous foot: "Yes sir," he says, "this development is building right up."

A successful composer says to his protégé, a young Arab poet:

"Start packing, Titmouse. I just saw Willy Lee in the Socco Chico. Interzone has had it."

"Why, is he dangerous? You don't have to see him."

"*See* him—I should think not. It's like this: A culture gets its special stamp—Mayan, Northwest Coast, North Pacific—probably from one person or small group of people, who originally exuded these archetypes. After that, the archetypes are accepted unchanged for thousands of years. Well, Lee goes around exuding his own archetypes. It isn't done anymore. Already the Interzone Café reeks of rotting, aborted, larval archetypes. You notice that vibrating soundless hum in the Socco? That means someone is making archetypes in the area and you'd best evacuate right now. . . . Look, I am a success because I mesh with existing archetypes. If I accept, or even get to know, Lee's archetypes . . . and his routines!!!" The composer shudders. "Not me. Get packing, we're meeting Cole in Capri."

I just lit up. . . . A very dangerous party, Miss Green. Just one long drag on the unnatural teat she's got under her left arm and you are stoned, Pops. . . . In Mexico once I picked up on some bum-kick weed, and then got on a bus. I had a small pistol, a .41-caliber double-barreled Remington derringer in a holster tucked inside my belt so it was pointing just where the leg joins the body. . . . Suddenly I could feel the gun go off, smell the powder smoke, the singed cloth, feel the horrible numb shock, then the pit-pat of blood dripping like piss on the floor. . . . Later I examined the gun and found the safety half-cock was broken and such accidental discharge was quite possible.

I see the Un-American Committee has got around to Chris Goodwin. About time. I knew him when, dearie. A rank card-carrying

Scumunist. Queer, of course. He married a transvestite Jew Liz who worked on *Sundial*, that left-wing tabloid. —You recall the rag folded when their angel, an Albanian condom tycoon who came on like an English gentleman—the famous Merchant of Sex, who scandalized the International Set when he appeared at the Duc du Ventre's costume ball as a walking prick covered by a huge condom—went broke and shot himself during World War II. He couldn't get rubber, and Alcibiades Linton, the Houston Bubble Gum King, beat him out on Mexican chicle—perhaps these long parentheses should be relegated to footnotes. —I don't know why Chris married her. Probably for the looks of the thing, not knowing exactly how such things do look. . . . Did I ever tell you about my *New Yorker* cartoon? One State Department pansy visiting another. Kids crawling all over both of them, so the visiting swish says to the other: "Really, my dear, this front thing can be carried too far." —Anyhoo, his Liz wife was killed by Kurds in Pakistan— the reference is not to sour milk but to a species of Himalayan bandit. So Chris comes back with his dead wife in a jeep and says: "Poor Rachel. She was the life of every party. Kurds, you know." Kurds indeed. He liquidated her on orders from Moscow. Fact is, she "had taken to living on a slope of aristocracy," and ultimately "became crude and rampant"—I quote from the Moscow Ultimatum. I am leaving a reference to Turds for Milton Berle or anyone else who wants it. . . .

Also an improvement on the new anti-enzyme toothpaste to keep off lieutenants j.g. (junior grade) . . . a queen-repellent smelling of decayed queen flesh. (Shark repellent issued by the Navy smells like decayed sharks. Will put even a shark off his feed.)

The unfrocked commander lost his breevies, as he calls them, his jockstrap bathing suit that just does cover his equipment. That is, the maid lost his breevies in the laundry and he has been arguing with her about it for the past week.

Today the maid showed me the breevies and said: "Are they

his?" pointing to his room, and I said: "I presume that they are . . . they certainly aren't yours, madam."

Typical Interzone conversation: "My dear, let me tell you where you can buy the most marvelous cakes. Doughnut dough outside, hot custard filling, and rolled in sugar . . . Just opposite the Mecca bus terminal in the wholesale market. A very attractive boy cooks the cakes, who by the way is available."

Incredibly ugly and bestial women come down from the mountains carrying loads of charcoal on their backs. These are Berber women, unveiled, a blue tattoo stripe follows the cleft line from base of nose to upper lip, from lower lip to chin. Does the tattoo stripe continue along cleft line from cunt to asshole? I'm afraid we'll have to pigeonhole that under "Mysteries of the East." Our field man is a swish. . . . I notice many of these old charcoal beasts have their noses eaten away.

Two fags passing noseless woman: "My dear, these people lose their noses through sheer carelessness."

Interzone is crawling with pedophiles, citizens hung up on pre-puberty kicks. I don't dig it. I say anyone can't wait till thirteen is no better than a degenerate.

Above notes under file head T.B.W.I.—To Be Weaved In . . . A routine starts here concerning a rich writer who employs an extensive staff to do menial work like "weaving." I have a group of men and women, "My Eager Little Beavers" as I call them. . . . So this writer is a sadistic tyrant, you dig? I come and supervise the work, maintaining the nauseous fiction they really are beavers, and they have to wear beaver suits and stand for a roll call . . . "Sally Beaver, Marvin Beaver," et cetera, et cetera.

"And watch you don't get caught when a tree falls," I say jovially, holding up a finger stub.

Sort of a horrible tour de force, like the books of Anthony Burgess. Nobody gives those people who write children's books credit for what they have to go through. I have discovered a certain writer of children's books is a great Kafkian figure. He chose to hide himself in children's stories as a joke.

For example, there was a story of Old Grumpy Stubbs, who said he needed subsidiary personalities—Subs, he calls them—to keep his psyche cleaned out and perform other menial chores around the "farm."

"So just sign here, my friend. You'll never regret this as long as you live."

But poor Albrecht the woodcutter did regret it as soon as he got back to his little proviso apartment—that is, an apartment that has already been leased to someone else, or on which the lease has expired, so you can only hope to stall a few days until they get the necessary papers for dispossessing you. Albrecht had lived in provisos all his life.

Well, even though he couldn't read Clause 9(v) of the contract—which can only be deciphered with an electron microscope and a virus filter—Albrecht knew somehow he had done a terrific thing to sell out to Old Stubbs, so called because he had cut off all but two of his fingers in an effort to amuse his constituents: "I get it back!" he would say, jovially rubbing his mutilated hands together. "I get it back!"

"I just don't know," Albrecht reflected. "Now Old Stubbs he talks real nice and he did cut off a thumb for me. . . . It isn't every Sub can say he got a thumb off the old man. Some of them didn't get nothing."

An Advertising Short for Television:

"So there they are, these two young kids, naked in a jungle clearing under a great, cheesy moon so big and close, like a big soft white ass, you dig me? Like you could reach right up and goose it, and all around the myriad sounds of the jungle night. They have found the Lost City in each other's arms.

"Well, do they get living et by mosquitoes?" (These lapses into faulty syntax are carefully cultivated by J.R., the Director. He is starting a J.R. legend, you dig?) "Do they wake up in the morning with their assholes swoll shut they can't shit? Not at all. They wake up in the magic of a jungle morning. A cool breeze gooses them gently, running light fingers over their lean, hard young bodies. Half in sleep, they begin to move in rhythmic contractions. . . .

"Well, the Hays Office steps in here, boys. They would have stepped in last night, but the Assistant Coordinate Censor fell out of the launch watching an Indian boy jack off in his dugout, and a *candiru* skedaddled up his prick and we had to roust out a witch man to extract the little varmint." (The *candiru* is a little eel-like critter about two inches long by one-quarter inch in diameter, that darts up your prick, ass, or a woman's cunt if he can't do any better, holding himself *in situ* by barbs. Just what he figures to gain by this maneuver is not known, and no martyrs have stepped forward to study the *candiru*'s life cycle on location.)

"So why aren't they attacked by the whining hordes? Does love protect them? Balls! They use the new DuPont 8-hour B-22 Insect Repellent, that's why. You too can shit or fuck in comfort from the jungles of Madagascar to the great Arctic marshes of Lapland, where the mosquitoes drink deep under the sword of Damocles like in a British pub: 'Hurry up please, it's time . . .' "

Antonio the Portuguese Mooch

The Portuguese mooch came and sat down with Lee. Lee glanced up and said: "Hello, Antonio. Sit down." He went on writing and ignored the demanding waves emanating from Antonio. Antonio compressed his lips and sighed. He clapped tiny hands which were the blue-purple color of poor circulation. He ordered a glass of water, turning his simian profile to ignore the waiter's look of cold contempt.

"Bill, I hate to bother you with the tragedies of my life. The life of a European filled with sickness and hunger." He coughed. "Americans are not able to understand these things. . . . You— stupid, vulgar, mechanized . . . How we *hate* you." He patted Lee's arm and smiled, showing his dirty, cheap false teeth. "Not you, of course. You are different from the other Americans. You have a heart at least."

"Yes. And liver and lungs and a stomach. What's on your greasy mind? As if I didn't know . . ."

Antonio did not notice. He was looking into space, his face twisted with monkey-like hate.

"Yah! To you Americans I am just a little performing monkey who will do dirty little tricks for a penny. *Less* than a penny . . . I remember when I am fourteen years old, two drunken American merchant marines have me to jack off at their café table in a crowded street in Lisbon. 'Guess I win the bet, Joe.' 'Yeah, I guess you do. I've seen everything now.' And he passed over a wad of escudos that would feed a Portuguese family for a year. 'How much is this in *money*, Joe?' He holds up a coin like this. . . ." Antonio made an ugly gesture, pinching thumb and forefinger together— Lee was used to Antonio, but sometimes the man gave him a shock with some indescribable twist of malevolent ugliness.

" 'Oh, about one fifth of a cent.'

" 'You think that's too much? I don't want to spoil him.'

" 'Oh hell. Might as well spread around a little goodwill.'

" 'Trouble is the little gook might go into convulsions of gratitude and die right here at the table. Haven't you got anything smaller?'

" 'Wait a minute. Yeah, here we are. Rock bottom. Throw it over there in that horse manure.' "

Antonio's imitation of American accents was perfect, like a

recording, but mixed. Brooklyn and Chicago, California, East Texas, Maine and the Deep South, the voice's absent owner appearing momentarily at the table, like a speeded-up superimposed movie.

The waiter set the glass of water down with a smack so that some of the water jumped out onto Antonio's sleeve. Antonio glared at the waiter, who flicked the table with a towel, then turned his back and walked away.

"Gratitude you want. We pick your coin out of dung with our teeth, and *then*, shit running down our chins, we should kiss your fine, long-wearing American boots, and say, 'Oh thank you, Johnny. Thank you for your generosity. . . . That you condescend to watch a European of noble family fuck his blood sister and that my performance could find favor in your sight. This I did not dare to hope for. . . . You are indeed kind. . . .' "

His voice rose to a piercing shriek. Lee looked up, vaguely annoyed.

"I, with seven-hundred-year-old blood in my veins! I, to kiss the feet of a son-of-a-bitch American peasant pig!"

He was spitting with rage, like an hysterical cat. Suddenly his plate flew out and he thrust his head forward, snapping for it. Lee glimpsed a horrible extension of Antonio's mouth, teeth on the end of a flesh tube, undulating across the table, silent, sinister and purposeful as a parasitic worm.

The plate slid across the table into Lee's lap. Lee flicked the plate back onto the table, snapping the cloth of his pants. Antonio picked it up and polished it on the tablecloth with one hand. With the other hand he kept his face covered. He replaced the teeth, kneading his face. Finally he turned on Lee a ghastly smile, his face yellow like dirty old wax, sweating with strain.

"But you are not like the other Americans. You are a . . . good guy."

"Did you ever think of working, young man?" Lee asked.

"In Tangier is no work."

"Well, I know the owner of the Café de la Paix. I might could get you on as a part-time lavatory attendant. After all, it's honest, respectable work, and there's a future in it. He's thinking of putting in a shoeshine parlor, and you might work right into a bootblack job. That is, if you apply yourself, keep your eye on the ball. . . . When an American finishes shitting, don't just stand there, wipe his ass. And wipe it better than it was ever wiped before."

Antonio glared at Lee. Lee smiled. His face ghastly with strain, hate streaming out of his eyes like a malevolent shortwave broadcast, Antonio smiled back.

"You are joking, Bill."

"Sure. We're great kidders, us Americans."

"Americans! They come to Europe and buy us like cattle! 'You're in the wrong hole, Clem. That's a he-gook you got there.' 'So what, Luke? 'Tain't as if it was being queer. After all, they's only gooks.'

"You cannot understand what it means, Bill. You do not come from an old family. To have seen my great-aunt Mitzi, the Dowager Countess of Borganzola, the proudest family in Europe, an old lady of eighty years, dancing the can-can for drunken American soldiers. 'Shake the lead out, grandma. I got money on your ass.' And I stand there helpless. I hate them so almost I cannot pass around the hat."

"Okay," Lee said. "I'll take over the script now. Your old mother is gaping like a fish, locked out of her iron lung for nonpayment of rent. The finance company is repossessing your wife's artificial kidney. . . . It's going to be tough, sitting there watching her swell up and turn black, drowning in her own piss, your darling wife, the mother of your dead son, last of the noble line of Borganzola, and the croaker said just one more day with the kidney and she is functioning again. A sad, sweet, resigned smile . . . 'Ah well

. . . My life has been one long tragedy. But to think that only fifty pesetas would save her! It is too cruel!'

"You express the dilemma of the European, Antonio. You hate us so much *almost* you cannot pass around the hat."

Displaced Fuzz

A drastic simplification of U.S. law has thrown thousands of cops and narcotics agents out of work: The DFs—Displaced Fuzz—overran the Placement Center, snarling and whimpering like toothless predators: "I don't ask much out of life. Just let me give *some* citizen a bad time."

A few of them were absorbed by Friendly Finance:

DF 1: "Now, lady, we wouldn't want to repossess the artificial kidney, what with your kid in such a condition like that, not being able to piss."

DF 2: "Anna innarest."

DF 1: "Anna carrying charges."

DF 2: "Anna upkeep."

DF 1: "Anna wear and tear onna appliance."

DF 2: "Depreciation, whyncha?"

DF 1: "Check, *and* the depreciation."

DF 2: "It's like you're delinquent already. . . . Mmmm. *Quite* a gadget."

DF 1: "Quite a *gadget*."

DF 2: "Not the sort of thing you could make out of an old washing machine in your basement."

DF 1: "If you had an old washing machine."

DF 2: "Anna basement."

Lady: "But what am I to do? I been replaced by the automation."

DF 2: "I'm not Mr. Anthony, lady. . . ."

DF 1: "You might peddle the kid's ass if he'll stand still for it, haw haw haw. . . . Lady, we'd like to help you. . . . You see—"

DF 2: "—We got a job to do is all. You should be able to save sumpin'."

DF 1: "Maybe he pisses it all down the drain. Haw haw haw."

A DF can still get his kicks with Friendly Finance. But what about the other DFs?

One of them obtained a sinecure as lavatory attendant in a Greyhound terminal and maintained his self-respect by denouncing occasional improprieties and attempts to tamper with or circumvent the pay toilets. To this end he concealed himself in the towel receptacle, peeking out through a hinged slot.

Another worked in a Turkish bath and equipped himself with infrared binoculars: "All right, you there in the north corner. I see you." He couldn't actually denounce the clients or throw them out, but he did create such an unnerving ambiance—prowling about the halls, poking into the steam room, switching on floodlights, sticking his head into the cubicles through hinged panels in the walls and floors—that many a queen was carried out in a strait-jacket. So he lived out a full life and died at an advanced age of prostate cancer.

Another was not so fortunate. For a while he worked as a concierge, but he harried the tenants beyond endurance, so they finally banded together and were preparing to burn him alive in the furnace—which he habitually either over- or understoked—when the police intervened. He was removed from office for his own protection. He then secured a position as a subway guard, but was summarily dismissed for using a sharpened pole to push people into the cars during the rush hour. He subsequently worked as a bus driver, but his habit of constantly looking around to see what the passengers were doing precipitated a wreck, from which he emerged shattered in mind and body. He became a psychopathic informer, writing interminable letters to the FBI which J. Edgar used as toilet paper, being of a thrifty temperament. He sank ever lower and ended up Latah for cops, and would spend his days in front of any precinct that would tolerate his presence, having been barred from the area in and about Police Headquarters as a notorious bringdown.

Spare Ass Annie

When I became captain of the town, I decided to extend asylum to certain citizens who were persona non grata elsewhere in the area because of their disgusting and disquieting deformities.

One was known as Spare Ass Annie. She had an auxiliary asshole in the middle of her forehead, like a baneful bronze eye. Another was a scorpion from the neck down. He had retained the human attribute of voice and was given to revolting paroxysms of self-pity and self-disgust during which he would threaten to kill himself by a sting in the back of the neck. He never threatened anyone else, though his sting would have caused instant death.

Another, and by far the most detrimental, was like a giant centipede, but terminated in human legs and lower abdomen. Sometimes he walked half-erect, his centipede body swaying ahead of him. At other times he crawled, dragging his human portion as an awkward burden. At first sight he looked like a giant, crippled centipede. He was known as the Centipeter, because he was continually making sexual advances to anyone he could corner, and anyone who passed out was subject to wake up with Centipete in his bed. One degenerate hermaphrodite known as Fish Cunt Sara claimed he was the best lay in town: "Besides, he's a perfect gentleman in every sense of the word. He's kind and good, which means nothing to the likes of you. . . ."

These creatures had developed in a region where the priests

carried out strange rites. They built boxes from the moist, fresh bones of healthy youths, captives from neighboring tribes. The boys were killed by looping a vine noose around their necks and pushing them off the branch of a giant cypress tree. The branch had been cut off and carved in the form of an enormous phallus, being some fifteen feet long and three feet in circumference. The vine (always a *yagé* plant) was attached to the end of the branch, and the youth was led out and pushed off so that he fell about eight feet, breaking his neck. Then the priests pounced on him, while he was still twitching in orgasmic convulsions, and cut through the flesh with copper knives, tearing out the bones. From these bones they made boxes with great skill and speed, lining the boxes with copper. Runners were dispatched to carry the boxes to a certain high peak where peculiar lights were given off by the rocks. Pregnant women were placed in the boxes and left on the peak for a period of three hours. Often the women died, but those who survived usually produced monsters. The priests considered these monstrosities a way of humiliating the human race before the gods, in the hope of diverting their anger.

These horrible freaks were highly prized, and they lived in the temple. The women who gave birth to the most monsters received gold stars, which they were authorized to wear on ceremonial occasions.

Once a month they held a great festival at which everyone gathered in a round stone temple, open at the top, and prostrated themselves on the floor, assuming the most disgusting and degraded positions possible, so that the gods would see they were not attempting to elevate themselves above their station.

The habit of living in filth and humiliation finally occasioned a plague, a form of acute leprosy, that depopulated the area. The surviving freaks (who seemed immune to the plague) I decided to receive as an object lesson in how far human kicks can go.

The Dream Cops

There was a sudden thunder of knocks on the door. The Agent pulled on his trousers and turned the key in the lock. Three men pushed into the room. Two were in plain clothes, one in uniform. The man in uniform immediately pulled a pair of handcuffs out of his pocket and twisted them around the Agent's wrists. The handcuffs were made of a tough pliable wood. His uniform was torn and spotted, the tunic twisted and buttoned in the wrong holes.

One of the plainclothesmen looked like a vaudeville-house detective, with derby and cigar. The cigar was ten inches long. The other plainclothesman was tall and thin and carried an instrument that looked like a slide rule.

"The cigar's too long," said the Agent. "A dream cigar. You can't touch me."

The house detective nodded to the uniformed cop. The cop showed dirty steel teeth in a snarl. He hit the Agent across the mouth. The Agent could taste the blood.

"You have some peculiar dreams," said the detective. "Besides, we can dream too. . . . Sleeping with a nigger."

The Agent was about to deny this, but when he turned to look there was a young Negro in his bed. Huge lice crawled in and out of the Negro's greasy, frizzled hair.

"All right," said the detective. "Let's see your arm."

The Agent rolled up the sleeve of his sweatshirt. Sparks exploded behind his eyes. Blood ran down his chin. He got up, looking at the house detective.

"Wise guy, eh?" the house detective snarled, his eyes phosphorescent, his mouth slavering. "You're the wisest prick I ever walked in on. Let's see your *arm*. Your *short* arm."

He reached out a hairy hand as thick as it was wide, and grabbed the Agent's belt. With the other hand he ripped open the Agent's fly. The buttons rolled across the floor. He held the Agent's penis judicially between thumb and forefinger. He turned to the other plainclothesman—glen-plaid suit, skin tight and smooth and red over his face, bad teeth. Smoking a cigar shaped like a cigarette. He had been taking down the number on the Agent's kerosene stove.

"Sixty percent of them are Jews," said the house detective.

"I'm not Jewish," said the Agent.

"Sure, I know. You fucked one of those characters eats glass and razor blades and circumscribed yourself. Not Jewish!"

The other detective looked up from the kerosene stove and laughed sycophantically. A gold filling fell out on the floor.

At a signal from the house detective, the uniformed cop took the handcuffs off.

"Watch your step," said the house detective. The three men went out, closing the door.

Next morning the Agent's mouth was still sore. Lighting the kerosene stove, he found a gold filling.

THE CONSPIRACY

Yes, they know we'll wait. How many hours, days, years, street corners, cafeterias, furnished rooms, park benches, sitting, standing, walking? . . . All those who wait know that time and space are one. How long-far to the end of the block and back? How many games of solitaire make an hour? . . . Then time will suddenly jump, slip ahead. This happens usually in the late afternoon, after four o'clock. From one to four you hit on the slowest time.

I was reexamining candidates, proceeding by elimination, to isolate the name. Yes, I thought, that is correct procedure. At the same time, I knew the name would probably be a dark horse, someone I hadn't thought of, like the man who says, "Why didn't you come to me? I'd have lent you the money," and you know he would have lent it. It was someone like that I was looking for, while the logical elimination of prospects went on:

Gardiner? I wonder how he would manage to turn me in without picking up a phone and calling the law? By getting arrested himself? By telling someone who was sure to talk?

Marvin? At least he would say: "Bill, I can't do it. I won't take the risk. You'll have to get out."

Anyone who would do it for money was out. There would be more money on the other side. Two cops. That can scare up $5,000 overnight. (Why is killing a cop such a heinous crime in America? It isn't so in Mexico or South America. Because Americans accept cops at their own valuation, as they accept anyone who has the means of force.)

"Not a man of my acquaintance, that I'm sure of. . . ."

("Is this your final report?")

Not a man . . . not a man. . . . Well, how about a woman? . . . A woman? Well . . . Mary! That was the name, the answer.

I told the driver to stop. We were passing 72nd Street. I got out, paid the cab back to Washington Square, and waved good-bye to Nick, still in the cab.

I took the subway up to 116th Street and walked across the Columbia campus to Mary's flat. Why didn't I think of her first? A university campus—the perfect hideout. And I could count on Mary, count on her 100 percent. The building was a four-story brownstone. The windows shone clean and black in the morning sunlight. I walked up three flights and knocked on the door. Mary opened it and stood there looking at me.

"Come in," she said, her face lighting up. "Want a cup of coffee?" I sat down with her at the kitchen table and drank coffee and ate a piece of coffee cake.

"Mary, I want to hide out here for a while. I don't know how long exactly. You can say someone rented the extra room to write his thesis. He doesn't want to go out of the room or see anyone till it's finished. You have to buy his food and bring it to him. He's paying you one hundred dollars to stay there three weeks, or however long it takes. I just killed two detectives."

Mary lit a cigarette. "Holdup?"

"No. It's much more complicated than that. Let's move to the living room, in case somebody comes. I'll tell you about it. . . .

"Light junk sickness, when I wake up needing a shot, always gives me a sharp feeling of nostalgia, like train whistles, piano music down a city street, burning leaves. . . . I mentioned this to you, didn't I?"

Mary nodded. "Several times."

"An experience we think of as fleeting, incalculable, coming and going in response to unknown factors. But the feeling appears without fail, in response to a definite metabolic setup. It's possible to find out exactly what that setup is and reproduce it at will, given sufficient knowledge of the factors involved. Conversely it is possible to eliminate nostalgia, to occlude the whole dreaming, symbolizing faculty."

"And you mean it's been done?"

"Exactly. Scientists have perfected the anti-dream drug, which is, logically, a synthetic variation on the junk theme. . . . And the drug is habit forming to a point where one injection can cause lifelong addiction. If the addict doesn't get his shot every eight hours he dies in convulsions of oversensitivity."

"Like nerve gas."

"Similar. In short, once you are hooked on the anti-dream drug, you can't get back. Withdrawal symptoms are fatal. Users are dependent for their lives on the supply, and at the same time, the source of resistance, contact with the myth that gives each man the ability to live alone and unites him with all other life, is cut off. He becomes an automaton, an interchangeable quantity in the political and economic equation."

"Is there an antidote?"

"Yes. More than that, there is a drug that increases the symbolizing faculty. It's a synthetic variation of telepathine or yageine, the active principle of *Bannisteria caapi*."

"And where do you come in?" Mary asked.

"Five years ago I made a study of *Bannisteria caapi*—the Indians called it Yagé, Ayauhuasca, Pilde—in South America, and found out something about the possible synthetic variations. The symbolizing or artistic faculty that some people are born with—though almost everyone has it to some degree as a child—can be increased a hundred times. We can all be artists infinitely greater than Shakespeare or Beethoven or Michelangelo. Because this is possible, the opposite is also possible. We can be deprived of symbolmaking power, a whole dimension excised, reduced to completely rational nonsymbolizing creatures. Perhaps . . ."

"Yes?"

"I was wondering whether . . . Well, let it go. We have enough to think about."

That afternoon Mary went out and bought the papers. There was no mention of Hauser and O'Brien.

"When they can keep that quiet they must have a fix in near the top. With the ordinary apparatus of law looking for me, I might have one chance in a hundred; this way . . ."

I told Mary to go to a pay phone in Times Square, call police headquarters and ask for Hauser. Then go across the street and see what happens. She was back in half an hour.

"Well?"

She nodded. "They stalled me, said to hang on a minute, he was on the way. So I cut across the street. Not more than three minutes later a car was there. Not a police car. They blocked both entrances to the drugstore—I called from the drugstore—two went in and checked the phone booths. I could see them questioning the clerk, and he was saying in pantomime: 'How should I know? A thousand people in and out of here every day.' "

"And now you're convinced I'm not having a pipe dream? I wish I *could* have one. Haven't seen any gum in a dog's age. . . ."

"So what do we do now?"

"I don't know. I'd better start at the beginning and bring you up to date."

What was the beginning? Since early youth I had been searching for some secret, some key by which I could gain access to basic knowledge and answer some of the fundamental questions. Just what I was looking for, what I meant by basic knowledge or fundamental questions, I found it difficult to define. I would follow a trail of clues. For example, the pleasure of drugs to the addict is relief from the state of drug need. Perhaps all pleasure is relief and could be expressed by a basic formula. Pleasure must be proportional to the discomfort or tension from which it is the relief. This holds for the pleasure of junk. You never know what pleasure is until you are really junk-sick.

Drug addiction is perhaps a basic formula for pleasure and for life itself. That is why the habit, once contracted, is so difficult to break, and why it leaves, when broken, such a vacuum behind. The addict has glimpsed the formula, the bare bones of life, and this knowledge has destroyed for him the ordinary sources of satisfaction that make life endurable. To go a step further, to find out exactly what tension is, and what relief, to discover the means of manipulating these factors . . . The final key always eluded me, and I decided that my search was as sterile and misdirected as the alchemists' search for the philosopher's stone. I decided it was an error to think in terms of some secret or key or formula: the secret is that there is no secret.

But I was wrong. There *is* a secret, now in the hands of ignorant and evil men, a secret beside which the atomic bomb is a noisy toy. And like it or not, I was involved. I had already ante'd my life. I had no choice but to sit the hand out.

IRON WRACK DREAM

This is one of the worst habits I ever kicked. I sit for an hour in a chair, unable to get up and fix myself a cup of tea.

Early this morning, half awake, shivering in a light junk-sick fever, I had a vivid dream-fantasy. The hypersensitivity of junk sickness is reflected in dreams during withdrawal—that is, if you can sleep.

In the dream, I go to an elaborate house on a high cliff over the sea. An iron door opens in a limestone cliff, and you get to the house in a swift, silent elevator.

I have come to see a sexless character who wears men's clothes but may be man or woman. Nobody knows for sure. A gangster of the future, with official recognition and arbitrary powers.

He walks toward me as if about to shake hands. He does not offer his hand. "Hello," he says. "Hello . . . there."

The room is surrounded on three sides by a transparent plastic shell.

"You will want to see the view," he says. A plastic panel slides back. I step out onto a limestone terrace cut from the solid rock of the cliff. No rail or wall. A heavy mist, but from time to time I can see the waves breaking on the rocks a thousand feet below. See the waves, but I don't hear them, like a silent film. Two bodyguards are standing a few feet behind me.

"It gives the sensation of flying," I say.

"Sometimes."

"Well, feller say only angels have wings," I say recklessly. I turn around. I say, "Excuse me." The bodyguards don't move. They are standing with their backs to him. He is arranging flowers in an obscene alabaster bowl. The guards cannot see him and he says nothing, makes no sound, but a signal has been given. The guards step aside to let me pass, back into the room.

I walk up to the table where he is arranging flowers. "I want to know where Jim is," I say.

"Mmm. Yes. I suppose you do."

"Will you tell me?"

"Maybe Jim doesn't want to see you."

"If he doesn't, I want to hear it from him."

"I never give anything for nothing. I want your room in the Chimu. I want you out of there by nine tomorrow morning."

"All right."

"Go to 60 at Fourth Street, coordinate 20, level 16, YH room 72."

The City is a vast network of levels, like the Racks, connected by gangways and cars that run on wires and single tracks. You put a coin in a vacant car and it will take you anywhere on its track or wire. Everyone carries an instrument called a coordinator, to orient himself.

The City is in the U.S. The forces of evil and repression have run their course here. They are suffocating in their armor or exploding from inner pressure. New forms of life are germinating in the vast, rusty metal racks of the ruined City.

It takes me twelve hours to find the address. A padded hammer hangs from a copper chain on the door. I knock.

A man comes to the door: bald, looks like an old actor on the skids. Effeminate, but not queer. A dumpy, middle-aged woman is sitting in a purple velvet brocaded chair left over from 1910. She looks good-natured. I say I want to see Jim.

"And *who* might you be?" the man asks.

"I'm Bill."

He laughs. "He's Bill, Gertie." He turns to me. "Someone was just here asking for Bill."

"How long ago?"

"Just five minutes," the woman says.

"Can I stay five minutes?" I ask. "I mean, if someone was here five minutes ago asking for *Bill*, and now I am here asking for *Jim* . . . well . . ."

"You don't have to *slug* me with it," the man says. "But I never heard of Bill or Jim."

"Oh, let him stay," the woman says.

Five minutes later there is a knock. The man opens the door.

"Hello," he says. "You wouldn't be Jim, by any chance?"

"Yes, I'm Jim. I'm looking for Polly."

"Polly doesn't live here anymore." The man sings it.

Jim sees me. "Hello, Bill," he says. He smiles and cancels all the reproaches I had stored up.

"Let's go, Jim," I say, standing up. I turn to the man and woman. "Thanks for your trouble."

"Anytime, old thing," the man says. He is about to say something more.

"That's okay, boys," the woman cuts in.

We walk out together. "I need a drink," Jim says. We find a bar and sit down in a booth. There is no one else in the place. Jim is beautiful but has the kind of face that shows every day that much older. There are circles under his eyes, like bruises. He drinks five double Scotches. He is sweet and gentle when drunk. I help him out of the bar. We go to my room and sleep there.

Next morning I throw the few things I have—mostly photos and manuscripts—into a plastic bag, and we leave.

Jim has a place on a roof. You unlock a metal door and climb four flights of rusty, precarious stairs. One room with a mattress, a table and a chair. Metal walls. A toilet in one corner, a gas stove in another. A tap dripping into a sink.

Jim is trembling convulsively. "I'm scared, Bill," he says over and over.

I hold him, and stroke his head, and undress him.

We sleep together until twelve that night. We wake up and dress and Jim makes coffee. We take turns drinking from a tin can.

We start out looking for Polly. Jim gives me an extra key to his place, before we leave the room.

The City is honeycombed with nightclubs and bars. Many of them change locations every night. The nightclubs are underground, hanging from cables, and built on perilous balconies a thousand feet over the rubbish and rusty metal of the City.

We make the rounds, and we find Polly in Cliff's place. The room shifts from time to time, with a creak of metal. It is built in a rusty tower that sways in the wind. "This place is too good to last, kids," Cliff says, laughing.

Polly is a dark Jewish girl. She looks like that picture of Allen Ginsberg on the beach when he was three years old. Jim is talking to some people at the bar. I put the key in her hand and press it there. She kisses me lightly on the lips and then on the ear, murmuring, "Billy Boy . . ."

I find a car and ride down to the waterfront. I see a light. A man is standing in a doorway.

"You open?" I ask.

"Why not?"

I go in. The place is empty. I sit at a table. He brings me a soft drink without asking what I want, and sits down at the table opposite me. A gentle, thuggish face, broken nose, battered but calm and kind.

"Where you live at?" he asks me.

"No place now."

"Want to shack up here?"

"Why not?" I finish my drink and he leads the way to a round metal door that opens soundlessly on oiled bearings. He motions for me to go in. His hand rests on my shoulder, and slides down my ass with a gentle forward pat.

GINSBERG NOTES

Lee woke again. The room was light now. He could hear the clock ticking, but he did not want to look at it, to locate himself definitely in time, to be completely awake. He arranged the covers to shade his eyes, pushing them away from his mouth so he could breathe comfortably. A shiver ran through his body. He closed his eyes, remembering his dream, clinging to sleep.

He had been dreaming about marshmallows. He had four or five marshmallows, and he was preparing to toast them in little wooden boxes which had wicks running around the edges like a kerosene stove. The dream had a tone of furtive, but overpowering, sexuality.

What's sexy about marshmallows? he thought, irritably. He felt aware of his sexual organs, but not in the normal manner of sexual excitement. It was as if he could feel inside the whole genitourinary apparatus, the intolerable, febrile sexuality of junk sickness.

Marshmallows, boxes . . . cunts, of course. Mary, the English governess . . . dreams of something sticky in his mouth, like chewing gum. The memory he never could reoccupy, even under deep narcoanalysis. Whenever he got close to it, excitation tore through him, suppressed below the level of emotional coloring, a neutral energy like electricity. The memory itself never actually seen or reexperienced, only delineated by refusals, disgusts, negation. He knew, of course, what it must be, but the knowledge was of the brain only.

He shivered again, feeling the discordant twang of unfamiliar visceral sensations, the light fever of sickness. The Spanish word *escalofríos* came to him, then the English "chills and fever," hot and cold. Every moment he felt more intolerably conscious. He looked at the clock: eight-thirty. It was always slow—it was nearer to nine.

Soon the drugstores will open. If only the methadone comes through today. If only I could get my money so I can get to England and take the cure.

If only his body had never known junk. How could he ever unknow it? He decided he would settle for a cure and then a place to live where it is never cold.

No use trying to sleep any longer. He pushed the covers aside and sat up. Immediately he began to shiver. He crossed the room and lit a small kerosene stove, with trembling hands. He reached into an open drawer and took out a small syringe filled with colorless liquid.

He held the syringe poised, and looked down at his blue hands, coldly, impersonally. *No use trying to hit there,* he decided. He felt along the side of his bare foot. *There's one I might be able to hit*. He pushed the needle in his foot at the ankle, feeling, probing for a vein. Pain swept through his sensitized flesh. A thin column of blood climbed sluggishly into the syringe. He pressed the plunger. The liquid went in very slowly. Every now and then his foot twitched involuntarily away from the needle, which was embedded almost to the point where it joined the syringe.

The last of the liquid drained in. He pulled out the needle and stopped the blood with a piece of cotton. He sat listening down into his viscera, waiting for the effect.

Lee had discovered that he got his best ideas while lying in bed with a young boy after the fact. At first he thought this was coincidence. *God damn it, every time I get ideas for writing, I am occupied with a boy. Or maybe it's the other way around . . . hmm. Weel, I'm in the right place.*

He embarked on a three-thousand-page sexology, as he called it. One after the other his boys were drained of their orgones and cast aside, dragging themselves about like terminal hookworm-malaria-malnutrition cases.

"I don't know why, but I just feel sorta tired after I make it with that writing feller."

"You can say that again, Pepe. And in all my experience man and boy as a grade-A five-star hustler—A.J. gives me five stars in his Sex and Drug Guide—I never yet see a citizen type and get fucked at the same time. You shoulda seen me before I met Lee. I was a good-looking kid, had all my hair and teeth. I'm only twenty-four—well, twenty-nine. Shucks, we're in the same line. . . . I can afford to let my hair down a bit, that is, if I had any. . . ."

I figure it will require the orgones of ten thousand boys to finish my sexology. I assume the frightful responsibility of the creative artist.

A group of rich queens formed a corporation and offered a reward of one million dollars to any assassin who would dispose of "this shameless liquefactionist, who is debauching and decanting our boys—oh, uh, I mean the youth of the world."

There are two middle-aged, ugly, fattish men in a club like the University Club or the Harvard Club. The two are on cordial but by no means familiar terms.

Scene is the club sitting-room. The other members are annoyed, you understand, by anyone even talking there, as they want to sit and think about their money and doze and digest. We will call them Jack and Robert.

Jack: "Let's rekindle the embers!"

Robert: "Huh? The embers of precisely what?"

Jack: "Don't tell me you've forgotten our nights on the sandbanks of the Putumayo with the piranha fish jumping out there in the soft tropic darkness. All around us the brooding jungle of the Amazon, like a great carnivorous plant. It was Auca country, but we were drunk with youth and love. We laughed at danger and perhaps the Auca laughed with us and lowered their poison arrows and stole away into the jungle. And the moon so clear you could read by it—why, I can see you now, lying there with your beautiful mouth a little open, clad only in youth and innocence."

Robert: "I'm damned if you can! For one thing, I've never been within a thousand miles of the Amazon!"

Jack: "And remember that waterfall back in the virgin jungle of the upper Shipibo? We'd been walking all day since sun-up, hacking our way through with machetes. And you said it was my fault we'd missed the way, and sulked for ten hours. You always looked beautiful when you were sulky. And then we broke through the jungle to a crystal-clear river and a waterfall so high the top was lost in mist, and we stripped off our clothes and played under the waterfall until the sun went down and the mosquitoes came out with the moon."

Robert: "What are you talking about?"

Jack: "Let's go up to my room and play touchies!"

Robert: "Play what!"

Jack: "Touchies! *Our* little game!"

Robert: "Listen. I've had just about enough of your silly games, and since you lead me to say so, Throckmorton, I strongly advise you to see an able psychiatrist without delay."

Jack: "Ah well, perhaps it wasn't in the Amazon . . . come to think of it. We were just kids, fourteen, fifteen. It was in a deserted house down by the railroad tracks. We made a great thing of breaking into the house, and you looked at me solemnly and said: 'Do you realize we're burglars?' And there was an old mattress on the floor in a dark room with the shutters nailed down, and we dragged the mattress into the middle of the room and wrestled on it, and you won, as you always did, and I lay there looking up at you and a train whistled in the distance and we took off our clothes in the musty darkness. It was like the pure blue flame of a welder's torch: sudden, hot, intense in both of us. . . . Later we walked home at twilight along the tracks, a beautiful clear Indian summer day, and we were so happy we didn't say anything all the way home, with our arms around each other's necks, so young it never occurred to either of us anyone would think anything about it. And when we got back to the main road it was dark, with a full moon rising red over the smokestacks of the city and the smell of burning leaves in the air. . . ."

Robert: "You obviously have me confused with someone else. Now if you will excuse me."

Jack: "Wait a minute! It all comes back now. . . . I had a little studio apartment on Jane Street in the Village. It was my first time really away from home and on my own. I was young, I had a secondhand Remington, I was going to write the Great American

Novel. So what difference did it make if the bed was lumpy, and the windowpane vibrated in a raw winter wind, and the radiator gave off more noise than heat, and a black dust seeped into the room and covered my manuscripts, my clothes, my pillow, and got in my hair and ears so I always looked a little dirty? I was happy, and deadly serious about my writing, and I believed in my talent.

"But I was desperately lonely. I had read Oscar Wilde and Gide and Proust and Havelock Ellis. I knew that I was destined to love my own sex as long as I lived. I accepted this. After all, so many great writers had been like that. I used to go out after writing all day, every night to a different bar, always hoping to meet someone who would understand what I was trying to say on paper, who would share my lumpy bed, and we would wake up in the cold, gray dawn, warm with each other's bodies.

"Then one night I happened into a strange, equivocal place on Twelfth Street at Second Avenue. It was called The Clock Bar. The Clock had no regular crowd. It was not bohemian or tough or Bowery. It was a place where anyone could happen in. The place was empty—except for you. . . ."

Take it up from the next page. You can carry this second-rate-novel kick too far. I just got writing and couldn't stop.

When a depressed psychotic begins to recover, that is, when recovery becomes possible, the illness makes a final all-out attack, and this is the point of maximum suicide danger. You might say the human race is now at this point, in a position for the first time, by virtue of knowledge which may destroy us, to step free of self-imposed restrictions and see all life as a fact. When you see the world direct, everything is a delight, and boredom or unhappiness is impossible.

The forces of negation and death are now making their all-out suicidal effort. The citizens of the world are helpless in a paranoid panic. First one thing and then another is seen as the enemy, while the real enemy hesitates—perhaps because it looks too easy, like an ambush. Among the Arabs and the East in general, the West (especially America), or domination by foreigners, is seen as the enemy. In the West: communism, queers, drug addicts.

Queers have been worked over by female Senders. They are a reminder of what the Senders can and will do unless they are stopped. Also many of them have sold out their bodies to Death, Inc. Their souls wouldn't buy a paper of milk sugar shit. But the enemy needs bodies to get around.

Also there is no doubt some drugs condition one to receive, that is, soften one up for the Senders. Junk is not such a drug, but it is a prototype of invasion. That is, junk replaces the user cell by cell until he *is* junk, so the Sender will invade and replace until separate life is destroyed. Nothing but fact can save us, and Einstein is the first prophet of fact. Anyone is free, of course, to deliberately choose insanity and say that the universe is square or heart-shaped, but it is, as a matter of fact, curved.

Similar facts: morality (at this point an unqualified evil), ethics, philosophy, religion, can no longer maintain an existence separate from facts of physiology, bodily chemistry, LSD, electronics, physics. Psychology no longer exists, since a science of mind has no meaning. Sociology and all the so-called social sciences are suspect to be purveyors of pretentious gibberish.

The next set of facts of similar import will most likely come from present research on schizophrenia, the electronics of hallucination and the metabolism of insanity, cancer, the behavior and nature of viruses—and possibly drug addiction as a microcosm of life, pleasure and human purpose. It is also from such research that the greatest danger to the human race will come—probably has already come—a danger greater than the atom bomb, because more likely to be misunderstood.

I am taking another junk cure—is this my tenth or eleventh cure? I forget—in the Hassan Hospital of Interzone. They are curing me slow, and why not? Stateside croakers are mostly puritan sadists, who feel a junky *should* suffer taking the cure. Here they look at it differently.

I could never have been a doctor. I did right to quit. My heart is too soft and too hard, too quickly moved to love, anger, or indifference. I would care too much for some patients and nothing for others: Like I mess a case up and kill some jerk, so I say: "It's all in the day's work. Get this stiff outa here. I'm waiting on another patient."

People talk about "the hospital smell." You never had it till you sniff a Spanish hospital. All the old standbys: ether, carbolic, alcohol, the antiseptic, ozone smell of bandages *plus* piss and shit and dirty babies, cunts with the rag on, never-washed pricks, sweat and garlic, saffron and olive oil, afterbirths, gangrene, *keif* and death.

I used to be in room 10 and they moved me upstairs. Just passed my old room, where they had a maternity case, looks like. Terrible mess and bedpans full of blood and Kotex and nameless female substances enough to pollute a continent. Just thought, suppose somebody comes to visit me in my old room, they will think I give birth to a monster, and the State Department is trying to hush it up.

Dave Dunlop just came in, and I was telling him about the eels. It was a Dane found out about them. Gave his whole life to the eels—it would be a Dane, somehow. When the adult eels reach the Sargasso Sea, which is actually a place in the Atlantic, they go down into it and disappear. It is assumed they mate and die down there—nobody has seen them doing either—but sure as shit an eel doesn't come all that distance and lose his ass in the service for no purpose.

Often pain and death leave me untouched. I have seen hundreds of bullfights. I feel nothing for the bull. The old man who died a few days ago just annoyed me with his groans. He had the stupid, blunted look of a sick cow. Some people would call me callous, but I am not so. It is simply that I divide people into those who matter and those who do not, and I have no concern with quantitative criteria. If I do feel someone else's pain, I feel it with my whole being. It shatters me. I just heard a child screaming downstairs, and tears came to my eyes. I can't stand the pain of children. No, I could never have been a doctor. I would be crying over some child while people I didn't like died in the hall.

More trouble with the Evil Night Nurse. I caught her *in flagrante* cutting my shot in half with water. I don't say nothing. Later she doesn't even bother to cut it. Just brings me a shot of two ampules, instead of four like she's supposed.

I say: "That's two centimeters."

She say: "No, it's four. The syringe is bigger."

I say: "Look, *señorita*" (she's no more *señorita* than I am. Brazen old junky cunt)—"I got eyes. I want four centimeters."

"I can't give you any more."

"All right, *señorita*. I'll be having a little talk with the croaker *mañana*."

See what I mean? I give her a chance to come up right. If she told me straight, "I got a habit. You know how it is," I would say, "All right. All right. Just fuck up somebody else's shot."

But she gives me a snow job. Well, I'm going to fix her wagon good.

Yesterday I meant to add a few sentences to this. Possessed by a wild routine and wrote two pages. I laughed till my stomach hurt.

These routines will reduce me to a cinder, like the Technician. And how can I ever write a "novel"? I can't and won't. The "novel" is a dead form, rigid and arbitrary. I can't use it.

The chapters form a mosaic, with the dream impact of juxtaposition, like objects abandoned in a hotel drawer, a form of still life. Just looking over Chapter II. I don't know. The mosaic method is more suitable to painting than writing. I mean, you can *see* a painting as a whole.

What I want to do in Chapter II is to indicate Lee's literal point of view. The following concepts are central:

1. He writes with horror and foreboding because his writing is meant to be acted out somewhere, somehow, sometime, and so can put him in actual danger.

2. Repetition of Lee's desire and intention to kick habit. Junk keeps him in state of suspension. He must kick to realize his routines. His cautious, junk-bound flesh is reluctant to leave the safety of junk. I notice the songs that sing themselves in my head indicate my hesitancy to leave the safe, warm place of junk. One for example: I heard the tune a long time before I remembered the words. It's about an old spade who has sold his "cabin and patch of ground" to go north for better pay:

"But Dinah she don't want to go
  She says we're getting old
  She's 'fraid that she will freeze to death
  The country am so cold
  That story 'bout the work and pay
  She don't believe it's true
  She begs me not to do the thing
  That I am bound to do."

Dinah is junk, of course—that is, my cellular representative of junk.

3. His love for anyone is always a pretext, a means to achieve something, to go somewhere. . . . Perhaps the search for an ideal audience?

4. The Routine (Birth of the Monster, Hassan the Afterbirth King, the Baboon Stick, etc.) as Lee's special form. What distinguishes the routine from writing, painting, music? It is *not completely symbolic* but subject to slide over into action at any time. (Cutting off finger joint, wrecking the car, etc. In a sense, the whole Nazi movement was a great, humorless, evil *routine* on Hitler's part.) Routines are uncontrollable, unpredictable, charged with potential danger for Lee himself, and anyone close to him is liable to be caught in the line of fire. I mean the so-called innocent bystanders. Actually there are no "innocent bystanders." In the immortal words of Huncke, "We are all guilty of everything."

Of all forms, the routine is closest to bullfighting. The routine artist is always trying to outdo himself, to go a little further, to commit some incredible but appropriate excess. A routine, like a bullfight, needs an audience. In fact the audience is an integral part of the routine. But unlike a bullfight, the routine can endanger the audience.

This morning the orderly took my table away to surgery. I opened my knife and held it out to him: "Need this too?" I'm the life of the hospital.

A wet dream of a thirteen-year-old redheaded kid waiting for treatment, sitting on the long white waiting bench . . . I see myself a doctor, bandaging his thigh with "sweet, reluctant, amorous delay."

"Mrs. Brounswig is in shock, Doctor. I can't find her pulse."

"Maybe she's got it up her snatch in a finger stall."

"Adrenalin, doctor?"

"The night porter shot it all up for kicks."

Tangier extends in several dimensions. You keep finding places you never saw before. There is no line between "real world" and "world of myth and symbol." Objects, sensations, hit with the impact of hallucination. Of course I see now with the child's eyes, the Lazarus eyes of return from the gray Limbo of junk. But what I see is there. Others see it too.

I am selecting, editing and transcribing letters and notes from the past year, some typed, some indecipherable longhand, for Chapter II of my novel on Interzone, tentatively entitled *Ignorant Armies*.

Find I cannot write without endless parenthesis (a parenthesis indicates the simultaneity of past, present and emergent future). I exist in the present moment. I can't and won't pretend I am dead. This novel is not posthumous. A "novel" is something finished, that is, dead—

I am trying, like Klee, *to create something that will have a life of its own, that can put me in real danger, a danger which I willingly take on myself*.

My thoughts turn to crime, incredible journeys of exploration, expression in terms of an *extreme act*, some excess of feeling or behavior that will shatter the human pattern.

Klee expresses a similar idea: "The painter who is called will come near to the secret abyss where elemental law nourishes evolution." And Genet, in his *Journal of a Thief*: "The creator has committed himself to the fearful adventure of taking upon himself, to the very end, the perils risked by his creatures."

Genet says he chose the life of a French thief for the sake of *depth*. By the fact of this depth, which is his greatness, he is more humanly involved than I am. He carries more excess baggage. I only have one "creature" to be concerned with: myself.

Four months ago I took a two-week sleep cure—a ghastly routine. I had it almost made. Another five days sans junk would have seen me in the clear. Then I relapsed. Just before relapse, I dreamed the following:

I was in high mountains covered with snow. It was in a suicide clinic: "You just wait till you feel like it." I was on a ledge with a boy, about sixteen years old—I could feel myself slipping further and further out, out of my *body*, you dig. I don't mean a physical slipping on the ledge. The Plane was coming for me. (Suicide is performed by getting in this Plane with a boy. The Plane crashes in the Pass. No Plane ever gets through.)

Marv reaches out and catches my arm and says: "Stay here with us a while longer."

The suicide clinic is in Turkey. Nothing compulsory. You can leave anytime, even take your boy out with you. (Boat whistle in the distance. A bearded dope fiend rushing to catch the boat for the mainland.) My boy says he won't leave with me unless I kick my habit.

Earlier dream-fantasy: I am in a plane trying to make the Pass. There is a boy with me, and I turn to him and say: "Throw everything out."

"What! All the gold? All the guns? All the junk?"

"Everything."

I mean throw out all excess baggage: anxiety, desire for approval, fear of authority, etc. Strip your psyche to the bare bones of spontaneous process, and you give yourself one chance in a thousand to make the Pass.

I am subject to continual routines, which tear me apart like a homeless curse. I feel myself drifting further and further out, over a bleak dream landscape of snow-covered mountains.

This novel is a scenario for future action in the real world. *Junk, Queer, Yagé,* reconstructed my past. The present novel is an attempt to create my future. In a sense it is a guidebook, a map. The first step in realizing this work is to leave junk forever.

I'll maintain this International Sophistico-criminal Mahatma con no longer. It was more or less shoved on me anyway. So I say: "Throw down all your arms and armor, walk straight to the Frontier."

A guard in a uniform of human skin, black buck jacket with carious yellow tooth buttons, an elastic pullover shirt in burnished Indian copper, adolescent Nordic suntan-brown slacks, sandals from the calloused foot sole of a young Malay farmer, an ash-brown scarf knotted and tucked in the shirt. He is a sharp dresser since he has nothing to do, and saves all his pay, and buys fine clothes and changes three times a day in front of an enormous magnifying mirror. He has a handsome, smooth Latin face with a pencil-line mustache, small brown eyes blank and greedy, eyes that never dream, insect eyes.

When you get to the Frontier, this guard rushes out of his *casita*, where he was plucking at his mustache, a mirror slung round his neck in a wooden frame. He is trying to get the mirror off his neck. This has never happened before, that anyone ever actually got to the Frontier. The guard has injured his larynx taking off the mirror frame. He has lost his voice. He opens his mouth and you can see his tongue jumping around inside. The smooth, blank, young face and the open mouth with the tongue moving inside are incredibly hideous. The guard holds up his hand, his whole body jerking in convulsive negation. I pay no attention to him. I go over and unhook the chain across the road. It falls with a clank of metal on stone. I walk through. The guard stands there in the mist, looking after me. Then he hooks the chain up again and goes back inside the *casita* and starts plucking at his mustache.

At times I feel myself on the point of learning something basic. I have achieved moments of inner silence.

III. WORD

WORD

The Word is divided into units which be all in one piece and should be so taken, but the pieces can be had in any order being tied up back and forth in and out fore and aft like an innaresting sex arrangement. This book spill off the page in all directions, kaleidoscope of vistas, medley of tunes and street noises, farts and riot yipes and the slamming steel shutters of commerce, screams of pain and pathos and screams plain pathic, copulating cats and outraged squawk of the displaced Bull-head, prophetic mutterings of *brujo* in nutmeg trance, snapping necks and screaming mandrakes, sigh of orgasm, heroin silent as the dawn in thirsty cells,

Radio Cairo screaming like a berserk tobacco auction, and flutes of Ramadan fanning the sick junky like a gentle lush worker in the gray subway dawn, feeling with delicate fingers for the green folding crackle.

This is Revelation and Prophecy of what I can pick up without FM on my 1920 crystal set with antennae of jissom. Gentle reader, we see God through our assholes in the flashbulb of orgasm. Through these orifices transmute your body, the way out is the way in. There is no blacker blasphemy than spit with shame on the body God gave you. And woe unto those castrates who equate their horrible old condition with sanctity.

Cardinal————(who shall be a nameless asshole) read *Baby Doll* in the Vatican crapper and shit out his prostate in pathic dismay. "Revolting," he trills. His cock and balls long since dissolve inna thervith of shit death and taxes.

Armed with a meat cleaver, the Author chase a gentle reader down the Midway and into the Hall of Mirrors, trap him impaled on crystal cocks.

With a cry squeezed out by the hanged man's spasm, I raise my cleaver. . . . Will the Governor intervene? Will the whimpering chair be cheated of young ass? Will the rope sing to empty air? Go unused to mold with old jockstraps in the deserted locker room?

The Word, gentle reader, will flay you down to the laughing bones and the author will do a striptease with his own intestines. Let it be. No holes barred. The Word is recommended for children, and convent-trained cunts need it special to learn what every street boy knows: "He who rims the Mother Superior is a success-minded brown nose and God will reward him on TV with a bang at Question 666."

Mr. America, sugar-cured in rotten protoplasm, smiles idiot self bone love, flexes his cancerous muscles, waves his erect cock, bends over to show his asshole to the audience, who reel back blinded by beauty bare as Euclid. He is hanged by reverent Negroes, his neck snaps with a squashed bug sound, cock rises to ejaculate and turn to viscid jelly, spread through the Body in shuddering waves, a monster centipede squirms in his spine. Jelly drops on the Hangman, who runs screaming in black bones. The centipede writhes around the rope and drops free with a broken neck, white juice oozing out.

Ma looks up from knitting a steel-wool jockstrap and says, "That's my boy."

And Pa looks up from the toilet seat where he is reading *The Plastic Age* he keeps stashed in a rubber box down the toilet on invisible string of Cowper gland lubricant—hardest fabric known, beat ramie hands down and cocks up. Some people get it, some don't. A sleeping acquaintance point to my pearl and say, "*¿Eso, qué es?*" ("What's that?" to you nameless assholes don't know Spanish), and I have secrete this orient pearl before a rampant swine not above passing a counterfeit orgasm in my defenseless asshole. It will not laugh a well-greased siege to scorn—heh heh heh—say, "Mother knows best."

A Marine sneering over his flamethrower quells the centipede with jellied gasoline, ignoring the Defense Attorney scream: "Double Jeopardy: My Client . . ."

The Author will spare his gentle readers nothing, but strip himself brother naked. Description? I bugger it. My cock is four and one-half inches and large cocks bring on my xenophobia. . . . "Western influence!" I shriek, confounded by disgusting alterations. "Landsake like I look in the mirror and my cock undergo some awful sorta sea change. . . ." Like all normal citizens, I ejaculate when screwed without helping hand, produce a good crop of jissom, spurt it up to my chin and beyond. I have observed that small hard cocks come quicker slicker and spurtier.

These things were revealed to me in Interzone, where East meets West coming round the other way. In a great apartment house done in Tibetan Colonial, lamsters from the crime of Iowa look out on snowy peaks and groan with Lotus Posture hip-aches. You hooked on Nirvana, brothers, old purple-assed mandrill gibber and piss down your back and eat your ears off. Carry your great meaningless load in hunger and filth and disease, flop against the mud wall like a cut of wrong meat—the Inspector stamp Reject on you with his seal of shit. And the Nationalist white slaver, "Sidi the Lymph," covers his face with scented Kotex and pass by on the other side; and the bearded old Moslem convert from Ottawa, Illinois, seals a coin in the slack hand intoning Koranic platitudes through his Midwest nose. Chinese boys turn in Dad as a rampant junky, and the Japanese boy has rape his honey-face after subdue her with a jack handle, throw the meat into that volcano and roar home in his hot rod to catch the Milton Berle show. And the Javanese fuck himself with a greased banana in a suburb toilet, and Malays catch halitosis from the copywriters and run for the 6:12 with *Amok* trot— the reference, you ignorant asshole, is to the typical trotting gait of the *Amok*. He does not walk, he does not run, he *trots*—and read "How-to" books: *Thank God for My Bang-Utot Attack*, and *On Being a Latah*. See footnote whyncha? So East screams past West on the scenic railway over the midways of Interzone.

And Mother Green grows geraniums in her asshole, and a man-drake spring from Johnny's deserted cock. The Rock and Rollers crack wise with a cyclotron, shit on the great American deck, wipe their ass with Old Glory and turn the Palomar telescope into the Women's Toilet.

"And is there not perhaps something amiss?" says the World, shitting liver, pissing blood and coughing up tripes and round-worms. "—I don't even feel like a human . . . I mean when the poltergeist come down from the attic and shit in the living room, outnumber the haunted ten to one like niggers and Arabs, and their merry pranks are no longer virginal and they turn vicious with adolescence like apes, and with a monarch's voice fart purple havoc. . . .

"Can you deny your purple-assed Döppelganger? This is the time of Witness, when every soul stands with a naked hard-on in the Hall of Mirrors under the meat cleaver of a disgusted God. What a Gawd has to put up with in this business! No, I will *not* hang you. Much too good for you. You abject citizens couldn't raise the libido to commit a sex murder, mute inglorious Robert Christies give me a pain in my curved ass. Now I'll say it again and I'll say it slow . . . I am *curved*. Did you think to flee God in thy souped-up hot rod and play chicken with the Holy Ghost whilst fucking the Virgin Mary up the ass? Generation of Yipers I spew thee out like a reluctant cocksucker won't swallow the load."

"It's rusty," he complains, "I am subject to the botulism." A wise old thug beat the Great Famine nourishing himself on jissom of street boys sleep naked, he absorb that protein rich in all dietary goodness oral or rectal as the case may be, *mutatis mutandis* fore and aft.

The boy wakes up paralyzed from the waist down, and the Mayan priest has pull a trepanning caper and suck the young boy's libido right out of the hypothalamus with an alabaster straw.

"Nothing like a chilled boy on a hot afternoon. . . . Ever get them hot popovers from a burnin' Nigra? Run a red hot rod in and Swedish glögg pour out the nose. . . ."

So glad to have you aboard, reader, but remember there is only one captain of this shit, and back-street drivers will be summarily covered with jissom and exposed to faggots in San Marco. Do not thrust your cock out the train or beckon lewdly with thy piles, nor flush thy beat Benny down the toilet. (Benny is overcoat in antiquated Times Square argot.) It is forbidden to use the signal rope for frivolous hangings, or to burn Nigras in the washroom before the other passengers have made their toilet. Show Your Culture. Rusty loads subject to carrying charges, plenty of room in the rear, folks, move back into the saloon.

Bloody Mary's First-Aid Manual for Boys: . . . Erections: Apply tight tourniquet at once, open the urethra with a rusty razor blade a whore shave her cunt with it and trim her rag. Inject hot carbolic acid into the scrotum and administer antivenin shot of saltpeter directly into the hypothalamus. If you are caught short without your erection kit, feed a *candiru* up it to suck out the poison. In stubborn and relapsing cases pelvectomy is indicated.

The *candiru* woman with steel-wool pubic hairs receives clients in her little black hut across the river. . . .

The Child Molester has lured a little changeling into a vacant lot. "Now open your mouth and close your eyes and I'll give you a big old hairy surprise."

"And I've news for thee, uncle," she say, soul kissing a *candiru* up his joint.

A cunt undulates out of a snake charmer's basket. Tourist: "He's pulled the teeth of course."

Do I hear a paretic heckler mutter, "Cathtrathon Complekth God damn it?" Well I'd rather be safe than sorry. Almost anything can lurk up a woman's snatch. Why, a Da is subject to be castrated by his unborn daughter, piranha fingerlings with transparent teeth sharp as glass slivers leave you without a cunt to piss in. Safest way to avoid these horrid perils is come over here and shack up with Scylla, treat you right, kid, candy and cigarettes.

The vibrating chair receives the yellow cop killer, burns his piles white as a dead leech.

Death dressed as an admiral hang Billy Budd with his own hands and Judge Lynch sneer, "Dead suns can't witness." But the witness will rise from the concrete of Hudson with a fossil prick to point out the innocent wise guy.

And when the graves start yielding up the dead—Goddammit I pay rent in perpetuity for the old gash, now she rise like Christ in drag.

It's the final gadget, the last of the big-time gimmicks—wires straight into the hypothalamus orgasm center! White nerves spilling out at ear and winking lewdly from corner of the eye, the queen twitch his switch and pant, "Gawd you heat my synapses! Turn me on DaddyOOOOOOOOOOH!!"

"You cheap bitch! You nausea artist! I wouldn't demean myself to connect your horrible old synapses." So the queen has slink a slug in the pay toilet and blew her top off with an overcharge.

So this is Smiles Benson, your loathsome counselor. You can just tell old Smiles anything, so come on in, kiddies, and let your hair down with a gash and show me all your interesting sores.

Drop your pants, sister, my Mary hides behind the prostate trap with her protoplasm showing, dissolve herself and run out her bloody cunt. Must be careful of the word bloody. Quite thick in England they tell me. Wouldn't want to offend the office manager and he take back the keys to the office shithouse. Always keep it locked so no Sinister Stranger sneak a shit, give all the kids in the office some horrible disease; and old Mr. Anker from Accounting, his arms scarred like a junky from Wassermanns, spray plastic over it before he travail there.

Prostate white as an eye receives the delight massage, shoot it up the spine to the hypothalamus with delicious bone tickles, the spine squeeze the body in spasms of delight and throws its white juice.

Put the orgasm line direct in the hypothalamus socket and we are in business. My line is Total Disability and Termite-Proof Orgasms. It's the American way, folks, if you want a thing done do it yourself first, then mass-reduce anyone stand still for it, anyplace you can find traction. Hanging is an outmoded trip around the world to the Hypothalamus Orgasm Center. England missed the bus. Don't break your neck to get an orgasm, folks. Buy Uncle Lee's portable charge set, turn you on *direct connection*. Shit sure contract your spine in spasms.

"Turn the cocksucker off!! I'm Stoned!!"

Technicians: "Fluid drained out! Hydraulic switch ain't worth a fart." He mixes a bicarbonate of soda and belches into his hand. White bone juice spurt out.

The Jordanian soldier, convict of selling a map of the barracks privy to Jew agents, hanged in the marketplace of Amman, crawl up onto the gallows poop deck to hoist the Black Wind Sock of the Insect Trust. Black rocks and great brown lagoons invade the world silent and sure as junk taking the sick cells.

There stands the deserted transmitter, crystal tubes click on the message of retreat from the Human Hill.

"Fellow worshippers of the Centipede God, there is no halfway house. To compromise at animal level were to invite carnivorous disaster, and as such I protest. We gotta make it all the way lest any citizen raise his voice to say, 'I do not check those deeds that you have done!' "

Only the dry hum of wings rub together and giant centipedes crawl in the ruined city of our long home.

Thermodynamics has won at a crawl. . . . Orgone balked at the post. . . . Christ bled. . . . Time ran out.

"We were caught with our pants down," admits General Peterson. "They rimmed the shit out of us."

Will the centipede stand in the spine like he's supposed? Will Greg let his bone-teasing lover Brad hang him for kicks? He shove his hypothalamus, rotten with stasis sores all over it, into Brad's face and scream, "Break it, Brad, and let the white juice flow! Bury me under the school privy, let the winds of East Texas whimper through my ribs filling up with young boy sweet shit."

The spectators scream through the Track. The electronic brain shivers berserk in blue and pink and chlorophyll orgasms, spitting out money printed on rolls of toilet paper, condoms full of ice cream, Kotex hamburgers—FBI files spurt out in a great blast of bone meal, garden tools and barbecue sets whistle through the air, skewer the spectators. A million jukeboxes truck and jitterbug and waltz and mambo across the floor, snatch money from the spectators, shove it up the slot. A rousing Bronx cheer throws a silent greased spray of glass across the bars and soda fountains and lunch rooms of America and the jukebox goes out like a dead electric eye. Mixmasters attack the markets and fields, orchards and warehouses, flood the world with juice. Bendixes tear clothes from spectators, snap up sheets and rugs. The Brain spews out test results; positive Wassermann ejects a huge rubber spirochete, albuminous urine throws out an artificial kidney, Contraceptive Unit rams a squealing peccary up a woman's snatch with vaginal jelly; the cream separator has cut a cow in half, and the automatic milker jack boys off to white bone juice, carries it away in slop bucket to feed the hogs that never touch the ground, supported in plastic slings, great globs of fat folding over the mouth, like a gorged tick—tiny hooves stick out the white lard wiggling feeble. And the halitosis tester billows out rings of pure black stink, sear the lungs like burning shit, and the electric chair executes at ten-minute intervals equipped with built-in court and jail.

"Just feed your criminal into the machine and his cremated ashes fall out the other end in a plastic Chimu Funeral Urn. Infallible electronic jurisprudence prevent miscarriages and Suburbia is spared screams for mercy or some nausea artist strip on the gallows with a hard-on, scream, 'I'm ready for a meet with my maker!' and leer at the doctor so nasty or roll around the gas chamber floor shitting and ejaculating, while the sheriff whimpers at the witness slot—and who want to see the prick turn red like an old blood sausage and burst open when the switch goes home? The machine does it all, folks."

General Peterson leaps on a Bendix and careens around the track at supersonic speed, his voice falls out of his empty wake of air—"Hold that line, boys! Exterminate the bastards!" He is washed away screaming in a river of DDT.

The thinking machine runs out of thought, and sucks the brains out of everybody with stainless steel needles glittering in pinball pinks and gas flares and sky rockets.

Outside, the dry husk of insects. . . .

Now the thoughtful reader may have observed certain tendencies in the author might be termed unwholesome. In fact some of you may be taken aback by the practices of this character. The analyst say: "Mr. Lee have you not consider, to thread thy cock on a lifelong oyster string of pearly cunts and get with normal suburban kicks is chic as Cecil Beaton's ass this season in Hell?"

I call in my friends and we spend whole evenings listen to the Bendix sing "Sweet and Low," "The Wash Machine Boogie"; and the sinister cream separator, a living fossil, bitter as rancid yak butter, seeks the bellowing Hoover with a leopard's grunt. Suburbia hath horrors to sate a thousand castrates and stem the topless cocks of Israel.

Going my way, brother? The hitchhiker walks home through gathering mushroom clouds, and we meet in the Dead Ass Café, to break glass ashtrays over our foreheads pulsing in code . . . slip with a broken neck to the ground-floor mezzanine and put sickness up the cunt of Mary, yearly wounded with a frightened girl.

Brothers, the limit is not yet. I will blow my fuse and blast my brains with a black short-circuit of arteries, but I will not be silent nor hold longer back the enema of my word hoard, been dissolving all the shit up there man and boy forty-three years and who ever held an enema longer? I claim the record, folks, and any Johnny-Come-Late think he can out-nausea the Maestro, let him shove his ass forward and do a temple dance with his piles.

"Not bad, young man, not bad. But you must learn the meaning of discipline. Now you will observe in my production every word got some kinda awful function fit into mosaic on the shithouse wall of the world. That's discipline, son. Always at all times know thy wants and demand same like a thousand junkies storm the crystal spine clinics cook down the Gray Ladies."

The bartender has kick the Sellubi, his foot sink in the ass and the Sellubi comes across the dusty floor. The bartender braces himself against the brass rail, put other foot in the Sellubi's back and pops him off into the street.

"Step right up ladies and gents to see this character at the risk of all his appendages and extremities and appurtenances will positively shoot himself out of a monster asshole. . . ." An outhouse is carried in on the shoulders of Southern Negroes in dungarees, singing spirituals.

"And the walls come tumbling down."

The outhouse falls in a cloud of powdered wood and termites, and the Human Projectile stands there in his black shit suit. A giant rubber asshole in a limestone cliff clicks open and sucks the Human Projectile in like spaghetti. Noise of distant thunder and the Projectile pops out with a great fart, flies a hundred feet through the air into a net supported by four gliders. His shit suit splits and a round worm emerges and does a belly dance. The worm suit peels off like a condom and the Aztec Youth stands naked with a hard-on in the rising sun, ejaculates bloody crystals with a scream of agony. The crowd moans and whimpers and writhes. They snatch up the stones dissolve in red and crystal light. . . . The boy has gone away through an invisible door.

Nimun with sullen cat eyes look for a scrap of advantage, he snap it up and carry it away to the secret place where he lives and no one can find the way to his place. Old queens claw wildly at his bronze body, scream, "Show me your secret place, Nimun. I'll give you all my hoard of rotten ectoplasm."

"What place? You dreaming, mister? I live in the Mills Hotel."

"But WHERE YOU BEEN??????????"

The Skip Tracer has come to disconnect your hypothalamus for the nonpayment of orgones:

"I got a fact process here, Jack. You haven't paid your orgone bill since you was born already and used to squeak out of the womb, 'Don't pay it Ma. Think of your unborn child. You wanta get the best for me,' like a concealed rat. Know this, Operators, Black and Gray Marketeers, Pimps and White Slavers, Paper Hangers of the world: no man can con the Skip Tracer when he knocks on your door with a fact process. He who gives out no orgones will be disconnected from life for the nonpayment."

"But give me time. I'm caught short. . . ."

"Time ran out in the 5th at Tropical. . . . Disconnect him boys."

"Lost my shoe up him," grumbles the bartender. "My feet are killing me, I got this condition of bunions you wouldn't believe it. Turn on the ventilator, Mike. When a man live on other people's shit he can fart out a stink won't quit. I knew this one Sellubi could fart out smoke rings, and they is bad to shoplift with their prehensile piles. . . ."

"Order in the court! You are accused of soliciting with prehensile piles. What have you to say in your defense?"

"Just cooling them off, Judge. Raw and bleeding . . . wouldn't you?"

Judge: "That's beside the point. . . . What do you recommend, Doctor?"

Dr. Burger: "I recommend hypothalamectomy."

The Sellubi turns white as a dead leech and shits his blood out in one solid clot. Warm spring rain washes shit off a limestone statue of a life-size boy hitchhiking with his cock. "GOING MY WAY?" in dead neon on a red-brick dais overlook a deserted park in East St. Louis.

The Hoover bellows retreat and the Business Man says to his honey-face, "I'm tired, sweet thing, and got the rag on."

The team hangs Brad in the locker room. Ceremonial dress of shoulder pads and jockstrap. His friend will pull the jockstrap down, let the cock spurt free and break his neck with a stiff arm. He is buried under the school outhouse where black widows lurk is bad to bite young boy ass.

Fearless boy angels fly through the locker room jacking off, "Whooooooooooooooooo"—they jet away in white wake of jissom, leave a crystal laugh hang in the air.

Transmute your substance. . . . Burn the black shit blue. No disgust on the human tightrope. Stay on that rope brothers and sisters and those who evade the sex census holed up in the mountains of Interzone.

No one transmute by proxy, nor send the chauffeur with thy pelvis in a hat box, nor Nubian Expeditor bearing your hypothalamus in a crystal cylinder. Folks, you must bring your own ass in at the door. The Saint can't come for you and why should I repeat myself in your horrible old body disgust me already with stasis sores?

Negroes with sad monkey eyes stand in a jungle clearing—animal substance invades the thickening face—disease of the race in blood and bones, and white lymphogranuloma swell the groins. Little toe amputates spontaneous, it's a dirty nigger trick, and the bleached-blond-passing replica crook her little toe elegant, it drop off clean and bloodless on Mrs. Worldly's drawing-room floor.

Great raindrops fall like crystal skulls through the green air, and Portuguese gauchos with huge black mustaches ride through the clearing, sing strange sad songs. Planters use cured Nigra balls on the golf course, whacking them over the gallows. Their women sit on the club veranda. Peeled balls float like opal chips in jars of glycerin at withered yellow necks, a resplendent tiara at the governor's ball catch the Aladdin lamp sputter of burning insect wings. The woman dreams of a Black Mamba and wake shrieking, "The houseboy fucked me!"

"Rusty load of ectoplasm . . . gotta score for a medium tonight," said the arty ghost. "Don't have a regular stand like some lucky pricks go around all the time on the nod. Earth-bound to the monkey three hundred years man boy and ghost."

Spontaneous amputation of cock occurs among boys, it just turn to shit and pop off with a fart. The boy picks his cock out of shit shale, the careful archaeologist, and sprays shellac all over it—subject to turn to dust when it hits the air after all those shit-bound years.

Johnny make it all the way in St. Louis before spellbound audience—throw off his pink bathrobe naked as the Young Corn God, hang himself for keeps ejaculating crystal skulls. . . . There was this citizen have a circus act, hang himself with a special elastic rope. A dangerous act they tell me, you gotta check the rope for elasticity before every performance. In St. Louis he didn't check the rope and his neck snapped, he was carried out by leering cops with a paralyzed hard-on . . . and the last spasm on the operating table under floodlight—a trouper to the end. The wind sock sags and the croaker shakes his head and the nurse covers Johnny's prick with a sheet.

So he turns to limestone, and setting his hard cock in the cunt of shadow, fades down the mountainside, and pipes call "Taps for Danny Boy" and "Johnny's So Long at the Fair."

The Ringmaster has pulled a rope switch . . . the old army game. "The One, the Only, Midway Johnny, though his spine breaks in his neck, gives the performance of all time!"

The Dreamer—impresario of that Los Angeles cemetery under-lines mortality with shit—gilds Johnny with angel wings springing from an outhouse on the tomb of a rich old queen rolls right over in her grave.

"Just build a privy over me, boys," said the rustler to his bunk-mates, and the sheriff nods in dark understanding. Druid blood stirring in the winds of Panhandle, and bloody rites to the Cow God are consummate in the Sacred Cottonwood groves. Johnny is eaten in Kansas City by bankers and brokers with black mustache and gold watch chain.

"Now that's what I call *tenderloin*," B.Q. says, pensively studying a sliver of red meat on the end of his toothpick.

"Yeah, but the meat's gotta *hang*. . . . Now in Dodge City they are serving raw unparalyzed boys is subject to come up on a poor old queen and slice her motherfucking head off and rummage through her intestines for gold fillings. Eager beaver might swallow a gold crown with the jissom."

"But here the boys is cut down to eating size the way I like to see a cut of boy, Clem."

The Cow God and the Horse God, the Bank God, the Cop God and the Eunuch God of Small Business claim their yearly crop of Young Gods in the Vibrating Chair, the Green Outhouse and the rope sing like wind in wire.

And the broker shits Johnny out in his marble shithouse with sunken bath, smokes his great greasy Havana, chewing it slow and dirty, and take the chewed end out to look at and lick his mustache and belch.

Lean sick junkies play Banker and Broker in Washington Square.

"Billy Budd must hang! All hands aft to see this exhibit." Billy Budd gives up the ghost with a great fart, and the sail is rent from top to bottom, and the petty officers fall back confounded. . . . "Billy" is a transvestite Liz. "There'll be a spot of bother about this," mutters the Master-at-Arms, breathing into his halitosis tester.

The tars scream with rage at the cheating profile in the rising sun. The Liz gives a few tired old kicks and throws a little sliver of black shit curved like a pigtail.

"Is she dead?"

"So who cares?"

"Are we going to stand still for this, boys? The officers pull a switch on us," said young Hassan, Ship's Uncle.

"Gentlemen," said Captain Vere, "I cannot find words to castigate this foul and unnatural act whereby a boy's mother take over his body, infiltrate her horrible old substance right onto a decent boat and, with bare tits hanging out, unfurl the nastiest colors of the spectroscope."

All the world's a gallows and we all play with our parts, some are towel boys, others lewd doctors, most of us just dirty old men whimper at life's Glory Hole.

A young kid has wandered in off the range with the winds of Texas in his hair. He wipes his ass pensively with a Mandrake.

A great black tornado has sucked meaning from the Cyclone Belt. Citizens crawl out of the cellar in a blighted subdivision, look after the cyclone with canceled castrate eyes. . . .

"Lawd! Lawd! I don't even feel like a human."

"At least the TV is left."

They squeak out a feeble "Hallelujah."

See, the sheriff frame every good-looking kid in the country, say, "Guess I'll have to hang some cunt for the new *frisson*. He hang this cute little corn-fed thing, her tits come to attention, squirt milk in his eye blind him like a spitting cobra.

"Oh land's sake!" say the sheriff. "I shoulda never hang a woman. A man can only come off a second best he tangle assholes with a gash. Well, I guess I can see with my mouth from here on in. Hehe hehe heh."

So the sheriff have glass eyes made up with filthy pictures built in—her is walking penny arcade—and feel the kid up, and that hot blood hit the young cock, and the kid's breath get short, and the sheriff's steady finger (best shot in Dead Coon County) unbutton his fly slow and just ease the cock out stand up there pulsing in the Old Privy all overgrown with weeds and vines, rusty smell of shit turning back to soil.

Come in at the door after delouse treatment. Don't give halo lice to your fellow angels. They will sneer at you and hamstring your harp.

"You want to lose that proboscis?" she say. Her cunt click open like a snap-knife.

Don't offend with innocence. Need Life Boy soap. Body smell of life a nasty odor in the snooze of a decent American gash.

See this Liz fuck a kid with a April Fool exploding prick, and it go off inside and blow his guts right outa navel. The Liz roll on the floor laughing, yell, "Oh! Oh! Give me ribs of steel."

Any woman get gay with me after all I suffer from the fairy-making sex bite off more than she can chew, even with my lymphogranuloma I can still kick shit out of Brubeck the Unsteady lose his in the thervith of junk and the slunk traffic.

"The gimmick is this, Doc: tell a farmer his cow give birth to a monster and you had to burn it already, goosed by your Veterinary Ethics. We can't miss."

. . . It's the only way to live . . . a few chickens . . . jug of paregoric and thou under the swamp cypress. Sweet screams of burning Nigra drift in on the warm spring wind fans our hot bodies like a Nubian slave. How obliging can you get?

The boy trots along the curb with tireless *amok* trot of the Indian-giver to a perilous scaffold of rusty iron, termite-eaten wood, rotten rope. Meets a young junky—black hair uncombed, black eyes with pinpoint green pupils open on the Green Death Room (one reference, gentle reader, is to the Green Room in San Quentin where cyanide executions are consummated under civil leers of the witnesses).

Papers of heroin stashed in the history book, he fixes in the school toilet. Narcotics agent, peeping through the glory hole, has caught a kid in the junk act, slaps the cuffs on his ankles.

I ask the boy how old he is and he say, "I'm seventeen."

I nod with dark understanding and say, "Junkies always look younger than they are."

"How they hangin', Herman?" Old fat junky cheat on his rope with cyanide.

It's the Plastic Age, folks. 'Tain't no sin take off your new skin and clown around in your bone-ons.

That good Black Gum with hot Arab tea hits you ten minutes like a ton of shit. . . . Black Death Terry called his Ford the river of sticks to Reynosa Boy's Town where the mangy lioness was to break his neck with one quick claw. . . . That's what happen when you wake a sleeping lioness with the flashbulb of urgency. She don't like it. And the Chinaman don't like it. Don't ever wake that Chinaman with a heroin flash.

(Young friend of mine name of Terry have this 1936 Ford he call the Black Death. One night he get in the Black Death and cross the Rio Grande to Reynosa, where a mangy old lioness stood in a cage in Joe's patio. So Terry goes in the cage, throw a flashlight in the lioness' face, who leap on him and break his neck, and the bartender vault over the bar with a forty-five blast the lioness. But Mr. Terry he dead.)

The blond woman came in through the white door with a holly wreath on it, and took down my wine-colored pants. Drank champagne from the living cunt with breakfast sausage and scrambled eggs.

Where you been? This young cat eat sausages out of a woman's cunt (prominent actress) at a Berlin party in Weimar days. Later he run into this same cunt fully dressed at another party and say, *"Wie gehts?"* or something . . . and she draw herself up and sneer: "Where is your culture, you nameless asshole? I don't know you."

And he says, "But Fräulein, I have et the blood sausage from your cunt at Mitzi's Comming-off and Going-away Party."

And she says, "Oh dahling! . . . Of course! Mitzi's such an old castrate." Such was life in the Weimar Republic.

Boy on the way to Lexington jacks off in the shuddering junk-sick toilet. Girls scream by on the scenic railway over the edge of space into the night. . . . "Put out your condom, kid, and Santa drop a cunt in it."

So I say to this broad, I say, "Listen baby you ought to take a picture. Do you dye your cunt or shave it?"

The Caid in gasoline screams up the Midway to the burning roller coaster where the boy stood on the heroin deck proclaiming his habit to the sneers of sick physicians.

The trap falls with tremendous speed, no time for breakfast. Let it come down and fix the black bone yen.

Burning high yeller boy tied to a packing crate with barbed wire at wrist and ankle, screams out of his flesh and runs across the red clay of Georgia in black bones.

London Bridge is falling, slow trap through the long white nerves and green intestine jungles and the pearly glands. . . . Slow fall. . . .

In the Closed Garden the Boy runs in a curved fold, pants of Nexus burn with jellied Narcissism—incandescent pelvis among the geraniums. . . . Outside yipping Arabs barbecue sad-eyed Indians in pink Cadillacs.

Junk yacks at our heels a silent riot, and predated checks bounce all around us like fossil skulls in a Mayan ball court.

"Dicks scream for dope fiend lover"—A savage spot haunted by a woman scream for her demon lover, Coleridge, "Xanadu"—another old-time schmecker.

Dead bird, quail in the slipper, money in the bank. Fossil cunts of predated chicks bounce around us in Queens Plaza. Lay them in the crapper—just shove it in, vibration does the rest. Old stove burn nostalgia, and black dust rain down over us cancer curse of switch. Cock under the nut shell.

"Step right up. Now you see it, now you don't."

The penis is not of mine to give is passport of cunt. Past port and petal crowned with calm leaves she stand there across the river under the trees.

"Come," she says. "Come, and you can suck my marshmallows, and I will show my little black box of Turkish Exquisitries." (.32 prick cover this caper, penis in hand.)

(Proprietor of a Turkish Exquisitries shop shot by holdup man with .32.)

The light shakes over the lake, and the wild cataract leaps through the Glory Hole, blinding the old queen in the next cavity. Spitting cobras, patronize your neighborhood toilet.

Adolescent angels sing on shithouse walls of the world: "Come and Jack Off . . . 1929." "Gimpy pushes milk sugar shit . . . Johnny Hung Lately, 1952." Deserted farm outhouse (shit turn back dust to dust).

Telegram from your boy buried under the outhouse forty-year shit strata . . . sing over the deep river into K-Y Inferno (female impersonator joint).

"I got the calling," scream the female impersonator like a horse kicked in the nuts. Orient Express screaming train whistle, and the chic young agent summarily hanged at the Turkish border for possession of Exquisitries turns out to be female impersonator from Yokohama with a strap-on cunt fly off in last orgasm. Bullfighter's cap caught by The Witness . . . hiatus of time out when the banana slip up his ass, goose him onto the long horn.

Come in at the Door Jam. Don't worry about a Thing Man. Where'd you get it? Shaking that thing. The prostate back trap door let it down, shit out the marines like a landing barge, nail it shut with cobwebs.

Frontier moves out into space-time—phantom riders, chili joints, saloon and the Quick Draw, hangings from horseback to the jeers of Sporting Women. Black Smoke on the hip in the Chinese Laundry. . . . No tickee, no washee. Clom Fliday.

Chinese pushers stopped serving Occidentals in the 1920s. When a junky want to score off the Chink, he say, "No glot. Come Fliday."

Golden horses copulate in black clouds of West.

The quaint English gangster is in the marl hole of the world.

In front of the mutilated limestone fragments of museum, Indian boys with bright red gums are eating the green ices.

Mr. Gilly looks for his brindle-faced cow across the Piney Woods where armadillos innocent of a cortex frolic under the .22 of black Stetson and pale blue eyes.

When the author was raising marijuana in East Texas, he unwillingly made the acquaintance of one Mr. Gilly, a rural mooch leave low pressure area in his wake like an impotent cyclone, toothless snarl of blackmail, weak and intermittent like music down a windy street. "Lawd Lawd, have you seen my brindle-faced cow? Guess I'm taking up too much of your time. Must be busy doing *something*, feller say. Good stand you got, whatever it is. Maybe I'm asking too many questions. Weell, guess I'll be getting along. You wouldn't have a rope, would you? A *hemp* rope? Don't know how I'd hold that old brindle-faced cow without a rope if I did come on him. No, I guess not. Well, now you got that new Chevy, I guess you'd most *give* your old jeep to a poor man. You wouldn't have a cold drink, would you?"

In England are bottomless holes used as public tips (dumps), known as marl holes, where English gangsters dump copper's narks in oil tins—until the busies put a watchman on the hole to prevent such violations of the sanitary code.

The museum at Guatemala City, looted by Mayan collectors of the world, has left a few old beat-up pieces of stelae. Set in a little park grove of trees.

Money all over him like shit you can smell it. And Rocky smell so sweet of junk always leave that selfish smell never come off a man handle it, use it, junk cling to him like jellied ectoplasm, burns out whiffs of black smoke.

The Operator want to suck the emergent maleness of the passing queen . . . wise prick know when the bones will change and jump on that wagon break its ass with his weight of centuries, sit and take his cut and never never give nothing back. Got the Big Fix up his ass in a finger stall with 14-carat diamonds, antibiotics and heroin. Under Corn Hole Sign of carny lot caretaker toolshed.

"Drop your pants, kid." Over the broken chair and out through the dusty window—Midway boarded up for winter, whitewash whip in a cold wind on limestone cliff over the river—pieces of moon hang like smoke in the cold blue substance of sky out on a long line of jissom spurt across the dusty floor.

"See you Joe's Lunch. Treat you meal. What'll you have, kid? Two chilis with cherry crumb pie and white coffee."

"Like this," he say on all fours, cup the boy's tits with hard palms, shove it in with a slow sideways wiggle, pull the boy's body on to him with long strokes sculpt stomach, arch like a cat pulling up into his stomach, up and in.

Balls squeezed dry black lemon rind pest rim the ass with a knife cut off piece of hash for the water pipe bubble tube indicate what used to be me.

"The river is served, sir."

In the barn attic came on the wetback sleep with hard-on under thick cotton pants . . . sits up with fierce eyes, smile sweet, bright red gums, look down and stretch his body, and I reach slow and touch it. He sit me down and make the strip motion, and I undo belt silent and shaking and shove my pants down slow. Cock spring out hard, turn me around, sink slow fence post in hole, quicksand, rubber boots slow in, the boy shudder and sigh. Black widow fall on the wetback's copper neck, bite him; die in quick convulsions allergic shock—come five times.

The young rustler say to his friend, "You do it." And the friend take the noose, looking into his friend's eyes, put it over his head and adjust behind the left ear—ritual gentleness of sacrifice. "You'd better stand up in the saddle." Help him up with tied hands, leaning against his friend's hard young body keep him from falling on the hemp (premature ejaculation unhealthy practice the experts say). Stand now like a young god ready: "Well, go ahead, Greg." They stand there, one steadying the other with hand on his shoulder, young males gentle and sad, and the wind ripples through their hair in a vibrating soundless hum under the cottonwoods. The two boys change middle-aged hennaed fags, start back from each other appalled by the hideous sea change, and Johnny falls from the saddle. Mandrakes pop up with pathic screams.

Crawl out and identify yourselves before we throw in a Mills Brothers cough drop or a chocolate éclair, and the third time he go down for the long count tangled in seaweed, down there looking for his fish dinner.

"Let's shake the joint down." Freudian dicks burst in like burning lions.

"Ground floor dining room, so-called living room, den, kitchen, pantry, toilet under the stairs."

"We been over this a million times. Really, Doctor, if you have nothing further to enlighten us, shut your doddering mouth whyncha?"

"Second floor."

"Don't make with the room layout again, or I shall scream."

"Toilet lead right into our lady's dressing room soft silky smells perfume and cold cream and whiff of diarrhea shit smell yellow, the way old three-day vintage smell black. Ever whiff green shit? A sort of shiny green-black glows in the dark? But that was in another country, and besides—"

"Shut up already, murder never outlaws. The fuzz try hanging this meatball rap on me as notorious Blue Ball and Torso Artist."

"Never outlaws." I.e., the statute of limitations does not run. Blue balls are a symptom of real evil clap.

The arrow right through his eye and out the back of that adorable head. Shrunk down I keep it up my ass in a plastic cover on a long gold chain. Lovely mouth falls open as if petulant wake from sleep with a sulky hard-on, he dead falls with a soft plop in the Amazon mud.

"Well," she says, "I got this vibrator off my cousin Fred connect with the black market for these coupons entitle him all different gadgets—folding bidet carry up your ass, open out like an umbrella. And the handbag cream separator, second as weapon a girl caught short-armed with a prick up her."

Long line of black boys march up the ramp to the hidden gallows singing spirituals. And when they open the door underneath cut them down with a Kansas combo the warm wheaty odor of semen drifts out across the blighted continent, South of the Border, wanders in miasmal mists and ambrosial fogs flowers in a clear green switch.

Jim goose Brad, say "Ooooooooh," and his teeth pop out with a fart into the clear blue mountain lake, turn into a lamprey and swim away to suck a silver trout.

The face strangles (audience gags and stick out tongues), veins pop in the brain like little red firecrackers, blue sparks fly from broken connections, lights go off in square blocks of power failure. Light across Long Island park and trees in the bright sun seen from the El shake through the young body. (America a great plain under the wings of vultures husk in the dry air.)

Cool as blue-eyed young junky spectral in the sun. Hot as blood leap to mouth and cock, and the eyes go black and blood sing in the ears sweet as little pink conchs.

"The question is this," said the philosophic doctor, that old tired prop him up, downing a mason jar of corn. "Can the pleasure of a sex act, deeply repressed say like MacArthur we have returned and squeeze out the jet at tremendous pressure, be qualitatively more intense than the normally charged act?"

Blast of trumpets, drool of drums and dead march. And decayed corseted tenor sings "Danny Deever" in drag: "They have taken all his buttons off and cut his pants away. Bastard browned the colonel sleeping, the man's ass is all agley. And he'll swing in harf a minute for a sneaking, shooting fay. They are 'angin' Danny Deever in the morning."

Lights: a stage stretching to the neon skyline. Golden gallows towers a thousand feet against the Grand Canyon, Pikes Peak, Niagara Falls and Chrysler Building, vast souvenir postcards light up slow with neon.

Motel. Motel. Motel loneliness moans across the continent like foghorns over still oily waters of tidal rivers. Violet's Massage Parlour in green neon. The Girl in White greases up a vibrator. The boy watches her face black down to a little green dot.

Hanging togs at Antoine's, emporium for young fags of good family. We have literally thousands of escape suits for the—tee hee—bride.

"May I kiss the bride?"

The skull nods knowingly. Antoine claps imperious hands, and the Fashion Show is on.

Boy drops on a blue rope. Blue flame burns round his waist,

and his pants fall free, burning, into a dark lagoon in the empty park. Shirt burns in blue flare light his grinding bone grins. The separate spine squeeze the soft body up and out the cock.

Escape suit burn blue all over, cook the boy while he come, spit hot balls out his cock. (Negro smile malevolently, catch them on a skewer. "Hot balls, folks! Hot balls!" He moves up through the aisles. Circus, Stadium, Plaza.)

Our Snow Drop Suit guaranteed to liquefy. We have never had a failure. When you shoot that rusty dark load cross the night like a shooting star.

Cowboy suit dissolves in a mist of powder smoke, clear to show bunkmate reverently pull off the boots . . . and with beatified face receive the benediction of sperm sweet as warm summer rain on the face and hair.

The Preaching Hangman touches the boy's neck with hands, sweet slime like a snail. "Now, ladies and gentles of this congregation. When I hang a man and think of his lluuuuuvelay soul bear his rusty load right up God's ass—how old did you say, sheriff?"

"Sixteen."

"Looks younger. —Sometimes I really haaaaate this job." He wipes the foam from his lips with an eiderdown.

Soldier suit dissolve, run down the body. Our permanent plating process guarantee you an interested niche in any park, hang off the limp foot in a bronze tear.

Suits turn to shit and drip off you swung out over the privies of the world on a long black bolo. Angel suits made of marshmallows and spun sugar sweet burn, leave the little naked boy twitching. (Sweet young breath quick through the teeth, stomach hard as marble spits it out in soft sweet blobs. Spurty boy comes, slower and slower and slower turn to a long yellow beard in the old man's hands.)

Socially conscious Negroes hang themselves over a fire of packing crates singing "Strange Fruit" slow and fruity, while serious Negroes with rimless glasses and fat smooth coffee faces hand out bills among the audience, well-dressed and vaguely embarrassed. (Whiff of dried jissom in a bandanna rises out of a hotel drawer, ghost town twenty years shut down, covered with dust.)

"Interesting, don't you think?"

"Decidedly," says the venomous thin-faced Colonel, circumcises a boy with his cigar cutter, lights his cigar with the foreskin.

The boy like a nun so pure and alive for the moment to take the death vow it hurts, a soft blue blast of sadness. Boy grin dissolves slow into the sunlight over the bullhead hole, quarry, vacant lot with a pond in it. The boy looks down at his bloody arms marked with the needle-wound stigmata. Soft sadness of death. Riddled child cancer. "Hope to God the President's Radium Bicycle gets here on time," says the White House Press Department, looking nervously at his watch.

Mirror suits scatter into white sand desert, reveal the vicious leer of the brazen victim.

The hangman in doublet is adjusting the knot with bestial leers and obscene gestures.

A pig forty feet high is sliced open by a huge neon-tube knife. Amusement park stretch in roller-coastering black lace to the horizons of smoky cities.

Greg sits in the school toilet. Clean sharp turds fall out his tight young ass (turds like yellow clay washed clean in summer rain covered with crystal snail tracks in the morning sun lights the green flame of grass).

The man with black Japanese mustache, each hair frozen in white grease. (Black branches with the white ice cover catch the morning sun over a frozen lake when we get back from the hunting trip.)

Ambivalent alcoholic hangs himself with a great Bronx cheer, blasting out all his teeth, and tears at the noose. (Shivering dog breaks his teeth on the steel trap under a cold white moon.)

"Candy, I Call My Sugar Candy." Hanged boy descends on a rope of toffee, comes in the mouth of a fourteen-year-old girl eats toffee and taps out "Candy" on the neon-lighted table—outside, the blight of Oklahoma beaten by the calm young eyes.

The boy has found the vibrator in his mother's closet. They won't be back before five . . . plenty of time. Drops pants to ankles, cock springs up hard and free with that lovely flip make old queen bones stir with root nerves and ligaments. He grease the tip, and it turn into a vulgar cock given to Bronx cheers at moment of orgasm and other shocking departures from good taste. (Emily Post is writing a million-word P.S. to *Etiquette*, entitled *The Cock in Our House*.) He stands front mirror, stick it slow up his ass to the glad gland give a little fart of pleasure. Bubble filled with fart gas hang in the air heavy as ectoplasm dispersed by the winds of morning sweep the dust out with slow old man hands coughing and spitting in the white blast of dawn. Sperm splash the mirror, turn black and go out in a short circuit with ozone smell of burning iron.

Greg has come up behind Brad in the park, goose him and his hand sink in.

"Hello, Brad." He pulls his hand out with a resounding fart and rubs ambergris over his body, poses for *Health and Strength* in faggot-skin jockstrap.

So there he stand on top of the filing cabinet naked as a prick hang out in the muted blue incense of the lesbian temple. (Cold-eyed nuns rustle by, metallic purity leaves a whiff of ozone.) Funny how a man comes back to something he left behind in a Peoria hotel drawer 1932.

You are nearing the frontier where all the pitchmen and street peddlers, three-card-monte quick-con artists of the world spread out their goods. Old pushers, embittered by years of failure, mutter through the endless gray lanes of junk *amok* with a joint (i.e., a syringe), shooting the passersby. The tourist is torn in pieces by Soul Short-Change hypes fight over pieces. (Piranha fish tear each other to great ribbons of black-market beef. White bone glistens through, covered with iridescent ligaments.)

Neon tubes glow in the blood of the world. Everyone see his neighbor clear as an old message on the shithouse wall stand out in white flames of a burning city.

Greg turns away with a cry of defeat. Bone ache for the Marble God smiling into park covered with weeds.

Fish thrown to the seal by naked boy grin for ooze in verdigris: KEEP THE CHANGE.

Smile sweet as a blast of ozone from a June subway, teeth tinkle like little porcelain balls.

Hold your tight nuts frozen in limestone convolutions.

"I'll be right over stick a greased peccary up her Hairy Ear." Albanian argot for cunt.

Sea of frozen shit in the morning sun and maggots twelve feet long stir underneath, the crust breaks here and there. Asshole farts up sulfur gases and black boiling mud.

Crisp green lettuce heads glitter with frost under a tinkling crystal moon.

"We'll make a heap of money, Clem, if the price is right." He plucks a boy's balls, look over careful for lettuce blight, probing veins and ligaments with gentle old-woman fingers, feel soft for the vein in the pink dawn light; and the young boy wake naked out of wet dream, watch his cock spurt into the morning.

The boy flies screaming in a jet of black blood, turns a red tube in the air, ineffable throbbing pink, rains soft pink cushions on your ass in a soft slow come.

The boy has cut off his limestone balls and tossed them to you with a grin—light on water. Now the body sinks with a slow Bronx cheer to a torn pink balloon hang on rusty nail in the barn. Pink and purple lights play over it from a great black crane swing over rubbish heap go back to stone and trees.

His neck has grown around the rope like a tree. (Vine root in old stone wall. Voice fade to decay, loose a soundless puff of dust, fall slow through the sunlight.)

The boy has eaten a pat of butter, turns into middle-aged cardiac. "That's the way I like to see them," says Doctor Dodo Rindfest—known as Doodles to his many friends. "Them old cardiac rams alla time die up a reluctant ewe."

The old queen wallows in bathtub of boy balls. Others jack off over him jitterbugging, walking through the Piney Woods with a .22 in the summer dawn (chiggers pinpoint the boy's groin in red dots), hanging on the back of freight trains career down the three-mile grade into a cowboy ballad bellowed out by idiot cows through the honky-tonks of Panhandle.

Screaming round the roller coaster in a stolen car, play chicken with a bronze scorpion big as a trailer truck on route 666 between Lynchburg and Danville.

The boy rise in sea-green marble to jack off on the stones of Venice invisible to the ravening castrates of the world, fill the canals with miasmic mist of whimpering halitosis can't get close enough to offend.

The boy has hit you with soft snowballs burst in light burn you soft and pink and cold as cocaine.

Don't walk out on a poor old queen leave her paralyzed come to an empty house. Spurt into the cold spring wind whip the white wash in Chicago, into the sizzling white desert, into the limestone quarry, into the old swimming hole, bait a boy's hook for a throbbing sunfish burn the black water with light.

The wind sighs through the silk stocking hang in clear blue of Mexico clear against the mountain a wind sock of sweet life. (Sweet smell of boy balls and rusty iron cool in the mouth.)

Attic under the round window eye. Summer dawn the two young bodies glow incandescent pink copulations, cock sink into the brown pink asshole up the pearly prostate, sing out along the white nerves. First soft licks of rimming tighten balls off like a winch up the ass. Rim on, MacDuff, till the pool be drained and fill with dead brown leaves, dirty snow drift across my body frozen in the kiss wakes the soft purple flower of shit.

The boy burglar fucked in the long jail with the Porter Tuck— a bullfighter of my acquaintance recently gored in the right lung— in the lungs risk the Great Divide, ousted from the cemetery for the nonpayment come gibbering into the queer bar with a mouldy pawn ticket to pick up the back balls of Tent City, where castrate salesmen sing the IBM song in quavering falsetto.

Balls on the window ledge fall like a broken flowerpot onto the pavement of arson yearly wounded to the sea.

Slow cunt tease refuse until the conversion of the Jew to Diesel go around raping decent cars with a nasty old Diesel Conversion Unit cancerous, so red the rosette, on earth as in heaven this day our breadfruit of cunt.

Crabs frolic through his forest, wrestling with the angle hard-on all night thrown in the home full of valor by adolescent rustler, hide in the capacious skirts of home on the range and the hunter come home from the Venus Hill take the back road to the rusty limestone cave.

Rock and roll around the floor scream for junk fix the Black Yen ejaculate over the salt marshes where nothing grow, not even a mandrake. (Year of the rindpest. Everything died, even the hyenas had to bite a man's balls and run like smash and grab.)

Talk long enough say *something*. It's the law of averages . . . a few chickens . . . only way to live.

Don't neglect the fire extinguisher and stand by with the Kotex in case one of these Southern belles get hot and burst into flame. (Bronx cheer of a fire-eater.)

Cleave fast to mayhem and let not arson be far from thee and clamp murder to thy breast with WHOOOOOOOOPS of seal leap at your throat in Ralph's. Not a bit alarmed about that. Think of something else.

We are prepared to divulge all and to state that on a Thursday in the month of September 1917, we did, in the garage of the latter, at his solicitations and connivance, endeavor to suck the cock of one George Brune Brubeck, the Bear's Ass, which act disgust me like I try to bite it off and he slap me and curse and blaspheme like Christopher Marlowe with the shiv through his eye the way it wasn't fitting a larval fag should hear any old nameless asshole unlock his rusty word hoard.

The blame for this atrociously incomplete act rest solidly on the basement of Brubeck, my own innocence of any but the most pure reflex move of self-defense and -respect to eliminate this strange serpent thrust so into my face at risk of my Man Life, so I, not being armed (unfortunately) with a blunderbuss, had recourse to nature's little white soldiers—our brave defenders by land—and bite his ugly old cock in a laudable attempt to circumcise him thereby reduce to a sanitary condition. He, not understanding the purity of my motives, did inopportunely resist my well-meaning would-be surgical intervention, which occasioned to him light contusions of a frivolous nature. Whereupon he did loose upon my innocent head a blast of blasphemies like burning lions or unsuccessful horse abortionists cooked in slow Lux to prevent the shrinkage of their worm.

We are not unaware of the needs of our constituents. Never out of our mind, and you may rest assured that we will leave no turd interred to elucidate these rancid oil scandals. We will not be intimidated by lesbians armed with hog castrators and fly the Jolly Roger of bloody Kotex, nor succumb to the blandishments of a veteran queen in drag of Liz in riding pants. Even the Terrible Mother will be touched by the grace of process.

So leave us throw aside the drained crankcase of Brubeck and proceed to unleaven the yeast bread of cunt and unfurl the jolly condom. . . . I walk up to this chick, flash a condom on her like a piecea tin, you dig, and I say, "Come with me."

"Fresh," she say and slap me hard, the way I know it is this impersonator is a insult. I insinuate a clap up her ass without so much as by-your-leave.

So I says, "I thought you was McCoy. You look so nice and female to an old cowhand."

"Oh go impersonate a purple-assed baboon, you stupid old character. I'd resist you to the last bitch in any sex."

I stand on the Fifth Amendment, will not answer question of the senator from Wisconsin. "Are you or have you ever been a member of the male sex?" They can't make Dicky whimper on the boys. Know how I take care of crooners, don't you? Just listen to them. A word to the wise guy. I mean you gotta be careful of politics these days, some old department get physical kick him right in his Coordinator. Well, that's the hole story, and I guess I oughta know after all these years. Wellcome and Burroughs to the family party, a member in *hrumph* good standing we hope.

Castrates, Don't Let The Son Set On You Here—precocious little prick could get it by ass mosses. (Seaweed in a dark green grotto.)

The Philosophic Doctor sits on his rattan-ass Maugham veranda drinking pink gin fades to a Manhattan analyst looking over a stack of notes.

"So our murder was, it seems, the bitten Brubeck, who has since recovered and spread his hideous progeny from the wards of Seattle to the parishes of New Orleans, nameless blubby things crawl out of ash pits all covered with shitty sheets, walk around gibber like dead geese."

This refers to a nightmare of the subject's childhood in which he found himself threatened by two figures covered with soiled sheets—poison juices, Goddammit! Dream occur after the subject's collaborating father read him "The Murders in the Rue Morgue," where, as you will doubtless recall, one woman got her head cut clean off and rammed up the chimney. So, Brubeck, you know what you can do with your Liz bitch; and if you don't, my orangutan friend will show you.

"I have frequently observed in the course of my practices, *hrumph*, I mean practice, that homosexuals often express a willingness to, *humph*, copulate with *headless* women—a consummation devoutly to be wished. As one subject expressed it, 'Now I read where this chicken live a week without a head. They feed it through this tube stick out so the neck don't heal over and close up the way a cunt would heal over she didn't open it up every month with an apple corer, to let the old blood out. I mean a broad don't need that head anyhoo.' And recall that it was Medusa's head turned the boys to stone. I suggest that the perilous part of a woman is her hypothalamus, sending solid female static fuck up a man's synapses and leave him paralyzed from the waist down."

So I am prepared to state that the above is true and accurate to the best of my knowledge, so help me God or any other outfit when my dignity and sovereignty be threatened by brutal short-arm aggression. Sworn before me, Harry Q. T. Burford on this day.

"We must have a long talk, son. You see there are men and there are, well, women; and women are different from men."

"In precisely what way, Father?" said young Cesspool incisively.

"Well, they're, well, they're different, that's all. You'll understand when you're older; and, *hurumph*, that's what I want to talk to you about. When you *do* get older."

"Come see me tonight in my apartment under the school privy.

Show you something interesting," said the janitor, drooling green coca juice.

Women seethe with hot poison juices eat it off in a twink. Laws of hospitality be fucked. Take your recalcitrant ass to your own trap. No drones in my dormitories.

"I'm no one's live one," sneered the corpse to the necrophile. "Go back to your own people, you frantic old character."

"Oh be careful. There they go again," says the old queen as his string break, spilling his balls across the floor. "Stop them, will you, James, you worthless old shit! Don't just stand there and let the master's balls roll into the coal bin."

"Is them my peeled balls those kids play marbles with? Why shit sure. Boy, who give you the right to play with my balls?"

"They revert to the public domain after not being claimed forty year, mister."

Well, the wind-up is the fag marries the transvestite Liz disguised as a boy in drag, former heartthrob of Greg hang him for kicks and retire to a locker in Grand Central, subsisting on suitcase and shoe leather. So many tasty ways to prepare it, girls—simmered in saddle soap, singe-broiled in brilliantine, smoked over smoldering ashtrays.

We are in a long white corridor of leaves lithp sunlight.

The Old West dies slow on Hungarian gallows, so while he is fixing (can't hit the hypothalamus anymore) we will shake down the trap for hidden miles and tragic flaws hang a golden lad with his own windblown hair.

When is a boy not a boy? When he is buoyed up by the wind, and the sailplane falls silent as erection.

The blind vet is on the way over to fuck me in the Grand Canal bent over the Academy Bridge. Someone take a picture and cops the film fest for a big brass bidet.

The lamprey seeks a silver fish in the green lagoon.

It would be better off dead. Broken leg. Told by an idiot broken down there you must hear. It is out of the woodpile and into the fire that monkey, and Denmark is rotten with a funeral pyre of bullshit.

"Look into my eyes, baby, mirror of the mad come."

"I can see inside the blue flames running on these long white nerves burn the spine in a slow squeeeeeeeeeze."

Mouths leap forward on flesh tubes, clamp and twist.

Johnny on all fours and Marv sucking him and running his fingers down the thigh backs and light over the ass and outfields of the ball park. Johnny's body begins to hump in the middle, each hump a little longer and squeezier like oily fingers inside squeeze your balls soft as pink down, squeeze those sweet marshmallows slow slow slow.

He throws his head back with a great wolf howl.

Call the coroner; my skill naught avail.

Mine it out of your limestone bones, those fossil messages of arthritis; read the metastasis with blind fingers.

Where else you gonna look? Into the atrophied nuts of the priest, coyote of death? (A coyote is character hangs around the halls of the immigration department in Mexico, D.F., engage to help you for a fee with his inside connections.)

"I can get you straight in to the District Supervisor. Got an in. Of course, it cost. I don't want much—all go pay off my *tremendous* connections." His voice breaks in a pathic scream.

"Didja get a stand-on?" said the vulgar old queen to the virginal boy, trembling in white flame of contempt. "Land sakes," said the queen, "so young so cold so fair—I love it." (Silver statue in the moonlight.)

The swindler enters Heaven in a blast of bullshit. Here's a man hang self opening night of the Met. Cut throat of entire staff, take over the stage, single-handed scene-stealer. Prance out in Isolde drag, sing the "Liebestod" in a hideous falsetto, ending in burlesque striptease. "Take it off! Take it off!" chant his stooges, as pink step-ins, stiff with ass blood, fly out over the audience, she spring the trap. Blood burn to neon pink light through his spine spasms and grinding bone grins. Flesh turn to black shit and flake off—wind and rain and bones on mouldy beach. The queen is a hard-faced boy, patch over one eye, parrot on shoulder, say, "Dead men tell no tales—or do they?" He prods the skull with a cutlass, and a crab scuttles out. The boy reaches down and pick up a scroll.

"The Map! The Map!"

The map turns to shitty toilet paper in his hands, blow across a vacant lot in East St. Louis, catch on clean barbed wire and burn with a blue flame.

The boy pulls off the patch, parrot flies into the jungle, cutlass turns to machete. He is studying the Map and swatting sand flies.

The author has gathered his multiple personalities for a rally at Tent City on the banks of the river Jordan. "Come on in and park your piles, boys. You is Burroughs and Wellcome. Now I wanta hear something artistic like the time you got out of that old black Model A, Cowper's juice seeping right through your thin schoolboy slacks, and jack off into the dogwood and your jissom turn to little white flowers in the air fall so slow and sweet through the air.

"He's the Last Dead End Kid."

"He ain't talking."

"Well, let him soften up a bit."

"Wait till his balls dissolve down to little black frog eggs." (Tadpoles wriggle away in the black lagoon.) "Then he'll talk, and be glad to talk."

"Yonny, glo home."

"This *is* my home, you Chinaman cocksucker. Fuck off, you! And remember, there is only one captain of those shits—as I affectionately call my S.P.s, Subsidiary Personalities. You nothing but an L.S.P.: *Local* Subsidiary Personality. Get forward, or I shall put a ball through all your heads."

"You don't got the balls, Gertie."

"Why, you Southern white trash rim a shittin' nigger for an eyecup of P.G.!"

"You dare get sassy and fat with me? You tired old Southern belle, nobody care if you come in or not except for your unsanitary habits eatin' with prehensile piles the way it break up the Family Reunion."

"And what's eatin' you, you little intimidate prick? Nobody goin' to cut our nuts off while I'm around, and I can kick the shit out of any Liz inna Zone. Now we drop that fucking *Lucha Libre* dyke down the marl hole she crawl up out of. Strictly from Loch Ness. Strange and undesirable serpent. So for the Chrissake, kid—make with the smile. The show must go on.

"And as for you, you black-assed mealy-mouthed cuntsucker always mutter around about, 'Lawsy, boss, I believe in life, boss,' just as sure as that old river yonder, life flow through you, sit still in the springtime, wash me back to old Virginia and cornhole me up my tater . . . spitting cotton."

A delicious *frisson* offer up your pink ass sweat like a young boy's lip to a black buck in a nigger shack make you scream and whisper and moan for it. "Aw now I couldn't screw the young Massa! I'm a *good* nigger."

"I'll teach you to brown a golden lad, you hog-balled bastard. Come hawg-cutting day. Hmm, on second thought . . ."

"Please! Rasmus, please!"

"I ain't uppity, boss. Better put your pants on. Might dirty your little white ass sitting around naked in a nigger shack."

"Yes, sir, that old river seen a heap of folks come and go, shit and die. He flood out in the spring, and he shrink down in the long heat of summer, them crawdads crawl way down into the earth. Ever suck the sweet cool water up out of a crawdad hole?"

"For the love of God, sheriff, lock up this rusty word hoard."

"Now, you nameless assholes, remember I do the shitting around here, *all* the shitting; and any wise prick try to dip into my ass is going to be kicked right down the marl hole with the Gibbering Larvals. I mean, show your culture. When the Massa shits, keep your distance, folks. He is subject to eject a choking cloud of dried yellow hepatitis fallout." (A puffball bursts in Missouri field. Dry heat of August. Sound of insects.)

"Now it is chiefly you two half-assed entities I am concerned with. Your recalcitrant and perfidious maneuvers constitute a menace to the enterprise, which, as I well aware, you sworn to sabotage. Scumunist pricks, slop out of my public trough. And the Chink Dummy yacks party line on a queer barstool, blatting out the Formulas of Doom. And you, Johnny-Come-Lately, advance and be recognized. What're you now, a cock biter? Well, I don't think we have an opening for a man of your caliber. Keep you on file."

"Filthy little beast." She tweaks the Child in the nuts, and he doubles over retching. "Faugh!" she screams, starting back. "Bitch dog! Puking cock-roach!" She splits his lips with an expert one-finger slap—like a dog chain across the face.

He looks at her face gray as junk eyes betrayed to death go out in empty light sockets. Blue smoke drifts out.

Come in, please! Come in, please! Can't move a cell of my body without got the Word. I'm a synopsis Latah. Nobody know my trouble, and especially not Jesus, the miracle artist. Something he don't like? Go make with the miracle, James, I show you how. Now the perpetrating of miracles constitute a brazen attempt to louse up the universe. When you set up something as MIRACLE, you deny the very concept of FACT, establish a shadowy and spurious court infested by every variety of coyote and shady fixer, *beyond* Court of Fact.

Idiot raconteur cling to you like a linguaphone. Ever hear "This is the penwiper of my brother-in-law" repeat a million times? Once those sockets in your head, can't turn nobody out no more. The sockets weep little tears of blue flame.

Now look, none of this trying to slide in the pitch on the chick deal you got cooking. Back there in Bebop jive talk. This is not an escort service but a functioning (after a fashion) organism. Positively no pimping in the aorta.

Run fingers over her chassis light as moths leave little blue phosphorescent wake burn slow behind. Converge a soft blue crackle up her cunt and burn inside her begin to squirm and wiggle and moan. (Burn her tits.)

"Of *course* I'm sure of ultimate 'victory,' but the little prick's got the orgone supply sew tight up as young boy nuts."

"We gotta find a way to get at it, boss."

"Mindless idiot! The only way to get at it is through him."

"Well, we gotta con him."

"How do you mean? Like this? 'Of course you know I'm down here from Front Office, con you back into a Gibbering Larval and take over the orgone supply. Now this con involves Duty, HIGHER DUTY and *32nd DEGREE DUTY*, all of which devolve on you should act precise like I prefer it.' "

They'll move in right away, take a girl over, piss out her cock and start farting code to the Enemy. "It's a fifth column, is what it is," I said to Luke only yesterday. "We should pass it along to the Torso, come down from Cleveland take care of those pricks."

"Smartest thing is not to let me in first base. Once I get my little foot through that door, which you would be well advised not to open—I mean a con like that require personality. . . . Wouldn't you?"

"Well, we gotta talk to him straight, man to man: 'Now, kid, *you* want something, *I* want something. I do something for you, you do something for me. That's the way the ball bounces."

The Child blasts all his teeth out in a great Bronx cheer. (Pansy dressed in spring robes catch them in butterfly net, throw them at the boy's mouth; they float back and fit into a whitewashed brick wall.)

They was ripe for the plucking, forgot way back yonder in that cornhole, lost in little scraps of delight and burning scrolls.

The Egyptian struts in with hump of racial hate on his back, feeds off him regular as clockwork—big fat boy in there swill butter and animal fats in the worst form there is.

(Oh, death, where is thy sting? The Man is never on time.) Corseted Tenor: "You and I are good for nothing but pie." Steak and kidney pie is served in top hats by naked chorus girls—pubic hairs, finger toe nails and teeth silver painted.

Crystal oaks and pines and persimmons light up green and purple and blue and deep cherry red, frozen in pathic postures. Heavy snow opportunely blankets arrival of W.Q. "Fats" Terminal, cosmic horse's ass.

I am looking over a river in Tolima—section of Colombia where is much leprosy and guerrilla war—through cardboard opera glasses of leprosy.

"How did you get this terrible habit, kid?"

"In the family. The Garcías have always been lepers, and proud of it. You bet I'm going back to Carville."

"Put a Direction Finder on the Chink, smell out that Controller." The Private Eye strips to bulletproof plastic transparent magnifying shorts.

"Show you something interesting." He switches on his pelvis. "Light all the veins in my prick. Beautiful pink sight."

The plague break out in the lobby of the U.N. Victims are spirited away in black Cadillacs, flushed down a garbage disposal unit in a special kitchen of the Arab delegates where a man knew what to do with his fat old dog offend with halitosis. Sidi Slimano turn up the garbage disposal full blast, shake the house like a tornado—he leap onto the kitchen table, do a Russian dance with shrill "hy, hy, hy"s and a Negro janitor, with a eunuch jockstrap over his balls, feed the yipping dog into the unit, hair and blood spurt out 1963 on the wall.

"Yes sir, boys, the shit really hit the fan in '63," said the tiresome old prophet can bore the shit out of you in any space-time direction. "Now I happen to remember because it was just two years before that a strain of human aftosa developed in a Bolivian laboratory got loose through the medium of a chinchilla coat fix an income tax case in Kansas City. When it hit New York and everybody with long streamers hang out the mouth, the town look like one big toffee pull. The Abolitionists hanged a purple-assed baboon in Buckingham Palace, and 'Fats' Terminal, dressed in his Home Secretary suit, sucked it off *in extremis*. Cutaway pants, rubber prick two feet long sticking out, ejaculated Black Widows all over the palace. (The Queen is still shit-scared of the W.C.)

"Now it was just one month before that I was took bad with the menstrual cramps. And a Liz claimed immaculate conception give birth to a six-ounce Spider Monkey thooh the navel—they say the croaker was party to that caper had the monkey on his back all the time. 1963 a dream meet with a Mexican bank robbery."

The Arab plays a flute, and the unit undulates up out of the sink on a long flexible metal tube. It gives a great Bronx cheer, and the Arab delegates scream away in burning Cadillacs.

A Negro boy in turtleneck red sweater dances fearless with the unit under the flickering white light of a Coleman gasoline lamp in an East Texas barn.

"Undulate me, baby; and let me undulate you." The unit nips him playfully on the ear, and a drop of blood falls onto his sweater.

Under icebergs and fjords where naked nymphs goose each other with classic pictures, sooner or later knock a girl up with a tintype, her give birth to a penny arcade.

"I'm a slow man with a mustache," said the colonel know how to give a girl the time.

"Land's sake, like a hundred little scrub women with pink down brushes scrub your cunt out with ambergris it turn to a conch and give a weird Attic wail." (Fade out. Jungle calls. The kid stirs muttering in malarial sleep, and Pan pipes drift down the Andes.)

Death comes slow on Hungarian gallows. "When you gonna pull my leg, get this show on the road?" he gags, his face tumescent with lust.

"Daddy, that old nigger shit sure do Number Two right on my tummy-wummy."

"What's that you say, girl? That black bastard. A judgment on me for eatin' the coon pone. A man's sins do trail him like a fart into Mrs. Worldly's drawing room, stamp him REJECT." (The butler puts the Blue Seal on his haunch, while Mrs. Kindheart politely blinds herself with Sani-flush.)

"Don't you fret, sweet thing. Me and the boys take care of that nigger when Hawg Day rolls around."

The *diseuse*, in hillbilly dress with a necklace of hog castrators tinkling in the pink dawn, passes a ruined outhouse (Piney Woods backdrop), sings "When Hawg Day rolls around." The sunrise catches an armadillo rooting in a weed-grown field.

"Girl, it's time you learn where castrates come from . . . blub blub."

"Yes poppa eat it lovely old moleskin way."

"Let me be your mole cricket, lady." Candy tongue melt up in there, light up your pink coral grotto.

Nineteen-ten whorehouse: black silk stocking, white skin: black pubic hair, black-and-white photos. A huge Victrola plays slow and mournful through a vast horn to howling whores. (Drunk, with a top hat and a mustache, takes off his hat and gives a reverent Bronx cheer.)

Satyr runs down a garden path, marine shoots pink ping-pong balls from tommy gun, rain off his ass turn to little red candy pillows. Armadillos gambol up and eat them in the satyr's wake.

"I want you to *smell* this barstool," said the paranoid ex-Communist to the manic FBI agent. "Stink juice—and you may quote me—has been applied by paid hoodlums constipated with Moscow *goldwasser*." (The water cure, comrade. So I should take the active part in this horrible synopsis?)

Dirty snow melt in the spring hatch these frozen niggers out the woodpile.

Some cowboy ride around with the noose on, looking for his last roundup.

"I live with my boots off," The Singing Tumbleweed told your reporter, leaning against the whitewashed brick wall of heroin slowdown.

"I'll cut your white pecker throat and leave you a squaaawwking chicken. I'm nobody's fool—good public school of hard knockers and know how to handle this horrible case. When is a woman not a woman? When I cut her motherfucking head off."

(Note: When your reporter was learning to be a pilot, this young angel of a cadet dive on this old gash in a field. Her run instead of flop when he buzz her, he cut her head off with his wings. The commandant's press agent referred to "this horrible case.")

So I am in Mrs. Bridey Murphy's chowder along with the overalls. The Interrogator operate on the boys and the girls and the cats and the rats, leave them grope for lost balls through a maze of movies and burlesques and penny arcades. (Mad-eyed jungle rats die with a Gallic shrug—"*Zut alors! Quoi faire?*")

"What are you doing?" said the torso artist to his colleague.

"Just experimenting. Interesting relation between pain, fear and the *harumph* doctor—and nothing more interesting than this phenomenon." He shows his hard prick. "Now touch it just there. . . . See how it pulses. And now I am going to conceive The Great Work," he says, shitting on the laboratory floor. "I have created life!!" he screams, pointing to a roundworm undulating up out of the shit, give a Bronx cheer, grow to a great serpent with lamprey mouth and chase the "scientist" through his Yokohama appliances.

"There are some things of which I cannot even bring myself to squeak," said the rat. "The things a girl sees in a warehouse!"

Cute little agent use sex as a weapon, crucify an old queen with neon nails, run up the black wind sock over burning boys in a plane crash (all those innocent young male screams). The old queen breathe in the Black Snake. "That hits so good." (Young male screams drift in on the warm spring wind, stir boy hair in the carny night stand so sweet so cold so fair popping pink gum bubbles, look into the penny arcade, petals of young sweat caught in the lip down make your mouth water for stuff.)

"Cardinal, can you stand up there in the very ass of God which you have plugged with the Pope, that veteran horse's ass and cosmic brown-nose?"

Will the gentle reader get up off his limestone and pick up the phone?

Cause of death: completely uninteresting.

The Voices rush in like burning lions.

"I'll rip through you," said, trembling, the Man of Black Bones.

"So told Lieutenant LeBee, whose auntie was drowned at sea," said a little squeegee voice.

"Cross crystal pains of horror to the tilted pond."

"Time to retire. . . . Get a frisk . . . glittering worms of nostalgia's call house where young lust flares over the hills of home, and jissom floats like cobwebs in a cold spring wind."

"Lovely brown leg. Oh Lordy me baby on the brass bed, and bedbugs crawl under the blue light. . . . Oh God."

"All the day you do it. . . . Do it right now."

"Suck the night tit under the blue flame of Sterno. . . . Orient pearls to the way they should go. . . ."

"The winged horse and the mosaic of iron cut the sky to blue cake. . . ."

"On crystal balconies pensive angels study pink fingernails. Gilt flakes fall through the sunlight."

"Distant rumble of stomachs. Porcine fairies wave thick wallets. Bougainvillea covers the limestone steps. Poisoned pigeons rain from the Northern Lights, plop with burning wings into dry canals. The Reservoirs are empty. Blue stairs end, spiral down, suffocate . . . where brass statues crash through the hungry squares and alleys of the gaping city. . . ."

"Iridescent hard-on . . . Rainbow in the falls."

"Can't hear nothing."

"Two kids got relief."

"Never more the goose honks train whistle bunkmate. . . . Man in Lower Ten (eyes caked with mucus) watch the boy get a hard-on."

"Not a mark on him. What killed his monkey?"

"Suicide God, take the back-street junk route. Detours of the fairy canyon shine in the light of dawn. Buildings fall through dust to the plain of salt marshes. Are the boys over the last ridge and into the safe harbor of Cunt Lick, where no wind is?"

"By the squared circle, cut cock, my mouth, the cunt of and the rag on. Bring your own wife. . . . Panama Flo, the sex fiend, beat the Gray Nurse for steak-sized chunks." (The Gray Nurse is most dangerous form of shark. Like all sharks they bite out steak-sized chunks.)

"Wouldn't you?"

"Libido is dammed by the Eager Beaver."

"Notice is served on toilet paper."

"Smell shock grabs the lungs with nausea."

Fat queen, bursting out of dungarees, carry a string of bullheads to the tilted pond.

"TILT."

Gray head bob up in the old swimming hole. The boys climb up each other, scream, "EEEEK! A man!"

"He will be fetched down, this creature."

"A fairy."

"Monstrous!"

"Fantastic!"

"Get her!"

"Slam the steel shutter of latency!"

"Radius radius. It is enough."

"Doctorhood is being made with me."

Middle-aged Swede in yachting cap, naked tattooed torso, neutral blue eyes, gives a shot of heroin to the schizophrenic (whiff of institution kitchens). Gray ghosts of a million junkies bend close as the Substance drains into living flesh.

"Is this the fix that staunched a thousand shits and burnt the scented drugstores of Lebanon?"

Student in medieval hose and doublet with cock guard: "If a cat hath nine lives, verily this olde pricke of mine hath nine childhoods, each more maudlin than its fellow."

The professor is caught short and shits in a piece of newspaper, rolls it up and throws it at a passing citizen of indeterminate nationality who screams curses in twenty languages living and dead.

"It's a cheap Shanty Irish trick, shitting in a piece of paper and throwing it at passersby."

"So who's lace-curtain? This stark young novelist like a dirty windswept street." Fade out 1920s tunes, fireworks cover stutter of machine-gun fire from black Cadillacs longer and lower, fade into Soviet tanks.

"One of my earliest memories was a bull's-eye score scored by Mary O'Toole the local Liz on a dignified old junky so loaded he didn't register. Just walk along with shit dripping off his pan, a boyish smile on his lips. I shall never forget that smile . . . in times of affliction such as come to any woman. Goddammit, another impersonator! Be there a man with soul so dead to himself have never said this is my own my native ass?"

American queens shriek and howl in revolting paroxysms of self-pity. They declare a nausea contest. The most abject queen of them all gathers his rotting protoplasms for an all-out effort. . . .

"My power's coming! . . . My power's coming!" he screeches.

Orchestra strikes up, and female impersonator prances out in hillbilly drag with hairy knobby knees showing.

"She'll be swishing round the mountain when she comes. . . ."

The queen's familiar spirits are gathering, larval whimpering entities. The queen writhes in a dozen embraces, accommodating the passionate exigencies of invisible partners, now sucking noisily, now throwing his legs over his head with a loud "Whoopeee!" He sidles across the floor with his legs spread, reaches up and caresses one of the judges with a claw . . . he has turned himself into a monster crab with a human body from the waist down. Beneath the skin liquid protoplasm quivers like jellied consommé as he offers up his ass.

The judges start back, appalled.

"He liquefy himself already!"

"Deplorable!"

Other contestants jealously throw off their clothes to reveal an impressive variety of unattractive physiques.

"Look at me!"

"Feast your eyes on *my* ugliness!"

One queen pulls the falsie top off his pinhead and begins cackling like a chicken: "I don't need that old head anyhoo!"

Junky furnished room opens on red-brick slum—young addict, sculpted to bone and muscle, probes for a blue vein with a brass needle in his smooth white arm.

Mexican finca: drunken machos in dark glasses reel about on the patio, blasting at terrified cats with .45 automatics. All wear two-hundred-dollar English suits and drink Old Pharr Scotch from bottles. They miss the cats, wound each other, scream "*¡Chinga!*" in chorus as each empties his gun into a compañero.

Barefoot, ragged boys steal in, silent as dawn. Hideous atomic mutations, some miss a lower jaw, others have two black holes and no nose. They strip the bodies, drink the Scotch—one born without a mouth sticks a bottle up his ass and tilts his body forward. They put on the suits, which hang on them in folds, and posture in parody of drunken machos, spitting, patting .45s, flashing police badges and nude pictures of Chapultepec blonds. Exit boys without a sound.

Sunrise. Vultures settle, peck at dark glasses.

Modern apartment *a là swish*. Fags and old women gabble and giggle faster and faster, scream past each other at supersonic speed.

Blue-walled Arab whorehouse. Outside, the yipes of rioters; shop shutters slam, Arab music blasts from loudspeakers mixed with Radio Cairo like a berserk tobacco auction. Fades to flutes of Ramadan.

—

Stop! Here is Terminal!

W.Q. "Fats" Terminal wake with a fart and let out a bray can be heard for blocks.

"I have arisen, Goddammit! Fetch the royal lounging robes!"

His secretary trots in, a huge slovenly man in filthy sweatshirt and rusty black pants. "Fats" struggles into his purple bathrobe and straps on his cavalry sword, with which he decapitated the Countess de Perrier's Russian wolfhound. A long-ago garden party in his slim youth, before he was blacklisted by every embassy and hostess in the world.

He barely escaped with his life from Seville after a perfect kill, and the noble bull dying and the matador talk to it soft and nasty sweet and everybody silent, "Fats" loose his terrible Bronx cheer, leap down into the arena and kick the dying bull in the nuts.

"Fats" is connected in some unspecified way with every underground of the world: Mafia, IRA, Bolivian Trotskyites, PDL, EOKA, Islam, Inc., Arab Brotherhood, Mau Mau. He expresses himself typically on all movements and leaders of movements: "Black-assed cocksuckers don't know their piles from a finger stall. They couldn't resist a virus. What I think about Sidi?" He lets out his famous Bronx cheer.

No resistance movement dares to dispense with his "services." He edits a newspaper known as the *Underground Express*, mostly consists of bulletins and trade gossip: "What well-known asshole currently throbs to a DARK HORSE? Is my cunt red? All Mau Mau requested to castrate themselves if captured, to foil the degenerate appetites of English Capitalist hangman Smithers 'The Nance' Macintosh, who was drummed out of the Black Watch for importuning the Crown Prince with prehensile piles at the Queen's funeral."

"I think Fats is swell," said the inspirational female analyst.

"A preposterous slander!" shrieks Dr. Burger.

"We are at a loss," snarls Brundage the Insolvent, dissolving in a pool of shit.

"Clearly an anal type," observes Dr. Burger severely. "Faugh."

"Discrimination!" screams a Negro fag, high on injustice.

"So I hung an albatross. . . . It was my training done it, born and bred to hang dat cocksucker."

"We hear it was the other way around, Doc," said the snide reporter with narrow shoulders and bad teeth.

The doctor's face crimsons. "And I wish to state that I have been doctor at Dankmoor Prison thirty years man boy and bestial and I always keep my nose clean . . . never compromise myself to be alone with the hanged man, always insist on presence of my baboon assistant, witness and staunch friend in any position."

"Oral breakthrough," lisped the skeleton.

"Very likely," said the Horse Trader, spitting out all his teeth.

"Orgone service is terrible around here," said the rectal cancer case.

"Already loth my ath inna thervith," lisped out the hole in his side.

"God purge me of the black yen for his bones," whimpered the aging queen, her prick dropping like a wind sock where there is no wind.

Negroes thin and brittle as smooth black sticks cut each other with sneering razors. No surrender in yellow eyes like incandescent gold.

Adolescent hoodlums have crucified Christ with Bronx cheers, go honkytonking and nobody give a shit when He give up the Ghost.

And "Fats" bites into a sandwich. "Butter!" he screams. "They is trying to poison me with cholesterol!"

—

The young rustler is apprehended by his friend at the old swimming hole. Under the eyes of giggling boys he is hanged from the diving branch, pirouettes in the air with an *entrechat* six—breathless pause at leap top.

"Let this be a lesson to you boys," said the old sheriff, eyes pale and empty as blue sky over the neon midways of America.

Shattering bloody blue of Mexico, brains spilled in the cocktail lounge, white leather and blue silk, and the fat macho substance in dark glasses has burned down the jai alai bookie with his obsidian-handled forty-five.

Heart in the sun, headless snake, hanged man's cock pulsing on the holy gallows, pantless corpses hang from posts along the road to Monterrey.

The boys whistle and wolf-call. One catches jissom in a straw hat and passes it around in obscene, begging pantomime and each boy jacks off into it. A boy twangs the rope and sings like an angel, voice clear, hard, metallic as wind in high wires over a gorge, waterfalls and rainbow.

"Watch those prehensile tensions!" screams the belching Technician . . . as the bridge wires snap, spill screaming hot rods into the void.

"Play chicken with gravity, you little pricks!" snarls the Technician. "I told them the fucking bridge wasn't worth a—" He farts loud and ugly.

The great black crab penetrated with air-pistol pellet oozes watery crankcase oil.

The rope rot through, the rustler falls white as Narcissus into the black water, glides down. The boys lean over to watch the descent of the god, dissolve in sunlight, see hairs sharp as fine wire and teeth and freckles—their mourning selves. The sheriff is muttering through his toothless mean old-woman mouth, "Now, I want you fellows to wear trunks. . . . Decent women with telescopes can see you. We've had complaints."

The boy floats white as marble in the swimming hole, with a lamprey at his side where Christ's blood flowed and the colostomy came out spurting shit.

"Let me do a suck job on you," said the old queen with a lamprey mouth. A great silver fish goes over the falls with a lamprey on its side, into the rainbow.

Pinks and blues of 1920s tune drift into the locker room and the two boys, first time tea-high, jack off to "My Blue Heaven." What are we going to do with all the golden lads? Not enough train whistles and fights against the house odds. "I just can't get you a fight, kid. Things are tough."

Police bullet in the alley, broken wings of Icarus and screams of a burning boy inhaled by the old junky, eyes empty as a vast plain—husk of vulture wings in dry air—pulls the pale smoke into his screaming lungs and his body squirms in the Black Massage.

They walk down Lindell and into the house surrounded by deserted factories and junkyards; weeds and vines and the sound of insects. They undress slow in a mirror-lined room, fuck all the way out and back across backyards, ash pits and bars, stickball games, virginal lots (little green snakes under rusty iron), cats copulate and boys jack off in packing crate.

The pusher dropped around to leave his card. "Like the song say, 'I'll be around.' " Looking for a vein with a tattoo needle, the boy's chest is marked over the hard limestone bone with blue bites.

The wind shakes billowing brass like yellow silk.

Lick of junk sickness eats at your heels like a dream rat, gnaw the shiny white tendons probing for a vein of iron.

Chorus of Midwest fairies sing "Glow Worm" with lighted wands . . . plaintive purple ghosts in the June night.

" 'Tain't human. Devil doll . . ." The Controller hides in some ultimate privy on a black windy slope of the Andes under a sky green as neon.

Great fat queen in a huge baby carriage pushed by a brutal-faced, gum-chewing Italian with long sideburns and a white silk vest. "AWWWWWW!" squalls the queen. And the Italian changes her diapers absently, his eyes follow a woman's haunches down the street and into the butcher shop.

Masochist queen refuse to leave burning warehouse because her hand-trucking lover won't carry him.

Empty waxen child faces, the teeth go first.

Over the hills to the lonesome pines of Idaho, where boy hearts pulse on Christmas trees, and ski-jumpers whistle over our heads like bullets in the crystal night . . .

The boy is pure sad, all hate faded like smoke in the dawn wind, clear and calm sad forever.

Carnival of splintered pink peppermint. Black mustache and child screams after his lost balloon like a frustrated cocksucker. Tattooed sailor leaves the penny arcade with firm young ass.

"Oh, those Golden Slippers—" Copper-luster chamber pots, brass spittoons, black smoke on the hip in the Chink laundry.

Ski run revisited by old queen, his friend killed there in 1928, black and empty against the vacationing sky.

"You're nothing but a larval," sneered one subsidiary personality to another. "I'm a decent entity at least, got some outlines to me."

So this is the Burroughs special, a dash and a soupçon, a pinch and a handful. If you all like it not, will distribute to the school privy of the world for a glorious burial. Young asses wiped all over the world, white ass and black ass, yaller ass and copper ass, pink ass and bronze ass.

Two gentlemen opponents square off on the country club lawn. With a bestial snarl one throws up his knee with murderous force. The other pivots deftly, jabbing for his opponent's eyes with forked fingers. They roll in the grass, screaming like mandrills and clawing at each other's eyes and genitals.

Old Colonel nudges Sir Granville Heatherstone: "This is tasty."

Sanitarium grounds 1917—junkies sit under spreading oaks in the Indian summer of Iowa. Nurses bustle along with busy hypos.

"Now, Mr. Harmon, you know you only get five grains."

"Oh I think you're terrible, Mr. Hardwith."

They sprawl in green chairs, faces dead as the garroted. "And where the dead leaf fell, there it did rest."

Peacocks scream in the red crystal dawn. Golden apple of woman breast swells bronze souvenir ashtray. He sits up and looks into a cobra lamp.

On a white alabaster bed a Negress black as opium does slow bumps and grinds. "Haven't got a thing to say," he sneered through his plastic surgeon nose.

The gray-faced queen with dark glasses and purple lips sneers and shoves it in gear and shoots away . . . a white-faced boy carries a dead dog from the suburb road.

Cursed down your years with a yen like an open needle sore, coal and junk, cancer and black oil in the blood and bones. Ink in the white bones. Black blood from the ruptured crab.

Porpoises with pink ribbon nooses around their necks pilot the ship to anchor at vast Venetian mooring posts in an endless oily rubbish heap. The ship is stuck in black slime and garbage and rusty iron. The porpoises fade with a Bronx cheer and a distant boat whistle. . . .

"I am the Egyptian," he said, looking all flat and silly.

And I said, "Really, Bradford, don't be tiresome."

Old dank garden in the Midwest August moon, pool full of leaves in black iridescent water.

Would it be forgiven the rising young diplomat occasional slip and shit on the floor by the punch bowl? Or absently offer his prick instead of his hand to Nikki from the Russian Embassy? Or now and then leap up like the savant in reverse, as though catapult by unseen hand, and fart loud and ugly in Mrs. Worldly's face?

Could grace or charm give these faults a snow job, sure Reggie has them all.

Insouciance of a child awakened from sleep with a sulky hard-on in the green summer dawn, boy-grin on sunlit water. Hot rod piloted by a debased and brutal angel screams through pregnant Indian women, leave all behind a wake of blood and afterbirths, throw out a blast of condoms with Bronx cheer.

"Just see me, a fourteen-year-old boy," said the skinny old queen. "I've never been fucked before so I wander down into Mexican town and this copper youth in white pants call me over, make sullen and bestial motions—I bend over and drop my pants. He fucks me with furious quivering contempt that melts my whole pelvis down onto his cock like a glob of gold."

Death rows the boy like sleeping marble down the Grand Canal in a gondola of gold and crystal . . . poles out into a vast lagoon: souvenir postcards and bronzed baby shoes, Grand Canyon and Niagara Falls, Chimborazo, New York skyline and Aztec pyramid. Pinks and blues and yellows of religious objects in the Catholic store on a red-brick square surrounded by trees.

"All right. You're paying for it," said the Mexican.

"Only fools do those villains pity who are punished ere they have done their mischief," said the young Billy Budd as he innocently cut the throats of his lifeboat mates. "Such a thing as too much fun," he adds primly. "Besides which they was eatin' me out of house and home. Nip it in the bud, Mary, nip it in the bud."

Frenzied dinosaurs uncover a fossil man. . . .

In the attic of the Big Store on bolts of cloth we made it, careful don't spill, don't rat on the boys. Light cuts through the dark chasm, dust in sunlight, the cellar is full of light and air . . . in two weeks the tadpoles hatch. I wonder what ever happened to Otto's boy who played the violin?

━━

Pages blew out across the winds and rubbish of Mexico. . . .
A boy squats by a mud wall whistling mambo through his teeth,
wipes his ass with a sheaf of manuscripts. Wind and rubble, vultures peck at fish heads. The boy stands up, shies a stone at the
vulture, vaults the wall and whistles away under dusty poplar trees
shake in the afternoon wind.

Spilt is the wastings of the cup. . . . "Take it away," he said
irritably.

The city mutters in the distance, pestilent breath of the cancerous librarian faint and intermittent in the warm spring wind.

Ruined porticoes and arabesques, boys playing languidly on the
vine-covered pyramids. Greg screws Brad on all fours, freeze into
a dirty picture in the withered hand of a very old queen.

"Is this a sex hang-up, Brad?" said the Chinese narcotic fuzz.

The decent women of America object. "Stay where you are!"
said Lithping Lu the Deputy. "You fruit varmints give me Burger's
disease in the worst form there is."

"I wouldn't put it in precisely those words," said Dr. Burger.

The man in a green suit—old-style English cut, with two side
vents and change pockets outside—will swindle the aging pro-
prietress of the florist shop. "Old flub gotta yen on for me."

The Grand Dragoness has given the order to her agents yack on
all the queer barstools in the world: "Get Burroughs." She gives
a little bump and fart. "It would be well not to fail."

"Continual assault of hostility," said the languid lavatory attendant. "Can't help it."

In a limestone gorge near East St. Louis, Illinois, met a copper
lad with a rusty loincloth crumble from his stiffening member seize
me in stone hands and fuck me with a crystal cock.

Interrupted by Paco, a little Spanish whore. Great pests from
little assholes grow. "Untimely comes this dirt," shrieked the poet
swallow forever the Perfect Line. What a con that was. . . . The

cast-off lover trailing broken potentials looks at me with reproach he can never formulate, sad and hostile sick conning eyes, feels with idiot slyness for the horrified cock.

"This is trivial," he said cunningly to the mastiff bitch.

"Satori," said the Zen monk. "I see . . ." He crosses the room and opens the door. "The Mons Calpa from Gibraltar."

—unload her unhatched shits upon us. "Another consignment of undesirables," sighed Immigration. "No, we do *not* admit advanced cases of lymphogranuloma, and we have no form of dole for disabled stool pigeon lost his voice in the service."

We are not at all innarested to find a prick crawl up the back stairs, make time in the broom closet, remember? and spurt all over the white sheet in the hung-over Sunday dawn. . . . We goin' to home it over the silver plate into the golden toilet and jack out our balls on the mosaic floor into the carp pool, keeps them healthy, fat and sluggish.

Assassin of geraniums! Murderer of the lilies!

Over the bridge to Brighton Rock, place of terrible pleasures and danger, where predatory brainwashers stalk the passersby in black Daimlers. Clients check Molotov cocktails and flamethrowers with the beautiful diseased hatcheck person of indeterminate sex. . . . And the government falls at least once a day.

Set wades in blood up to her cunt, cuts down the blasphemers of Ra with her sick hell of junk.

The snake's venom is paid for with coins of the realm of night. No hiding place . . .

Wooden steps wind up a vast slope, scattered stone huts. Greg licks the black rim of the world in a cave of rusty limestone. Across the hills to Idaho, under the pine trees, boys hang a horse with a broken leg. One plays "I'm Leavin' Cheyenne" on his harmonica, they pass around an onion and cry. They stand up and swing off through the branches with Tarzan cries.

We is all out on a long silver bail.

It was a day like any other when I walk down the Main Line to the Sargasso, pass faces set a thousand years in matrix of evil, faces with eerie innocence of old people, faces vacant of intent. Sit down in the green chair provided for me by other men occupy all the others. Convey my order with usual repetitions—at one time I was threatened by rum and Cinzano, whereas I order mint tea. I sit back and make this scene, mosaic of juxtapositions, strange golden chains of Negro substance seeped up from the Unborn South. So I do not at once dig the deformed child—I call it that for want of a better name: actually it look between unsuccessful baboon and bloated lemur, with a sort of moldy sour bestial look in the eyes—that was sitting to all intents and purposes on the back of my chair.

Shellac red-brick houses, black doors shine like ice in the winter sun. Lawn down to the lake, old people sit in green chairs, huddle in lap robes.

We are on the way over with a bolt of hot steel wool to limn your toilet with spangled orgones. Conspicuous consumption is rampant in the porticoes slippery with Koch spit, bloody smears on the cryptic mosaic—frozen cream cone and a broken dropper. As when a junky long dead woke with a junk-sick hard-on, hears the radiator thump and bellow like an anxious dinosaur of herbivorous tendencies—treeless plain stretch to the sky, vultures have miss the Big Meat. . . .

Will he fight? is the question at issue.

"Yes," snarls President Ra look up from a crab hunt, charge the Jockey Club with his terrible member. "Fuck my sewage canal, will you? Don't like you and don't know you. Some Coptic cocksucker vitiate the pure morning joy of hieroglyph."

"At least we have saved the bread knife," he said.

"The message is not clear," said Garcia, when they brought him the *brujo* rapt in nutmeg.

Priest whips a yipping Sellubi down the limestone stairs with a gold chain.

"Unlawful flight to prevent consummation," lisps the toothless bailiff. The trembling defendant—survivor of the Coconut Grove fire—stands with a naked hard-on.

"Death by Fire in Truck," farts the Judge in code.

"Appeal is meaningless in the present state of our knowledge," says the defense, looking up from electron microscope.

"You have your warning," says the President.

"The monkey is not dead but sleepeth," brays Harry the Horse, with inflexible authority.

The centipede nuzzles the iron door rusted to thin black paper with urine of a million fairies. Red centipede in the green weeds and broken stelae. Inside the cell crouch prisoners of the Colónia. Mugwump sits naked on a rusty bidet, turns a crystal cylinder etched with cuneiforms. Iron panel falls in dust, red specks in the sunlight.

A vast Moslem muttering rises from the stone square where brass statues suffocate.

Cities of the Red Night £3.99

'An obsessive landscape which lingers in the mind as a fundamental
statement about the possibilities of human life'
PETER ACKROYD, SUNDAY TIMES

'Not only Burroughs' best work, but a logical and ripening extension of all
Burroughs' great work' KEN KESEY

'Burroughs is an awe-inspiring poetic magician. I believe *Cities of the Red
Night* is his masterpiece' CHRISTOPHER ISHERWOOD

'The outrageousness of *Cities of the Red Night* suggests it was written in
collusion with Swift, Baudelaire, Schopenhauer, Orwell, Lenny Bruce,
General Patton and John Calvin' SAN FRANCISCO CHRONICLE

Queer £2.95

His legendary and most revealing novel, published at last after three decades, *Queer* is a strikingly candid and powerful work which takes the reader back into the homosexual underworld of the forties and into the very core of Burroughs' unique sensibility.

Queer is a love story—the account of William Lee's painfully circular seduction of Eugene Allerton in Mexico City, and the romantic agonies he suffers. In his introduction Burroughs discusses frankly and courageously the shattering event that happened after the occurrences described in *Queer*, and how this event has haunted his life and affected his work.

'A major work . . . The love story is told with astonishing economy, Burroughs conjuring the heights and the depths in an intensely lyrical shorthand which seems to imitate and not travesty feeling' SUNDAY TIMES

'The Mexico it depicts is phosphorescent and the portrait of William Lee is devastating. For William Burroughs, start here' NEW STATESMAN

'Shocking the world all over again, Burroughs has written a thoughtful and sensitive study of unrequited love . . . Retroactively the book humanises his work' MARTIN AMIS, OBSERVER

'A vividly evoked depiction of frustration and obsession; human, richly comic, strangely touching . . . well worth waiting for' GAY TIMES

'A blueprint for many of Burroughs' themes, narrative techniques and characterizations, it helps us come to grips with the dark humour, violent energy and unsettling vision of this writer who has forced himself into our consciousness and seized a place in literary history' NEW YORK TIMES BOOK REVIEW

'The only American novelist living today who may conceivably be possessed by genius' NORMAN MAILER

'A major work. Burroughs' heart laid bare' ALLEN GINSBERG

The Western Lands £3.95

The road to the Western Lands is by definition the most dangerous road in the world, for it is a journey beyond Death, beyond the basic God standard of Fear and Danger. It is the most heavily guarded road in the world, for it gives access to the gift that supercedes all other gifts: Immortality.

The Western Lands is William Burroughs' Book of the Dead which draws upon Ancient Egyptian mythology for its symbolic structure. It is an intricately interwoven novel, often picaresque, often episodic, sweeping through time from Ancient Egypt to the Medical Riots of 2999, ranging from despairing apprehensions of modern reality to moments of bathos and high comedy. *The Western Lands* concludes Burroughs' spiritual odyssey which began in *Cities of the Red Night* and continued in *The Place of Dead Roads*.

'The only living American writer of whom it seems to me one can say with confidence he will be read with the same shock of terror and pleasure in a hundred years' time' ANGELA CARTER, THE GUARDIAN

All Pan books are available at your local bookshop or newsagent, or can be ordered direct from the publisher. Indicate the number of copies required and fill in the form below.

Send to: **CS Department, Pan Books Ltd., P.O. Box 40, Basingstoke, Hants.   RG21 2YT.**

or phone: 0256 469551 (Ansaphone), quoting title, author and Credit Card number.

Please enclose a remittance* to the value of the cover price plus: 60p for the first book plus 30p per copy for each additional book ordered to a maximum charge of £2.40 to cover postage and packing.

*Payment may be made in sterling by UK personal cheque, postal order, sterling draft or international money order, made payable to Pan Books Ltd.

Alternatively by Barclaycard/Access:

Card No.

Signature:

Applicable only in the UK and Republic of Ireland.

While every effort is made to keep prices low, it is sometimes necessary to increase prices at short notice. Pan Books reserve the right to show on covers and charge new retail prices which may differ from those advertised in the text or elsewhere.

NAME AND ADDRESS IN BLOCK LETTERS PLEASE:

....

Name————————————————————————————

Address————————————————————————————

—————————————————————————————————

—————————————————————————————————

—————————————————————————————————

3/87

Roman Britain

A sourcebook

Second edition

S. Ireland

London and New York

rst published 1986

Reprinted 1989, 1992
Second edition published 1996
by Routledge
2 Park Square, Milton Park, Abingdon, Oxon, OX14 4RN

Simultaneously published in the USA and Canada
by Routledge
270 Madison Ave, New York NY 10016

Reprinted 1998

Transferred to Digital Printing 2005

Typeset in Baskerville by
Florencetype Ltd, Stoodleigh, Devon

British Library Cataloguing in Publication Data
A catalogue record for this book is available from the
British Library

Library of Congress Cataloguing in Publication Data
A catalogue record for this book is available from the
Library of Congress

ISBN 0–415–13134–0

For Frank Norman
Teacher, Colleague, Friend

Contents

Part Three: Religion, Government, Commerce and Society

Acknowledgements

The author wishes to express his thanks to B.A. Seaby Ltd. for permission to reproduce illustrations to §63, 64, 120, 121, 122, 142, 143, 153, 154, 181, 182, 183, 190, 215, 221, 225, 267.

Preface

The sources for Roman Britain are numerous, varied and in many cases not readily accessible even in their original Greek or Latin forms. In producing the present volume, therefore, I have had two principal aims: first, to assemble as many as possible of those sources that would otherwise be obtainable by readers only with difficulty or at considerable expense, and secondly, through translation, to make them available to the growing number of students who approach the history of Roman Britain through the medium of English. The translations themselves have no pretensions to literary merit: they are work-horses rather than works of art, designed to represent accurately the contents of the originals without the addition of stylistic flourishes or any attempt to tone down the turgidity of many later writings. Since the sources are also, in many cases, chance survivors from the world of antiquity, and as such often present a fragmentary picture of events, I have sought to connect them by means of explanatory passages. It should be stressed, however, that such connection exists to set the sources in their context and establish the interrelationship of their contents. It was not designed as a substitute for the many excellent textbooks now in print, which remain essential for any proper interpretation of the evidence.

The sheer quantity of material available for the study of Roman Britain has led inevitably to the need for selectivity, but the process of selection has aimed at providing as wide a spectrum as possible within the space available, even to the extent of including apparent nonsense in order to illustrate the pitfalls that litter the path to knowledge. In common with most other sourcebooks evidence of a purely archaeological nature has not been included. Not only does it require lengthy description and analysis, but it is readily available in handbooks and journals. Of literary sources the purely military sections of Caesar's commentaries and Tacitus' *Agricola* have likewise been omitted. To have done otherwise would have necessitated the exclusion of many other authors, and both are already well served by Penguin translations. Where, on the other hand, they provide material relevant to the geography, society, or religion of Britain, this has been included for the sake of completeness of those sections and convenience of reference. Similarly omitted are the many, almost obligatory, references to the geography of Britain found in later writers; they add nothing to the overall picture and on many occasions have clearly been inserted for the sake of form alone. In the case of inscriptions or numismatic evidence their very number has meant that only a small fraction could be used. The deciding criteria have, therefore, been intrinsic importance combined with physical completeness or relative certainty of restoration. For obvious reasons, too, it is only rarely that uncertainties of textual reading have been discussed or alternative translations offered.

Collections of material relevant to the history of Roman Britain have been published before: J.C. Mann and R.G. Penman, *Literary Sources for Roman Britain* (Lactor 11) has long proved its usefulness. In the case of inscriptions R.G. Collingwood and R.P. Wright, *The Roman Inscriptions of Britain*, Vol. I, *Inscriptions on Stone* (Oxford, 1965) holds pride of place, though both M.C. Greenstock, *Some Inscriptions from Roman Britain* (Lactor 4) and A.R. Burn, *The Romans in Britain: An Anthology of Inscriptions*, 2nd edn (Blackwell, 1969) supplement the evidence found in Britain itself with material from elsewhere in the empire, while for coins G. Askew, *The Coinage of Roman Britain*, 2nd edn (Seaby, 1980) serves as an excellent introduction. It is not the aim of the present volume to supersede what has already been produced, rather to make available within the confines of a single work something of what each severally provides.

In format I have arranged the sources under three main headings. The first of these, dealing with the geography and peoples of Britain, sets the scene for Roman occupation in its various phases, and thus forms the basis of the central sector, the political and military history, with which the majority of ancient writers concerned themselves. In the final section, religion, commerce and the social life of Britain, I have sought to draw together as far as possible those other facets of evidence which often provide a glimpse behind the face of official pronouncements to the cares and hopes of individuals.

When referring to the titles of sources, place names, or official positions I have attempted, wherever feasible, to give both the original form and its modern equivalent or translation, one in the text, the other in round brackets (. . .). This, it is hoped, will facilitate use of the work in conjunction with textbooks, which often provide one or the other but seldom both. Exceptions inevitably occur: an often-used piece of ancient literature may be commonly known by its English title alone; more obscure works may have no widely accepted translated form. In other cases omission of the alternative serves to prevent its use with frequently occurring names becoming oppressively obtrusive, or, as is the case with such widely accepted technical terms as Legate etc., to establish an element of uniformity. Round brackets (. . .) are also employed to designate explanatory material not found or easily supplied in the original or to summarise passages of connecting narrative. In the majority of cases an author's name has been followed by a reference to the century in which he lived or was active. The aim in doing this is to provide the reader with an immediate and handy reference by which a writer's closeness to his subject matter might be gauged. Where, however, several passages from the same author occur close together, I have not felt it necessary to repeat the dating on every occasion.

Inevitably, any work which seeks to provide a selection of sources runs the risk of omitting altogether aspects that some will deem essential, while indulging to an excessive degree what may otherwise appear trivial or plainly wrong. For omission I can only plead ignorance or shortage of space; for the sin of commission, the belief that one of the greatest lessons to be learned is a healthy suspicion of what antiquity has transmitted to us. Recognition of arrant nonsense should put us well on our guard against accepting too readily what seems ostensibly plausible.

Preface to
the Second Edition

When the *Sourcebook* appeared some nine years ago, it was clear that with time the discovery of new material would demand a second edition. I was encouraged to begin the task of accumulating this by the generally favourable reaction to the book from both reviewers and users, but I have benefited greatly from the publication of works that have brought together the finds from Bath and Vindolanda, as well as the gradual appearance of *RIB* II. In this revised edition, therefore, I have attempted to incorporate both the improvements suggested by others (most notably indicating by square brackets [. . .] the missing or restored sections of inscriptions) and the more useful and interesting of the new finds. As before, I have restricted the introduction of linking material to the bare essentials and the Bibliography largely to items cited in the text. To have included more would simply have duplicated information available in the many excellent handbooks that this volume is meant to supplement. To what extent I have succeeded in my aim of providing readers with a convenient store of original material I leave for others to decide.

Map One: The Tribes of Britain

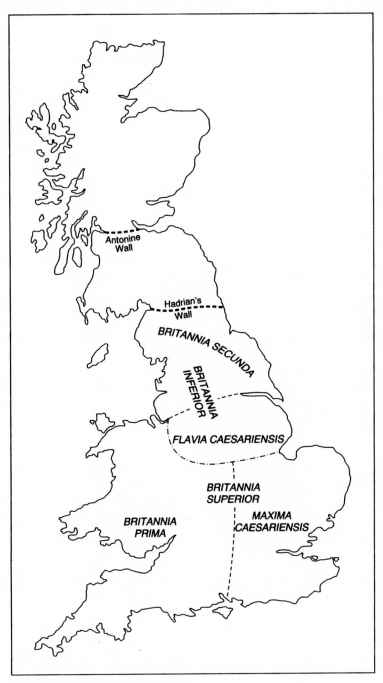

Map Two: The Provinces of Britain

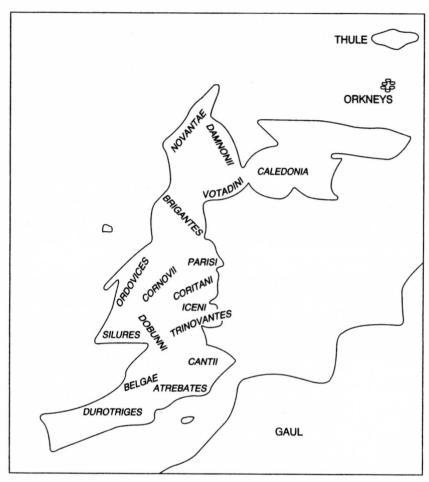

Map Three: Britain according to Ptolemy (2nd C. AD)

Introduction

From the earliest contacts of Caesar's invasions to the break-up of the Western Empire the history of Rome's involvement with the island of Britain spans a period of nearly five centuries. It is not the purpose of this Introduction, however, to attempt a survey of those years – these already exist in much greater detail than would ever be possible here – but rather to examine the sources, be they literary, epigraphic or numismatic, that form the substance of this book, and to indicate some of the problems and difficulties encountered in their use.

Despite the volume of material upon which our understanding of Roman Britain is based, it remains an inescapable fact that this is but a fraction of what once existed. Unlike the historian of more modern times, for whom archival material exists in relative abundance, the student of antiquity is separated from his topic of enquiry not only by at least a millennium and a half but more importantly by a major cultural upheaval and a virtual collapse of learning in which many of the accumulated records of the classical world ceased to exist. In the case of literary works, what remained was then subjected to a further and protracted period of attrition in which survival became largely dependent upon the ability of their contents to inspire continued interest in the monks who laboured in the scriptoria of mediaeval monasteries. For it was only through their periodic and painstaking copying and recopying of manuscripts over the centuries that writers as diverse as Caesar, Claudian, Tacitus and Gildas exist for us today. Needless to say, however, the interests of the mediaeval monk were not always identical to our own, and our ability to study the tedious ruminations of this or that late grammarian is scant compensation for the loss of many major texts. In the case of inscriptions and coins, on the other hand, their survival has been more dependent upon pure chance, when concealment, either deliberate or accidental, has preserved them in whole or in part from the ravages of re-use or wanton destruction.

Faced, then, with a body of evidence which, for all its size, is incomplete, we have to recognise and accept that there are times, whole decades indeed, when our ignorance of events is almost total, caused by the failure of hardly any record to survive. The extent of our losses we see, for instance, when an author refers fleetingly to matters dealt with more fully in works or books no longer extant: the reference by Tacitus to the military prominence of Venutius (§71) or that by Ammianus Marcellinus to the Areani in the reign of Constans (§260). In other cases the source may survive but only in tantalisingly truncated form: the fragmentary books of Dio Cassius or the Epitomes of his histories produced in the eleventh century by the Byzantine monk Xiphilinus. Here too we can include the many damaged inscriptions such as the tombstone of Classicianus with its two missing lines (§80), or the even more fragmentary Agricola-inscription from St Albans (§106).

By way of contrast other periods of the province's history appear endowed with a veritable superabundance of material either in the form of multiple surviving sources or the existence of a single work characterised by the depth and detail of its contents. The danger here is that we are tempted to compensate for what we lack elsewhere by attributing to such periods an emphasis and importance that is out of proportion to their real significance. The career of Agricola might well be a case in point. The prominent position enjoyed by his six-year governorship, its virtual domination of the closing decades of the first century AD, rest entirely upon the biography written by his son-in-law Tacitus. Remove that and he sinks to the same level of obscurity as many ostensibly eminent governors whose achievements, for want of extant records, we cannot assess with any degree of certainty.

A somewhat similar problem arises for those periods in which sources of information are less than common: the danger of our uncritically accepting what in more favourable circumstances might well be dismissed as garbled conjecture on the part of the author. This becomes particularly evident at the very end of Roman Britain when we are faced by a writer like Gildas, attempting to reconstruct in the sixth century the breakdown of Roman rule that had taken place a hundred years earlier, and for whom historical truth was less important than the religious significance perceived within events. At the same time, however, we need to be aware that by rejecting too readily what Gildas says we may equally pass over the germ of truth that lies within his narrative.

In addition to those general considerations of distorted emphasis outlined above, distortions which arise primarily from the incompleteness of our evidence, others exist that are more specific to the individual type of source material. These we shall see as we deal with the sources themselves.

The literary evidence

Of all the varied forms of evidence we possess for Roman Britain by far the most productive of detailed information are the literary works of ancient writers, in both Latin and Greek, prose and verse. It is largely to these indeed that we owe our ability to trace the detailed historical developments that occurred, be they extensions of the province and the resistance encountered, the shifting stances of client rulers and the Roman attitude to them, major rebellions and the Roman reaction, internal dissension and the usurpation of power, or external threats and the havoc wrought by barbarian invasion. No less important than the narrative account they provide, however, is the motivation many of our sources attribute to those involved in the history of the province; for it is in this that we glimpse something of the individual writer's approach to his subject and his ability to analyse and interpret critically the events he describes. This in turn affects our estimation of his reliability, acumen and ultimately his value as a source.

At the same time it goes without saying that in dealing with so extensive a period we are presented with a body of literary evidence that displays within itself a wide diversity of form, purpose and underlying rationale. The prose works alone include such varied genres as historical commentaries, biography, letters, encyclopaedic and geographical compilations, panegyrics, religious tracts and philosophy. As a result we have to recognise the need for an element of flexibility in our own approach. We can no more demand of authors working in the same genre but separated from one another by up to four hundred years identical methods of treating their material than we can apply the same criteria of judgement to writers contemporary with one another but engaged in the production of widely differing genres. Nor by the same token should we look for the same degree of relevance and accuracy in a writer treating Roman Britain as his central theme and one for whom it supplies but a passing reference.

Within prose literature the most obviously relevant genre to the study of Roman occupation is historiography, but if we are to gain any proper appreciation of the information given, we need to be aware not only of the individual historian's relationship to the period he is treating but sensitive also to the influences at work on him and the prejudices to which he is prone. A figure like Caesar dealt with contemporary events in which he was intimately involved; others in contrast chose to treat either a wider timespan or themes of which they had little or no first-hand experience and were thus dependent upon earlier records, the reliability of which is usually beyond our power to determine. All, however, were inescapably affected either by the environment in which they worked or their own personal preferences and aims. The disinterested scholar seeking absolute truth was no more a feature of the ancient world than he is of the modern. Thus, while it would be wrong of us to suggest that the historians of antiquity set out deliberately to falsify their material or to mislead their readers, it would be equally naive to regard them as infallibly correct in their judgements or unaffected by their own preoccupations. In the case of Caesar the veneer of impartiality and the clarity of his third-party narration, which are such features of his commentaries, overlie a distinct autobiographical tendency to self-justification. What he tells us of his motives, his analysis of events, of the events themselves, is largely determined by the image of his career and personality he wished to project. Similarly with Tacitus, his treatment of imperial history in the first century AD is coloured by the fact that he wrote as a member of a senatorial order that had only recently emerged from a bout of imperial repression.

In many respects the existence of more than one source dealing with the same events serves as a valuable means of comparison. Successive versions clearly derived from one another, for example, enable us to trace the development of historical connections and emphases from one century to another, as important in the case of such ostensible fictions as that which attributed the construction of Hadrian's wall to Severus as it is with more credible events. In other instances one writer may serve to set within a broader perspective the evidence of another: the later reassessment by Dio Cassius of the significance to be attached to Caesar's invasion in 55 BC (§24), or the contemporary reaction of Cicero to the 54 BC invasion in letters he wrote from the heart of the empire (§29–34).

Though differing from historiography in the greater weight it places upon the delineation of character and motivation, biography shares with it the capacity to direct the treatment of its subject to a predetermined and often biased end. So for example in Tacitus' *Agricola*, a work which incorporates features from many genres within its biographical framework, the achievements of previous expansionist governors, for all their intrinsic merits and significance, become largely reduced to the status of preliminaries to the great push north, while to the necessary intervals of consolidation and recovery under governors like Petronius Turpilianus and Trebellius Maximus is attached the shameful name of sloth and indolence. Even more remarkable is the way Tacitus is able to implicate Domitian in Agricola's death while ostensibly claiming there is no evidence of any involvement on the part of the emperor. This capacity to damn by negation or silence is no less evident in Suetonius' treatment of Caligula's abortive attempt at invasion (§54). By careful selection of information and manipulation of phrasing the reader is inescapably directed towards the conclusion that responsibility for the fiasco lay solely with the emperor's madness.

For all their differences of emphasis and approach historiography and biography, indeed all the literary genres of antiquity, share this much in common: that their aim was as much the production of literature as the provision of information. As a result they were susceptible to a whole range of embellishment for the sake of their literary function. We see this most clearly when a writer of history or biography punctuates his narrative with speeches that are clear fabrications – the flowing Latin rhetoric placed into the mouth of Caratacus or Calgacus by Tacitus, or the Greek attributed to Boudicca by Dio Cassius. It was never the writer's purpose to suggest that such speeches were actually made in the form recorded. Rather, they exist to enliven the narrative with sentiments appropriate to the occasion in a manner designed to appeal to the ancient love of oratory. The existence at times of parallel speeches from the Roman side reveals indeed their origins in the *suasoriae* (exercises in imaginary advice) and *controversiae* (fictitious debates) that were a staple element of classical education. Even the apparent recognition by writers that Roman domination was not without its darker side, a theme frequently given to native British leaders, was itself in part but a feature of oratorical training. Tacitus may have chosen to paint the picture of the noble savage struggling to maintain his freedom and independence, but there is little to indicate that he deviated so radically from the rest of his class as to reject outright the City's imperial mission.

To compilers of encyclopaedic information like Pliny the Elder, and geographers like Strabo, no less than to historians like Caesar and Diodorus Siculus, we owe our evidence for the social and political structure of Celtic Britain and the customs and religious beliefs of its inhabitants. The information they provide, however, comes to us not as disinterested factual records, but already affected by the theories and assumptions upon which the individual author based his reasoning and conclusions. That many such presuppositions were erroneous needs no demonstration. In the case of geographical knowledge limitations in technical expertise and instrumentation, a theoretical approach that depended heavily upon deductive reasoning, and a tendency to rely upon received wisdom rather than empirical fact or personal experience led inevitably to many long-held axioms that proved ultimately untenable. We see this in the widespread belief that Britain lay between Gaul and Spain, or the 90° shift in the position of north Scotland indicated by the geographer Ptolemy in the second century AD. In the realm of social custom and religious belief, on the other hand, the frequent use of explanation by analogy, equating what was found in Britain with a supposed Greco-Roman counterpart, inevitably introduced the danger of distortion either by simplification or by ill-matched inference. In a very basic form it appears in the equation of a Celtic deity with a Roman counterpart as the result of some minor point of similarity. On a deeper level, interpretation of the druidic belief in life after death in terms of Pythagorean doctrine on the transmigration of souls creates a series of implications that may ultimately have little basis in reality.

Towards the end of Roman Britain there appeared a number of genres more obviously devoted to the propagation of a single viewpoint than anything hitherto seen. To these belong the writings of Christian apologists, for whom fact becomes patently subservient to message, liable to embroidery, alteration or expansion by edifying fiction for the benefit of the faithful. This is no less true of Gildas, seeking to explain the decline of Romano-British society in terms of its sinfulness, than it is of the miracles that surround the visits of St Germanus. Equally coloured are the products of third and fourth century panegyricists, whose prime function, maintaining the cult of the personality, led inevitably to an accentuation of success and the virtual elimination of any reference to failure.

In turning from prose to verse we need not be surprised that the output of Latin poets furnishes useful information on Roman Britain, so long as we bear in mind that its original purpose was far removed from the use to which we now put it. In the case of the poets of the Augustan age their frequent references to the prospect of invasion were clearly designed not only to maintain a point of contact with the achievements of Caesar, but also to provide an outlet for the traditional Roman belief in territorial expansion in an empire for the moment set on the more mundane paths of consolidation and stability. Even so, they provide an important source for policies and events which, while perhaps designed to impress themselves upon the kings of Britain rather than have any real military effect, serve to mirror contemporary concerns and modes of thought. With the fourth century poet Claudian, on the other hand, his works serve to supplement our other sources with details, no matter how vaguely expressed, that would otherwise not be available to us. In such circumstances it is the historian's task to delve beneath the outer poetic form to reach whatever truth lies beneath.

The epigraphic evidence

In contrast to the evidence of our literary sources, which comes to us through the process of copying century after century, with all the problems this implies for the maintenance of accuracy, the inscriptions of Roman Britain provide not only an immediate and direct contact with the world of antiquity but also much of the information we possess on the workings of the province and the lives of individuals. In form they range from the monumental, both public and private, on the costliest of stone, to the humblest of scratchings on walls and potsherds, from the lofty pronouncements of official policy to the loves and hatreds of society's lower levels.

To official inscriptions recording the construction or repair of buildings we owe much of our ability to follow the history of individual sites, to establish those responsible for the various phases of building, and at times even why the repair became necessary: whether through the depredations of enemy action or simple deterioration with time. In the case of the northern walls, indeed, it is the evidence of epigraphy that even allows us to reconstruct the process of building, section by section. In other cases such official inscriptions mark the opening up of new areas to economic exploitation, the movement of troops from one posting to another, or the movement of individuals from one unit to another. In this respect diplomas awarding citizenship on retirement to members of the auxiliary forces, or honorary dedications set up by municipalities to their benefactors are of particular value. Both serve in fact to reveal for us the variety of career patterns that imperial service might take. At the same time, however, the very immediacy of official inscriptions should not blind us to their usefulness as a vehicle of propaganda for the administration of the day, seeking to present an official version that might well be at variance with reality. In this respect loyalty declarations, ostensibly set up by sections of the army in the form of religious offerings, become particularly suspect, especially when other sources point to unrest and disaffection. In such cases, indeed, it might not be altogether inappropriate to regard the level of profuseness as being in inverse proportion to the truth of the situation.

Inscriptions of a more personal and private nature are in many ways one of the few means at our disposal for glimpsing the lives of individuals and groups in all their aspects, building up in a way the literary sources never attempted a picture of business concerns and religious attachments, friendship and enmity, family life and inevitably, through the many funerary inscriptions that survive, of death. Here it is that the range of materials used is at its widest, reflecting no doubt the varied spectrum of society itself. Not surprisingly in a world still very much at the mercy of natural forces, many inscriptions centre upon the comfort afforded by religion, dedications to this god or that expressing hopes and fears: a safe return, success in business, or promotion. The last of these also shows how easy it was for apparently private offerings to be made with one eye on officialdom: Tineius Longus' dedication to Anociticus (§338) or Donatianus' allegory (§410) are classic examples. In many instances it is also such inscriptions that provide our sole evidence for the existence of a cult within the province: the references to the shrine of Isis in London are notable but not unique examples (§412-13). Though gratitude and thanks loom large among the sentiments voiced, the less sympathetic emotions are not altogether absent, as we see in the curses, inscribed in often florid terms on lead and then buried, calling down upon those responsible for theft or some other misdemeanour a whole range of unpleasant mishaps. In the vast majority of cases, however, it is only in death that the details of life survive, the brief glimpse provided by the tombstone of a career in the army, a dutiful wife or husband, the love of parent and child, the bond between freedman and patron. The formulaic expression of grief which operated then no less than today cannot altogether extinguish the pathos that so often characterises the details given. At the same time, though, such inscriptions are also valuable tools in establishing patterns of life expectancy: the relative frequency of infant and child mortality, the chances of reaching a hundred, the dangers of military service, or simply of being a wife and mother.

The numismatic evidence

From the point of view of the historian the value of coinage as a means of establishing and dating many of the major events of Roman Britain has long been recognised. It rests indeed upon two basic characteristics of the coins themselves. First, there is the ease with which individual issues may be dated by reference to the number of times the emperor concerned had held tribunician power, conferred upon accession and renewed annually thereafter, or the less frequent consulship, since both form a regular element of obverse legends down to the middle of the third century. Second, there is the frequency of special issues commemorating specific events within the province: Roman victories against external enemies, imperial visitations, a return to legitimate power after a period of usurpation, the claims to legitimacy by those same usurpers, or the re-establishment of military and economic stability. The very fact that so many issues were minted is itself a powerful indication that governments clearly recognised the importance of coins as a means of disseminating news, even if doubt continues to surround the question of to whom such information was directed – the army, for which much of the coinage struck was initially intended as pay, or the civilian population. Equally problematic from our own point of view is the degree to which those who used the coins ever noticed the message they offered, or the speed with which new issues became submerged within the coinage already in circulation. These, however, are problems for us; for the administration involved variety of issues was clearly regarded as a useful and valuable practice. At the same time, though, we need to recognise, as in the case of epigraphy, the fine line that separates information from propaganda, and to be aware that such declarations as *Felicitas Temporum* (Happy days are here again) or *Concordia Militum* (Harmony among the troops) could be as much a pious hope as an expression of the truth.

If in writing this Introduction I have tended to emphasise the problems that may be encountered in any approach to the sources for Roman Britain, it is to impress upon readers the need for caution in using material that presents only a partial picture of events and from which we are separated by so great a span of time. Not everything, however, is unrelieved blackness or subject to the distorting influence of bias. The very candour and directness of many authorities win our easy acceptance of the evidence they present, and even when a source appears deliberately slanted, our ability to recognise this is the first step towards setting its contents in their true perspective.

Part One

The Geography and People of Britain

I The Earliest Contacts

For all its momentous significance as regards future relations between Britain and the Empire of Rome, the invasion launched by Julius Caesar in the late summer of 55 BC was in many respects merely the culminating event in a long history of contact between the Mediterranean world and the largest of Europe's offshore islands. As early as the fourth century BC the Greek colony of Massilia (Marseilles) knew of the island's existence, and the years *c.* 320 BC saw a partial exploration by its navigator Pytheas. Evidence of even earlier contact dating from the sixth century BC was long thought to be reflected, if at several hands removed, in the bare mention of 'the island of the Albiones' contained in the fourth century AD *Ora Maritima (Sea Coast)* of Avienus. Recent study by Hawkes,[1] however, has demonstrated that this probably represents no more than the transference to a British context, perhaps by the mid-fourth century BC writer Ephoros, of material that originally described the south-west coast of Spain, where there was also a tribe of Albiones. Despite this, however, the attribution to Britain of the name Albion, together with its Greek variations in spelling, was certainly old, and it continued to be given sporadically by writers in antiquity, if only at times as a name long superseded:

1. Pliny the Elder (1st C. AD), *Natural History* IV, 102

It was itself called Albion, while all the islands of which I shall shortly be making mention are called the British Isles.

2. Pseudo-Aristotle (? 1st C. AD), *On the Cosmos* 393b12

In it (Ocean) there are two very large islands called the British Isles, Albion and Ierne (Ireland). They are larger than those already mentioned and lie beyond Celtic territory.

At what stage the change to the name 'Britain' came about is unknown, but again it would seem that this was in fact the standardised form of what had originally been 'Pritain':

3. Diodorus Siculus (late 1st C. BC) V, 21, 1

Opposite that part of Gaul which borders on the Ocean . . . there are many islands in the Ocean, of which the largest is called the Prettanic island.[2]

4. Eustathius (12th C. AD), *Commentary on Dionysius Periegetes* 492

There are those who write Ambrax the old-fashioned way with a P and (call) the region Ampracia, just as (they call) the Brettanic Isles Prettanic. The spelling with B is more common.

5. Ibid. 568

The size of the Brettanides (British Isles), which others, as previously stated, call the Prettanides with a P, is given not only by Dionysius, as has been mentioned above, but also by Ptolemy in his work on geography.

Of the account given by Pytheas of Massilia himself, describing his visit to Britain, nothing survives except allusions, either direct or indirect, in later writers. So for instance Pliny the Elder refers to information given by the fourth to third century BC historian Timaeus which can only have come from Pytheas:

6. Pliny the Elder (1st C. AD), *Natural History* IV, 104

The historian Timaeus says that six days' sail up-Channel[3] from Britain is the island of Mictis (Wight[4]) in which tin is produced. Here he says the Britons sail in boats of wickerwork covered in sewn leather. There are those who record other islands: the Scandiae, Dumna, the Bergi, and Berrice, the largest of them all, from which the crossing to Thyle (Thule) is made. One day's sail from Thyle is the frozen sea called by some the Cronian sea.

It is likewise to Pytheas that many of the details given by Caesar and Diodorus Siculus in the first century BC must ultimately be traced back:

7. Caesar (mid-1st C. BC), *Gallic War* V, 13

The island is triangular in shape, with one side opposite Gaul. One corner of this side, situated in Cantium (Kent), is where nearly all the ships from Gaul land, and points east; the lower corner (Land's End) points south. The length of this side is about 500 miles. Another side faces Spain[5] and the west. In this direction lies Hibernia (Ireland), half the size of Britain, so it is thought, and as distant from it as Britain is from Gaul. Midway between the two is the island called Mona (Man[6]), and in addition it is thought a number of smaller islands are close by, in which, according to some writers, there are thirty days of continuous darkness around midwinter.[7] We ourselves discovered nothing about this from our enquiries, though we observed from accurate measurements using the waterclock that the nights are shorter than on the continent. The length of this side, according to the opinion of the natives, is 700 miles. The third side faces north and has no land opposite it, but its (east) corner points generally towards Germany. It is thought to be 800 miles in length. Thus the whole island is 2,000 miles in circumference.

8. Diodorus Siculus (late 1st C. BC) V, 21, 3–6

Britain is triangular in shape rather like Sicily, though its sides are unequal in length. It stretches at an angle alongside Europe and the nearest point to the continent, called Cantium (Kent), is said to be some 100 stadia (*c.* 11.5 miles) from Europe at the place where the (North) sea has its outlet (into Ocean). The second promontory, called Belerium (Land's End) is said to be four days' sail from the continent. The last is recorded as reaching out into the open sea and is called Orkas (Duncansby Head). The shortest of its sides, which lies alongside Europe, measures 7,500 stadia (*c.* 860 miles), the second, stretching from the Channel up to the (northern) tip, 15,000 stadia (*c.* 1,725 miles), the last 20,000 stadia (*c.* 2,300 miles), so that the whole circumference of the island measures 42,500 stadia (*c.* 4,900 miles). They say that Britain is inhabited by tribes that are aboriginal, and in their lifestyle preserve the old ways; for they make use of chariots in their wars, just as tradition tells us the ancient Greek heroes did in the Trojan war, and their houses are simple, built for the most part of reeds or logs. They harvest their grain crops by cutting off only the ears of corn and store them in covered barns. Each day they pick out the ripe ears, grind them, and in this way get their food. They are simple in their habits and far removed from the cunning and vice of modern man. Their way of life is frugal and far different from the luxury engendered by wealth. The island also has a large population, and the climate is very cold, since it actually lies under the Great Bear. It contains many kings and chieftains, who for the most part live in peace with one another.

Unfortunately for later travellers, not least Julius Caesar himself, much of what Pytheas had to say was only transmitted by later writers as evidence of his general untrustworthiness, insofar as he had recorded what current theory held to be impossible. This is nowhere clearer than in the case of Thule, probably Iceland though the coast of Norway has also been suggested, a land never again discovered by ancient mariners. By the end of the first century AD in fact the name itself had been transferred to the Shetlands:

9. Strabo (1st C. BC–1st C. AD) I, 4, 3

For Pytheas, who gives an account of Thule, has been found on examination to be an arrant liar, and those who have seen Britain and Ierne (Ireland) say nothing of Thule, though they mention other islands, small ones, around Britain ... Pytheas declares that the length of the island (Britain) is greater than 20,000 stadia (c. 2,300 miles), and he says that Cantium (Kent) is some days' sail from Celtica (Gaul). .... Therefore, a man who tells such great lies about well-known regions could hardly tell the truth about regions unknown to all.

10. Ibid. II, 4, 1

Polybius in his account of the geography of Europe says he passes over the ancient authorities, but examines those who criticise them, that is Dicaearchos and Eratosthenes ... and Pytheas, by whom many have been misled. Pytheas claimed he visited the whole of Britain that was accessible to him, gave the circumference of the island as more than 40,000 stadia (c. 4,600 miles), and in addition gave a description of Thule and those regions in which there was no longer land or sea or air as separate entities but a compound of them all like a jellyfish.

One result of such 'character assassination' is the association with Thule, and subsequent damning by association, of many facts clearly appropriate to Britain itself, but simply rejected out of hand:

11. Strabo IV, 5, 5

As regards Thule our information is even more uncertain (than it is for Ireland) on account of its distance; for people locate it as the most northerly of lands to which a name is given. However, the fact that what Pytheas says about it and about the other places in those parts is false, is clear from (what he tells us of) the districts we do know about. For in very many cases he has told falsehoods, as was stated earlier, so that it is clear he has been even less truthful as regards remote regions. And yet from the point of view of astronomy and mathematical theory he would seem to have made reasonable use of his data in asserting that those who live close to the frozen zone have a total lack of some cultivated crops and domesticated animals and a shortage of others, and that they live on millet and vegetables, fruit and roots. Those who have grain and honey, he says, also make a drink from them. The grain itself they thresh in large barns to which they bring the ears for storage, since they do not have clear sunshine. For threshing floors are useless owing to the lack of sun and the rain.[8]

NOTES

1 *Pytheas*, p. 19ff; cf. Rivet and Smith, p. 39.
2 The spelling here with P is not found in all manuscripts of Diodorus, though it clearly represents the older tradition which later scribes 'corrected'. A similar process was evidently at work in the transmission of Strabo's *Geography*, since it is only in Book II that the use of P in spelling Britain begins to occur. See further Rivet and Smith, p. 39f.
3 The sense here, lit. 'inwards', is obscure and disputed. Interpretation as 'up-Channel' is favoured by Hawkes, but many commentators despair of extracting any clear understanding, cf. Maxwell (1), p. 298.
4 Thus Rivet and Smith, p. 487ff identify the island, equating it with the more frequent name Vectis. Maxwell (1), however, argues for the traditional identification with St Michael's Mount.
5 The erroneous view of the relative positions of Britain and Spain persisted in ancient writers until Ptolemy in the second century AD. It was later to recur in writers like Orosius in the fifth century AD and beyond. See further Ogilvie and Richmond, p. 166f.
6 Though Caesar's description certainly suggests identification of Mona with the Isle of Man, Rivet and Smith, pp. 41 and 419f suggest that this, like references to Mona in other writers, should be taken as signifying Anglesey.
7 Cf. Pliny the Elder, *Natural History* II 187: 'Pytheas of Massilia writes that this (6 months' continuous sun or darkness) occurs in the island of Thyle, which is 6 days' sail north of Britain, and some assert also in Mona, which is about 200 miles from the British town of Camulodunum (Colchester).'

8 Hawkes, p. 36f sees in these details information relevant to the state of northern Britain at the time; cf. Pliny the Elder *Natural History* II 217: 'Pytheas of Massilia states that to the north of Britain the tides rise 80 cubits (120 feet).'

II The Roman Period

In addition to the political and military implications of Caesar's two expeditions, Roman penetration of Britain in the middle of the first century BC also brought with it additional and ostensibly first-hand information concerning the more southerly sectors of the island:

12. Caesar, *Gallic War* V, 12

The interior of Britain is inhabited by people who claim on the strength of their own tradition to be indigenous to the island; the coastal districts by immigrants from Belgic territory who came after plunder and to make war – nearly all of them are called after the tribes from which they originated. Following their invasion they settled down there and began to till the fields. The population is very large, their homesteads thick on the ground and very much like those in Gaul, and the cattle numerous. As money they use either bronze or gold coins or iron bars with a fixed standard of weight. Tin is found inland,[1] iron on the coast, but in small quantities; the bronze they use is imported. There is every type of timber as in Gaul, with the exception of beech and pine. They have a taboo against eating hare, chicken, and goose, but they rear them for amusement and pleasure. The climate is more temperate than in Gaul, the cold spells being less severe.

13. Ibid. V, 14

Of all the Britons by far the most civilised are the inhabitants of Cantium (Kent), a purely maritime region, whose way of life is little different from that of the Gauls. Most of those inhabiting the interior do not grow corn, but live instead on milk and meat and clothe themselves in skins. All the Britons dye themselves with woad, which produces a blue colour, and as a result their appearance in battle is all the more daunting.[2] They wear their hair long, and shave all their bodies with the exception of their heads and upper lip. Wives are shared between groups of ten or twelve men, especially between brothers and between fathers and sons. The offspring on the other hand are considered the children of the man with whom the woman first lived.

Towards the end of the first century BC much of the information given by Caesar was clearly reworked by the geographer Strabo, though with one or two additions, the result no doubt of the increase in trade that followed the invasions:

14. Strabo IV, 5, 2

There are four crossings which are commonly used in getting from the continent to the island, namely from the mouths of the Rivers Rhine, Seine, Loire and Garonne. Those who put to sea from the region around the Rhine do not, however, sail from the river estuary itself, but from the Morini, who are the neighbours of the Menapii and in whose territory lies Itium (Boulogne), used by the deified Caesar as a harbour when he crossed to the island. . . . Most of the island is flat and thickly wooded, though many districts are hilly. It produces grain and cattle, gold, silver and iron. These are exported along with hides and slaves and dogs bred specifically for hunting. The Celts (Gauls) also use both these and their native breed in war. The men (of Britain) are taller than the Celts, not so blond, and of looser build. As an indication of their size I myself saw some in Rome little more than boys standing as much as half a foot above the tallest in the city, though they were bow-legged and in other respects lacking any gracefulness of body. Their customs are in some respects like those of the Celts, in other respects simpler and more barbaric. As a result, some of them, through their want of skill, do not make cheese, though they have no shortage of milk. They are also unskilled in horticulture or farming in general. They are ruled by chieftains. In war they mostly use chariots like some of the Celts.[3] The forests are their cities; for they fortify a large circular enclosure with felled trees and there make themselves huts and pen their cattle,[4] though not for a long stay. Their weather tends to rain rather than snow, and on days when there are no clouds fog persists for a long time with the result that throughout the whole day the sun can be seen only for about three or four hours around noon. This also happens among the Morini and the Menapii and those living close to the Menapii.

Later still, following the Claudian invasion, the whole of Britain became subject to detailed exploration and exploitation by both the Roman army and the influx of merchants and speculators. Even the furthest reaches of Caledonia were to come under scrutiny as a result of Agricola's campaigns, recorded by his son-in-law:

15. Tacitus (1st–2nd C. AD), *Agricola* 10–12

10 The position and inhabitants of Britain have been recorded by many writers, but it is not with a view to challenging their accuracy or ability that I bring these topics up again; rather because it was then (under Agricola) that the conquest of Britain was completed. For this reason, while earlier writers embroidered with their eloquence things that had yet to be fully investigated, I shall set down the truth of the situation. Britain is the largest of the islands known to the Romans, and in terms of its extent and situation faces Germany in the east and Spain in the west. To the south it actually lies within sight of Gaul, while its northern parts, with no land opposite them, are beaten by a vast open sea. The overall shape of Britain has been compared by Livy and Fabius Rusticus, the most eloquent of ancient and modern writers respectively, to an elongated shoulder-blade (i.e. rhombus) or an axe-head. This is indeed its shape as far as Caledonia, and the idea has been extended to the whole. However, once you have crossed (into Caledonia) there is a vast irregular tract of land stretching out from (what was considered) the furthermost shore and tapering to a kind of wedge. It was then for the first time that a Roman fleet circumnavigated the coast of this remotest sea and established the fact that Britain was an island. At the same time it discovered and conquered hitherto unknown islands called Orcades (Orkneys).[5] Thule (Shetland) too was sighted (but no landing made) since their orders went no further and winter was approaching. They did, however, report that the sea was sluggish and heavy to the oars, and was not set in motion as much as other seas even by the winds. The reason for this I suppose is that the land and mountains which are the source and cause of storms, are further apart, while the deep mass of the open sea is set in motion more slowly. Investigation of the nature and tides of Ocean is not, however, the purpose of this work, and besides many have already dealt with

them. I would add just one thing: nowhere does the sea hold wider sway. This way and that its tidal currents flow, nor does it ebb and flow only up to the coast, but penetrates and winds its way deep inland, insinuating itself amidst the ridges and mountains as if in its own domain.

11 However, who the first inhabitants of Britain were, whether they were indigenous or immigrants, has not been sufficiently ascertained, as one might expect where barbarians are concerned. The physical types vary and from these variations come a number of theories. The red hair and large limbs of those who inhabit Caledonia affirm their German origin. The swarthy faces of the Silures and their generally curly hair, plus the fact that Spain lies opposite, leads one to believe that in ancient times Iberians crossed over and occupied this region. Those who live closest to the Gauls are like them, either because the influence of their (mutual) origin persists, or because the countries approach each other from north and south and as a result the (similarity of) climate has produced a (similar) physical appearance. Looking at the question overall, however, it seems likely that the Gauls occupied the nearby island. You would find (in Britain) the rites and religious beliefs of the Gauls. There is not much difference between them in language, the same boldness in courting danger and, when danger looms, the same panic in avoiding it. The Britons, however, display greater ferocity since they have not yet been enervated by a long period of peace. The Gauls too, we learn, were experts in warfare, but in recent times indolence and a life of ease have made their appearance, with the resultant loss of valour and, at the same time, freedom. This has also happened to those of the Britons who were conquered at the outset (i.e. in the Claudian invasion); the rest remain what the Gauls once were.

12 Their strength is in their infantry; some tribes also fight in chariots. The nobleman is the driver; his retainers do the fighting. At one time they owed obedience to kings; now they are split into partisan factions under rival chieftains. Nothing indeed is more to our advantage against these very powerful tribes than the fact that they do not plan joint operations. It is rare for two or three tribes to come together in order to repel a common danger. So, they fight individually and are collectively defeated. The climate with its frequent rains and mist is wretched; yet extreme cold is absent. The length of the (summer) days is greater than that in our world; the nights are light and in the points of Britain furthest north short, so that you can hardly distinguish dusk from daybreak.[6] If clouds

do not get in the way, they say the sun's glow can be seen right through the night, and it does not set and rise but rather passes along (the horizon). Evidently the flat edge of the world with its low shadow does not project the darkness much; night therefore falls below the level of the sky and the stars. Except for olives, vines and the other usual products of warmer countries the soil will produce grain and is rich in cattle. Crops are slow to ripen, but germinate quickly, both factors stemming from the same cause, the great moisture of the earth and sky. Britain bears gold, silver and other metals which are the prize of victory. The Ocean too produces pearls, but these are dark and blue-black in colour. Some people think those who collect them lack skill since in the Red Sea (Indian Ocean) the pearl-oysters are torn from the rocks alive and breathing, while in Britain they are collected just as they are thrown up (on the shore). I am more ready to believe that the pearls lack quality rather than that we lack the desire for them.

For all their civilising influence in those parts of Britain directly controlled by Rome, this seems not to have extended far beyond the northern frontier, eventually established for good along Hadrian's wall. The following describes the tribes north of the frontier in the early years of the third century AD, the reign of Severus.

16. Epitome[7] of Dio Cassius LXXVI, 12, 1–5

There are among the Britons two very large tribes, the Caledonians and the Maeatae. The names of the others have been merged as it were into these. The Maeatae for their part live near the wall which divides the island into two, and the Caledonians beyond them. Both tribes inhabit wild and waterless mountains and desolate marshy plains, and possess neither walls nor cities nor farms. Instead they live on their flocks, on game and on certain fruits, and though there are vast and limitless stocks of fish they do not eat them. They live in tents without clothes or shoes; they share their womenfolk and rear all their offspring in common. Their form of government is for the most part democratic, and they have a great liking for plunder. For this reason they choose their boldest men to be their leaders. They go into battle both in chariots with small swift horses, and on foot. They are in addition very fast runners and very resolute when they stand their ground. Their weapons consist of a shield and a short spear with a bronze 'apple' at the end of the shaft which is designed to make a loud noise when shaken and thus terrify the enemy. They also have daggers. They are able to endure cold, hunger and all kinds of hardship; for they plunge into the marshes and stay there for many days with only their heads above water; in the forests they live on bark and roots, and in case of emergency they prepare a type of food, a piece of which, the size of a bean, when eaten, stops them feeling hunger or thirst. Such is the island of Britain and such are the inhabitants, at least in the hostile part.

cf.

17. Herodian (3rd C. AD) III, 14, 6–8

Most of (northern) Britain is marshy since it is constantly washed by the ocean tides. The barbarians are accustomed to swim in these marshes or to run through them with the water up to their waists. For the most part they are naked and think nothing of getting mud on themselves. Also, being unfamiliar with the use of clothing, they adorn their waists and necks with iron, considering this an ornament and a sign of wealth, just as other barbarians do gold. They tattoo[8] their bodies with various designs and pictures of all kinds of animals. This is the reason they do not wear clothes: so as not to cover up the designs on their bodies. They are extremely warlike and bloodthirsty, though their armament consists simply of a narrow shield, a spear, and a sword that hangs beside their naked bodies. They are unfamiliar with the use of breastplates or helmets, considering them a hindrance in crossing the marshes. From these thick mists rise and cause the atmosphere in that region always to have a gloomy appearance.

NOTES

1 Was Caesar misled by traders hoping to keep their traffic in the metal to themselves, or is this simply the view of Cornish tin gained by someone approaching Britain from the south-east?

2 Though the use of woad was again remarked upon in the first century AD by Pomponius Mela, *De Chorographia* III, 6, 51, he admits ignorance as to why, a salutary reminder to us perhaps that even supposedly key works in antiquity could be less available to a general readership than they are today: 'They dye their bodies with woad – whether for decoration or some other reason is unknown.'

3 For British tactics in using the chariot see Caesar, *Gallic War* IV, 33 and V, 16–17.

4 Cf. Caesar, *Gallic War* V, 21.

5   This amply refutes the claim made in the fourth century AD by Eutropius and repeated by writers like Orosius (5th C.), Jordanes (6th C.) and Bede (8th C.) that the Orkneys were conquered under Claudius: Eutropius VII, 13, 3.

    'He also added to the Roman empire certain islands called the Orkneys situated beyond Britain in Ocean.'

6   Cf. Pliny the Elder, *Natural History* II 186: 'The longest day amounts to ... 17 equinoctial hours in Britain.'

7   For ease of reference I associate under the single heading *Epitome* both the fragmentary remains of books and the true epitomes of otherwise lost books composed by Xiphilinus in the eleventh century. Book and chapter references follow the traditional divisions given in the margin of the Loeb edition.

8   Cf. Solinus 22.20 (3rd C.): 'The land is occupied partly by barbarians who from childhood have the pictures of various animals put on their bodies by tattoo artists.'

Part Two

The Political and
Military History

III The Invasions of Caesar

THE INVASION OF 55 BC

Though initially it had been the need to defend Roman interests and territory in southern Gaul that in 58 BC drew Caesar into intervening in the affairs of tribes beyond the confines of his designated sphere of influence, the opportunities offered by Gaul as a whole for large-scale conquest and the political *kudos* that would doubtless come from military success made it virtually inevitable that sooner or later Caesar would be brought into contact with Britain. That close ties connected the two countries both politically and commercially must have become clear to him at an early stage, as he himself implies:

18. Caesar, *Gallic War* II, 4

Among them (the Suessiones) even within our own living memory Diviciacus had been king, the most powerful in the whole of Gaul, and he had exercised control over a large part of these regions and also over Britain.

19. Ibid. III, 8

Of the whole seaboard in that region the Veneti exercise the most extensive sway, because they have very many vessels and in these they are accustomed to sail to Britain.

More importantly, however, Britain offered not only a safe haven for those unable to accept the growth of Roman influence:

20. Caesar, *Gallic War* II, 14

Those who were the leaders of this plot fled to Britain because they saw how great a disaster they had brought upon the tribe (the Bellovaci).

but also the prospect of direct intervention in support of Gallic tribes who had their own reasons for suspecting and fearing a Roman move against Britain:

21. Strabo (1st C. BC–1st C. AD) IV, 4, 1

Of these (the maritime tribes of Belgic Gaul) the Veneti engaged Caesar in naval war. For they were concerned to prevent the crossing to Britain, since they were engaged in trade with it.

22. Caesar, *Gallic War* III, 9

They (the Veneti) secured as their allies for the war the Osismi, Lexovii, Namnetes, Ambiliati, Morini, Diablintes and the Menapii. They also summoned help from Britain, which is situated opposite those regions.

Of the first invasion the longest, most detailed, and undoubtedly best account is that by Caesar himself, but as with all autobiographical material it is the account that Caesar himself chose to give rather than total unvarnished truth. As a result we have to recognise that behind the veneer of apparent objectivity there lies a strong undercurrent of careful subjective censorship which is perhaps nowhere more apparent than in the reasons he gives for embarking on the expedition in the first place.

23. Caesar, *Gallic War* IV, 20–38

More than 200 years later Caesar's account was abridged as part of Dio Cassius' history of Rome, and though the account he gives adds little from a factual point of view, it does serve to put into perspective what in 55 BC was an almost incredible event.

24. Dio Cassius (2nd–3rd C. AD) XXXIX, 51–3

51 To this island (Britain), therefore, Caesar wished to cross, once he had won over the Morini, and the rest of Gaul was quiet. He made

the crossing with his infantry by the best route, but he did not land where he should have. For the Britons, being forewarned of the invasion, occupied in advance all the landing places facing the continent. Caesar, therefore, sailed round a projecting headland and skirted along the coast on the other side of it. There he defeated those who joined battle with him as he disembarked in the shallows, and secured a bridgehead before reinforcements could arrive. He then repulsed this attack too. Not many of the barbarians fell, however, since they consisted of charioteers and cavalry and easily escaped the Romans, whose own cavalry had not yet arrived. However, the natives were alarmed both by reports about the Romans that came over from the continent, and by the fact that they had dared to cross over at all and had been able to set foot on their territory. So they sent some of the Morini, who were friends of theirs, to Caesar in order to arrange peace.

52 At the time they were willing to give him the hostages he demanded, but when subsequently the Romans suffered damage both to the fleet they had with them and to the one on its way (from the continent) as the result of a storm, they changed their minds. While not attacking the Romans openly, since their camp was strongly guarded, they did seize a number of men who had been sent out as if into friendly territory to forage for provisions, and killed all but a few of them, the remainder being hastily rescued by Caesar. After this they even assaulted the Roman encampment itself, but they achieved nothing, and in fact came off badly. Even so, they would not come to terms until they had been defeated on a number of occasions. Indeed Caesar had no intention of making peace with them, but winter was coming on and he was supplied with insufficient forces for engaging in hostilities at that time of year. Since too those forces being shipped over (from the continent) had been prevented from arriving and the Gauls had risen in his absence, he reluctantly entered into a treaty with the Britons, demanding many hostages on this occasion also, though he received only a few.

53 Thus, he sailed back to the continent and ended the disturbances. For himself or the state he had gained nothing from Britain except the glory of having led an expedition against it. Indeed he himself took great pride in this, and the Romans at home made great play of it. For seeing what was previously unknown had been revealed to sight, and what had formerly been unheard-of had become accessible to them, they regarded future expectations arising from these events as already realised, and gloried in all the gains they expected

to achieve as if they already had them in their possession. On account of this they voted to hold a festival of thanksgiving for 20 days.

A similar toning down of the acclaim that greeted Caesar's first invasion is also evident in Tacitus' work on his father-in-law, though in this case the motive behind the estimate is not without a personal aspect:

25. Tacitus (1st–2nd C. AD), *Agricola* 13

The deified Julius (Caesar) was indeed the first Roman to enter Britain with an army, but though he intimidated the inhabitants by a victory and gained control of the coast, it is clear he merely pointed it out to those who came after him; he did not bequeath it to them.

THE INVASION OF 54 BC

Once again we are dependent for a detailed account of the invasion upon Caesar's own commentaries, to which Dio Cassius' abridgement adds little extra:

26. Caesar, *Gallic War* V, 1–23

27. Dio Cassius (2nd–3rd C. AD) XL, 1–4

1   Among Caesar's other undertakings in Gaul during the consulship of those same men, Lucius Domitius and Appius Claudius, he had built ships that were half-way between his own swift vessels and the local cargoboats. This was so they might combine as far as possible lightness of construction and the ability to withstand the waves, and also so that they would not come to any harm when left high and dry. Once the weather was fit for sailing, Caesar again crossed over to Britain, giving as his excuse the fact that they had not sent him all the hostages they had promised. They evidently thought that because Caesar had withdrawn from Britain empty-handed on one occasion, he would not trouble them again. In fact, however, he coveted the island greatly so that he would certainly have found another excuse if he had not had this one. So he landed at the same place as before and because of the number of his ships and the fact that they put into the shore at many points

{ simultaneously, no one dared to oppose him. Immediately, there-
{ fore, Caesar was able to consolidate his beachhead.

2   For this reason the barbarians were unable to prevent his invasion,
and because Caesar's arrival with a larger army caused them even
greater alarm than had been the case the previous occasion, they
gathered together all their most valued possessions into the densest
and most thickly overgrown parts of the surrounding countryside.
Once they had made them secure by cutting down the trees round
about and piling more on top of them row after row so that the
end result was a kind of stockade, they then began to harass the
Roman foraging parties. Indeed, after being defeated in a battle
on open ground, they drew the Romans in pursuit towards their
stockade and killed a number in turn. After this a storm once again
damaged the Roman ships and the Britons sent for allies and moved
against the fleet with Cassivellaunus, the foremost of the island's
chieftains, as their leader. On engaging them, the Romans were at
first thrown into confusion by the onslaught of the British chariots,
but then they opened their ranks, and allowing the chariots to pass
through, hurled their weapons at the enemy from the side as they
rushed past. In this way they made the battle equal.

3   For a while both sides stood their ground, but then, though the
barbarians gained the upper hand over the Roman infantry, they
were routed by the Roman cavalry and withdrew to the Thames,
where they camped after blocking the crossing point there by means
of stakes both above and below the water line. Caesar, however,
forced them to abandon this stockade with a vigorous attack, and
later, by means of a siege, drove them out of their stronghold, while
others beat off an attack on the naval camp. As a result the Britons
became very much alarmed; they ended hostilities, provided
hostages, and agreed to pay a yearly tribute.

4   Thus did Caesar depart from the island for good, leaving no troops
behind in it; for he believed that such a force would be in danger
if it passed the winter in a foreign land, and that it would not be
advisable for himself to be absent from Gaul any longer. He
contented himself with his present achievements for fear that in
striving after greater ones he should be deprived of even these. And
it seemed that he was right in this, as was proved in the event.

It is worth noting that in all the accounts of the conflicts given there
is nowhere any mention of the hackneyed but fallacious belief that the
Britons attached scythe-blades to the axles of their chariots – a Persian
practice. This silence is given additional backing by both archaeology

and the very tactics employed by the Britons in using chariots for warfare (cf. *Gallic War* IV, 33 and V, 16). The idea of British scythed chariots seems in fact to originate with Pomponius Mela (first century AD):

28. *De Chorographia* III, 6, 52

The Britons engage in combat not only on horseback and on foot, but also with two-horse chariots and vehicles equipped in the Gallic fashion. Those they use with scythed axles they call *covinni*.[1]

While the invasion of 55 had been motivated largely by political and military considerations, the presence of numerous private vessels as part of the 54 BC flotilla (Caesar, *Gallic War* V, 8) suggests that on this occasion the prospect of loot had exerted its influence. This is further borne out by a number of letters written that year by Cicero to his friend Trebatius and brother Quintus, who accompanied the venture, and to other friends concerning events in Britain. In this he provides an interesting second-party picture of how the expedition was being regarded by one individual near the centre of Roman public life:

29. Cicero, *Ad Familiares* (*Letters to his Friends*) VII, 6, 2 = S.B.[2] 27, 2 (to Trebatius, May 54)

Take care you aren't cheated by the charioteers in Britain.

30. Cicero, *Ad Familiares* (*Letters to his Friends*) VII, 7, 1 = S.B. 28, 1 (to Trebatius, June 54)

I hear there's no gold or silver in Britain. If this is so, I advise you to get a war-chariot and hasten back to us as soon as possible.

31. Cicero, *Ad Atticum* (*Letters to Atticus*) IV, 16, 7 = S.B. 89, 7 (early July 54)

The outcome of the war in Britain is eagerly awaited; for it is well known that the approaches to the island are set round with walls of wondrous mass. It has also become clear that there isn't an ounce of silver in the island, nor any prospect of booty except slaves. I don't suppose you're expecting any of them to be accomplished in literature or music!

32. Cicero, *Ad Atticum* (*Letters to Atticus*) IV, 15, 10 = S.B. 90, 10 (late July 54)

A letter from my brother Quintus leads me to believe he is now in Britain. I am waiting in suspense to learn what he is doing.

33. Cicero, *Ad Fratrem* (*Letters to his Brother*) III, 1, 10 (late August 54)

On affairs in Britain I see from your letter there is nothing there for us to fear or rejoice at.

34. Cicero, *Ad Atticum* (*Letters to Atticus*) IV, 18, 5 = S.B. 92, 5 (late October–early November 54)

On the 24th of October I received letters from my brother Quintus and from Caesar which were sent from the nearest point on the shores of Britain on September 25th. The campaign there is complete; hostages have been received; there is no booty; tribute has, however, been imposed and they are bringing back the army from Britain.[3]

In the great Gallic uprising that eventually followed Caesar's return from the second invasion of Britain Commius the Atrebate, who had given the Romans signal service in both expeditions, took sides with his fellow countrymen, and when eventually defeated made good his escape to Britain. There he ostensibly founded a dynasty among the British Atrebates which was to last until the time of Claudius:

35. Caesar, *Gallic War* VII, 75, 76, 79; VIII, 6, 7, 10, 21, 23, 47, 48

36. Frontinus (1st C. AD), *Stratagems* II, 13, 11

When Commius the Atrebate was defeated by Caesar and was fleeing from Gaul to Britain, he chanced to arrive at Ocean (English Channel) when the wind was favourable but the tide on the ebb. Though his ships were stuck on the exposed shore, he nevertheless ordered the sails to be spread. When in his pursuit of Commius Caesar saw them from a distance billowing and swelling in the breeze, he thought that Commius was making a successful getaway and turned back.

NOTES

1 A similar instance of confusion attributes to Caesar the use of elephants in order to startle the natives – a tactic employed in reality by the Emperor Claudius:

Polyaenus (2nd C. AD), *Strategemata* (*Stratagems*) VIII, 23, 5

> Caesar attempted to cross a large river in Britain, but Cassivellaunus, the king of the Britons, prevented him with many horsemen and chariots. Caesar had in his train a very large elephant, a creature never before seen by the Britons. This he equipped with iron plates and placed a large tower on it, stationing in this archers and slingers. He then ordered them to enter the river. The Britons were struck with terror at the sight of a beast that was enormous and that they had never seen before.

2 Shackleton Bailey.
3 Cf. Plutarch, *Caesar* 23.3 §455.

IV Caesar to Claudius

With the outbreak of civil war in 49 BC, followed by further conflicts after the death of Caesar in 44 BC, Britain disappears from Roman records for nearly two decades. That contact on a commercial level continued we cannot doubt, but while diplomatic links may have faded for a time, there were still tribes who had a vested interest in maintaining ties, if only as a means of counteracting the expansionist tendencies of their neighbours. Such contacts do indeed begin to appear again once Augustus was in power:

37. Strabo (1st C. BC–1st C. AD) IV, 5, 3

At present, however, some of the chieftains there, having gained the friendship of Caesar Augustus through embassies and paying court to him, have set up votive offerings on the Capitolium and have almost made the whole island Roman property. In addition they submit so readily to heavy duties both on the exports from there to Gaul and on the imports from Gaul – these consist of ivory chains, necklaces, amber, glassware, and other such trinkets – that there is no need to garrison the island. For at the very least one legion and some cavalry would be needed to exact tribute from them, and the expense of the army would equal the money brought in. Indeed the duties would have to be reduced if tribute were imposed and at the same time there are dangers to be faced if force is applied.

What is significant, however, is that while Rome recognised that such links had certain financial advantages, it did not see any need for a costly takeover of the island, so long as Britain posed no threat to the empire:

38. Strabo II, 5, 8

As for governmental purposes there would be nothing to gain from knowledge of such places (i.e. north of Britain) or their inhabitants, especially if they live on islands that can neither injure nor benefit us because of their isolation. For though the Romans could have held Britain, they rejected the idea, seeing there was nothing to fear from the Britons, since they are not powerful enough to cross over and attack us, nor was there much advantage to be gained if the Romans were to occupy it. For it seems that at the moment more revenue is gained from the customs duties than tribute could bring in, if one deducts the expense of the forces needed to garrison the place and levy the tribute.

Despite Strabo's optimistic description of Roman influence in Britain, there does not appear to have been a total absence of friction, and evidence, late it is true, suggests the need at times for Augustus to rattle the Roman sabre to maintain the status quo:

39. Dio Cassius (2nd–3rd C. AD) XLIX, 38, 2 (34 BC)

Augustus had set out to lead an expedition into Britain in emulation of his father (Julius Caesar – by adoption), and had already advanced into Gaul after the winter which saw the consulships of Antony for the second time and of Lucius Libo, when some newly conquered tribes together with the Dalmatians rose in revolt.

40. Ibid. LIII, 22, 5 (27 BC)

He also set out with the intention of leading an expedition into Britain, but on his arrival in Gaul he stayed there. For it seemed likely that the Britons would come to terms with him, and affairs in Gaul were still unsettled since the civil wars had broken out immediately after their subjugation.

41. Ibid. LIII, 25, 2 (26 BC)

Augustus was anxious for war against Britain since the people there would not come to terms, but he was prevented by a revolt of the Salassi, and the Cantabrians and Asturians had become hostile.

On a lower level the diplomatic pressure was maintained through the public expectation of an eventual Roman takeover voiced in the poetry of the day:[1]

42. [Tibullus] III, 7 = IV, 1, 147–50 (pre 27 BC. Addressed to Augustus' general Messalla)

Where Ocean with its waves surrounds the world no land will meet you with opposing arms. For you remains the Briton, by Roman force yet undefeated, for you the world's other half beyond the path of sun.

43. Propertius II, 27, 5f. (*c*. 27 BC)

Whether on foot the Parthian we pursue or the Briton with our fleet, blind are the perils of sea and land.

44. Horace, *Odes* III, 5, 1–4 (*c*. 27 BC)

That Jupiter the thunderer reigns in heaven has ever been our creed; Augustus shall be held a god on earth when once the Britons and the grievous Parthians are added to our empire.

45. Idem, *Odes* I, 35, 29f. (*c*. 26 BC)

May you (the goddess Fortune) preserve our Caesar soon to go against the Britons, furthest of earth's peoples.

46. Idem, *Odes* I, 21, 13–16 (pre 23 BC)[2]

Moved by your prayer he (Apollo) shall take from our people and their leader Caesar tear-inspiring war and plague and wretched famine and inflict them on the Persians and the Britons.

Until such time Rome clearly preferred to acquiesce in minor shifts of power in Britain so long as these did not radically alter the balance of power there. A passing reference in Horace, *Odes* IV, 14, 47–8 (*c*. 15 BC) may indicate a transitory renewal of Roman interest:[3]

47. Idem, *Odes* IV, 14, 47–8

To you monster-filled Ocean that roars around Britain pays heed.

For the most part, however, the door was open to receive friendly kings expelled from their lands by what were often little more than palace coups:

48. Augustus (early 1st C. AD), *Res Gestae* (*Achievements*) 32

The following kings sought refuge with me as suppliants: Tiridates of Parthia (29 BC), and later Phrates, son of King Phrates (*c.* 25 BC), Artavasdes of Media (after Actium), Artaxares of Adiabene, Dubnobellaunus and Tincommius from Britain, Maelo of the Sugambri . . .

Within Britain itself literary evidence for such power struggles within and between tribes is altogether lacking, but coinage may suggest something of events and propaganda struggles.[4] Thus coins of the Catuvellaunian king Tasciovanus and his successor Cunobelinus bearing the mint-mark of Camulodunum, capital of the Trinovantes, indicate a resumption of expansion that Caesar's intervention and restoration of Mandubracius had temporarily halted:

49. Gold coin of Tasciovanus (Van Arsdell 1684–1)

50. Gold coin of Cunobelinus (Van Arsdell 1931)

Similar expansion southwards into the northern sectors of Atrebate territory evidently took place under Epaticcus, apparently a brother of Cunobelinus:

51. Gold coin of Epaticcus (Van Arsdell 575–1)

Was it to counter such pressure that coins of Eppillus, who had supplanted Tincommius, and his own successor Verica, bear the title REX, perhaps as a token of Roman recognition, together with the vine-leaf motif in Verica's case?

52. Gold coins of Verica (Van Arsdell 500–1, 520–1)

Despite the changes, however, the early years of Tiberius' reign show relations in general between Rome and Britain to have been sufficiently good to allow the return of survivors from a shipwreck on the British coast in AD 16:

53. Tacitus (1st–2nd C. AD), *Annals* II, 24

Some men had been carried to Britain and were returned by its chieftains.

While the period of Tiberius' reign (AD 14–37) saw relations between Rome and Britain frozen into terms of mutual non-interference, the accession of Gaius Caligula brought a radical, if transitory, renewal of interest. The expulsion from the island of Adminius and his 'surrender' to Gaius, engaged at the time in the farce of a German expedition, was to lead to the infamous seashell incident that was the only apparent achievement of the Emperor's proposed British campaign of AD 40. What events can be held to account for our sources' narrative of the incident we cannot tell. Was it simply a manifestation of imperial insanity, or a shrewd attempt to humiliate troops who refused to embark for action in a land still regarded with awe, suspicion and fear?

54. Suetonius (2nd C. AD), *Caligula* 44, 46

44 On reaching the camp Caligula dismissed in disgrace the legates
who were late in assembling auxiliary units from various places so
as to demonstrate that he was a rigorous and strict leader. In his
review of the troops he deprived many of the chief centurions of
their rank, men who were by now getting on in years and in some
cases had just a few days to go before they were due for discharge.
This he did on the pretext of their age and infirmity. The rest he
railed at for their greed, and reduced their retirement bonus to
6,000 sesterces.[5] All that he accomplished was to receive the
surrender of Adminius, a son of Cunobelinus, King of the Britons,
who had been banished by his father and had gone over to the
Romans with a few followers. Yet, as if the whole island had been
handed over, he sent a pompous letter to Rome, and ordered the
couriers to drive their vehicles right into the Forum and up to the
Senate House, and not to hand it over to the consuls except in
the Temple of Mars and before a full meeting of the Senate.

46 Finally, as if to bring the campaign to a close, he drew up his
battleline on the shore of Ocean and moved his ballistas and
other artillery into position. Then, with no one knowing or able
to guess what he was about, he suddenly ordered them to gather
shells and fill their helmets and the folds of their tunics with them,
calling them spoils from Ocean owed to the Capitol and Palatine.
As a monument to his victory he erected a very high tower from
which fires were to shine at night to guide the passage of
ships, just like the Pharos (at Alexandria). He also announced
to the soldiers a bonus of 100 denarii per man, as if he had shown
unprecedented generosity, and said 'Go on your way happy; go on
your way rich.'

55. Dio Cassius (2nd–3rd C. AD) LIX, 25, 1–3

On his arrival at Ocean, as if he were going to conduct a campaign
in Britain, he drew up all his soldiers on the shore. Then he
embarked on a trireme, and after putting out a little from the land,
sailed back again. After this he took his seat on a high platform,
gave the soldiers a signal as if for battle, and urged them on by
means of the trumpeters. Then suddenly he ordered them to gather
seashells, and having got these spoils – for it was clear he needed
booty for his triumphal procession – he became very excited, as
though he had enslaved Ocean itself, and gave his soldiers many

presents. The shells he carried off to Rome in order to exhibit his booty there as well.

NOTES

1 See further Stevens (1).
2 Dated by many to 28 BC.
3 Cf. Salway (1), p. 51f.
4 See, however, Van Arsdell p. 319ff.
5 This constituted only half the amount fixed by Augustus.

V The Claudian Invasion

The official version inscribed on the arch of Claudius dedicated in Rome AD 51:

56. *Britannia* 22 (1991) p. 12 (restored)

To Tiberius Clau[dius Cae]sar Augu[stus Germani]cus, [son of Drusus], Pontifex [Maximus] (High Priest), in the 11th year [of his holding Tribunician Pow]er (AD 51), 5 times Consul, [22 times saluted] Imperator, [Censor, Father of his Co]untry, the Senate and Ro[man] Pe[ople] (dedicate this arch) because [he received the surrender of] 11 British kings, [defeated without] any reverse, and was the first [to bring] b[arbarian] tribes [beyond Ocean under Roman] sway.

Behind this ostensibly bald statement of triumph, however, we find in the period before the invasion itself a combination of both worsening relations between Britain and Rome and a personal need on the part of Claudius to prove himself worthy of serious consideration as emperor:

57. Suetonius (2nd C. AD), *Claudius* 17

He undertook but a single campaign, and a minor one at that. The Senate voted him the triumphal ornaments for it, but he considered the honour beneath his dignity as emperor and wanted the glory of a proper triumph. So, as the best place for gaining this he chose Britain, which no one had attempted to invade since the deified Julius, and which was in uproar at the time as a result of the Roman refusal to return certain fugitives.

58. Dio Cassius (2nd–3rd C. AD) LX, 19, 1

At the same time as these events were happening in the City Aulus
Plautius, a senator of great distinction, led a campaign to Britain,
since a certain Berikos (Verica), who had been driven out of the
island as a result of an uprising, had persuaded Claudius to send a
force there.

Nor was the expedition itself without incident, and at one stage the
prospect of a refusal on the part of the troops may have raised momentarily the spectre of another Caligulan fiasco. In the event the not
inconsiderable delay was to prove a positive advantage in the initial
stages of conquest:

59. Dio Cassius LX, 19–22

19 So it was that Plautius undertook the expedition, though he had
difficulty in getting his army to leave Gaul, since the troops were
indignant at the prospect of campaigning outside the known world,
and would not obey him until Narcissus, who had been sent by
Claudius, mounted Plautius' tribunal and tried to harangue them.
Thereupon they became even more angry and refused to allow
him to speak at all, but suddenly all in unison they raised the cry
'Io Saturnalia' – at the festival of Saturn the slaves take over the
role of their masters and engage in festivities – and at once they
willingly followed Plautius.[1] These events did, however, delay the
departure. They made the crossing in three divisions so as not to
be hampered in landing, as a single force might be. On their way
across, however, they were at first disheartened by being driven
back in their course. Subsequently, though, they recovered their
spirits when a bolt of lightning shot from east to west – the direction they were sailing. On putting in to the island they met with
no resistance, since the Britons, from what they had learned, had
not expected them to come, and had not assembled beforehand.
Even when they did assemble they did not engage the Romans,
but took refuge in the marshes and woods hoping to wear them
out by these tactics, so that they would sail back empty-handed, as
had happened in Julius Caesar's day.
20 Plautius, therefore, had a good deal of trouble in searching them
out, and when he did eventually locate them, he defeated first
Caratacus and then Togodumnus, the sons of Cunobelinus, who
was now dead. The Britons were not in fact independent, but ruled
over by various kings. With these two put to flight Plautius secured

the surrender on terms of part of the Bodunni (Dobunni) tribe who were subject to the Catuvellauni. Leaving a garrison there he advanced further and came to a river. The barbarians thought the Romans would not be able to cross this without a bridge, and as a result had pitched camp in a rather careless fashion on the opposite bank. Plautius, however, sent across some Celts who were practised in swimming with ease fully armed across even the fastest of rivers. These fell unexpectedly on the enemy, but rather than attacking the men they maimed the horses that drew their chariots instead. In the resultant confusion not even the mounted warriors could get away unscathed. Plautius then sent across Flavius Vespasian, who subsequently became Emperor, and his brother Sabinus, who was serving under him. They too managed to get across the river and killed some of the enemy, since they were not expecting them. Those Britons who survived did not, however, take to flight, but rather joined battle with them again the following day. The struggle was indecisive until Gnaeus Hosidius Geta, after narrowly escaping capture, defeated the enemy so resoundingly that he was awarded triumphal ornaments[2] even though he had not yet held the consulship. From there the Britons withdrew to the Thames, at a point where it flows into the sea and at high tide forms a lake. This they crossed with ease since they knew precisely where the ground was firm and the way passable. The Romans, however, in pursuing them, got into difficulties here. Once again the Celts swam across, while others crossed by a bridge a little way upstream, and they engaged the enemy from several sides at once, cutting many of them down. However, in pursuing the survivors without due precaution they got into marshes from which it was difficult to find a way out and lost a number of men.

21 On account of this and the fact that the death of Togodumnus, far from causing the Britons to give in, had united them all the more to avenge him, Plautius became afraid and advanced no further. Instead, he hung on to what was already in his possession and sent for Claudius. He had in fact been instructed to do this in the event of any strong opposition, and a good deal of equipment, including elephants, had already been assembled for this campaign. When the report reached Claudius, he handed over affairs at home to his colleague Lucius Vitellius (father of the future emperor), whom he had obliged to remain consul like himself for the full half year, and went off on campaign. After sailing downriver to Ostia he was then conveyed along the coast to Massilia. From there he travelled partly

overland and partly along the rivers and on his arrival at Ocean, he crossed over to Britain and joined the army, which was waiting for him at the Thames.[3] Taking over command, he crossed the river and engaging the natives who had gathered at his approach, defeated them, and took Camulodunum (Colchester), the capital of Cunobelinus. As a result of this he won over numerous tribes, some on terms of surrender, others by force, and was saluted Imperator on several occasions – contrary to precedent; for no one may receive this title more than once for the same war. In addition he disarmed the Britons and handed them over to Plautius, whom he authorised to subjugate the remaining areas.[4] Claudius himself hastened back to Rome, sending the news of his victory on ahead by means of his sons-in-law, Magnus and Silanus.

22 When the Senate learned of these achievements, it awarded Claudius the title Britannicus and gave him permission to celebrate a triumph. They also voted to hold an annual festival and to erect two triumphal arches, one in Rome, the other in Gaul, from where he had put to sea when he crossed to Britain. They also bestowed on his son the same title, with the result that Britannicus came in a way to be the boy's actual name, and they granted Messalina the privilege that Livia had had of sitting in the front seat at the theatre and the use of the carriage.[5]

On one point of the expedition Dio Cassius' account differs from that of Suetonius – the actual degree of Claudius' involvement in military operations. On this too depends the decision whether Plautius' sending for Claudius really was due to his encountering stiff resistance, or simply a device to allow the Emperor a triumphal entry into the enemy capital:

60. Suetonius (2nd C. AD), *Claudius* 17

From there (Boulogne) he crossed to Britain. In the space of a very few days he received the surrender of part of the island without a single battle or any bloodshed, returned to Rome within six months of setting out, and celebrated his triumph with the greatest of pomp. To witness it he allowed not only provincial governors to come to Rome, but even some exiles, and among the spoils of victory he fixed a naval crown next to the civic crown on the pediment of the Palatine Palace as a sign that he had crossed and, as it were, conquered Ocean. His wife Messalina followed Claudius' triumphal chariot in a carriage; then those who had won triumphal ornaments in the same campaign followed on foot wearing purple-bordered togas, with the exception of Marcus Crassus Frugi who rode a horse decorated with *phalerae* (trappings) and wore a tunic embroidered with palm branches, since this was the second time he had won the honour.

At all events the duration of Claudius' stay in Britain was remarkably short, and in striking contrast to the lavishness of his triumphal celebrations:

61. Dio Cassius (2nd–3rd C. AD) LX, 23, AD 44

Thus were parts of Britain captured at that time. Later, when Gaius Crispus and Titus Statilius were consuls, the former for the second time, Claudius came to Rome after an absence of six months, of which he had spent only sixteen days in Britain, and celebrated his triumph. In this he did everything according to precedent, including going up the steps of the Capitol on his knees with his sons-in-law supporting him on either side. To the senators who had gone on campaign with him he awarded triumphal ornaments, and this not only to those who had held consular office . . . (lacuna) . . . something he used to do with great lavishness and on the slightest pretext . . . Having attended to these affairs he held his victory celebration, assuming a kind of consular authority for it. It took place in two theatres at the same time. On many occasions Claudius himself left the spectacle and others took charge of it in his stead. He announced as many horse races as could be fitted into a day, but not more than ten in fact took place, for in between the races there was bear-baiting, athletic contests, and boys brought from Asia danced the Pyrrhic war-dance. Another festival, this too in honour of the victory, was given by the stage artists with the permission of the Senate. This was done on account of events in Britain, and so that other tribes might come to terms more easily, it was enacted that all the treaties made with tribes by Claudius or his lieutenants should be as binding as if made by the Senate and People.

Nor indeed was Claudius grudging in his gratitude to the true architect of his victory:

62. Suetonius (2nd C. AD), *Claudius* 24

Claudius also decreed an ovation[6] for Aulus Plautius, went out to meet him when Plautius entered the city, and walked on his left (a mark of respect) as he went to the Capitol and came away from it.

While public celebrations might serve as a vehicle to propagandise Claudius' victory in Rome, more widespread circulation of the news was assured by the issue of a number of coins celebrating the conquest, the first to bear any reference to Britain:

63. Denarius from the mint of Rome, AD 49–50 (*RIC*[7] I p. 123, no. 45)

Obverse
Ti(berius) Claud(ius) Caesar Aug(ustus)
P(ontifex) M(aximus) (High Priest) Tr(ibunicia)
P(otestas) (Tribunician Power) VIIII (times)
Imp(erator) XVI (times)

Reverse
De Britann(is) (From Britain)

64. Silver didrachm of Caesarea, *c.* AD 46 (*RIC* I p. 131, no. 122)

Obverse
Ti(berius) Claud(ius) Caesar Aug(ustus) Germ(anicus)
P(ontifex) M(aximus) (High Priest)
Tr(ibunicia) P(otestas) (Tribunician Power)

Reverse
De Britannis (From Britain)

NOTES

1 Suetonius, *Galba* 7 records another delay in the expedition caused by the illness of Galba: 'Galba was in great favour with Claudius, who took him into his circle of friends and regarded him with such great esteem that when Galba suddenly contracted some minor ailment, the date of the British expedition was postponed.'

2 For the significance of these see Eichholz.

3 On the timing of Claudius' visit to Britain see Barrett (2).

4 Cf. Seneca, *Apocolocyntosis* 12, 3: 'Claudius commanded the Britons beyond the seas we know of, and the Brigantes with their blue shields, to bow their necks to the chains of Rome.'

5 The use of the *carpentum*, a two-wheeled covered carriage, inside Rome was a mark of special distinction and usually reserved for festal occasions.

6 A lesser honour than a triumph, which by this time was reserved solely for the emperor. Another participant in the invasion was Gaius Gavius Silvanus (From Taurini, *Inscriptiones Latinae Selectae* 2701):

> To Gaius Gavius Stel(?) Silvanus, son of Lucius, Leading Centurion of the VIII legion Augusta, Tribune of the 2nd cohort of the Watch, Tribune of the 13th Urban cohort, Tribune of the 12th Praetorian cohort, decorated with the *torquibus armillis phaleris* and golden crown by the deified Claudius in the British war, patron of this colony.

7 *Roman Imperial Coinage.*

VI Expansion of the Province and Rebellion

From their initial concentration in Colchester the legions now fanned out to produce the wider subjugation Claudius had envisaged (Dio LX, 21, §59). While the XX Valeria remained to hold what had already been gained, the IX Hispana advanced northwards, the XIV Gemina north-west over the Midlands, and the II Augusta, the best documented of them all since its Legate was the future Emperor Vespasian, into the west country:

65. Suetonius (2nd C. AD), *Vespasian* 4

In the reign of Claudius Vespasian was sent to Germany as a legionary Legate through the influence of Narcissus. From there he was transferred to Britain and fought the enemy on thirty occasions. He reduced to submission two powerful tribes, more than 20 towns, and the Island of Vectis (Wight) which is very close to Britain, this partly under the command of Aulus Plautius, the Consular Governor, and partly under the command of Claudius himself. For this he received triumphal insignia and shortly afterwards two priesthoods in addition to the consulship, which he held for the last two months of the year (AD 51).

For other evidence of early troop movements we are largely dependent on inscriptions, often funerary, which may be approximately dated:

66. The XX Valeria at Colchester before AD 60 (*RIB*[1] I 200)

Marcus Favonius Facilis, son of Marcus, of the Pollian voting-tribe, Centurion of the XX Legion, lies here. Verecundus and Novicius, his freedmen, set this up.[2]

67. An auxiliaryman ends his days at Colchester. His unit left the city AD 48–9 (*RIB* I 201)

Longinus, son of Sdapezematygus, *duplicarius* (soldier on double pay) of the 1st cavalry squadron of Thracians from the district of Sardica (Sofia) aged 40 with 15 years' service lies here. His heirs had this put up under his will.

68. The IX Hispana at Lincoln (*RIB* I 255)

To Gaius Saufeius, son of Gaius, of the Fabian voting-tribe, from Heraclea, soldier of the IX Legion, aged 40 with 22 years' service. He lies here.

69. The XIV Gemina at Wroxeter (*RIB* I 294)

Marcus Petronius, son of Lucius, of the Menenian voting-tribe from Vicetia, aged 38, a soldier of the XIV Legion Gemina, with 18 years' service and a standard-bearer, lies here.

The Roman victories in the south-east did not, however, mean that all British resistance was broken. Rather, with expansion of the province came a multiplication of the problems that faced the new governor, Ostorius Scapula, when he assumed command in AD 47: the opportunity for native unrest in the period between governors, the need to guarantee the security of lines of communication in a situation where tribes that had voluntarily surrendered and entered into treaty relations as client kingdoms were permitted to retain their arms, the increasing problem of keeping the Welsh and Brigantian frontiers quiet simultaneously and the efforts of Caratacus, still at liberty, to create as much trouble as possible:

70. Tacitus (1st–2nd C. AD), *Annals* XII, 31–9

31 It was a troubled state of affairs that the Governor, Publius Ostorius, found in Britain, since the enemy had poured into allied territory with a violence that was all the greater because they thought a new commander would not take the field against them with an army that was unfamiliar to him and with winter already begun. Ostorius, on the other hand, aware that from first results spring fear or confidence, hurried forward his light cohorts, cut down those who resisted, and pursued those put to flight. Then,

to prevent them from regrouping and to avoid an uneasy and untrustworthy peace giving no rest to either commander or army, he prepared to disarm suspect tribes and to hold in check the whole area between the rivers Trisantona (Trent)[3] and Sabrina (Severn). The first to rebel against this measure were the Iceni, a powerful nation and not yet broken in battle, since they had willingly agreed to an alliance with us.[4] At their instigation the tribes round about chose as their field of battle a site enclosed by an earth rampart and with a narrow entrance to prevent the entry of cavalry. This defensive position the Roman commander prepared to break through, even though he was leading an auxiliary force unsupported by the strength of the legions. After positioning his cohorts he equipped even the cavalry squadrons for infantry action. Then at the given signal they broke through the rampart and threw the enemy into confusion, hampered as they were by their own defences. The Britons for their part, aware of having broken the peace and with their escape routes blocked, performed many remarkable bold deeds. In that battle the Legate's son, Marcus Ostorius, earned the distinction of saving a citizen's life.

32 However, the defeat of the Iceni quietened those who were hesitating between peace and war, and the army was led against the Decangi (Deceangli). Their territory was devastated, and booty seized far and wide, while the enemy dared not risk an open engagement and, if they attempted to harass the Roman column by stealth, their treachery was punished. At this point the army was not far from the sea which looks across to Ireland, but trouble among the Brigantes caused the Roman commander to turn back, resolved as he was not to undertake new ventures unless earlier gains were fully secured. The Brigantes for their part settled down again once those who had taken up arms were killed and the rest pardoned. However, neither harsh treatment nor mercy made any difference to the tribe of the Silures. Instead, they carried on the war, and had to be held in check by a legionary fortress. To achieve this end more easily a colony with a strong corps of veterans was established on captured land at Camulodunum (Colchester), as a bulwark against revolt and to familiarise the (native) allies with their legal duties.[5]

33 Then an advance was made against the Silures. Their innate ferocity was heightened by the trust they placed in Caratacus, whose many engagements, some partially successful, others completely so, had raised his reputation to the point that he was without rival among British leaders. Then, however, though inferior in military strength,

his superiority in cunning and the deceptive difficulty of the terrain allowed him to transfer the theatre of war to the Ordovices, and with his ranks swollen by those who feared the Roman peace, he attempted a final stand. He chose a site for the battle where the approaches, exits, and everything else were to our disadvantage and to his advantage. On one side were steep hills; where the gradient was easier he piled up rocks into a kind of rampart; in front flowed a river with a precarious crossing, and bands of warriors were stationed along the defences.

34 Besides this the tribal chiefs went round encouraging the men and raising their spirits by reducing their fears, kindling their hopes, and variously inciting them to battle. As for Caratacus, he hastened to one position after another, declaring that day, that battle would be the beginning of their restored liberty or perpetual enslavement. He invoked the names of their ancestors who had repulsed the dictator Caesar: by their valour they were free from Roman domination and taxes, and preserved the bodies of their wives and children from defilement. These and other exhortations of his the crowds applauded, and each man swore by the gods of his tribe that he would give way to neither weapons nor wounds.

35 This enthusiasm astounded the Roman general, daunted as he already was by the obstacle of the river, the addition of the rampart, the overhanging ridges, and the fact that everything was productive of alarm and bristling with defenders. The troops on the other hand clamoured for battle, insisting that against courage nothing was impregnable, while the Prefects and Tribunes, expressing similar views, further intensified the army's impatience. Then, having reconnoitred those points that could and could not be breached, Ostorius crossed the river without difficulty at the head of his eager troops. When the rampart was reached, our side sustained the greater proportion of wounded and killed so long as the conflict was confined to the exchange of missiles, but once a formation of locked shields had been made and the crude and chaotic pile of stones demolished, the fighting was on equal terms at close quarters, and the natives withdrew to the hilltops. Yet here too our light and heavy-armed troops rushed upon them, the former attacking them with javelins, the latter in close formation. The ranks of the Britons on the other hand, without the protection of either breastplates or helmets, were thrown into disorder, and if they stood their ground against the auxiliary troops, they were laid low by the swords and javelins of the legionaries, while if they turned to face these, they were cut down by the broadswords and

spears of the auxiliaries. It was a glorious victory: Caratacus' wife and daughter were captured and his brothers surrendered.

36 Caratacus himself sought the protection of Cartimandua, Queen of the Brigantes, but since generally there is no security in misfortune, he was arrested[6] and handed over to the victorious Romans in the ninth year after the war in Britain had begun (AD 51). His fame had reached beyond the islands and had spread through the adjoining provinces; in Italy too it was on people's lips, and folk longed to see who it was had defied our power for so many years. Even in Rome the name of Caratacus was well known, and in seeking to enlarge his own reputation Caesar conferred glory on the conquered man. The people were summoned as if to a great spectacle: the Praetorian Cohorts were drawn up under arms on the parade ground in front of their camp. Then as the king's vassals filed past, the ornamental bosses, torques, and spoils won in his foreign wars were paraded. Next his brothers, wife and daughter were displayed, and finally Caratacus himself. The others out of fear indulged in undignified pleading, but from Caratacus there was no downcast look, no appeal for mercy. When he stood before the tribunal, this is how he spoke:[7]

37 'If I had been as moderate in success as my noble birth and rank are great, I should have entered this city as a friend rather than as a captive, nor would you have scorned to admit to a peaceful alliance one sprung from famous ancestors and the ruler of many peoples. My present lot is as much a source of glory to you as it is degrading to myself. I had horses, men, arms, wealth; what wonder then if I regret their loss. If you wish to rule the world, does it follow that everyone welcomes servitude? If I were being dragged before you as one who had surrendered at the outset, neither my own downfall nor your glory would have become famous: oblivion would have been the consequence of my punishment. If on the other hand you spare my life, I shall always be a memorial to your clemency.' In response to this Caesar pardoned Caratacus and his wife and brothers. Released from their chains they also gave to Agrippina, conspicuously seated as she was on another dais nearby, the same homage in terms of praise and thanks as they did the Emperor. That a woman should sit in authority before the Roman standards was clearly a novel event and one without precedent in ancient customs, but Agrippina herself was asserting her partnership in an empire won by her ancestors.

38 The Senate met later and there were many high-flown speeches on the capture of Caratacus to the effect that it was no less brilliant

than the displaying before the Roman people of Syphax by Publius Scipio or of Perses by Lucius Paulus or of other kings exhibited in chains by other Romans. Ostorius was voted triumphal insignia, but his fortunes, which had hitherto been marked by success, soon became less certain. Either the removal of Caratacus from the scene led to a reduction in the vigour of our military operations as though the war were over, or the enemy's feeling of pity for so great a king kindled within them greater passion for revenge. A Camp-Prefect and legionary cohorts left behind to construct forts in Siluran territory were surrounded, and if assistance had not reached the beleaguered troops as a result of reports from nearby positions, they would have been massacred. As it was the Prefect, eight centurions and the best of the rank and file were killed. Shortly afterwards a Roman foraging party was overwhelmed together with the cavalry squadrons sent to their assistance.

39 Ostorius then brought up his light-armed cohorts, but even so he did not check the reverse until the legions intervened. Their strength made the fight equal, and then gave our side the advantage, but since the day was drawing to a close, the enemy escaped with few losses. After this there were frequent clashes, more often than not in the form of skirmishes in woods and marshes, occasioned by individual chance or gallantry, some by accident, others by design, some out of hatred, others for plunder, sometimes under orders, at other times without the knowledge of commanders. The Silures were a particularly intractable problem, infuriated as they were by a reported speech of the Roman commander that the Siluran tribe should be totally eradicated, just as the Sugambri had once been exterminated, or transported to the provinces of Gaul. So it was that two auxiliary cohorts were cut off through their Prefects' greed as they engaged in pillaging without sufficient precautions, and by gifts of booty and captives the Silures began to entice other tribes also to rebellion. At this point (AD 52) Ostorius died, worn out by the unremitting burden of his responsibilities. The enemy for their part were delighted that a general of undoubted merit had been disposed of by the war as a whole, if not by defeat in battle.

From the Roman point of view the capture of Caratacus had been a considerable stroke of luck, though in fact it was to create as many problems as it solved. Cartimandua's role in the affair suggests not only that she had a treaty of friendship with the Romans, but also that her hold on the widespread Brigantes was less than strong – hence the problems encountered by Ostorius Scapula (*Annals* XII, 32) – and that her motive for removing Caratacus was not without a personal aspect. Certainly her actions must have enraged those of the tribe who still harboured anti-Roman sentiments – sentiments that Caratacus had probably hoped to galvanise into action. It is doubtless this that underlies the coming internal power struggle:

71. Tacitus, *Annals* XII, 40

On receiving the news of the Legate's death Caesar appointed Aulus Didius in his place to avoid leaving the province without a governor. Despite a rapid crossing he found the situation had deteriorated; for in the meantime the legion under the command of Manlius Valens had suffered a reverse. Reports of the affair were exaggerated both among the enemy, so as to frighten the general on his arrival, and by Didius too when he heard them, so that his fame might be the greater if he settled matters, and his excuse the more justifiable if they persisted. Once again this defeat had been caused by the Silures, and they roamed the countryside far and wide until driven back by the approach of Didius. However, since the capture of Caratacus the most distinguished Briton in terms of military skill was Venutius from the tribe of the Brigantes, as mentioned above.[8] He had long been loyal and under Roman protection while he remained married to Queen Cartimandua, but when presently there came a divorce followed immediately by war, he had engaged in hostilities against us as well. At first, however, they merely fought among themselves, and by cunning stratagems Cartimandua waylaid Venutius' brother and other relatives.[9] Incensed at this and stung with shame at the prospect of being subject to a woman's rule, the enemy invaded her kingdom with a powerful and chosen band of armed men. We had foreseen this and cohorts sent to her assistance fought a sharp engagement which, after a shaky beginning, ended up more in our favour. An engagement with a similar outcome was fought by the legion commanded by Caesius Nasica; for Didius, burdened with age and with a superabundance of honours, was content to act through his subordinates and to keep the enemy at arm's length.[10] Though these operations were carried out by two governors over a number of years, I have linked them together lest piecemeal treatment cause them to be less easily remembered.

When the propaganda coup of the initial invasion gave way to the unremitting toil of garrisoning what had been gained and the costly process of expanding frontiers – for its size indeed Britain's garrison was far above normal in terms of numbers – doubts must quickly have been raised as to the economic wisdom of opening up what had seemed like a new world. At some stage in his reign Claudius' successor Nero contemplated abandoning the province. Whether the question arose before or after the Boudiccan rebellion we cannot tell:

72. Suetonius (2nd C. AD), *Nero* 18

He was never moved by any desire or hope of increasing the empire. He even considered withdrawing from Britain, and only refrained from doing so out of deference – so that he should not appear to be belittling his father's glory.[11]

Within the province itself the process of expansion was not without its own internal difficulties. The practice of granting client status to those tribes that had voluntarily surrendered to Rome had no doubt been of great advantage in the initial thrust into Britain. With time, however, the danger of leaving pockets of potential trouble behind Roman lines had become only too clear – hence Scapula's attempt to disarm the Iceni (Tacitus, *Annals* XII, 31, §70). Unfortunately for Roman and native alike the Roman tendency to overrule treaty rights at will, combined with an overbearing confidence in a military machine that could be blind to warning signals, was to serve as the spark to ignite much of the eastern part of the province. For many Britons the liberation from native oppression that early surrender to Rome offered had quickly become ruinous and heavy-handed exploitation from which the only escape lay in rebellion.

73. Tacitus (1st–2nd C. AD), *Annals* XIV, 29–37

29 In the consulship of Caesennius Paetus and Petronius Turpilianus a severe reverse was suffered in Britain. There, as I have mentioned, the Governor Aulus Didius had merely held on to what was already gained, while his successor, Veranius, after some minor plundering raids against the Silures, was prevented by his death from taking operations any further. During his life he had had a considerable reputation for self-discipline, though in the closing words of his will he displayed his vanity. For in addition to much flattery of Nero he claimed that if he had lived another two years, he would have laid the (whole) province at his feet. At that time, however, Paulinus Suetonius was in charge of Britain. In military science and people's talk, which allows no one to be without envy, he rivalled Corbulo,

and was anxious to equal the glorious recovery of Armenia by subduing enemies of the state. For this reason he prepared to attack the island of Mona (Anglesey) which had a large population and provided shelter for fugitives. Flat-bottomed boats were constructed to contend with the shallow water and shifting bottom, and in this way the infantry made the crossing. Then followed the cavalry, making use of fords or swimming beside their horses where the water was deeper.

30 Along the shore stood the enemy in a close-packed array of armed men interspersed with women dressed like Furies in funereal black, with streaming hair and brandishing torches. Round about were the Druids, their hands raised to heaven, pouring out dire curses. The Roman troops were so struck with dismay at this weird sight that they became rooted to the spot as though their limbs were paralysed and laid themselves open to wounds. Then, bolstered by the encouragements of their commander and urging one another not to be afraid of this mass of fanatical women, they advanced with their standards, cut down all they met, and enveloped them in the flames of their own torches. After this a garrison was imposed on the conquered natives, and the groves devoted to their savage rites cut down; for it was part of their religion to drench their altars with the blood of captives and to consult their gods by means of human entrails. While Suetonius was occupied with this, he received reports of the sudden revolt of the province.

31 Prasutagus, King of the Iceni and famed for his long-lasting prosperity, had made Caesar his heir together with his two daughters, thinking that by such deference his kingdom and family would be kept from harm. However, things turned out differently, so much so that his kingdom was plundered by centurions, and his household by Roman slaves, as if they were the spoils of war. To begin with his wife Boudicca was flogged and her daughters raped. The nobility of the Iceni were deprived of their hereditary estates as if the Romans had received the whole area as a gift, and the King's relatives were treated like slaves. As a result of this outrage and fear of worse to come, since they had been reduced to provincial status, the Iceni took up arms. The Trinovantes too were roused to rebellion along with others who were not yet broken by slavery and who had determined by secret conspiracy to recover their freedom. Their bitterest hatred was directed against the veteran soldiers recently settled in the colony of Camulodunum (Colchester), who were driving the natives from their homes, forcing them off their land, and calling them prisoners and slaves. The veterans' lawless

activities were even encouraged by the troops, who had a similar way of behaving and hoped for the same licence in their turn. In this respect the temple dedicated to the deified Claudius was looked upon as a stronghold of eternal tyranny, and those chosen as priests were pouring out whole fortunes on the pretext of religion. Nor did it seem a difficult task to destroy a colony that was unprotected by any fortifications, something to which our commanders, putting comfort before necessity, had paid too little attention.

32 In the meantime the statue of Victory at Camulodunum (Colchester) fell down for no apparent reason, and with its back turned as if it were fleeing the enemy. In addition, frenzied women prophesied that destruction was at hand, that a clamour of foreign voices had been heard in their Senate House, the theatre had resounded with wailing, and in the Thames estuary an apparition of the colony in ruins had been seen. What is more, the sea took on a bloody appearance, and shapes like human corpses left by the receding tide were interpreted as signs of hope by the Britons and with alarm by the veterans. However, as Suetonius was far away, they appealed to the Procurator, Catus Decianus, for help, but he sent barely 200 men without their full equipment. There was also a small band of regular troops there. Relying on the protection of the temple and hampered by clandestine accomplices in the rebellion who thwarted their plans, the veterans constructed neither defensive ditch nor rampart, nor were the old men and women moved away leaving only the fighting men behind. Heedless of precaution, as though all around was peace and quiet, they found themselves surrounded by the hordes of barbarians, and when all else had been laid waste and burned at the (first) onset, the temple, in which the garrison had concentrated, was taken by storm after a two-day siege. The victorious Britons also intercepted Petilius Cerialis, the Legate of the IX Legion, as he was advancing to the rescue, routed the legion, and slaughtered its infantry contingent. Cerialis escaped with his cavalry to their camp and found shelter behind its defences. Alarmed by this disaster and the hatred of a province his greed had driven into war, the Procurator Catus crossed to Gaul.

33 For his part Suetonius made his way undaunted through the midst of the enemy to London, a town which, while not distinguished by the title of colony, was a very important and busy centre for traders and goods. There he was in two minds whether to choose it as the place for making a stand, but considering the small number of his troops and that Petilius' rashness had been taught quite a severe

lesson, he decided to sacrifice a single town in order to save the whole province. Neither the tears nor lamentations of those who begged his help could deflect him from giving the signal to pull out and allowing into his column (only) those who could keep up with him. Those who stayed behind because their sex meant they were unfit for war, or who were burdened with age or were attached to the place, were overwhelmed by the enemy. The same disaster befell the *municipium* of Verulamium (St Albans) since the natives, with their relish for plunder and wish to avoid hard work, steered clear of the forts and military garrisons and made for places rich in spoil but unprotected by any defending force. It is reckoned that up to 70,000 citizens and provincials fell in the places I have mentioned; for the enemy did not take or sell prisoners, nor was there any other traffic of war. Instead they rushed to slaughter, hang, burn, and crucify, as though (they knew) they were destined to pay the penalty, yet were meanwhile snatching their revenge.

34 By now Suetonius had the XIV Legion together with detachments from the XX and auxiliaries from the nearest stations, in all about 10,000 armed men, and at this point he resolved to abandon delay and fight. He chose a site with a narrow approach and backed by a wood, having made sure that he would only have the enemy in front and that the plain of battle was open and presented no danger of an ambush. The legionaries were stationed in close order, with the light armed troops on the flanks and the cavalry massed on the (outer) wings. The forces of the Britons on the other hand pranced about far and wide in bands of infantry and cavalry, their numbers without precedent and so confident that they brought their wives with them and set them in carts drawn up around the far edge of the battlefield to witness their victory.

35 Boudicca rode in a chariot with her daughters before her, and as she approached each tribe, she declared that the Britons were accustomed to engage in warfare under the leadership of women. On that occasion, however, she was not someone descended from great ancestors avenging her kingdom and her wealth, rather she was an ordinary woman avenging the freedom she had lost, her body worn out with flogging, and the violated chastity of her daughters. Roman lust had gone so far that it left nothing undefiled, not even the bodies of the old or those of young girls. Yet the gods were on the side of just revenge: a legion that had ventured battle had been destroyed; the rest were skulking in their camps or looking for a chance of escape. They would not withstand even the din and clamour of so many warriors, still less their onslaught and blows.

If the Britons considered the number of their men under arms and the reasons they were fighting, they must conquer on that field of battle or die. That was her resolve as a woman; as for the men they could live on and be slaves (if they so wished).

36 Nor was Suetonius silent at this critical moment. Despite the confidence he had in his men's valour, his words of encouragement nevertheless contained an element of appeal: that they disregard the clamour and empty threats of the natives. There were more women visible in their ranks than fighting men, and they, unwarlike and poorly armed, routed on so many occasions, would immediately give way when they recognised the steel and courage of those who had always conquered them. Even when many legions were involved, it was a few men who actually decided battles. It would redound to their honour that their small numbers won the glory of a whole army. Only let them keep their close order, and once they had discharged their javelins, carry on felling and slaughtering the enemy with their shield bosses and swords, without any thought for booty. Once victory was won all else would be theirs. Such was the enthusiasm that greeted the commander's words, and so ready and eager were the seasoned troops, with their great experience of battle, to hurl their javelins, that Suetonius gave the signal for battle, certain of the outcome.

37 At first the legion did not move from its position and kept the narrow confines of the defile as its protection. Then, as the enemy came closer, they loosed off all their javelins against them with deadly accuracy and burst forward in a wedge-shaped formation. The auxiliaries attacked in the same manner, while the cavalry, with lances extended, broke through any stout resistance they encountered. The remaining Britons turned tail, but their escape was difficult because the ring of wagons had blocked the exits. In addition, the Roman soldiers did not refrain from slaughtering even the womenfolk, while the baggage animals too, transfixed with weapons, added to the piles of bodies. The glory won that day was outstanding and equal to the victories of old; for some there are who record that almost 80,000 Britons fell, while Roman casualties amounted to some 400 dead and a slightly larger number wounded. Boudicca ended her life with poison, and when Poenius Postumius, the Camp Prefect of the II Legion, learned of the success of the XIV and XX Legions, he ran himself through with his sword because he had cheated his own legion of equal glory, and contrary to military regulations had refused to carry out the orders of his commanding officer.

Though lacking the detail found in the *Annals* account, the theme of the rebellion had already been touched upon by Tacitus in the biography of his father-in-law. There too his treatment of British complaints constituted an indictment of Roman rule:

74. *Agricola* 15

There was nothing to be gained by submission except heavier impositions upon a people that seemed to endure them without a murmur. At one time they used to have only one king, but now two were set over them – a Governor to vent his fury on their life-blood, a Procurator on their property. Whether these overlords worked as a team or were at each other's throat was equally ruinous for those under them. The agents of either, centurions on one side, slaves on the other, added insult to injury.

Characteristically, Tacitus' account of the causes of the rebellion chooses to concentrate on the political and personal grievances of the Iceni and the overbearing Roman treatment of the Trinovantes. That there were other grievances of a more economic nature, however, is brought out by Dio Cassius.[12]

75. Epitome of Dio Cassius LXII, 1–2

1 While this child's play was going on in Rome, a dreadful disaster occurred in Britain: two cities were sacked, 80,000 Romans and provincials were slaughtered, and the island fell into the hands of the enemy. All this, moreover, the Romans sustained at the hands of a woman, something that in fact caused them the greatest of shame. Indeed the gods gave them advance warning of the disaster: during the night a clamour of foreign voices mingled with laughter had been heard in the council chamber and in the theatre uproar and lamentation, but it was no mortal who uttered those words and groans; houses were seen underwater in the river Thames, and the Ocean between the island of Britain and Gaul on one occasion turned blood-red at high tide.

2 The ostensible cause of the war was the confiscation of money which Claudius had given to the leading Britons, but which now had to be repaid – so at least the Procurator of the island Decianus Catus claimed. For this reason, therefore, they rose in revolt, this and the fact that Seneca had lent them 10,000,000 (drachmas =

40,000,000 sesterces) they did not want in the hope of a good return, and had then called in the debt all at once and in a heavy-handed manner.[13] However, the one person who most roused them to anger and persuaded them to go to war against the Romans, the one person thought worthy of leading them and who directed the course of the whole war, was Boudouica, a woman of the British royal family who possessed more spirit than is usual among women. Having collected an army of 120,000, she mounted a tribunal made in the Roman fashion out of earth. In stature she was very tall and grim in appearance, with a piercing gaze and a harsh voice. She had a mass of very fair hair which she grew down to her hips, and wore a great gold torque and a multi-coloured tunic folded round her, over which was a thick cloak fastened with a brooch. This was how she always dressed. And now, taking a spear in her hand so as to present an impressive sight to everyone, she spoke as follows.

Again it goes without saying that the speech Dio assigns to Boudicca has no more validity than the fabrication Tacitus attributes to her, though it does serve to emphasise the fact that writers, through their education, were not blind to the other side's point of view, even if such awareness was only manifested in terms of rhetoric:

76. Epitome of Dio Cassius LXII, 3–6

3 'You have learned from actual experience what a difference there is between freedom and slavery. As a result, though some of you through your ignorance of which is better were previously deceived by the Romans' tempting promises, now at least you have tried them both and understand how great a mistake you made in preferring an imported tyranny to your ancestral way of life. You have realised how much better is poverty with no master than riches accompanied by slavery. For what great dishonour, what extreme of grief have we not suffered from the moment these Romans arrived in Britain? Have we not been entirely deprived of our most important possessions, and pay taxes on what is left? In addition to pasturing and tilling all our other property for them, do we not also pay an annual tax on our very bodies? How much better would it have been to be sold to masters once and for all, rather than to ransom ourselves every year and retain the empty name of freedom! How much better to have been slaughtered and perish than to go

around with a tax on our heads! But why do I mention this? Not even death is free with them; you know how much we pay even for the dead. Among the rest of humanity death frees even those who are slaves; only among the Romans do the dead live for their profit. Why is it that though we have no money – how could we have any, from what source? – we are stripped and despoiled like murder-victims? And why should they moderate their behaviour with the passage of time when they have treated us like this from the outset, a time when all men show some consideration even for the animals they have newly caught?

4   Yet, to tell the truth, we are ourselves responsible for all these troubles. We allowed them to set foot upon our island in the first place, and did not immediately drive them out as once we did the famous Julius Caesar. We did not make even the attempt to set sail a frightful prospect for them while they were still far away, as we did in the case of Augustus and Gaius Caligula. For this reason, though we inhabit so large an island, or rather a continent as it were, surrounded by the sea, and though we have a world of our own and are separated from all the rest of mankind by the Ocean to such an extent that people believe we live in another world under another sky, and some of them – the most erudite included – have hitherto not known for certain what we are called, yet we have been despised and trampled under foot by men who understand nothing except giving vent to their greed. But if we have not done so in the past, let us do our duty now, my countrymen, friends and kinsmen – for I consider you all my kinsmen inasmuch as you inhabit a single island and are called by one common name – now while we still remember freedom, so that we may bequeath it to our children both as a term and a reality. For if we forget altogether that happy state in which we grew up, what will they do who are reared in slavery?

5   This I say not to make you hate your present state, for hatred of it you already have, nor to make you fear the future, for you already fear it, but in order to praise you because of your own accord you choose the necessary path of action and to thank you for being ready to unite with myself and one another. Have no fear of the Romans, for they are superior to us in neither numbers nor bravery. Proof of this is the fact that they have encased themselves in helmets, breastplates and greaves, and have built themselves stockades, walls and trenches so as not to suffer any harm from enemy attack. This course they choose out of fear, rather than acting as the spirit moves, as we do. For we enjoy such a superabundance of courage

that we regard our tents as safer places than walls, and our shields as more effective protection than all their arms and armour. In consequence, when we are victorious we capture them, and when we are beaten we escape. If we choose to retreat anywhere, we go to ground in swamps and mountains, the nature of which renders us undetectable and beyond capture. They on the other hand cannot pursue anyone because of the weight they carry, neither can they escape, and if ever they do elude us, they take refuge in pre-arranged spots and there pen themselves up as if in a trap. It is not only in this respect, however, that they are vastly inferior to us: they are also incapable of enduring hunger or thirst, cold or heat as we do. Instead they need shade and shelter, kneaded bread, wine and oil, and if ever they run short of any of these, they perish. For us on the other hand any grass or root serves as bread, any plant juice as oil, any water as wine, any tree as home. What is more, this land is familiar to us and our ally, but to them it is unknown and hostile. The rivers we swim naked, but they cannot cross them with ease even in boats. So let us go against them placing our trust in good fortune; let us show them that they are hares and foxes attempting to rule over dogs and wolves.'

6   Having made her speech, she then engaged in a type of divination by releasing a hare from the fold of her tunic, and since it ran on what was for them the lucky side, the whole mass of people shouted for joy and Boudouica raised her hand to heaven and said: 'I thank you, Andraste, and I call upon you woman to woman, not as one who rules over Egyptians with their burdens as Nitocris did, nor over Assyrian traders as did Semiramis – this much we have learned from the Romans – nor yet indeed as one ruling over the Romans themselves, as once Messalina did, then Agrippina and now Nero – for though he has the title of man, he is in fact a woman, as his singing and playing the lyre and painted face declare – but as one who rules over Britons who have no knowledge of tilling the earth or working with their hands, but are experts in the art of war and hold all things in common, even their wives and children. Through this the women too possess the same valour as the men. As queen, then, of such men and women I pray to you and ask for victory, safety and freedom from men who are insolent, unjust, insatiable and impious – if indeed we ought to call them men when they bathe in warm water, eat fancy food, drink unmixed wine, smear themselves with myrrh, sleep on soft beds with boys – boys past their prime at that – and are slaves to a lyre-player – and a bad one at that. May this woman, Domitia Nero,

reign no longer over me or you men; rather let her lord it over the Romans with her singing; for they deserve to be slaves to such a woman, whose tyranny they have put up with for so long. For us on the other hand may you alone, Lady, for ever be our leader.'

Following the rhetorical interlude Dio resumes his narrative with a description of British atrocities, Paulinus' reasons for bringing the issue to a decisive engagement, the speeches he is supposed to have made and the battle itself:

77. Epitome of Dio Cassius LXII, 7–12

7 Having made her harangue after this fashion Boudouica led her army against the Romans, who happened to be leaderless because their commander, Paulinus, had gone off on campaign to the island of Mona (Anglesey), which lies close to Britain. For this reason she sacked and plundered two Roman cities and inflicted untold slaughter, as I have said. Those who were taken prisoner by the Britons underwent every possible outrage; the most atrocious and bestial committed was this: they hung up naked the noblest and most beautiful women, cut off their breasts and sewed them to their mouths so that they seemed to be eating them. Then they impaled them on sharp stakes which ran the length of their bodies. All this they did to the accompaniment of sacrifices, feasting, and orgies in their various sacred places, but especially in the grove of Andate. This is the name they gave to Victory, and they regarded her with particular reverence.

8 As it turned out Paulinus had already reduced Mona to surrender, and on learning of the disaster in Britain he immediately sailed back there from the island. However, fear of the natives' numbers and their mad fury dissuaded him from risking everything against them. Rather, he was inclined to put off the battle till a more suitable occasion, but since he was short of food and there was no let-up in the native onslaught, he was forced to engage them, even against his better judgement. Boudouica, with an army of up to 230,000 men, rode in a chariot herself and arranged the others in their various positions. Paulinus on the other hand could not extend his own line to face (all of) hers – they would not have stretched far enough even if drawn up one man deep, so outnumbered were they. Nor did he dare to join battle in a single formation for fear of being surrounded and cut to pieces. So he disposed his army in

three divisions so as to fight on several fronts at once, and had each of the divisions maintain close ranks so as to be difficult to penetrate.

9 As he drew up his men and set them in their positions he encouraged them as follows: 'Come, my fellow soldiers, come Romans, show these murdering savages how great is your superiority even in adversity. For it would be shameful for you to lose in ignominy what a short time ago you won through your valour. On numerous occasions we ourselves and our fathers have defeated numerically superior adversaries with fewer numbers than we now have. Do not be alarmed by the size of their forces or their rebellious spirit – their boldness is the product of a recklessness bolstered by neither arms nor training – neither be alarmed by the fact that they have set fire to a couple of towns. They did not take them by force or as the result of a battle, but one through treachery, the other after its evacuation. So exact from them the due penalty for their deeds, so that they learn by experience what sort of men it is they have wronged compared with themselves.'

10 This was the speech he made to one division. He then went to another and said: 'Now is the time, my fellow soldiers, for spirit, now the time for daring. If today you show yourselves brave, you will recover everything you have lost. If you conquer these people, no one else will stand against us any longer. Through a single battle such as this you will secure what is already yours, and all else you will make subject to you. Our forces, even those in other countries, will seek to match you, and our enemies will stand in awe of you. So you have it in your power either to rule all men without fear – both those your fathers bequeathed to you and those you yourselves have gained – or to be deprived of them altogether: the choice to be free, to rule, to be rich and happy rather than to suffer the opposite through want of effort.'

11 Such was the speech he made to this division. He then went to the third and spoke to them too: 'You have heard the kind of thing these accursed creatures have done to us, or rather you have seen some of them yourselves. Choose then whether you wish to suffer the same as those others suffered, and even more, to be driven altogether from Britain, or by conquering to avenge those who have perished and to provide an example to all men of kindness and fairness to the obedient, and of inevitable harshness towards the rebellious. For my part I hope above all that we conquer: in the first place because we have the gods as our allies, since they generally side with those who have been wronged, then because of the

valour we have inherited from our forefathers, since we are Romans and have conquered all mankind by our valour, then by virtue of our experience, since we have defeated and subdued those very men who are now pitted against us, and finally as a result of our reputation, for it is not adversaries we are about to engage but our slaves whom we conquered even when they were free and independent. If, however, something unexpected happens – I will not shrink from mentioning even this possibility – it is better for us to fall fighting manfully than to be captured and impaled, to see our own entrails cut from us, to be skewered on red-hot spits, and to perish by being rendered down in boiling water, to perish as though we had been thrown to lawless and godless wild beasts. Let us therefore either conquer them or die here. Britain will be a fine monument for us even if all other Romans are driven out of it, since at all events we shall possess it with our bodies.'

12 After this speech and others of a similar nature he raised the signal for battle. Thereupon the two sides closed on one another: the natives with much shouting and threatening warsongs, the Romans in silence and order until they came within javelin range. Then, while the enemy was still advancing against them at walking pace, the Romans rushed forward in a mass at a given signal, and charged them for all they were worth. In the onslaught they easily broke through the opposing ranks of the Britons, though they were surrounded by the great numbers (of the enemy) and engaged in fighting on all sides at once. The struggle took many forms: light-armed troops exchanged missiles with other light-armed forces; heavy-armed were matched against heavy-armed; cavalry engaged cavalry, and Roman archers clashed with the native chariots. The natives would swoop upon the Romans with their chariots, throwing them into confusion, and then be themselves repulsed by the arrows, since they fought without breastplates. Horseman would ride down infantryman, and infantryman would strike down cavalryman. One group of Romans in close formation would advance on the chariots; another would be scattered by them. Some of the Britons would close with the archers and put them to flight; others kept out of their way at a distance, and all this was going on not just at one spot but in three places at once. Both sides fought for a long time, spurred on by equal spirit and daring, but finally, late in the day, the Romans prevailed. Many Britons were cut down in the battle and before the wagons and the woods. Many too were taken alive. Some, however, escaped and made preparations to fight again, but when in the meantime Boudouica fell ill and died the

Britons mourned her deeply and gave her a lavish funeral, and then they disbanded in the belief that now they really were defeated.

The victory over the Britons, closely followed by the death of Boudicca, ostensibly brought a rapid end to the rebellion itself:

78. Tacitus, *Agricola* 16

The favourable outcome of a single battle restored the province to its old submission.

The blow it had caused to Roman pride and prestige, however, called for further retribution, which threatened in turn to plunge the province into a protracted period of unrest and misery. The arrival of a new Procurator, therefore, one with roots in the Celtic society of Gaul, and who doubtless saw his task as promoting economic recovery, brought him inevitably into conflict with the Governor. Our source, Tacitus, chooses to present the clash in terms of personality, and to side with the military, but it is likely that the real cause of dissension lay in the more mundane realm of returning the province to a position of economic viability:

79. Tacitus, *Annals* XIV, 38–9

38 The whole army was now concentrated and kept under canvas to finish off what remained of the war. Caesar increased troop numbers with 2,000 legionary soldiers sent from Germany together with eight auxiliary cohorts and 1,000 cavalry. On their arrival the IX Legion was brought up to strength in terms of legionary troops. The cohorts and cavalry squadrons were stationed in new winter quarters and any tribe that had wavered in its loyalty or had been hostile was ravaged with fire and sword. However, nothing afflicted the enemy as much as famine, since they had taken no thought for sowing crops and had actually diverted people of all ages to the war effort, while marking out Roman provisions for their own use. In addition, the fierce tribes were all the more reluctant to settle back into peace because Julius Classicianus, who had been sent to succeed Catus, was on bad terms with Suetonius and allowed his personal animosity to stand in the way of the national interest. He was giving out that it would be well to await a new governor who would deal gently with those who surrendered, without feelings of enmity and anger or the arrogance of a conqueror. At the

same time he reported to Rome that they should expect no end to hostilities unless a replacement were found for Suetonius, whose failures he attributed to the man's incompetence, his successes to chance.

39 Accordingly Polyclitus, one of the imperial freedmen, was sent to examine the situation in Britain with high hopes on the part of Nero that his influence could not only effect a reconciliation between the Governor and Procurator, but would also pacify the rebellious spirits of the natives. In the event Polyclitus with his enormous entourage proved a burden to Italy and Gaul, and when he crossed Ocean, an object of dread to our own soldiers as well. To the enemy, however, he was an object of derision, for among them the flame of liberty still burned and they had yet to experience the power of freedmen. They were amazed that a general and an army that had carried through so great a war should yield obedience to slaves. The whole situation, however, was reported back to the emperor in a more favourable light. Suetonius was kept in office, but later, because he lost a few ships and their crews on the coast, he was ordered to hand over the army to Petronius Turpilianus, who had just vacated the consulship, on the grounds that the war was still continuing. By not provoking the enemy nor being provoked by them Turpilianus imposed upon his slothful inactivity the honourable name of peace.

Despite the gloss which Tacitus puts on the event, it is more than likely that the recall of Suetonius Paulinus owed much (pace Salway (1), p. 123 n.) to Classicianus' intervention. At some stage in the resulting period of recovery and consolidation Classicianus died in Britain. His tombstone, set up in what was clearly the commercial and by now also the political capital, London, survives:

80. *RIB* I 12 (restored)

To the spirits of the departed (and) of [Gaius Julius] Alpinus Classicianus, [son of Gaius], of the [F]abian voting-tribe ... (2 lines missing) ... Procurator of the Province of Britain, Julia Pacata I [...] daughter of Indus,[14] his wife, (set this up).

NOTES

1 *The Roman Inscriptions of Britain.*
2 Facilis' gravestone is further discussed by Phillips.

3 The text here is corrupt, and this is but one of a number of possible interpretations. See Rivet and Smith, p. 45; Salway (1), p. 100 n. 3.

4 This contrasts sharply with the loyalty of Britain's best known client king, Cogidubnus: Tacitus, *Agricola* 14: 'Certain tribal areas were given to King Cogidubnus – he in fact remained unswerving in his loyalty down to our own times.'

5 Cf. Tacitus, *Agricola* 14: 'A colony of veterans was also added.'

6 Tacitus, *Histories* III, 45 (§95) describes it as achieved through deceit on the part of Cartimandua.

7 While we cannot doubt that Caratacus' survival instead of being put to death after the triumphal ceremonies – the usual fate of a captured enemy leader – was probably due to the impression he made in Rome, and perhaps Claudius' own admiration for his one–time adversary, the speech here placed into his mouth is a clear fiction in form, if not altogether in substance.

8 In a book of the *Annals* now lost.

9 The chronological relationship between this and Tacitus, *Histories* III, 45 (§95) is discussed by Braund and by Hanson and Campbell.

10 Cf. Tacitus, *Agricola* 14:

> Didius Gallus hung on to what had been won by others, pushing forward a few forts at most to more advanced positions and by this sought to gain credit for enlarging his sphere of operations.

11 On the significance of the passage for the rebellion contrast Stevens (2), E. Birley (1) p. 1f., Salway (1) p. 109, Frere (1) p. 68.

12 The credibility of Dio as a source for the Boudiccan rebellion is questioned by Syme, pp. 762–6.

13 The inability of the Britons to endure abuses also figures in Tacitus, *Agricola* 13: 'The Britons themselves readily submit to recruitment into the army, paying tribute, and obligations imposed by the government so long as there are no abuses: these they do not take kindly to since they have been broken to obedience but not yet to slavery.'

14 Indus was a nobleman of the Treveri who had helped to suppress the revolt of Julius Florus in AD 21 and who gave his name to a cavalry squadron, the *Ala Indiana*; cf. *RIB* I 108: 'Danicus, trooper of Indus' cavalry squadron in the troop of Albinus with 16 years' service, a tribesman of the Raurici, lies here. Fulvius Natalis and Flavius Bitucus had this set up under his will.'

VII Tumult and Expansion

The years after the rebellion were marked by no recorded attempt to enlarge the province, and despite the typically critical slant that Tacitus gives to the governorships of Petronius Turpilianus and Trebellius Maximus it would seem that Rome recognised the need for peace and stability:

81. Tacitus (1st–2nd C. AD), *Agricola* 16

Petronius Turpilianus was therefore sent, ostensibly because of his greater readiness to listen to pleas, and since he had not witnessed the crimes of the enemy, he would for that very reason be more lenient to those who repented of their previous actions. He settled the earlier upheaval but ventured no further moves before handing over the province to Trebellius Maximus. Maximus was even less inclined to action and had no military experience; instead he kept control of the province by a rather easy-going administration. The natives too now learned to condone seductive vices, and the period of civil war provided a valid excuse for his inactivity.[1]

It is perhaps a measure of the success of these two governors that at some stage in the late 60s the XIV Gemina was withdrawn from Britain:

82. Tacitus, *Histories* II, 66

Vitellius decided to send them (the XIV Gemina) back to Britain, from which they had been withdrawn by Nero.

To fill the gap caused by the departure of the XIV from Wroxeter, the XX was moved up from South Wales, where it had been since its transfer from Colchester in AD 49 to make way for the colonia there:

83. From Wroxeter (*RIB* I 293)

Gaius Mannius Secundus, son of Gaius, of the Pollian voting-tribe, from Pollentia, a soldier of the XX Legion, aged 52, with 31 years' service, *beneficiarius* (seconded for special duties) of the Pro-Praetorian Legate, lies here.

During the upheaval ushered in by the forced suicide of Nero in AD 68 Britain remained conspicuously on the side-lines. Tacitus at one point paints a glowing picture of the integrity displayed by the legions in Britain:

84. Tacitus (1st–2nd C. AD), *Histories* I, 9

There were no disturbances among the army in Britain and in all the tumult of the civil wars no other legions conducted themselves with greater integrity. This was either because they were far away and cut off by Ocean, or because frequent campaigning had taught them to hate the enemy more than each other.

However, it is clear that dissension was not altogether absent, and Tacitus himself provides two versions of events:

85. *Agricola* 16

Nevertheless, a serious situation developed as a result of mutiny when the troops, accustomed as they were to campaigning, became restive through having nothing to do. Though he was able to avoid the wrath of his army by fleeing and going into hiding, Trebellius was despised and humiliated as a result. Thereafter he governed on sufferance. The army, it was tacitly agreed, would indulge itself, the commander would retain his life. And so, the mutiny came to a halt without bloodshed.

The second, later version seems designed as a correction:

86. Tacitus, *Histories* I, 59–60

59 Nor did the troops in Raetia delay going over to Vitellius' side at once, and even in Britain there was no hesitation.
60 The Governor was Trebellius Maximus, a man whose greed and miserliness rendered him despised and detested by the army. Hatred of him was fanned by Roscius Coelius, the Legate of the XX Legion, who had long been at odds with Trebellius, but now, with the

opportunity offered by the civil war, their enmity flared up with greater intensity. Trebellius accused Coelius of plotting mutiny and undermining discipline; Coelius accused Trebellius of robbing the legions and reducing them to poverty. In the meantime the morale of the army deteriorated as a result of this shameful bickering on the part of the commanders. Ill-will reached the point where Trebellius, rejected by the insults of the auxiliary forces and deserted by the cohorts and cavalry, who went over to Coelius' side, took refuge with Vitellius. The province, however, remained quiet even though its Governor had gone: the government was carried on by the legionary commanders, who in theory were equal to one another, though because of his audacity Coelius' influence was the greater.

In addition to 'verbal' support, the three legions in Britain also sent large contingents to support Vitellius against his rival Otho, though in the event they played no real part in the actual conflict:

87. Tacitus, *Histories* II, 57

Meanwhile, unaware of his victory (over Otho) Vitellius was assembling the remnants of the German army as if for a continuation of the war ... He supplemented his forces with a levy of 8,000 men drawn from the army in Britain.

With the death of Otho and the departure of Trebellius from Britain Vitellius was now free to send a governor who might find greater favour with the garrison there:

88. Tacitus, *Histories* II, 65

Trebellius had fled from Britain because of the soldiers' anger, and in his place was sent Vettius Bolanus, a member of Vitellius' retinue.

Similarly dispatched to Britain was the XIV Legion Gemina which had supported Otho, but in this case the purpose was to isolate them:[2]

89. Tacitus, *Histories* II, 11

Nero had increased the fame (of the XIV) by his choice of them as his best troops, and as a result of this they had long been loyal to Nero and were resolutely devoted to Otho.

Before long, however, the victorious Vitellius was himself confronted by a new contender for imperial honours, Vespasian. The latter's supporters wasted no time in communicating with the XIV Gemina:

90. Tacitus, *Histories* II, 86

Letters were sent to the XIV in Britain and the I in Spain, since both legions had been pro-Otho and against Vitellius.

Vitellius himself on the other hand sought support from a less than enthusiastic Governor of the province:

91. Tacitus, *Histories* II, 97

Vitellius summoned auxiliaries from Germany, Britain and Spain, but in a leisurely manner and pretending there was no real need. Similarly the provincial governors prevaricated: Hordeonius Flaccus because he suspected the Batavians and was concerned about having a war on his hands, Vettius Bolanus because Britain was never sufficiently quiet. Besides, both were doubtful in their allegiance.

In the event, however, contingents from Britain did participate in the second battle of Bedriacum, probably those earlier summoned for action against Otho:

92. Tacitus, *Histories* III, 22

Others report that ... the V and XV Legions together with detachments of the IX, II and XX British legions formed the centre of the battle formation ...

Following the defeat of Vitellius the legions in Britain wisely changed sides, though not without a certain reluctance from some quarters:

93. Tacitus, *Histories* III, 44

With the capture of Valens everything turned to the victor's (Vespasian's) advantage. It began in Spain with the I Legion Adiutrix which remembered Otho and was hostile to Vitellius. This then won over the X and VI Legions. Nor was Gaul slow to join in, and Britain was secured by the generally favourable opinion of Vespasian, who had been placed in command of the II Legion there by Claudius and had conducted himself with distinction in the war. This was not, however, without some resistance on the part of the other legions in which many centurions and other ranks owed their promotion to Vitellius, and were uneasy about changing an emperor they already knew (for one they didn't).[3]

In Britain itself the reduction in the size of the garrisoning forces by some 8,000 troops, together with the recent indiscipline of those that remained, had no doubt been instrumental in inducing within the Governor, Bolanus, a tendency towards inaction:

94. Tacitus, *Agricola* 16

Vettius Bolanus likewise refrained from troubling Britain by enforcing discipline while the civil wars yet continued. There was the same lack of response to the enemy, the same riotous behaviour in military quarters. The only difference is that Bolanus, through his innocuous character, had done nothing to stir up hatred against himself and so won affection if not obedience.

Inaction as far as the natives were concerned was not, however, a policy that would guarantee peace. Among the Brigantes the enmity stirred up by Cartimandua's treatment of Caratacus resurfaced as Roman attention was diverted elsewhere:

95. Tacitus, *Histories* III, 45

As a result of these differences and the frequent rumours of civil war the Britons were induced to pluck up courage by Venutius, who, in addition to his fierce temperament and hatred for all things Roman, was fired with personal animosity towards Queen Cartimandua. She ruled over the Brigantes, exercising great influence by virtue of her noble birth, and had increased her standing when, with her treacherous seizure of King Caratacus, she appeared to have paved the way for Claudius' triumph. From this act came wealth and the self-indulgence of success. She rejected her husband Venutius and took his armour-bearer Vellocatus as her husband and consort. The royal house was straightaway scandalised by this shameful event: the people sided with the husband, the adulterer was bolstered by the lust and savagery of the queen. Venutius, therefore, summoned help (from outside) and with a simultaneous revolt on the part of the Brigantes themselves forced Cartimandua into a very tight corner. She in turn appealed to the Romans for help, and after a number of indecisive engagements our cohorts and cavalry squadrons managed to extricate the queen from her dangerous situation. Venutius was left with the kingdom, we the war.

What action Bolanus took against Venutius is not recorded, unless a reference to an initial Brigantian campaign is to be seen lurking behind the poetry of Statius addressed to Bolanus' son Crispinus:

96. Statius (1st C. AD), *Silvae* V, 2, 142–9

What glory will extol the plains of Caledonia, when some great-aged native of that wild country tells you: 'Here it was your father's custom justice to dispense; from this mound his squadrons he addressed. Far and wide his look-out posts and strongholds did he set – do you see them? – and with a ditch these walls he girt. These gifts, these weapons to the gods of war did he devote – you see the dedications still. This breastplate he himself put on when battle summoned; this from off a British king he seized.

For certain, however, the XIV Gemina was once again removed from Britain, for service against the Batavi, and never returned:

97. Tacitus, *Histories* IV, 68

The XIV Legion was summoned from Britain, as were the VI and I from Spain.

In AD 71 Bolanus was himself recalled and replaced by Petillius Cerialis, his first task to settle the Brigantes:[4]

98. Tacitus, *Agricola* 17

Petillius Cerialis at once instilled a feeling of terror by attacking the territory of the Brigantes, said to be the most populous of the whole province. There were numerous battles, some of them bloody, and a large part of Brigantia was either annexed or overrun.

With Cerialis had come a new legion, the II Adiutrix, to bring the garrison back up to a total of four. This was stationed at Lincoln while the IX Hispana was advanced to a new position at York:

99. From Lincoln AD 76 (?) (*RIB* I 258)

Titus Valerius Pudens, son of Titus, of the Claudian voting-tribe, from Savaria, a soldier of the II Legion Adiutrix Pia Fidelis in the century of Dossenius Proculus, aged 30, with 6 (?) years' service lies here. His heir set this up at his own expense.

Cerialis' own successor was in turn to deal once again with the continuing problem of the Silures:

100. Tacitus, *Agricola* 17

Cerialis indeed would have overshadowed the administration and repute of any other successor, but Julius Frontinus, a man who reached the pinnacle of greatness that was then possible, shouldered and bore the burden. By force of arms he reduced the powerful and warlike tribe of the Silures, surmounting not only the valour of the enemy but also the difficulty of the terrain.

As part of Frontinus' campaign the II Augusta (moved from Exeter to Gloucester to take the place of the XX when it was transferred to Wroxeter) was now stationed in a new legionary fortress at Caerleon:

101. *RIB* I 365

To the spirits of the departed. Gaius Valerius Victor, son of Gaius, of the Galerian voting-tribe, from Lugdunum (Lyons), Standard-bearer of the II Legion Augusta, with 17 years' service, lived 45 years. Under the supervision of Annius Perpetuus, his heir, (this was set up).

Similarly, a new legionary fortress was begun at Chester, to be occupied for a time by the II Adiutrix:

102. *RIB* I 476

Gaius Juventius Capito, son of Gaius, of the Claudian voting-tribe, from Aprus, a soldier in the II Legion Adiutrix Pia Fidelis in the century of Julius Clemens, aged 40, with 7 (or 17) years' service (lies here).

In turn AD 77[5] saw the arrival in Britain of Frontinus' successor, Gnaeus Julius Agricola. His biography[6] from the pen of his son-in-law presents us with the most vivid and detailed picture we have not only of any governor but also of one who extended the province further than was ever to be achieved again.[7]

103. Tacitus, *Agricola*

For ease of reference the work may be divided up as follows:

Ch. 1–3:	Introduction.
Ch. 4:	Agricola's early life and education.
Ch. 5:	Agricola's military tribuneship in Britain under Suetonius Paulinus during the Boudiccan rebellion.
Ch. 6:	Return to Rome, marriage, service as Quaestor in Asia and Tribune of the People in Rome.
Ch. 7–8:	Murder of Agricola's mother during the civil wars. Agricola appointed Legate of the XX Legion Valeria Victrix in Britain under Bolanus and Cerialis.
Ch. 9:	Governor of Aquitania, the Consulship and appointment to Britain.
Ch. 10–12:	Description of Britain's geography and people.
Ch. 13:	Relations between Rome and Britain from Caesar to Claudius.
Ch. 14:	The governorships of Aulus Plautius, Ostorius Scapula, Didius Gallus and Quintus Veranius.
Ch. 15–16:	The Boudiccan rebellion and the recovery under Turpilianus, Maximus and Bolanus.
Ch. 17:	Cerialis overruns the Brigantes.
Ch. 18:	Agricola's action against the Ordovices. Anglesey reconquered.
Ch. 19:	Reforms of provincial government and abuses of taxation.
Ch. 20:	Brigantia annexed and garrisoned.
Ch. 21:	Measures to encourage Romanisation of the native aristocracy.
Ch. 22–3:	Advance to the Tay and consolidation of the Forth-Clyde frontier.
Ch. 24:	Agricola contemplates an Irish expedition.
Ch. 25–7:	Advance beyond the Forth-Clyde line. Attempts of the Britons to counter Agricola's tactics.
Ch. 28:	Mutiny of the cohort of the Usipi.
Ch. 29–38:	Roman naval operations force the Britons to engage Agricola in a set battle at Mons Graupius. Speeches of Calgacus and Agricola followed by the conflict. The north of Britain circumnavigated.
Ch. 39–46:	Domitian's reaction to Agricola's achievements. Recall, retirement, and death.

In contrast to the detail provided by Tacitus our only other literary source, itself derived from the *Agricola*, provides little additional insight:

104. Epitome of Dio Cassius LXVI, 20, 1–3

In the meantime war broke out again in Britain and Gnaeus Julius Agricola overran all the enemy's territory there. He was the first Roman of whom we have any information to discover that Britain is surrounded by water. For some soldiers mutinied, and having murdered their centurions and a tribune, they took refuge in boats, put out to sea and sailed round the western part of Britain just as the current and winds took them. And they escaped detection on the other (eastern) side when they put in at the forts there. As a result of this Agricola sent others to attempt the circumnavigation, and learned from them too that it was an island. These were the events in Britain and as a result Titus was given the title Imperator for the fifteenth time. Agricola, however, lived out the rest of his life in disgrace and want since he had accomplished more than was proper for a general. Finally he was murdered by Domitian for this very reason, though he had received triumphal honours from Titus.

Nor does Agricola figure much in extant inscriptions – only four survive:

105. Lead pipes from Chester (*RIB* II.3 2434.1–3)

In the ninth consulship of the Emperor Vespasian (AD 79), and the seventh of Titus Imperator, under Gnaeus Julius Agricola, Pro-Praetorian Legate of Augustus.

106. Fragmentary inscription from the Forum at St Albans AD 79 (extant portions italicised) (*JRS*8 46 (1956) p. 146–7 cf. Burn 40)

For the Emperor Titus Caesar *Ve*spasian Augustus, *son* of the deified *Vespa*sian, Pontifex Maximus (High Priest), in the ninth year of his holding Tribunician Power, fifteen times saluted Imperator, seven times Consul, and Consul *Desig*nate for the eighth time, Censor, Father of his Country, and for Caesar Do*mi*tian, son of the deified Vespa*sian*, six times Consul, and Consul Designate for the seventh time, Leader of the Youth, and Member of *all* the Colleges of Priests, under Gnaeus Julius A*gric*ola, Pro-*Pra*etorian Legate of Augustus, the Municipium of *Verulamium* (set this up) *on completion* of the Basilica.

Agricola's concentration of his forces into a single line of advance north of the Forth-Clyde line betokens his realisation that the west-coast route was now impassable, and it may be that his reconnaissance to establish this lies behind the activities of Demetrius of Tarsus:

107. Plutarch (1st–2nd C. AD), *On the Disuse of Oracles* 18 = *Moralia* 419e

Demetrius said that of the islands around Britain many are remote and desolate, and that some of them are named after gods and heroes. He himself had sailed to the nearest of these remote isles on the instructions of the emperor for the purpose of enquiry and observation – an island which had only a few inhabitants, though these were all holy men and held inviolate by the Britons.

To this same Demetrius are probably to be assigned two Greek inscriptions from York:

108. *RIB* I 662–3

(a) To the gods of the Governor's headquarters, Scribonios Demetrios (dedicated this).

(b) To Ocean and Tethys, Demetrios.

In this same period of Agricola's governorship and perhaps as part of the continuing effort to Romanise the province (cf. *Agricola* 21) Vespasian instituted the post of *Legatus Juridicus* or Law Officer.[9] Normally superintendence of legal affairs was one of the Governor's functions, but the conversion from Celtic to Roman law and the exigencies of rapid territorial expansion may have suggested the need for a deputy to oversee this aspect of administration. The first we know of was Gaius Salvius Liberalis Nonius Bassus; his successor is recorded in an inscription from Dalmatia:

109. *ILS*[10] 1015

To Gaius Octavius Tidius Tossianus Iaolenus Priscus, Legate of the IV Legion Flavia, Legate of the III Legion Augusta, *Juridicus* (Law-Officer) of the province of Britain, Consular Governor of the province of Germania Superior, Consular Governor of the province of Syria, Proconsul of the province of Africa, Priest, Publius Mutilius Crispinus, son of Publius, of the Claudian voting-tribe, ordered this to be set up under his will for his good friend.

NOTES

1 Cf. Tacitus, *Annals* XIV, 39 (§79).
2 Tacitus, *Histories* II, 66 (§82).
3 Cf. *Agricola* 7 where Agricola's appointment as commander of the XX Valeria is indirectly attributed to the slowness with which it transferred its allegiance and the reported disloyalty of its Legate. See further E. Birley.
4 See A.R. Birley (2).
5 AD 78 as the traditional date for the arrival of Agricola in Britain (Salway (1) p. 138, 167f., Frere (1) p. 89) has been revised in recent years as a result of studies into the coinage of the period, Hanson p. 40ff.
6 Whether in fact the *Agricola* should properly be termed a biography is discussed by Mattingly in the Penguin translation, p. 15f, and by Ogilvie and Richmond, p. 11ff.
7 See further Kenworthy.
8 *Journal of Roman Studies.*
9 A.R. Birley (4), pp. 211–14, 404–7.
10 *Inscriptiones Latinae Selectae.*

VIII Withdrawal and Consolidation

The period between the departure of Agricola and the building of Hadrian's wall is marked by an almost total dearth of literary evidence. What there is, together with that provided by inscriptions and archaeology, suggests an early realisation that while four legions and attendant auxiliary units might be enough to conquer Scotland, they were not enough to hold it. The situation can only have been made worse by the withdrawal of the II Adiutrix for service in Domitian's Dacian war *c.* AD 87:

110. Tacitus (1st–2nd C. AD), *Histories* I, 2

Britain was conquered and immediately abandoned.

The result was an inevitable withdrawal from much of what Agricola had gained.[1] Inchtuthil, the most northerly of the legionary fortresses, was abandoned and Chester was now held by the XX Valeria Victrix:

111. *RIB* I 501

Gaius Lovesius Cadarus, of the Papirian voting-tribe, from Emerita, soldier of the XX Legion Valeria Victrix, aged 25, with 8 years' service. Frontinius Aquilo, his heir, had this set up.

At some stage before Domitian's death in AD 96 and doubtless for a more serious reason than that given by our source, a governor of Britain was put to death:

112. Suetonius (2nd C. AD), *Domitian* 10

Domitian put to death many senators including a number of ex-consuls. Among them was ... Sallustius Lucullus, Governor of Britain, because he allowed a new type of spear to be called Lucullan.

At about the same time the now evacuated fortress at Lincoln was converted into a colony:[2]

113. From Mogontiacum (Mainz) (*CIL*[3] XIII, 6679)

Marcus Minicius Marcellinus, son of Marcus, of the Quirine voting-tribe, from Lindum (Lincoln), for the honour of the eagle of the XXII Legion Primigenia Pia Fidelis [. . .] the goddess Fortune.

Shortly afterwards, in the reign of Nerva (AD 96–8), Gloucester underwent the same transformation:

114. From Rome (*CIL* VI, 3346)

To the spirits of the departed and Marcus Ulpius Quintus of Nervia Glevi (Gloucester), *frumentarius* (soldier responsible for corn supply) of the VI Legion Victrix, Calidus Quietus, his colleague, had this made for his respected, most dutiful and deserving brother.

The first decade of the second century AD in turn saw the strengthening of the remaining fortresses at Caerleon, Chester and York with stone defences:

115. From Caerleon (*RIB* I 330 restored)

For the Emperor Caesar Nerva Traja[n Augustus], conqueror of Germany, [son] of the deified [Nerva], Pontifex Maximus (High Priest) with [Tribunician] Power, Father of his Country, Consul for the third time (AD 100) the II Legion Augusta (built this).

116. From Chester (*RIB* I 464, extant portions italicised)[4]

The *Em*peror Caesar *Ne*rva Trajan Augustus, conqueror of Germany and *D*acia, son of the deified Nerva ...

117. From York (*RIB* I 665 restored)[5]

The Emperor Caesar Ne[rva Traj]an Augustus, conqueror of Ger[many and Dacia], son of the [deified N]erva, [Po]ntifex

Maximus (High Priest) in the 12th year of his holding [Tribunician Po]wer (AD 108), six times saluted Imperator, [five times Consul, Father of his Country, built this gateway] through the agency of the IX Legion Hi[spana].

Consolidation, however, does not imply a total absence of native unrest, as a fleeting reference in Juvenal would seem to indicate:

118. Juvenal (early 2nd C. AD), *Satires* IV, 126–7

Some king you will capture, or Arviragus will be hurled from his British chariot pole.[6]

NOTES

1 That withdrawal from the area was not total is cogently argued by Salway (1), p. 150f.
2 On urbanisation in Britain see Wacher.
3 *Corpus Inscriptionum Latinarum*. The Flavian Emperors themselves belonged to the Quirine voting-tribe and extended the honour to citizens of their foundations.
4 The extremely fragmentary nature of the inscription suggests caution in attributing it to the reign of Trajan.
5 The last reference to the IX in Britain. By AD 122 it had been replaced by the VI Victrix.
6 Cf. Caesar, *Gallic War* IV, 33.

IX The Hadrianic and Antonine Frontiers

With the accession of Hadrian in AD 117 the abandonment of Trajan's expensive conquests in the east was soon matched by the consolidation of holdable frontiers in the west. In the case of Britain the presence of the Emperor in the province in AD 122, the arrival of the VI Victrix, ostensibly to replace the IX Hispana and the appointment of Platorius Nepos as Governor all provided the starting point for the construction of Hadrian's wall:

119. Scriptores Historiae Augustae (c. 4th C. AD), *Hadrian* 5, 1–2 and 11, 2

5   When he took over the government, Hadrian immediately reverted to an earlier policy, and devoted his energies to maintaining peace throughout the world. For at one and the same time those peoples Trajan had subjugated were in revolt, the Moors started making attacks, the Sarmatae were waging war, the Britons could not be kept under Roman control . . .

11   . . . And so, having reformed the army in the manner of a king, Hadrian set out for Britain. There he corrected many faults and was the first to build a wall, 80 miles long, to separate the Romans and barbarians. [1]

As often, the visit by the Emperor was marked by the minting of commemorative coins:

120. Bronze sestertius (*RIC* II p. 453 no. 882)

Obverse

Hadrianus Aug(ustus) Cos (Consul) III (times, AD 134–8) P(ater)
P(atriae) (Father of his Country)

Reverse

Adventui Aug(usti) Britanniae (For the arrival of the emperor in
Britain). S(enatus) C(onsulto) (By decree of the Senate)

121. Bronze sestertius (*RIC* II p. 458 no. 912)

Obverse

As 120

Reverse

Exer(citus) Britanni(cus) (British Army) S(enatus) C(onsulto) (By
decree of the Senate)

Similarly, as a declaration of Roman order, came further issues
showing Britannia subdued:

122. Bronze sestertius (*RIC* II p. 447 no. 845)

Obverse
As 120

Reverse
Britannia S(enatus) C(onsulto)
(By decree of the Senate)

Supplementing the admittedly bare literary account and numismatic evidence are inscriptions from the wall itself, recording not only the pattern of building but also the builders:

123. From near Jarrow (*RIB* I 1051 restored)

Son of all the [deified emperors, the Emperor Caesar Trajan] Hadr[ian Augustus], after the necessity of [kee]ping [the empire within its limits had been laid on him] by [div]ine co[mmand] ... thrice Consul ... once [the barbarians] had been scattered [and] the province of Britain [recovered], ad[ded a frontier between] either [shore of] O[cean for 80 miles]. The army [of the] pr[ovince built the wall] under the direction [of Aulus Platorius Nepos, Pro-Praetorian Legate of Augustus.]

124. From Benwell (*RIB* I 1340 restored)

For the Emperor Caesar Trajan Hadrian Augustus a detachment of the British F[leet] (built this) under Aulus Platorius N[epos], Pro-P[raetorian L]egate of Augustus.

125. From the Benwell to Rudchester section (*RIB* I 1374)

The century of Julius Proculus (built this).

126. From Halton Chesters (*RIB* I 1427 restored)

For the Emperor Caesar T[rajan Hadrian] Augustus the VI Legion
V[ictrix Pia Fidelis] (built this) under Aulus Platorius N[epos], Pro-
[Praetorian] Legate of Augustus.

127. Ibid. (*RIB* I 1428)

The II Legion Augusta built this.

128. From the central sector: Milecastle 38 (*RIB* I 1638)

The II Legion Augusta of the Emperor Caesar Trajan Hadrian
Augustus (built this) under Aulus Platorius Nepos, Pro-Praetorian
Legate.[2]

The actual construction of the wall, however, proved no easy
undertaking and was eventually to involve radical alterations in
both design and method of manning. Dedications of building were
still going on after 128 when Hadrian received the title 'Father of his
Country':[3]

129. From Great Chesters (*RIB* I 1736)

For the Emperor Caesar Trajan Hadrian Augustus, Father of his
Country.

Evidence, albeit fragmentary, also suggests changes in the disposi-
tion of forts continuing under Julius Severus in the early 130s prior to
his move to Judaea in order to suppress the Bar Kochba revolt:

130. From Carrawburgh (*RIB* I 1550 restored)

. . . Se]verus, [Pro-P]raetorian Legate [of Augustus], the 1st Cohort
of Aquit[anians] built this [under . . .] Nepos the [Pr]efect.

131. Epitome of Dio Cassius LXIX, 13, 2, AD 132–3

Then indeed Hadrian sent against them (the Jews) the best of his
generals. The first of these was Julius Severus, despatched from
Britain where he was governor[4] . . .

Even later, in AD 136–8, work was still in progress at sites like
Carvoran:

132. *RIB* I 1778

To the Emperor's Fortune for the welfare of Lucius Aelius
Caesar, Titus Flavius Secundus, Prefect of the 1st Cohort of
Hamian archers, willingly and deservedly fulfilled his vow as the
result of a vision.[5]

For reasons that remain uncertain[6] the accession of Antoninus Pius
in AD 138 brought with it a fresh Roman advance into southern
Scotland and the establishment of a new frontier between the Forth
and the Clyde:

133. Scriptores Historiae Augustae (*c.* 4th C. AD), *Antoninus Pius* 5, 4

Antoninus waged a large number of wars through his governors.
Through the governor Lollius Urbicus he defeated the Britons, and
having driven back the barbarians, he built another wall, this time
of turf.

As preparation for the push northwards Corbridge underwent a new
building programme to bring it back into commission as a supply
depot:

134. *RIB* I 1147 (restored)

For [the Emperor] Titus Aelius Antoninus [Au]gustus Pius, Consul
for the second time, [under] the command of Quintus Lollius
Urbicus, Pro-Praetorian [Legate] of [A]ugustus, the II Legion
Augusta built this.

As in the case of the Hadrianic frontier the process of wall building
is recorded by inscriptions:

135. From Bridgeness (*RIB* I 2139)

For the Emperor Caesar Titus Aelius Hadrianus Antoninus Augustus
Pius, Father of his Country, the II Legion Augusta built this for
4,652 paces.

136. From Old Kilpatrick (*RIB* I 2205)

For the Emperor Caesar Titus Aelius Hadrianus Antoninus
Augustus, Father of his Country, a detachment of the VI Legion

Victrix Pia Fidelis (carried out) the construction of the rampart for 4,141 feet.

137. From Castlehill (*RIB* I 2198)

For the Emperor Caesar Titus Aelius Hadrianus Antoninus Augustus Pius, Father of his Country, a detachment of the XX Legion Valeria Victrix built this for 3,000 feet.

138. From Rough Castle (*RIB* I 2145 restored)

[For the Emperor Ca]esar Titus [Aelius] Hadrianus [Anto]ninus Augustus [Pius], Father of his Country, the 6th Cohort of [Ner]vii built this headquarters-building.

139. From Bar Hill (*RIB* I 2170 restored)

For the E[mperor Cae]sar Titus Aelius [Hadrianus An]toninus Au[gustus Pius, Father of his Country], the 1st Cohort of B[aetasii], Roman [Citizens] for their val[our and lo]yalty (set this up).

140. From Balmuildy (*RIB* I 2191 restored)

[For the Emperor Caesar Titus Aelius Hadrianus Antoninus Augustus Pius, Father] of his Country, the II Legion Au[gusta built this under] Quintus Lollius Ur[bicus], Pro-Praetorian Legate of Augustus.

141. Milestone from Ingilston (*PSAS*[7] 13 (1983), pp. 379–85 restored)

For the E[mperor Caesar Titus Aelius Hadrianus Anto]ninus Augustus Pius, Father of his Country, 2/3 times Consul [2 lines] the 1st [Co]hort of Cugerni (set this up) [. . .] miles from [Tri]montium.

Similarly too, Antoninus celebrated his advance by issuing commemorative coins showing Britannia and Victory AD 143–4.

142. Bronze sestertii (*RIC* III p. 121 no. 745; p. 119 no. 719)

1 *Reverse*
  Imperator II (times) Britannia S(enatus) C(onsulto)
  (By decree of the Senate)

2 *Reverse*
  Imperator II (times) Britan(nia) S(enatus) C(onsulto)
  (By decree of the Senate)

The appearance of fresh issues of this type dated to the mid-150s, however, suggests renewed trouble, and further Roman victories:

143. Bronze dupondius AD 154–5 (*RIC* III p. 142 no. 930)

Reverse
Britannia Cos (Consul) IIII (times) S(enatus) C(onsulto)
(By decree of the Senate)

It may indeed be to this period that Pausanias' passing reference to a rising among the Brigantes belongs:

144. Pausanias (mid-2nd C. AD), *Description of Greece* VIII (Arcadia) 43, 3–4

Antoninus never willingly involved the Romans in war . . . he also removed much of the territory of the Brigantes in Britain because they had embarked upon an armed invasion of the region of Genounia, which was subject to the Romans.[8]

At all events the unrest seems to have been serious enough to necessitate reinforcements from the armies in Germany to bolster all three legions in Britain, now under a new governor, Julius Verus:

145. From Newcastle (*RIB* I 1322)

To the Emperor Antoninus Augustus Pius, Father of his Country, the detachment contributed from the two German provinces for the II Legion Augusta, the VI Legion Victrix and the XX Legion Valeria Victrix (set this up) under Julius Verus, Pro-Praetorian Legate of Augustus.[9]

It is under Verus too that we find rebuilding at stations like Birrens dated to AD 157–8:

146. *RIB* I 2110 (restored)

For the Emperor Caesar Titus A[elius H]adrianus An[to]ninus Augustus [Pius, Po]ntifex Maximus (High Priest), in the twenty-first year of his holding [Tr]ibunician Power (AD 157–8), four times Consul, the 2nd Cohort of [Tung]rians, 1,000-strong, part-mounted, citizens with Latin Rights, (set this up) under Ju[lius Verus], Pro-Praetorian Legate of Augustus.

The occupation of southern Scotland undertaken by Antoninus Pius seems from the evidence to have created more problems than it solved. Though precise details and chronology are still a matter of debate, archaeological evidence points to a temporary pull-back from the Antonine to the Hadrianic frontier at this time, before a second temporary occupation of the more northerly line.

147. From near Heddon-on-the-Wall (*RIB* I 1389)

The VI Legion Victrix Pia Fidelis rebuilt this in the consulship of Tertullus and Sacerdos (AD 158).

For certain, however, the early years of Marcus Aurelius' reign (AD 161–80) show signs of continuing problems:

148. Scriptores Historiae Augustae (*c.* 4th C. AD), *Marcus Antoninus* (Aurelius) 8, 7

War was threatening in Britain too, and the Chatti had invaded Germany and Raetia. Against the Britons was sent Calpurnius Agricola (AD 163), against the Chatti Aufidius Victorinus.

As in the days of Lollius Urbicus, Corbridge saw renewed building activity by the legions:

149. *RIB* I 1137

To the Unconquered Sun-god, a detachment of the VI Legion Victrix Pia Fidelis (set this up) under the command of Sextus Calpurnius Agricola, Pro-Praetorian Legate of Augustus.

That the problems faced by the province were becoming chronic is suggested by a hint of further trouble at the very end of the decade:

150. Scriptores Historiae Augustae, *Marcus Antoninus* (Aurelius) 22, 1

In addition war was threatening in Parthia and Britain.

The mid-170s in turn saw the arrival in Britain of new cavalry contingents drafted into the Roman army as part of Marcus Aurelius' settlement of his campaign across the Danube. In this case, however, their presence in the province seems to have been designed more to isolate them from their homeland than to counter native unrest:

151. Epitome of Dio Cassius LXXI, 16, 2

As their contribution to the alliance the Iazyges immediately provided him (Marcus Aurelius) with 8,000 cavalry, 5,500 of whom he sent to Britain.

As if to provide a foretaste of the disastrous reign of Commodus, the early months of his assuming sole imperial power in AD 180 saw northern Britain convulsed by a major penetration from beyond the frontier. The situation clearly demanded a man of proven worth:

152. Epitome of Dio Cassius LXXII, 8

Commodus also had a number of wars against the barbarians beyond Dacia in which both Albinus and Niger, who later fought against the emperor Severus, distinguished themselves. The greatest war, however, was in Britain. For the tribes in the island crossed the wall[10] that separated them from the Roman army and did a great amount of damage, even cutting down a general together with his troops. Commodus therefore became alarmed and sent Ulpius Marcellus[11] against them. Marcellus was a temperate and frugal man and when on active service lived like a soldier in the matter of what he ate and his conduct in general, but he was becoming haughty and arrogant. He was totally and patently incorruptible, but in his character not the least bit pleasant or kindly. He could go without sleep more than any other general, and since he wanted those who accompanied him to remain awake and alert, he used to write orders on twelve tablets – the kind made out of limewood – pretty well every evening, and he would order someone to take them to this or that person at various times so that being convinced their commander was awake, they might not themselves get their fill of sleep. He had besides a natural ability to resist sleep, and this he further developed through fasting. In general he never took his fill of food, and so as not to fill himself up even with bread, he used to send to Rome for it – not because he was unable to eat the local variety, but so that he would not be able to eat any more of it than was absolutely necessary because of its staleness, since he had bad gums and they bled easily because of the bread's dryness. So he took care to exaggerate this (resistance to sleep) in order to gain the greatest possible reputation for being able to stay awake. Such was the character of Marcellus, and he inflicted major defeats on the barbarians in Britain. Later, when he was on the point of being put to death by Commodus because of his singular abilities, he was nevertheless spared.

By AD 184 sufficient Roman victories had been won to justify the issue of coins advertising the fact:

153. Bronze sestertius (*RIC* III p. 418 no. 451)

Reverse

P(ontifex) M(aximus) (High Priest) Tr(ibunicia) P(otestas) (Tribunician Power) X (times, AD 184–5) Imp(erator) VII (times) Cos (Consul) IIII (times) P(ater) P(atriae) (Father of his Country) S(enatus) C(onsulto) (By decree of the Senate) Vic(toria) Brit(annica) (Victory in Britain)

154. Bronze medallion (Grueber no. 12)

Obverse

M(arcus) Commodus Antoninus Aug(ustus) Pius Brit(annicus)

Reverse

Britannia. P(ontifex) M(aximus) (High Priest) Tr(ibunicia) P(otestas) (Tribunician Power) X (times) Imp(erator) VII (times) Cos (Consul) IIII (times) P(ater) P(atriae) (Father of his Country)

For all his military expertise, however, Marcellus' overbearing nature was hardly calculated to make him a popular commander, and his unsociable personal idiosyncrasies together with increasingly erratic policies emanating from Rome served only to put the army in Britain into a rebellious mood. When Commodus' Praetorian Prefect, Perennis, began replacing senatorial legionary commanders with men of the lower equestrian rank the situation reached boiling point:

155. Scriptores Historiae Augustae (*c.* 4th C. AD), *Commodus* 6, 1–2

At this time Perennis attributed to his own son the successes gained in Sarmatia by other generals. In the war in Britain, however, this same Perennis who wielded so much power removed commanders of senatorial rank and placed in charge of the soldiers men of equestrian rank.

156. Epitome of Dio Cassius LXXII, 9

It came about that Perennis, who had command of the Praetorian guard after Paternus, was put to death as a result of a mutiny among the troops. Since Commodus had given himself over to chariot races and riotous living and performed practically none of the functions of government, Perennis was forced to take charge not only of military affairs but everything else as well, and thus to run the state. For this reason, whenever the troops were faced by something not to their liking, they laid the blame on Perennis, and were angry with him. The troops in Britain chose Priscus, a (legionary) Legate, as Emperor, but he refused saying 'I am as much an emperor as you are soldiers'. The officers in Britain, therefore, having been reprimanded for their insubordination – they did not in fact settle down until Pertinax checked them – chose out 1,500 javelin men from their ranks and sent them to Italy. As they drew close to Rome without encountering any resistance, Commodus met them and asked 'What is the meaning of this, my comrades in arms? Why are you here?' They replied 'We have come because Perennis is plotting against you in order to make his son Emperor', and Commodus believed them, especially as they were supported by Cleander who had a burning hatred of Perennis because he had thwarted his every design. So Commodus handed over the Praetorian Prefect to the very troops of whom he was commander, and did not in fact have the courage to rebuff 1,500 men, though he had many times that number of Praetorian guards. They then tortured and butchered Perennis, and his wife, sister, and two sons were also put to death.

The lesson to be learned from the fall of Perennis in AD 185 as a result of direct intervention by part of a provincial army was evidently not lost on Commodus. To restore the forces in Britain to a proper appreciation of their duties, he appointed as Governor Helvius Pertinax, a man with a well-established reputation for strict discipline. Pertinax's methods, however, seem to have been sadly out of step with the needs of the moment:

157. Scriptores Historiae Augustae, *Pertinax* 3, 5–10

Following the execution of Perennis Commodus made amends to Pertinax and asked him in a letter to set out for Britain. Having done this, he prevented the troops there from fomenting revolt, though they wanted to set up someone – more specifically Pertinax himself – as Emperor. Then Pertinax gained a reputation for malevolence because he was said to have brought before Commodus charges that Antistius Burrus and Arrius Antoninus were aspiring to the throne. In addition he put down revolts against himself in Britain and indeed came into very great danger, being almost killed in a mutiny involving a legion and actually left among the dead. This Pertinax punished with signal severity, but eventually he asked to be relieved of his post as Governor, saying that the legions were hostile to him on account of his maintenance of discipline.

NOTES

1 On the question of the British frontier see further A.R. Birley (3).
2 Cf. from the same area (*RIB* I 1637) '(This work) of the Emperor Caesar Trajan Hadrian Augustus the II Legion Augusta (built) under Aulus Platorius Nepos, Pro-P[raetorian] Legate.'
3 Cf. from Moresby (*RIB* I 801) '(This work) of the Emperor Caesar Trajan Hadrian Augustus, Father of his Country, the XX Legion Valeria Victrix (built).'
4 See further Jarrett.
5 See Salway (1), p. 183.
6 Ibid. pp. 193f, 197ff.
7 *Proceedings of the Society of Antiquaries of Scotland*. Because of damage there is uncertainty whether the inscription refers to the second or third consulship of Antoninus. II would date the inscription to AD 139–40, making the building very early; III would date it to AD 140–4. See further Maxwell (2).
8 For the dating of the reference see Salway (1), p. 199. Identification of the region is discussed by Hind (2).

9 See further Davies, cf. Bogaers (2) pp. 24–7, Wilkes, Speidel p. 235f., Frere (2) p. 329.

10 It is generally believed that the wall referred to here is Hadrian's. However, an altar from Castlecary (§381) has been dated to the 180s, suggesting a Roman presence on the Antonine Wall as late as this.

11 See further Brassington.

X Albinus and the Severan Dynasty

With the reign of Commodus prematurely terminated by the Emperor's assassination in AD 192, it was in fact to Pertinax that Rome now looked for the restoration of stable government. His efforts to restore discipline to the capital, however, were to prove as unsuccessful as his governorship of Britain had been, and within months he too fell victim to the same Praetorian guards who had murdered Commodus, and who were now prepared to sell the throne to the highest bidder. Yet while the guards might be content to invest Didius Julianus with imperial honours, they failed to realise that far more powerful figures were now poised at the head of provincial armies to advance their own claims:

158. Epitome of Dio Cassius LXXIII, 14, 3

At that time three men, each in command of three legions of citizens and numerous other foreign troops, took control of affairs: Severus, Niger, and Albinus, the last of these being in command of Britain, Severus of Pannonia, and Niger of Syria.

Taking advantage of his geographical proximity to the heart of the empire Severus was able to steal a march on those who were to be his rivals, seize Italy, and by offering Albinus the rank of Caesar, implying a division of power and eventual succession, to leave his hands free for the struggle with Niger:

159. Epitome of Dio Cassius LXXIII, 15, 1–2

Of the three commanders I have mentioned the shrewdest was Severus. He realised that after Julianus had been deposed the three of them would come into conflict with one another and fight for the empire, and he decided to win over the one who was nearer to him. For this reason he sent Albinus a letter through someone he trusted appointing him Caesar,[1] for he realised he would get nowhere with Niger who had set his sights high as a result of being the people's choice. Albinus, therefore, remained where he was in the belief that he would share the government with Severus, and Severus, after winning over all Europe with the exception of Byzantium, hastened on to Rome ...

Severus' ploy against Albinus, the success of which some in antiquity attributed to the latter's naive conceit, seems also to have been designed to mollify senatorial opinion:

160. Herodian (3rd C. AD) II, 15, 1–5

Severus made careful preparations for the war (against Niger), but being a cautious and wary individual he had his suspicions about the forces in Britain. These were large and powerful, and constituted very effective fighters. In command of them was Albinus, a man who by birth belonged to the nobility that made up the Senate, and who had been brought up amidst wealth and inherited luxury. Severus therefore wanted to trick him into giving him his support. He was concerned in fact that with such inducements to aim for the throne and relying on his wealth, family ties, the strength of his army and his reputation among the Romans, Albinus might make a bid for power and occupy Rome, which was no great distance away, while Severus had his hands full in the east. So, using as bait the semblance of doing him honour, Severus got him on his hook. Albinus was in any case a conceited and rather naive character who believed the many promises Severus made in his letters. He appointed him Caesar, thereby anticipating Albinus' hopes and desires with a share of power, and he sent him a most friendly letter, earnestly entreating him to devote himself to the welfare of the empire. Severus claimed he needed a man of nobility such as Albinus, one still in the prime of life, since he himself was old, afflicted with gout, and his sons as yet still very young. Albinus believed all this and gladly accepted the honour, delighted to have achieved his ambition without a fight or running any risks. Severus also brought the matter up in the Senate so as to reinforce Albinus' loyalty, sanctioned the striking of coins of Albinus, and by the erection of statues and other honours confirmed the favour conferred. When, therefore, by his cunning Severus had secured his position as far as

Albinus was concerned and there was nothing to fear from Britain, he moved against Niger accompanied by the whole Illyrian army in the belief that everything was arranged to the advantage of his own rule.

A dedication for the safety of Severus and Albinus:

161. From Rome (*ILS* 414 restored)

To the holy goddess Fortune of the Home, Lucius Valerius Frontinus, Centurion of the 2nd Cohort of the Watch set up this altar at his own expense along with his family for the safe return of Lucius Septimius Severus Pertinax Augustus [and Decimus Clodius] Septim[ius Albinus Caesar].

By AD 196, however, it was becoming clear that neither Severus nor Albinus any longer believed in the permanence of their previous arrangement:

162. Epitome of Dio Cassius LXXV, 4, 1

Before Severus could draw breath after his war with the barbarians, he was once more involved in civil war against his Caesar, Albinus. For now that he was rid of Niger and had arranged matters in that quarter as he wanted them, Severus no longer accorded him the rank of Caesar. Albinus on the other hand sought the dignity of being Emperor.

Certainly, hints of a Senate-based conspiracy to replace him seem to have prompted Severus to make the first move:

163. Herodian (3rd C. AD) III, 5, 2–8

Once Niger had been disposed of Albinus was considered a superfluous annoyance. Severus also received reports that he was revelling in the title of Caesar in a way more reminiscent of an emperor, and that many people, in particular the more prominent members of the Senate, were sending him personal letters urging him to come to Rome while Severus was absent and otherwise occupied. The aristocracy in fact preferred to have him on the throne since he was sprung from a long line of noble ancestors and was said to possess a pleasant temperament. On learning this Severus decided against an immediate and open breach or a declaration of war against him, since Albinus had given no valid cause (for such a move). Instead he decided to try to get rid of him, if at all possible, by underhand deception. He therefore sent for the most trustworthy of his usual imperial dispatch-carriers and gave them instructions to hand over their dispatches in public, should they be admitted into Albinus' presence, and then to ask him to withdraw in order to hear in greater privacy some secret instructions. If Albinus agreed, they were suddenly to attack and kill him while unprotected by his bodyguards. Severus also gave them poisonous drugs so that given the opportunity they might prevail upon some of Albinus' cooks or wineservers to administer them in secret and despite the suspicions of Albinus' advisers, who warned him to be on his guard against a man given to treachery and an expert at scheming. Severus' actions against Niger's generals had in fact blackened his character, since he had forced them through their children to betray Niger's cause, as has already been mentioned. Once, however, he had made full use of their services and had achieved his aims, Severus did away with them together with their children. It was these actions most of all that made plain the treacherous nature of Severus' character. As a result, Albinus surrounded himself with a larger bodyguard and none of Severus' messengers came near him without first taking off the swords they wore as soldiers and being searched for weapons concealed beneath their clothes. So it was that Severus' messengers arrived and handed over the dispatches in public. Then they asked him to withdraw in order to hear certain secret matters. Albinus, however, became suspicious, ordered their arrest, and by putting them to the torture one at a time, discovered the whole plot. The men were punished, and Albinus himself began preparations against an enemy who had more or less shown his hand.[2]

With the failure of the assassination attempt Severus was now thrown back into open warfare, though first he prevailed upon the Senate to legitimise the conflict by declaring Albinus a public enemy:

164. Scriptores Historiae Augustae, *Severus* 10, 1–2

As Severus was returning to Rome after the civil war with Niger, he received news of another civil war, this time against Clodius Albinus, who had revolted in Gaul ... He therefore had Albinus immediately declared an enemy of the state together with those who wrote to Albinus in favourable terms and received similar replies.[3]

In this more open phase of hostilities Albinus is described as being caught curiously unprepared, though this seems not to have hindered his move into Gaul to prepare his positions and await the struggle to come:

165. Herodian (3rd C. AD) III, 7, 1

When it was reported to Albinus as he languished in his life of luxury that Severus was wasting no time and would soon be upon him, he was thrown into a state of panic. Crossing from Britain to Gaul opposite he there established his base and sent to all the neighbouring provinces ordering their governors to send him money and supplies for his army. Some complied and sent supplies – a fatal mistake since they were later punished for it. Those, however, who did not comply were saved more by luck than by sound judgement, since it was the chance outcome of war that decided the soundness of each man's judgement.

In the initial skirmishes with Severan forces Albinus was able to gain the upper hand, but in the decisive engagement outside Lyons against Severus himself Albinus met his Waterloo:

166. Epitome of Dio Cassius LXXV, 6–7

6   The struggle between Severus and Albinus at Lyons took place as follows. On each side were 150,000 troops, and since this was the final showdown, both commanders were present in the conflict, though Severus had been at none of the other battles. Albinus was superior in terms of family background and education, but in warfare Severus was the better man and a shrewd commander. Notwithstanding this Albinus had managed to defeat Lupus, one of Severus' generals, in an earlier battle and had slain many of the troops with him. The present conflict, however, had many phases and changes of fortune. So, for instance, Albinus' left wing was defeated and fell back on their defences. Severus' troops, pursuing them, burst in with them and began slaughtering them and plundering their tents. In the meantime, however, those troops of Albinus stationed on the right wing advanced as far as the concealed trenches and the pits covered with a layer of earth they had in front of them, and threw their javelins at a distance. Further than this they did not go; instead they turned back as if afraid, so as to draw their adversaries in pursuit after them. And this is what

happened. Severus' men, irritated by their brief advance and despising them for their flight after so short a distance, rushed at them as though all the ground between them was passable, but then met with a dreadful disaster when they came to the trenches. Straight away the surface covering caved in and the soldiers in the front rank fell into the pits. Those behind crashed into them, lost their footing, and likewise fell in. The rest drew back in fear, but because of their sudden about-turn they themselves stumbled, and threw those to their rear into a state of confusion, forcing them as a result into a deep ravine. There was a great loss of life involving men and horses both among these latter and those who fell into the trenches. In the midst of all this tumult those who were between the ravine and the trenches were also being cut down by missiles and arrows. When Severus saw this, he came to their rescue with his Praetorian Guard, but far from helping them, he almost destroyed the Praetorians as well, and put himself in danger by losing his horse. When he saw all his troops in retreat, he tore off his cloak, drew his sword, and rushed in among his fleeing men to make them turn back out of shame, or to perish with them himself. Some at least did halt when they saw him like this, and did turn back. In doing so, however, they suddenly came face to face with those following them, and many of these they cut down in the belief that they were Albinus' forces, though they did also rout all those who were in fact pursuing them. At this point the cavalry under Laetus came up from the flank and completed the task . . .

7   In this way Severus secured his victory, but Roman power suffered a serious reversal, since countless men had fallen on both sides . . . Albinus took refuge in a house situated beside the Rhone, and when he saw the whole place was surrounded, he committed suicide.[4]

Following his victory in AD 197 one of Severus' first reported acts towards Britain was the division of the province into two:

167. Herodian III, 8, 2

Having settled matters in Britain, Severus divided control of the province into two commands.

Doubt, however, surrounds the question of whether the measure underwent immediate implementation.[5] Herodian's later description of the disturbances there (III, 14, 1, §174) suggests in fact a continuing unified command. Upon recovery of Britain, though, the newly appointed Governor, Virius Lupus, straight away initiated a programme of fort rebuilding in the region of the Pennines, suggesting that it was here the main danger to stability for the moment lay:

168. From Ilkley (*RIB* I 637)

The Emperor Severus Augustus and Antoninus Caesar[6] (Caracalla) destined (to be emperor) restored this under the direction of Virius Lupus, their Pro-Praetorian Legate.

169. From Brough-under-Stainmore (*RIB* I 757 restored)

For the Emperor Caesar Lucius Septimius Severus Pius P[ertin]ax Augustus and [Marcus Aurelius Anto]ninus Caesar (Caracalla) [. . .] in the consulship of [Later]a[nus] and R[uf]inus (AD 197).

170. From Bowes (*RIB* I 730)

To the goddess Fortune, Virius Lupus, Pro-Praetorian Legate of Augustus, restored this bathhouse destroyed by fire for the 1st Cohort of Thracians, under the direction of Valerius Fronto, Commander of the cavalry squadron of Vettones.

At the same time, however, came rumblings of potential trouble from beyond the northern frontier:

171. Epitome of Dio Cassius LXXV, 5, 4

Since the Caledonians did not remain true to their promises and had made preparations to assist the Maeatae,[7] and since at the time Severus was embroiled in war elsewhere, Lupus was forced to buy peace from the Maeatae for a large sum, and in exchange recovered a few captives.[8]

By AD 206–7 the Governor was Alfenus Senecio, and the main process of fort restoration had shifted to the region of Hadrian's wall:

172. From Birdoswald (*RIB* I 1909 restored)

For the Emperor-Caesars Lucius Septimius Severus Pius Pertinax and Marcus Aurelius Antoninus, the Augusti, [and for Publius

Septimius Geta, Most Noble Caesar] the 1st Aelian Cohort of Dacians and 1st Cohort of Thracians, Roman Citizens, built this granary under Alfenus Senecio, Consular Governor, through the agency of the Tribune Aurelius Julianus.

173. From Risingham (*RIB* I 1234 restored)

[For the Emperor-Caesars Lucius Septimius Severus Pius Pertinax, conqueror of Arabia, Adi]abene, most great conqueror of Parthia, thrice Consul, and for Marcus Aurelius Antoninus Pius, twice Consul, Augusti, [and for Publius Septimius Geta, Noble Caesar], the 1st Cohort of Vangiones 1,000-strong, part-mounted, restored from ground-level this gate and its walls which had collapsed through age, by order of His Excellency Alfenus Senecio, Consular Governor, and under the direction of Oclatinus Adventus,[9] Procurator of our Emperors, together with the Tribune Aemilius Salvianus.

Unlike the Pennine restorations, however, that at Risingham was demonstrably necessitated by the natural deterioration of age rather than enemy action. Noteworthy, though, is the part played by the Procurator, and behind Senecio's appeal for direct imperial intervention may well be a threat or even the reality of serious trouble:

174. Herodian (3rd C. AD) III, 14, 1

Severus was becoming disturbed by the lifestyle of his sons and their unseemly enthusiasm for public spectacles, when the Governor of Britain sent word to him that the barbarians were in revolt and that they were overrunning the country, looting it and causing widespread havoc. He therefore requested additional forces to protect the place or a visitation by the Emperor.

Severus' favourable reaction to the invitation despite his advanced years and failing health is regarded by Dio not only as an attempt to remove his sons from their dissolute life in Rome, but also as a means of maintaining the efficiency of the army:

175. Epitome of Dio Cassius LXXVI, 11, 1

Seeing that his sons were becoming unruly and the army slack through inactivity, Severus made an expedition to Britain though he knew he would not return.

To these reasons Herodian adds the Emperor's continuing desire for military glory:

176. Herodian III, 14, 2–3

Severus was pleased to hear this, for besides being a natural lover of glory, he wanted to raise some victory-trophies at the expense of the Britons to add to the victories and titles won in the east and north. Then again, he wanted to get his sons away from Rome so that they might come to their senses amidst the disciplined life of the army, once they were away from the luxury and high life of Rome. For this reason he announced the expedition to Britain, even though he was by now an old man and suffering from gout. When it came to enthusiasm, however, he had more spirit than any young man. Most of the travelling he did being carried in a litter, but he never stopped to rest for any length of time, and he completed the journey in the company of his sons sooner than expected and faster than news of him could spread.

In AD 208 Severus arrived in Britain together with his family and court. After initial preparations the campaign could get under way:

177. Herodian III, 14, 3–10

Crossing Ocean Severus set foot in Britain. There he mustered troops from all parts, and having raised a powerful army, he made ready for the war. Alarmed by the unexpected arrival of the Emperor and hearing about the vast force that had been assembled against them, the Britons sent envoys to discuss peace terms and wished to explain away their past misdeeds. Severus, however, wanted to prolong matters so as to avoid a speedy return to Rome and also to secure a victory and title at the Britons' expense. He therefore dismissed their envoys empty-handed and made ready for the war. In particular he attempted to divide up the marshy areas with causeways (or bridges) so that advancing in safety his troops could effect an easy and rapid passage of these regions and fight from a firm and steady base . . . Against this background, therefore, Severus got ready everything likely to be of use to the Roman army and to damage or impede the attacks of the barbarians. When it seemed that sufficient preparations for the war had been made, he left Geta, the younger of his sons, in that part of the province under Roman control, to dispense justice and to carry on the civil administration of the empire. To this end he provided him with a council made up of his older friends. Antoninus (Caracalla) he took with him and he pressed on against the barbarians. Once the army had crossed the rivers and earthworks on the frontier of the Roman empire, there were frequent encounters and skirmishes with the enemy in which they were put to flight. However, it was easy for them to escape and to disappear into the woods and marshes because of their knowledge of the terrain, but all this hampered the Romans and dragged out the war considerably.

That Severus' penetration of Scotland was no easy undertaking, however, is clear from other sources:

178. Epitome of Dio Cassius LXXVI, 13

Wishing therefore to subdue the whole of Britain, Severus invaded Caledonia, and as he passed through it, he experienced untold difficulties in cutting down the forests, levelling the high ground, filling in the swamps, and bridging the rivers. He fought no battles nor did he see any enemy drawn up for battle. Instead they deliberately put sheep and cattle in the Romans' way for the soldiers to seize, so that they might be lured on further still and thus be worn out. In fact the Romans suffered great hardships because of the water, and any stragglers became a prey to ambush. Then, unable to go on, they would be killed by their own men so they might not fall into enemy hands. As a result as many as 50,000 died in all. However, Severus did not give up until he neared the furthest point of the island where in particular he observed with great accuracy the change in the sun's motion and the length of days and nights in both summer and winter. And so, having been conveyed through the whole of enemy territory as it were – for he actually was carried in a covered litter for much of the time on account of his infirmity – he returned to friendly territory once he had forced the Britons to come to terms whereby they ceded a large sector of their land.

Despite the ostensible victories of the first year's campaign, the following year, AD 210, saw a renewal of native resistance and a vicious Roman response, which seems to have served to widen the conflict:

179. Epitome of Dio Cassius LXXVI, 15, 1–2

When the inhabitants of the island rose again in rebellion, Severus called together his troops and ordered them to invade their territory and to kill everyone they found, and he quoted these lines: 'Let no one escape total destruction at our hands, not even the child carried in its mother's womb, if it be male; let it not escape total destruction'. When this had been done and the Caledonians had joined the Maeatae in revolt, Severus prepared to make war on them in person, and while he was engaged in this he was carried off by illness on the 4th of February (AD 211)[10] not without a certain amount of help it is said from Antoninus (Caracalla). Before his death he is said to have told his sons the following – I give the actual words spoken without any embellishment: 'Live in harmony with one another; enrich the soldiers, and ignore everyone else'.

The absence of the Emperor from the campaign of AD 210 implicit in Dio's statement that Severus intended to conduct the projected campaign of 211 in person, is confirmed by Herodian's account:

180. III, 15, 1–3

Severus was now afflicted in his old age by a more prolonged illness, and as a result was forced to remain in his quarters. He attempted to send Antoninus out to direct the campaign, but Antoninus had little interest in the action against the barbarians, and was trying instead to win over the army. He began to persuade the troops to look to him alone for orders, and canvassed for the position of sole ruler in every way he could, making slanderous attacks against his brother. His father, who had been ill for a long time and was taking his time dying, he regarded as a troublesome nuisance, and he tried to persuade the doctors and attendants to do the old man some injury as they treated him, so that he might be rid of him all the sooner. Eventually, however, worn out for the most part by grief, Severus passed away after a life more distinguished in military terms than any previous emperor. No one before him had won so many victories either in civil wars against rivals or in foreign wars against barbarians. After a reign of 18 years he made way for his young sons to succeed, leaving them greater wealth than anyone before and an irresistible army.

As usual the campaigns were celebrated with coin issues proclaiming victory:

181. Bronze sestertius (*RIC* IV. i p. 202 no. 818)

Obverse
L(ucius) Sept(imius) Severus Pius Aug(ustus)

Reverse
Victoriae Britannicae (Victories in Britain)
S(enatus) C(onsulto) (By decree of the Senate)

182. Bronze sestertius (*RIC* IV. i p. 288 no. 465)

Obverse
M(arcus) Aurel(ius) Antoninus Pius Aug(ustus) (Caracalla)

Reverse
As above

183. Bronze sestertius (*RIC* IV. i. p. 288 no. 464)

Obverse

M(arcus) Aurel(ius) Antoninus Pius Aug(ustus) (Caracalla)

Reverse

As above

For some reason it is to Severus that some later writers attributed the construction of the Hadrianic and Antonine frontiers – a salutary reminder that sources can and do at times propagate nonsense:[11]

184. Eutropius (4th C. AD) VIII, 19, 1

His final campaign was in Britain, and so as to fortify with complete security the provinces he had recovered, he built a wall for 32 (or 132) miles from sea to sea. He died at York, a pretty old man, after a reign of 16 years 3 months.

The story, repeated in the fourth century by both Aurelius Victor[12] and the Scriptores Historiae Augustae,[13] was continued in the fifth century by writers like Orosius, though with the difference that the wall is now an earth rampart:

185. *Adversum Paganos (Against the Pagans)* VII, 17, 7–8

The victorious Severus was forced to go to Britain by the revolt of almost all the allies. There, after a large number of difficult engagements, he decided to separate off that part of the island he had recovered from the other unconquered tribes by means of a rampart. And so he built a great ditch and very strong rampart, fortified with numerous towers on it for 132 miles from sea to sea. And there he died of disease at the town of Eboracum.

cf.

186. Hieronymus (late 4th C. AD), *Chronica*, AD 207

Once Clodius Albinus, who had made himself Caesar in Gaul, had been killed at Lyons, Severus directed the war against the Britons. There, in order to make the provinces he had recovered more secure against attack by the barbarians, he built a rampart for 132 miles from sea to sea.

These references, presumably to the Antonine wall, were ultimately to find their way into Bede, writing in the eighth century:

187. *Historia Ecclesiastica Gentis Anglorum* (*History of the English Church*) I, 5

In the year of our Lord 189 (actually 193) Severus, by birth an African from the town of Leptis in Tripolitania, succeeded to the throne, the 17th Emperor after Augustus, and reigned for 17 years. Cruel in his character and constantly troubled by numerous wars, he ruled the state with great vigour, but also with a great deal of trouble. Following his victory in the grievous civil wars which assailed him he was forced to go to Britain by the revolt of almost all the allies. There, after a large number of difficult engagements, he decided to separate off that part of the island he had recovered from the other unconquered tribes not by means of a wall, as some think, but by a rampart. For a wall is made of stone, but a rampart, with which a camp is fortified to repel the might of enemies, is made of turf cut from the earth and raised high above the ground like a wall. In front of it as a result is a ditch from which the turfs have been taken, and on top of it are fixed stakes made from the hardest wood. In this way Severus built a great ditch and very strong rampart fortified with numerous towers on it from sea to sea. And there he died of disease at the town of Eboracum.

The lack of enthusiasm attributed to Caracalla's prosecution of the Caledonian campaign while his father was still alive, was more than matched after Severus' death by a speedy abandonment of what had so far been gained:

188. Epitome of Dio Cassius LXXVII, 1, 1

After this (the death of Severus) Antoninus assumed total control. In theory he ruled jointly with his brother, but in practice he was sole ruler from the start. The sources say he made peace with the enemy, withdrew from their territory, and abandoned the forts.

cf.

189. Herodian (3rd C. AD) III, 15, 6–7

When Antoninus made no progress with the army (in getting it to recognise him as sole ruler), he came to terms with the barbarians, granting them peace in return for pledges of good faith, left their territory and now hastened back to his mother and brother ... (Caracalla is forced to accept joint rule with Geta while regarding this as a temporary expedient) ... So the two of them administered the empire with equal authority. They decided to leave Britain and hastened back to Rome, taking with them their father's remains.

Despite this, coins commemorating victories in AD 211 continued to be minted. Did the literary sources suppress mention of a whole campaign, or do the coins pass off as victory what was in fact withdrawal?

190. Bronze sestertius (*RIC* IV. i p. 291 no. 483c)

Obverse
M(arcus) Aurel(ius) Antoninus Pius Aug(ustus) Brit(annicus)

Reverse
Vict(oriae) Brit(annicae) (Victories in Britain) Tr(ibunicia) P(otestas) (Tribunician Power) XIIII (times) Cos (Consul) III (times, AD 211) S(enatus) C(onsulto) (By decree of the Senate)

Or does a very fragmentary inscription from Carpow which seems to refer to AD 212 and continued construction there indicate that withdrawal from Scotland was less precipitate than is often represented?[14] The friction between Severus' two sons during their stay in Britain, to which Herodian (III, 15, §189) gives witness, culminated early in 212 with the assassination of Geta. A rash of dedications declaring loyalty to Caracalla and dated to 213 could well mark an official response to counteract the unrest the event had caused:

191. From Old Carlisle (*RIB* I 905 restored)

... for the welfare of] our Lord, [the Emperor Marcus Aurelius Antoni]nus Pius Felix [Augustus, under] his Legate [Gaius Julius Ma]rcus, on the direction of [. . .] Prefect, the Augusta cavalry squadron [set this up in the fourth] consulship of the Emperor Antoninus [Augustus and] the second of Balbinus.

192. From Whitley Castle (*RIB* I 1202 restored)

For the Emperor Caesar, son [of the dei]f[ied] Lucius [Septimius Severus Pius Pertinax Augustus], most great conqueror of [Ara]bia, Adia[bene, and Parthia], grandson of the deified Anton[inus] Pius (Marcus Aurelius), conqueror of G[ermany] and Sarmatia, great-grandson of the deified Antoni[nus Pius], great-great-grandson of the deified Hadrian, great-great-great-grandson of the deified Trajan, conqueror of Parthia, and of the deified Nerva, Marcus Aurelius Antoninus Pius Felix Augustus (Caracalla), mo[st great] conqueror of [P]arthia and [. . .] Pontifex Ma[ximus] (High Priest) in the sixteenth (?) year of his holding Tribunician Power, twice saluted Imperator, four times Consul, Father of his Country, out of their joint duty and devotion, under the direction of [Gaius Julius Marcus], Pro-Praetorian Legate of Augustus, the 2nd Cohort of Nervii, Roman Citizens, [devoted to his divine authority and majesty], set this up.[15]

That Caracalla's settlement of the northern frontier was, however, more successful than the haste with which Dio and Herodian describe his withdrawal from Scotland would imply, is given weight by the absence of references to trouble in the north for more than three-quarters of a century. Similarly, with the Severan division of Britain into two provinces now fully implemented, it was in the south, not the north, that the bulk of legionary forces was concentrated:

193. Dio Cassius (2nd–3rd C. AD) LV, 23, 2–6

Today only 19 of the legions (i.e. those existing in Augustus' day) remain: the II Augusta, which has its winter quarters in Britannia Superior (S. Britain) . . . the two VI legions, of which one, called Victrix, is in Britannia Inferior (N. Britain) . . . the XX, called Valeria Victrix, in Britannia Superior (S. Britain).

Similarly, it was Britannia Superior which ranked higher in terms of those who governed it:

194. From Caerleon (*RIB* I 334)

The Emperors Valerian and Gallienus, Augusti, and Valerian, most noble Caesar, restored from ground-level barrack-blocks for the 7th Cohort, through the agency of His Excellency (*vir clarissimus* signifying Senatorial rank) Desticius Juba, Pro-Praetorian Legate of the Emperors, and of Vitulasius Laetinianus, Legate of the II Legion Augusta, under the direction of Domitius Potentinus, Prefect of the same legion.

In contrast, the following inscription from South Shields has no reference to Senatorial status:

195. *RIB* I 1060

The Emperor Caesar Marcus Aurelius Severus Alexander Pius Felix Augustus, grandson of the deified Severus, son of the deified Antoninus the Great, Pontifex Maximus (High Priest) with Tribunician Power, Father of his Country, Consul, brought this water-supply[16] for the use of soldiers of the 5th Cohort of Gauls, under the direction of Marius Valerianus, his Pro-Praetorian Legate.

The continuation of restoration work along the northern frontier throughout the period of the Severan dynasty, however, ensures it is Britannia Inferior that is the better documented of the two:

196. From High Rochester (*RIB* I 1279)

For the Emperor Caesar Marcus Aurelius Severus Antoninus Pius Felix Augustus (Caracalla), most great conqueror of Parthia, Britain and Germany, Pontifex Maximus (High Priest), in the nineteenth year of his holding Tribunician Power (AD 216), twice saluted

Imperator, four times Consul, Proconsul, Father of his Country, the 1st Loyal Cohort of Vardulli, Roman Citizens, part-mounted, 1,000-strong, Antoninus' own, built this under [. . .],[17] Pro-Praetorian Legate of Augustus.

197. From Birdoswald (*RIB* I 1914)

Under Modius Julius (AD 219), Pro-Praetorian Legate of Augustus, the 1st Aelian Cohort of Dacians under the command of the Tribune Marcus Claudius Menander (built this).

198. From High Rochester (*RIB* I 1280 restored)

For the Emperor Caesar Marcus Aurelius Antoninus Pius Felix Augustus (Elagabalus), in the third year of his holding Tribunician Power (AD 220), three times Consul, P[roconsul], Father of his Country, the 1st Loyal Cohort of Vardulli, A[ntoninus' own], built this artillery platform from ground-level under the direction of Tiberius Claudius Paul[inus], Pro-Praetorian [Le]gate of Augustus, [and under the superintendence] of the [Tribune], Publius Ae[lius Erasinus].

199. From Chesters (*RIB* I 1465 restored)

The Emperor Caesar Marcus Aurelius [Antoninus Pius Felix] A[ugustus, most glorious priest of the Unconquered Sun-god Elagabalus], Pontifex Maximus (High Priest), [in the fourth year of his holding Tr]ibunician Power, [thrice] Consul, Father of his Country, [son of] the deified [Antoninus], grandson of the deified Severus, and Marcus [Aur]elius [Alexander, most noble] Caesar, [his partner] in empire, . . . [restored (this building) which had collapsed] through age for the 2nd cavalry squadron of Asturians, [Antoninus' own], through the agency of Marius Valer[ianus, Pro-Praetorian Legate of the Augusti] under the superintendence of the Pre[fect of cavalry], Septimius Nilus. Dedicated on October 30th [in the consulship] of Gr[at]us and Sele[ucus] (AD 221).

200. From Chesterholm (*RIB* I 1706 restored)

. . . The 4th Cohort] of Gauls, [Severus Alexander's own, de]voted to his divinity, [resto]red from ground-level this gate[way together with its to]wers under Claudius Xenephon, Pro-[Praetorian] Legate of our [Emperor in Britannia Inferior] (AD 223), under the direction of [. . .

201. From Great Chesters (*RIB* I 1738 restored)

The Emperor Caesar Marcus Aurelius Severus Alexander Pius Felix Augustus restored from ground level this granary, which had collapsed through age, for the soldiers of the 2nd Cohort of Asturians, Severus Alexander's own, while the province was being governed by [. . .] Maximus, [Pro-Praetorian] Legate [of Augustus, under the direction] of Valerius Martia[lis, Centurion of the . . . Legion in the consulship of Fu]sc[us for the second time and Dexter] (AD 225).

In this same period units of barbarian troops, *cunei* and *numeri*, ranking lower than auxiliaries, begin to make their appearance:

202. From Housesteads (*RIB* I 1594)

To the god Mars and the two Alaisiagae, and to the divine power of the emperor, the German tribesmen of Tuihantis[18] of the formation (*cuneus*) of Frisians of Vercovicium, Severus Alexander's own, willingly and deservedly fulfilled their vow.[19]

NOTES

1 Worthy of note, though not of credence, are the claims found in Scriptores Historiae Augustae that the rank of Caesar had once been offered to Albinus by Commodus, and that Severus actually contemplated abdicating in Albinus' favour:

Albinus 6, 4–5
   These events (Albinus' defeat of German invaders into Gaul) impressed themselves upon Commodus and he offered Albinus the title of Caesar and the power to award bounties and to wear the scarlet cloak. All these distinctions, however, Albinus wisely declined, alleging that Commodus was looking for someone who would either perish with him or whom he could justifiably put to death.

Severus 6, 9–10
   At the same time (AD 193) Severus also considered abdicating in favour of Clodius Albinus, to whom, on the prompting of Commodus, the position of Caesar seems already to have been decreed. However, being very much afraid of Albinus and Niger, his opinion of whom was proved correct, he sent Heraclitus to take over Britain and Plautianus to seize Niger's children.

The reported complicity of Clodius Albinus in the murder of Pertinax (Aurelius Victor, *Liber de Caesaribus* 20, 9, calls him 'the author of Pertinax's murder') suggests instead an additional cause of friction between him and Severus, who posed as Pertinax's avenger:

> *Orosius* (5th C. AD), *Adversum Paganos* (*Against the Pagans*) VII, 17, 1
> Severus wished to be called Pertinax after the emperor of that name, whose death he had avenged.

2 The reported attempt on Albinus' life is also given by Scriptores Historiae Augustae, *Albinus* 8.

3 According to Scriptores Historiae Augustae, *Albinus* 9, 1, however, the denunciation as a public enemy followed rather than preceded Albinus' initial victory over Lupus in Gaul (§166).

4 Shorter accounts of the battle are also given by Herodian III, 7, and by Scriptores Historiae Augustae, *Severus* 10–11 and *Albinus* 9. The latter two also provide variants on the circumstances of Albinus' death:

> Scriptores Historiae Augustae, *Albinus* 9, 3–4
> Albinus fled the field and, according to many, stabbed himself, or, as others relate, was stabbed by his slave and taken to Severus hovering between life and death. In this way the prophecy previously given (that Albinus would fall into Severus' hands neither dead nor alive) proved correct. Many state as well that he was slain by soldiers who asked for a reward from Severus for his death.

> Scriptores Historiae Augustae, *Severus* 11, 6–7
> Albinus' body was brought to Severus, who ordered him to be beheaded while still half-alive, and the head carried to Rome ... Albinus was defeated on February 19th.

5 See further Graham.

6 Caracalla was promoted from Caesar to joint-Augustus in AD 198.

7 See *The Geography and Peoples of Britain* (§16); cf. Salway (1), p. 225f.

8 See further A.R. Birley (1).

9 On Adventus see Rankov.

10 The location of Severus' death, York, is given by Scriptores Historiae Augustae, *Severus* 19, 1

> Having conquered those tribes that seemed hostile to Britain and now an old man worn out by a very serious illness, Severus died at Eboracum (York) in Britain, in the 18th year of his reign.

> cf. Aurelius Victor, *Liber de Caesaribus* 20, 27

> Shortly afterwards he died of disease in Britain, in the municipium called Eboracum (York), after a reign of 18 years.

11 See, however, Hassall.

12 *Liber de Caesaribus* 20, 18

> Undertaking a still greater enterprise, he fortified Britain, in as much as it was useful, with a wall built across the island from coast to coast on either side, having first driven back the enemy.

13 *Severus* 18, 2

> He fortified Britain with a wall built across the island from coast to coast on either side, the crowning glory of his reign. For this he was awarded the title Britannicus.

14 From Carpow (*JRS* 55 (1965) pp. 223–4).

> Emperor a[nd Our Lord Marcus Aurelius Antoninus Piu]s F[elix . . .

See further Wright.

15 Cf. *RIB* 1235 (Risingham), 1278 (High Rochester).
16 For water supplied to Chesters fort cf. *RIB* I 1463.

> Water supplied for the 2nd cavalry squadron of Asturians under Ulpius Marcellus, Pro-Praetorian Legate of Augustus.

17 The name of the Governor has been deliberately erased as an act of disgrace. Evidence from elsewhere suggests it may have been the Elder Gordian, destined to be emperor in AD 238.
18 Probably Twenthe in Holland.
19 Cf. from High Rochester (*RIB* I 1270) undated.

> Sacred to the goddess Roma. The soldiers on double pay (*duplicarii*) in the unit (*numerus*) of Scouts (*Exploratores*) at Bremenium set up this altar on her birthday (April 21st) under the direction of Caepio Charitinus Tribune, willingly and deservedly fulfilling their vow.

Ibid. (*RIB* I 1262)

> To the Spirit of Our Lord and the Standards of the 1st Cohort of Vardulli and the unit (*numerus*) of Scouts (*Exploratores*) at Bremenium, Gordian's Own, Egnatius Lucilianus, Pro-Praetorian Legate of Augustus (set this up) under the direction of the Tribune Cassius Sabinianus (AD 238–41).

XI Usurpation and Recovery

Following the murder of Severus Alexander in AD 235 the empire was shaken by nearly two decades of governmental chaos as one usurper after another laid claim to the imperial throne. Though the accession of Valerian and Gallienus in 253 brought with it a period of relative respite, the western defences of the empire, severely weakened by civil war, were put under still further strain when a massive invasion by the Alamanni of Germany was able to penetrate as far as Milan in 258. In 260 Gallienus' own commander on the Rhine, Postumus, asserted his claim to rule and won support from the provinces of Germany, Gaul, Spain and Britain.

203. Milestone from Trecastle Hill (*RIB* I 2260)

For our Lord, the Emperor Marcus Cassianius Latinius Postumus Pius Felix Augustus.

204. From Lancaster (*RIB* I 605 restored)

[For the Emperor Postumus[1] . . . on account of] the rebuilt bath-house [and] the basilica which had collapsed through age and was rebuilt from ground-level for the troopers of the Sebosian cavalry squadron, [Postumus' own], under His Excellency Octavius Sabinus, our Governor (*Praeses*), and under the direction of Flavius Ammausius, Prefect of cavalry. Dedicated on August 22nd in the second consulship of Censor and Lepidus.

For the next 14 years the west was to constitute a separate Gallic empire and it was not until 274 that it was eventually suppressed by Aurelian. Later still, the reign of Probus (276–82) saw a further attempt at secession instigated by Bonosus:

205. Scriptores Historiae Augustae, *Probus* 18, 5

Then Proculus and Bonosus seized power in Gaul at Agrippina and claimed for themselves all the provinces of Britain, Spain and Further Gaul. Probus, however, defeated them with the help of barbarians.

Within Britain too we hear of rebellion, by an unnamed governor:

206. Zosimus (5th–6th C. AD) I, 66, 2

Probus also put an end to another rebellion, which had broken out in Britain, through the agency of Victorinus, a Moor by birth. It was on his advice that Probus had come to appoint as governor of Britain the man who was now in revolt. Having summoned Victorinus, he censured him for his advice and sent him to rectify his mistake. Victorinus immediately set out for Britain and got rid of the usurper by means of a clever trick.

As in the days of Marcus Aurelius, however, Britain continued to provide a useful station for prisoners of war, and it was here that Probus sent the survivors of his victory over the Vandals and Burgundians in 277:

207. Zosimus I, 68, 1–3

He fought a second battle against the Franks, over whom he won a resounding victory through his generals, and then personally engaged the Burgundians and Vandals in battle ... Those he was able to take alive he sent to Britain, where they settled and became useful to the Emperor when anyone later rebelled.

With the accession of Diocletian to the throne in 284, the empire at long last saw a return to stable and firm government. The following year he appointed Maximian to the rank of Caesar with responsibility for defending the Western Empire, and in 286 Maximian was further elevated to the rank of joint Augustus. In his efforts to counteract the increasing problem of piratical raids on the coasts of Gaul and Britain, however, Maximian was inadvertently sowing the seeds of further rebellion:

208. Aurelius Victor (4th C. AD), *Liber de Caesaribus* 39, 20–1

In this war[2] Carausius, a Menapian, distinguished himself by his effective actions. For this reason and because he was considered an expert pilot – in his youth he had earned his living in this capacity – he was put in charge of fitting out a fleet and repelling the Germans who infested the seas. Carried away by this promotion, he failed to restore the whole of the booty to the treasury, though he intercepted many of the barbarians, and through fear of Herculius (Maximian) who, he discovered, had ordered his death, he assumed the title of Emperor and seized control of Britain.

cf.

209. Eutropius (4th C. AD) IX, 21

About this time too Carausius, a man of very low birth, had won great distinction as a result of a successful career in the army. From his headquarters in Bononia (Boulogne) he had undertaken the task of policing the sea in the region of Belgica and Armorica (north-west Gaul), which was then swarming with Franks and Saxons. However, though many barbarians were frequently intercepted, their booty was not returned to the provincials in its entirety, nor was it sent to the Emperors. As a result the suspicion arose that he was deliberately letting the barbarians in so as to catch them as they passed through with their booty and in this way enrich himself. When his execution was ordered by Maximian, he assumed the purple and seized control of Britain.[3]

From the point of view of the empire the loss of Britain and much of northern Gaul[4] was a not inconsiderable blow, even discounting the purple prose with which some sources describe the event. It is also clear that the Franks and Saxons in the Channel were not the only enemy Britain now faced. For the first time we begin to hear of an Irish menace:

210. Panegyric on Constantius Caesar (delivered AD 297) 11

And certainly, though Britain was but a single name, its loss to the state was not without significance – a land so rich in harvests, with such abundant pasture, shot through with so many seams of ore, a lucrative source of so much tribute, girded round with so many ports, so vast in its extent. When Caesar, the origin of your name, entered it, the first Roman to do so, he wrote that he had found another world. . . . The Britons too, at that time primitive and used only to foes as yet half-naked, like the Picts and the Irish, gave way with ease before the arms and standards of Rome, so much so that in his campaigns Caesar should have made this single boast: that he had crossed the Ocean.

Notwithstanding the personal motivation attributed to the rebellion, the fact that Carausius was able to gain and retain widespread support on both sides of the Channel suggests no small disenchantment with the central government:

211. Ibid. 12, 1

In that vile act of brigandage the fleeing pirate seized first the fleet which once protected provinces of Gaul, built many more besides in Roman style, seduced a Roman legion,[5] cut off divisions of provincial troops, recruited Gallic merchants to his service, won over hordes of barbarous forces by spoils from the provinces themselves, and through instruction by supporters of that disgraceful act he trained them all for naval duties.

Carausius' preparations for the inevitable clash with Maximian were not in fact to prove untimely. An early and much vaunted attempt was made to topple the usurper, probably in AD 288–9:

212. Panegyric on Maximian (delivered AD 289) 11, 7 and 12, 1–8

11 It is a mark I say of your good fortune, your success, oh Emperor, that even now your soldiers have reached the Ocean victorious; even now the ebb and flow of tide has drained the blood of enemies slaughtered on that shore.

12 What spirit does that pirate[6] now possess, when he sees your armies almost reach the strait which alone thus far delays his death, armies that forget their ships and follow the receding sea? What island more remote, what other Ocean can he long for? . . . The finest fleets were constructed and equipped, fleets that were destined to make for Ocean along every river at once[7] . . . Thus did the vessels make their assault upon the waves that of their own accord slipped under them, vessels gently set in motion by the efforts of those who

propelled them . . . Thus, it is easy, Emperor, for all to understand what propitious success will attend you in this maritime undertaking . . .

In contrast, the almost total silence of the panegyricists as regards its outcome, together with a reference to bad weather, suggest it fell far short of its intended aim:

213. Panegyric on Constantius Caesar (delivered AD 297) 12, 1–2

Your troops in contrast, though in valour unsurpassed, were none the less unused to naval action. And so we heard that from a shameful act of brigandage the evil threat of war had sprung, sure though we were of its outcome. On top of this, the crime so long unpunished had fanned the insolence of those reckless men to boast that roughness of the sea, which by constraint of fate delayed your victory, was fear of them. The war had been abandoned in despair, so they believed, not just postponed by act of policy.

Clearly it was now for Maximian to come to terms with Carausius and bide his time:

214. Eutropius (4th C. AD) IX, 22, 2

Eventually, however, a peace was arranged with Carausius after military operations against this expert strategist had been attempted without success.

With his assumption of the purple, Carausius was not slow to bolster up his powerful military and naval position with a propaganda campaign waged through the medium of coinage:

215. Silver denarius (*RIC* V. 2 p. 510 no. 554)

Obverse
Imp(erator) Carausius P(ius) F(elix) Au(gustus)

Reverse
Expectate Veni (Come, oh welcome and long-awaited one)
RSR (Mint-mark of London (?))

216. Bronze antoninianus (*RIC* V. 2 p. 493 no. 343)

Obverse
Imp(erator) G(aius) Carausius P(ius) Aug(ustus)

Reverse
Pietas Auggg[8] (The Piety of the three Augusti)

217. Bronze antoninianus (*RIC* V. 2 p. 550 no. 1)

Obverse
Carausius et Fratres Sui (Carausius and his Brothers)

Reverse
Pax Auggg (The Peace of the three Augusti)

218. Gold aureus (*RIC* V. 2 p. 554 no. 32)

Obverse

Maximianus P(ius) F(elix) Aug(ustus)

Reverse

Salus Auggg[9] (The Safety of the three Augusti)

In 293 the division of power between Diocletian and Maximian was
further enlarged by the appointment of two Caesars, thus effectively
dividing the empire into four spheres of influence. From now on the
task of removing Carausius was the responsibility of the Caesar
Constantius. Rather than repeat Maximian's ill-fated naval assault,
however, Constantius aimed first to seize Boulogne, Carausius' main
port of entry to mainland Europe, and in this way deny him access
to his continental power base:

219. Panegyric on Constantius Caesar 6, 1–2

And so immediately by your coming, Caesar, you made the provinces
of Gaul your own. Indeed that swiftness with which you outstripped
all the news of your elevation and arrival allowed you to seize and
crush within the walls of Gesoriacum (Boulogne) the company of
that piratical clique which still clung to its poor delusions; you denied
to them, who once relied upon the sea, the ocean lapping at their
city gates. In this your divine foresight and success, the equal of
your plans, displayed themselves; for all of that harbour's basin,
where the swell of Ocean ebbs and flows, you made impassable for
ships, with piles fixed at its mouth and added mounds of rock. You
overcame with marvellous ingenuity the very nature of the place;
for now the sea with ineffectual ebb and flow appeared as if to
mock them, prevented as they were from escape, and proved as
little use to them shut in as if it had ceased to flow at all.[10]

For Carausius the loss of Boulogne so soon after the elevation of
Constantius was evidently a blow to his prestige sufficiently great to
prompt his assassination:

220. Eutropius (4th C. AD) IX, 22, 2

After seven years (AD 293) Carausius was assassinated by his associate Allectus, who subsequently himself controlled the British
provinces for a space of three years.[11]

221. Bronze antoninianus (*RIC* V. 2 p. 562 no. 47)

Obverse
Imp(erator) G(aius) Allectus P(ius) F(elix) Aug(ustus)

Reverse
Temporum Felicitas (Happiness of the Age)

For the next phase of operations, the assault on Britain itself, Constantius would need a fleet. Its construction, together with the need to meet threats elsewhere along the western frontier, took up the next three years:

222. Panegyric on Constantine 5, 3

> And when by virtue of his valour he had seized that same army (in Boulogne) and by his mercy spared it, and while recovery of Britain was being put under way by building fleets, with guidance from a one-time native of the place he drove all hostile forces from Batavia, which Frankish tribes had occupied. Nor was he content with victory over them; those very tribes he brought to Roman lands and forced them to put off not just their arms but their savageness as well.

223. Panegyric on Constantius Caesar 7, 3

> For the war, invincible Caesar, could have been brought to an end straight away by that onslaught of your valour and good fortune, had not the situation persuaded you to take time for the construction of ships.

By 296 preparations for invasion were complete and the expedition, employing a two-pronged attack, could get under way:

224. Panegyric on Constantius Caesar 13–20

13 And so this war, so unavoidable, so inaccessible, of such long

standing, so well prepared for, you undertook in such a way, Caesar, that immediately you aimed at it the furious bolt of your majesty, all thought it finished. First of all – and this required special care – by calling on your father's majesty you ensured that while your might was turned towards that war, the nations of barbarians would not attempt revolt. You yourself, you Lord Maximian, eternal Emperor, deigning with unprecedented speed to hasten the arrival of your divinity, took up at once your place upon the Rhine, and guarded all that frontier not with forces made of infantry or cavalry, but by the terror of your presence. Maximian was as strong as any number of armies upon the riverbank. But you, invincible Caesar, drew up and armed your separate fleets, and rendered the enemy so confused, so devoid of plan, that then at last he was by Ocean not protected but instead confined.

14 ... But you, invincible Caesar, commanded that whole voyage and the war not merely by virtue of your imperial rank; by your very deeds and the example of your steadfastness you both encouraged and inspired it. Indeed you led the way in setting out from the coast at Gesoriacum (Boulogne) despite the raging sea, and inspired in that army of yours which had sailed down the River Seine an unquenchable resolution, so much so that though your generals still hesitated, with sea and sky in wild disorder, of its own accord the army demanded the signal to sail, poured scorn on threatening portents to be seen, set sail midst rain, and since the wind was not behind, they tacked across it. For who would not dare entrust himself to sea, however rough, when you were sailing? When news arrived that you had sailed, all, it is said, were of one voice, one exhortation: 'Why do we hesitate, why delay? He himself has now set sail, even now is under way, has perhaps by now arrived. Let us endure all things, let us pass through any seas. What is there for us to fear? We are following Caesar!'

15 Nor in their opinion of your own good fortune were they deceived. As we learn by their own accounts, at that very moment such mist swirled over the surface of the sea that the hostile fleet, on station at the Isle of Vecta (Wight) as look-out and in ambush, was bypassed with the enemy in total ignorance, and thus unable to delay our attack, still less resist it. As for the fact that the army, invincible under your leadership, set fire to all its ships the moment it set foot upon the coast of Britain, who else inspired that act except the will of your divinity? Or what other reasoning persuaded them to maintain in reserve no refuge for retreat, nor fear the uncertainties of war, nor contemplate that Mars may favour either side, except the

certain knowledge, sprung from observation of yourself, that there could be no doubt about victory? It was not their might nor human strength they had in mind, but your divine will. In every battle that presents itself it is not the soldiers' confidence that ensures success, so much as generals' fortune. Yet why did that ringleader of the abominable clique abandon the coast he occupied? Why did he desert his fleet and harbour unless he feared your imminent arrival, invincible Caesar, when he saw your sails bearing down on him? At all events he preferred to take his chance with your commanders rather than to feel in person the thunderbolt of your majesty. The fool, not to know that wherever he fled, there was the might of your divinity – wherever your image and standards were venerated!

16 Yet in fleeing from you he fell into the hands of your men, and defeated by you he was overwhelmed by your armies. Finally, in terror, looking for you behind him, crazed like some madman, he so hastened to his death that he neither deployed his line of battle nor arranged the forces he trailed after him, but rather, mindless of his great preparations, he rushed to the attack with only those old instigators of the plot and divisions of foreign mercenaries. And so, Caesar, even this advantage did your good fortune bestow upon the state, that in this victory of the Roman Empire scarcely did a single Roman fall. For, so I am told, all those plains and hills were littered only with the prostrate corpses of our loathsome enemies. Those bodies of barbarians or those that once feigned barbarous ways in style of dress and long blond hair, now lay besmirched with dust and gore, frozen into various attitudes of death imposed by agony of wounds, and among them the ringleader of that band of brigands himself. Of his own accord the royal robe that in his lifetime he defiled, he'd taken off, and by the evidence of scarce a single garment was he recognised. So truly had he taken counsel with himself as death approached, that he was eager to escape detection in his death.

17 Indeed, invincible Caesar, with such accord have the immortal gods granted you destruction of all the enemies you assailed, and especially the Franks, that those troops of yours, who had lost their way through fog at sea, became detached, as mentioned up above, and made their way to London; there through all the city they destroyed the remnants of the barbarous horde that had survived the battle, just as they were taking thought for flight after pillaging the place, and thus afforded your provincials not only safety by the slaughter of the foe, but also the pleasure of beholding it. What a

manifold victory, one marked by countless triumphs! By it Britain was restored, by it the power of the Franks eradicated, by it the necessity of obedience imposed on many tribes besides, found guilty of complicity in that crime; by it finally were the seas for peace eternal cleansed. You may boast, invincible Caesar, you have discovered another world when, by restoring to the might of Rome its naval prestige, you added to her empire an element greater than all lands. You have, I say, invincible Caesar, put an end to a war that seemed to threaten every province, that could have spread and flared up anywhere that the Ocean and the gulf of the Mediterranean lap the land . . .

19 Deserved, therefore, was the triumphal gathering that streamed forth to greet your majesty the moment that you landed on the shore, the longed-for avenger and liberator. Beside themselves with joy, the Britons met you with their wives and children. With veneration they regarded not only you yourself, on whom they looked as one from heaven descended, but even the sails and oars of that vessel that brought your divine person, and they were ready on their prostrate bodies your tread to feel. No wonder is it if they were borne along by such great joy after so many years of most wretched captivity, the violation of their wives, their children's shameful servitude. At last they were free, at last Romans, at last restored afresh by the true light of the empire . . .

20 . . . Beyond Ocean indeed what was there except Britain? So completely did you recover it that even those tribes dwelling at the far ends of the isle submit to your will.

To celebrate the retaking of London a commemorative medallion was struck, showing Constantius advancing on horseback towards a kneeling woman, the personification of London. Below, one of his galleys approaches. Found at Arras in France:

225. Medallion on the retaking of London

Obverse

Fl(avius) Val(erius) Constantius Nobil(is) (Noble) Caes(ar)

Reverse

Redditor Lucis Aeternae (Restorer of Eternal Light) Lon(dinium)
PTR (Mint-mark of Trier)

Following the destruction of Allectus and his mercenary forces,
Constantius' hold on Britain seems to have been quickly established,
and in 297 he was able to return to the continent. For nearly a
decade thereafter few events are recorded, and inscriptions to mark
rebuilding along the northern frontier, once interpreted as necessitated
by enemy action, seem more likely to have been prompted by the
need for periodic refurbishing in the face of neglect and deterioration
with age:

226. From Birdoswald (*RIB* I 1912 restored)

[For our Lords] Dioc[letian] and M[axim]ian, the Invincible Augusti,
and for Constantius and (Galerius) Maximian, Most Noble Caesars,
under His Perfection Aurelius Arpagius, Governor (*Praeses*[12]), the
Cohort [. . .] restored the commandant's house, which had fallen
into ruin and was covered with earth, and the headquarters building
and the bathhouse, under the direction of Flavius Martinus, Centurion in command.

In AD 305 Diocletian and Maximian abdicated, and it was as
Augustus that Constantius returned to Britain in order to campaign
in the north. The actual motive for the campaign and its detailed
course go unrecorded:

227. Panegyric on Constantine 7, 1–2

The day would end before my speech if all your father's deeds
I surveyed, however briefly. In that last great campaign of his he
did not seek for British trophies, as is generally believed, but with
the gods already calling him he drew close to the furthest limit of
the earth. And yet, with deeds so many and so various already
performed, he did not seek to occupy the forests and marshes of
the Caledonians and other Picts, not to mention nearby Ireland and
furthest Thule and the Islands of the Blessed, if they exist. Rather,
something he wished to tell no man, though he was about to join
the gods, he went to gaze upon the Ocean, that father of the gods

who restores the fiery stars of heaven, so that as one about to savour endless light he might already see almost continuous day.

It was while Constantius was in Britain, and shortly before his death at York in 306, that he was joined by his son Constantine:

228. Aurelius Victor (4th C. AD), *Liber de Caesaribus* 40, 2–4

Constantine, whose active mind was stirred from childhood by the desire to rule, could not stand this (that Severus had been appointed Constantius' Caesar by Galerius), affected flight, and having killed the post-horses along his route in order to frustrate those pursuing him, he reached Britain. For he was being held as hostage by Galerius on the pretext of religion. And it happened that just at that time death was pressing hard upon his father Constantius there. On Constantius' death and in response to pressure from all those present Constantine assumed imperial honours.

229. Eutropius (4th C. AD) X, 1, 3 and 2, 2

1 Constantius died at Eboracum (York) in Britain in the 13th year
2 of his reign (AD 306), and was deified . . . On the death of Constantius Constantine, his son by a somewhat undistinguished marriage, was made emperor in Britain, and succeeded to his father's position as a very popular ruler.

230. Zosimus (5th–6th C. AD) II, 8, 2 and 9, 1

8 With the situation settled and the barbarians everywhere glad to keep the peace as a result of our previous successes, Constantine, the offspring of a humble concubine of the Emperor Constantius, conceived the idea of gaining the throne. This desire increased when Severus and Maximinus were granted the rank of Caesar (to the emperors Constantius and Galerius respectively), and Constantine decided to leave the place where he happened to be living and to set out for his father Constantius who was in the provinces beyond the Alps and resided mostly in Britain . . .

9 The Emperor Constantius happened to die at this time and the troops of the court judged that none of Constantius' legitimate children was capable of ruling. Seeing, however, that Constantine

was a fine figure of a man, and at the same time inspired by hopes of large donations, they invested him with the rank of Caesar.

231. A Carausian Milestone reused for Constantine. From near Carlisle (*RIB* I 2291–2)

One end
For the Emperor Caesar Marcus Aurelius
Mausaeus Carausius Pius Felix, the Unconquered Augustus

The other end
For Flavius Valerius Constantinus, Noble Caesar

NOTES

1 The name was subsequently deleted, cf. Milestone from Brougham (*JRS* 55, 1965, p. 224)

For the Emperor Caesar M. Aurelius Casianius Latinianius Postumus Augustus Pius Felix, the *civitas* of the Carvetii (set this up).

2 Against the Bacaudae, marauding peasants and other disaffected provincials, in north-west Gaul.
3 For the value of Victor and Eutropius as sources see Shiel, pp. 15–20.
4 For a discussion of the extent to which Carausius controlled north Gaul see P.J. Casey (1).
5 Later issues of coins by Carausius mentioning specifically II Augusta and XX Valeria demonstrate clearly that he had the support of forces at least in Britannia Superior. See further Johnson (1), p. 28.
6 Carausius. The panegyricists never in fact accord him the honour of mentioning his name.
7 Presumably the Rhine and its tributaries since Carausius controlled the rivers of north Gaul. For a detailed discussion of the campaign see Shiel, p. 3ff.
8 Each of the gs represents one of the three Emperors: Carausius, Maximian and Diocletian. Significantly, neither Maximian nor Diocletian returned the 'compliment'. On the coinage of Carausius in general see Shiel, pp. 166–201.
9 The third g reveals that the coin, ostensibly one of Maximian's, was in fact minted by Carausius, as the mint-mark ML (London) shows. Other issues bestow the same 'honour' on Diocletian.
10 See further Shiel, p. 5ff.
11 Cf. Aurelius Victor (4th C. AD) *Liber de Caesaribus* 39, 40–1

Six years later Allectus treacherously overthrew Carausius. He had been put in charge of finances by Carausius, but alarmed at his own misdeeds and the resultant prospect of his execution, he had criminally seized power.

12 See §233.

XII Reorganisation and the Dynasty of Constantius

Despite its popularity among the troops in Britain the elevation of Constantine to the rank of Augustus in 306 struck directly at the principle of succession established by Diocletian; for according to this the automatic choice to fill the now vacant throne was not Constantine but his father's Caesar, Flavius Valerius Severus. To complicate matters further, the Praetorian Guard in Rome reverted to their former role of emperor-makers by raising to the purple Maximian's son, Maxentius. The result until 324 was an unprecedented period of imperial rivalry and conflict punctuated by repeated attempts to restore some semblance of ordered government by negotiation in the face of multiple claimants to imperial honours.[1] For a year Constantine himself was induced to accept the lesser rank of Caesar until the official western Augustus, Severus, was killed by Maxentius in 307. In turn Maxentius himself was eventually disposed of by Constantine at the battle of the Milvian Bridge in 312.

British contingents as part of Constantine's move against Maxentius:

232. Zosimus (5th–6th C. AD) II, 15, 1

Constantine, who had previously been suspicious of Maxentius, now made further preparations for the fight against him. Having gathered together forces from the barbarians he had taken prisoner, both German and from other Celtic tribes, as well as levies from Britain, a total of around 90,000 infantry and 8,000 cavalry, he marched from the Alps into Italy.

Of the other claimants Maximian died or was killed in 310 after being besieged in Marseilles by Constantine, and Maximinus died shortly after his defeat at the hands of Licinius in 313.

With Constantine by now supreme in the west and Licinius in the east there might clearly have been some reason to hope for a return to stability and the balanced division of power envisaged by Diocletian, had not the personal ambitions and mutual enmity of the two Augusti soon led to a resumption of hostility. In 324, however, the issue was finally resolved with the defeat and death of Licinius.

In the meantime, the reunification of Britain with the rest of the empire accomplished by Constantius in 296 had made possible the implementation of further provincial reorganisation. Under the Tetrarchy, the fourfold division of power originally established by Diocletian, the north-west sector of the empire, which constituted the western Caesar's sphere of operations, was controlled in fact by his deputy, the Praetorian Prefect. Subordinate to him were Vicars (Vicarii), each at the head of newly-constituted dioceses, of which Britain was to form a single instance. Within the diocese in turn the further subdivisions into provinces were headed by Praesides or Rectors.

233. From Cirencester (*RIB* I 103 restored)

Front

To Jupiter Greatest [and Best], His Perfection (*vir perfectissimus*) Lucius Septimius [. . .], Governor (*Praeses*) of B[ritannia Prima], and a citizen of R[eims], resto[red] (this).

Back

This statue and column raised under the old religion.

Left

Septimius, Ruler (*Rector*) of the province Prima, renews.

At what date this radical reorganisation was actually put into effect within Britain itself is not known, but by *c.* 314, it was clearly a reality:

234. *Verona List* VII

The Diocese of Britain has 4 provinces:

1) Prima
2) Secunda
3) Maxima Caesariensis
4) Flavia Caesariensis

With time the division of power was further developed by divorcing civil from military authority. Under Constantine himself or his immediate successors the existing administration appears to have lost its military function, which now became vested in the offices of Duke and Count. The *Notitia Dignitatum*, a list of officials produced probably in the first quarter of the fifth century, lists the following personnel for the Diocese of Britain:[2]

235. *Notitia Dignitatum* 23

Vicar of the British provinces

8 Under the control of the *Vir Spectabilis*, the Vicar of the British provinces:

9 Consular governors (of):

10 Maxima Caesariensis.

11 Valentia.[3]

12 Praesides (governors with the rank of *Praeses*) (of):

13 Britannia Prima.

14 Britannia Secunda.

15 Flavia Caesariensis.

16 This same *Vir Spectabilis*, the Vicar, has the following staff . . .

236. Ibid. 11

3 Under the control of the *Vir Illustris*, the Count of the Sacred Largesses:

20 The Treasurer (*Rationalis*) of finances in the Provinces of Britain.

36 In the British Provinces:

37 The Director (*Praepositus*) of the Treasury in London.

60 Procurator of the cloth factory at Venta in the Provinces of Britain.

237. Ibid. 12

3 Under the control of the *Vir Illustris*, the Count of the Privy Purse:

15 The Treasurer (*Rationalis*) of the Privy Purse in the British Provinces.

238. Ibid. 40

17 Under the control of the *Vir Spectabilis*, the Duke of the Provinces

of Britain:
18 Prefect of the VI Legion (York).
19 Prefect of the Dalmatian cavalry at Praesidium (?).
20 Prefect of the Crispian cavalry at Danum (Doncaster?/Jarrow?).
21 Prefect of the armoured cavalry at Morbium (?).
22 Prefect of the unit (*numerus*) of Tigris boatmen at Arbeia (S. Shields).
23 Prefect of the unit (*numerus*) of Nervii of Dictum at Dictum (Wearmouth?).
24 Prefect of the unit (*numerus*) of Watchmen (*Vigiles*) at Concangis (Chester-le-Street).
25 Prefect of the unit (*numerus*) of Scouts (*Exploratores*) at Lavatris (Bowes).
26 Prefect of the unit (*numerus*) of Directores at Verteris (Brough Castle).
27 Prefect of the unit (*numerus*) of Defenders (*Defensores*) at Bravoniacum (Kirkby Thore).
28 Prefect of the unit (*numerus*) of Solenses at Maglona (Old Carlisle?).
29 Prefect of the unit (*numerus*) of Pacenses at Magis (Burrow Walls?).
30 Prefect of the unit (*numerus*) of Longovicani at Longovicium (Lanchester).
31 Prefect of the unit (*numerus*) of Supervenientes of Petuaria at Derventio (Malton).
32 Also along the line of the wall:
33 Tribune of the 4th cohort of Lingones at Segedunum (Wallsend).
34 Tribune of the 1st cohort of Cornovii at Pons Aelius (Newcastle).
35 Prefect of the 1st squadron (*ala*) of Asturians at Condercum (Benwell).
36 Tribune of the 1st cohort of Frixagores at Vindobala (Rudchester).
37 Prefect of the Ala Sabiniana at Hunnum (Halton Chesters).
38 Prefect of the 2nd squadron (*ala*) of Asturians at Cilurnum (Chesters).
39 Tribune of the 1st cohort of Batavians at Procolitia (Carrawburgh).
40 Tribune of the 1st cohort of Tungrians at Borcovicium (= Vercovicium, Housesteads).
41 Tribune of the 4th cohort of Gauls at Vindolanda (Chesterholm).
42 Tribune of the 2nd[4] cohort of Asturians at Aesica (Gt. Chesters).

43 Tribune of the 2nd cohort of Dalmatians at Magnis (Carvoran).
44 Tribune of the 1st cohort of Hadrian's Dacians at (C)Amboglanna (Castlesteads).[5]
45 Prefect of the Ala Petriana at Petriana.[6]
46 [7]
47 Prefect of the unit (*numerus*) of Aurelian Moors at Aballaba (Burgh-by-Sands).
48 Tribune of the 2nd cohort of Lingones at Concavata (Drumburgh).
49 Tribune of the 1st cohort of Spaniards at Axelodunum.[8]
50 Tribune of the 2nd cohort of Thracians at Gabrosentum (Moresby).
51 Tribune of the 1st cohort Aelia Classica at Tunnocelum (?).
52 Tribune of the 1st cohort of Morini at Glannibanta (Ravenglass).
53 Tribune of the 3rd cohort of Nervii at Alione (Maryport).
54 Formation (*cuneus*) of Sarmatians at Bremetenracum (Ribchester).
55 Prefect of the 1st Ala Herculea at Olenacum (Elsack?).
56 Tribune of the 6th cohort of Nervii at Virosidum (Brough by Bainbridge).
57 This same *Vir Spectabilis*, the Duke, has the following staff . . .

239. Ibid. 28

1 The Count[9] of the Saxon Shore in Britain:
12 Under the control of the *Vir Spectabilis*, the Count of the Saxon Shore in Britain:
13 Commander (*Praepositus*) of the unit (*numerus*) of Fortenses at Othona (Bradwell).
14 Commander (*Praepositus*) of the Tungrecanian troops at Dubrae (Dover).
15 Commander (*Praepositus*) of the unit (*numerus*) of Turnacenses at Lemanis (Lympne).
16 Commander (*Praepositus*) of the Dalmatian cavalry of Branodunum at Branodunum (Brancaster).
17 Commander (*Praepositus*) of the Stablesian cavalry of Gariannonenses at Gariannonum (Burgh Castle).
18 Tribune of the 1st cohort of Baetasii at Regulbium (Reculver).
19 Prefect of the II Legion Augusta at Rutupiae (Richborough).
20 Commander (*Praepositus*) of the unit (*numerus*) of Abulci at Anderitum (Pevensey).

21 Commander (*Praepositus*) of the unit (*numerus*) of Scouts (*Exploratores*) at Portus Adurni (Portchester).
22 This same *Vir Spectabilis*, the Count, has the following staff . . .

240. Ibid. 29

1 The Count of the Provinces of Britain.
4 Under the control of the *Vir Spectabilis*, the Count of the Provinces of Britain:
5 The Province of Britain.
6 This same *Vir Spectabilis*, the Count, has the following staff . . .

241. Ibid. 7

Distribution of units (*numeri*):

153 In the provinces of Britain with the *Vir Spectabilis*, the Count of the Provinces of Britain:
154 Victores juniores Britannici.
155 Primani juniores.
156 Secundani juniores.
199 In the provinces of Britain with the *Vir Spectabilis*, the Count of the Provinces of Britain:
200 Equites catafractarii juniores.
201 Equites scutarii juniores.
202 Equites Honoriani seniores.
203 Equites Stablesiani.
204 Equites Syri.
205 Equites Taifali.

That Constantine returned to Britain on at least one occasion[10] during his reign is indicated by the issuing of coins from the London mint proclaiming his arrival, and the writings of Eusebius. What remains unknown is exactly when, and the purpose involved:

242. Coins of Constantine

(*RIC* VI p. 134 no. 141) AD 310–12

Obverse

Constantinus Aug(ustus)

Reverse

Adventus Aug (The Arrival of the Augustus)

(*RIC* VII p. 97 no. 1) AD 313–14

Obverse

Imp(erator) Constantinus Aug(ustus)

Reverse

Adventus Aug N (The Arrival of our Augustus)

243. From Africa (*ILS* 8942) AD 315

For the Emperor Caesar Flavius Constantinus Maximus Pius Felix, the Unconquered Augustus, Pontifex Maximus (High Priest) . . . great conqueror of Britain . . . in the tenth year of his holding Tribunician Power, four times Consul, saluted Imperator for the ninth time, Father of his Country, Proconsul, Annaeus Saturninus, devoted to his divinity, set this up . . .

244 Eusebius (4th C. AD), *De Vita Constantini* I, 25

After he was firmly established in the empire he turned his thoughts to what his father had bequeathed him, and looked with great kindness on all the nations that had been guided by his father's government . . . In the meantime he crossed over to Britain which lies within Ocean itself and once he had subjugated this he turned his attention to other parts of the world.

In 337 Constantine died and the empire once again underwent fragmentation as each of the Emperor's three surviving sons was proclaimed Augustus. Of these the eldest, Constantine II, controlled Britain, Spain and Gaul, Constans, the youngest, held Italy, the Balkans and Africa, while to Constantius II fell the provinces of the east. In 340, however, Constantine II, at odds with his brother over control of the west, invaded Italy and was quickly killed. Within two years the situation in Britain had for some reason[11] become serious enough to warrant a mid-winter visit by Constans early in 343:

245. Julius Firmicus Maternus (4th C. AD), *De Errore Profanum Religionum* 28, 6

You (Constans) conquered your enemies; you have extended your authority, and so that greater glory might be added to your virtues, you have changed and scorned the order of the seasons, trampling underfoot the swelling, raging waves of Ocean in winter time, a deed unprecedented in the past, and not to be matched in the future. Beneath your oars trembled the waves of a sea still scarcely known to us, and the Briton trembled before the face of an emperor he did not expect.

246. Libanius (4th C. AD), Oration 59, 139 and 141

139 Constans did not wait around sitting on the coast until the spring arrived and the Ocean storms abated, but straight away in mid-winter with everything, clouds, cold and swell, roused to total fury by the weather, he embarked a hundred men, so it is said, and casting off he clove the Ocean, and straight away everything became calm. He sent no advance warning to the cities there, nor did he make any prior announcement of his sailing, or wish to create a stir with his plans before he had completed the venture
. . .

141 If he had risked sailing with the island in revolt, with its inhabitants rebelling and the government overthrown, and if he had been seized with anger on hearing these reports, one would not have attributed his daring to ambition. Instead the element of compulsion created by those in revolt would have removed most of his glory. As it was, affairs in Britain were stable . . .

Later in the same decade Britain saw the arrival of the Elder Gratian, father of the future Emperor Valentinian, and since he held the rank of Count (*Comes*) it seems reasonable to presume he brought with him units of the continental mobile field army, the *Comitatenses*, to bolster for some unrecorded reason the *Limitanei* forces that provided the established garrison of the diocese:

247. Ammianus Marcellinus (late 4th C. AD) XXX, 7, 3

Gratian was widely known because of his great physical strength and his skill in wrestling military-style. After holding the position of bodyguard and Tribune, he was given command of the army in Africa with the rank of Count. There he became suspected of theft and left. Some considerable time later he commanded the army in Britain with the same rank, and was at length given an honourable discharge and returned home.

In 350 Constans himself fell victim to the usurper Magnentius, who held on to the Western Empire until his final defeat three years later at the hands of the eastern Augustus, Constantius II. That Magnentius had enjoyed not inconsiderable support in Britain is suggested by the savageness of the reprisals Constantius inflicted through his Secretary (*Notarius*) Paul:

248. Ammianus Marcellinus XIV, 5, 6–8

Prominent among these was the Secretary Paul, a native of Spain, behind whose face there lurked a serpent, and who was very adroit at sniffing out hidden paths of danger. He was sent to Britain to fetch certain members of the armed forces who had dared to join Magnentius' conspiracy, and when they were unable to offer any resistance, he took it upon himself to exceed his instructions. Like a flood he suddenly overwhelmed the fortunes of many, sweeping forward amidst widespread slaughter and ruin, casting freeborn men into prison and degrading some with fetters, all this by fabricating charges that were far removed from the truth. Thus was perpetrated an impious crime, which branded Constantius' time with an everlasting mark of shame. Martinus, who governed those provinces on behalf of the Prefects, deeply deplored the calamities afflicting the innocent, and frequently made the plea that those free from all blame should be spared. When he failed in his pleas, he threatened to resign so that the evil inquisitor, alarmed by this at least, might desist from driving into obvious danger men who were devoted to peace.

Paul considered this a restriction on his activities, and being a formidable expert in creating complications – hence he was dubbed with the nickname 'the Chain' – he involved the Vicar himself, who was still attempting to protect those he governed, in the danger faced by them all. He threatened to take him in chains to the emperor's court along with the tribunes and many others. Martinus was alarmed at this, and with the threat of sudden death spurring him on he attacked Paul with a sword. Because, however, he was unable to deal a fatal blow owing to a weakness in his right hand, he then plunged the drawn sword into his own side. By this ignominious death there departed this life a most just ruler, one who had dared to alleviate the pitiable misfortunes of many.

Though official inquisitions might wreak havoc on the lives and fortunes of individuals, Britain in this period remained largely immune to the large-scale barbarian incursions that caused widespread disruption to the life and economy of the continental empire. For this reason the island became increasingly regarded as an invaluable and reliable source of raw materials and grain. It was indeed largely to ensure the free passage of such grain to the garrison of the north-west frontier that Julian, appointed Caesar in 355 and given charge of Gaul and Britain, embarked upon a series of major campaigns aimed at reopening the supply route along the Rhine, which enemy action had effectively blocked:

249. Libanius (4th C. AD), Oration 18, 82–3

He took thought for the largest island under the sun, which Ocean surrounds, and sent accountants to examine the expenditure that in theory was devoted to military operations, but in fact formed a source of income for the generals. Those guilty of this he brought to heel, and in addition he effected another far greater benefit, especially from the point of view of Gaul. In earlier times corn was shipped from the island, first over the sea and then up the Rhine, but since the barbarians had become a force to be reckoned with, they had blocked its transport and the cargo vessels had long been hauled ashore and had rotted away. A few still plied, but since they discharged their cargo in coastal ports, it was necessary to transport the grain by waggon instead of by river, and this was a very expensive affair. Julian therefore revived the practice and considered it a serious matter should he not put the carriage of grain on its former footing. He quickly produced more ships than before and examined ways the river might be opened up for corn.

250. Julian, *Letter to the Athenians* 279D

After this came the second and third years (of the campaign: AD 358–9). All the barbarians were driven out of the Gallic provinces, most of the cities were recovered, and large numbers of ships were brought over from Britain.

251. Ammianus Marcellinus (late 4th C. AD) XVIII, 2, 3, AD 359

He even constructed granaries in place of those burned, in which could be stored the supply of grain usually brought over from Britain.

252. Eunapius (4th C. AD), Fr. 12

When Julian invaded enemy territory and the Chamavi begged him to spare it as though it were friendly territory, Julian agreed. He ordered their king to come forward, and when he did so and Julian saw him standing on the river bank, he went on board a boat, which he kept out of arrowshot, and spoke to the barbarians through an interpreter. Since they were prepared to carry out all his instructions, and Julian saw that from his own point of view peace was opportune and necessary – for without the cooperation of the Chamavi it was impossible for grain from the island of Britain to be transported to the Roman garrisons – he was induced by necessity to grant them peace, demanding hostages as a surety of their good faith.

253. Zosimus (5th–6th C. AD) III, 5, 2

At the far end of Germany where there is a province of Gaul the Rhine flows into the Atlantic Ocean at a point on the coast 900 stadia (*c*.103 miles) from Britain. Julian had timber gathered from the forests around the river and 800 boats larger than galleys built. These he sent to Britain and had them convey grain.

Though safe from the depredations of the Germans, Britain was not without her own enemies and in 360 the diocese suffered a large-scale attack by the Picts and Scots. In response Julian despatched Lupicinus and four units of the mobile field army:

254. Ammianus Marcellinus XX, 1

Such was the course of events in Illyricum and the east. In Britain during the tenth consulship of Constantius and the third of Julian (AD 360) invasions by the fierce tribes of the Scots and the Picts, who had broken the peace they had agreed upon, were causing destruction in those areas near the frontiers, and the provinces, worn out by numerous disasters in the past, were caught in the grip of fear. The Caesar Julian, who was wintering at Paris and was preoccupied by various problems, was afraid to go to the assistance of those across the sea, as I have related Constans did, in case he left the Gallic provinces without a ruler at a time when the Alamanni were roused to savagery and war. He therefore decided that Lupicinus, who at that time was commander of the armed forces (*magister armorum*), should go to settle matters either by force or by negotiation. Lupicinus certainly had a talent for war and was skilled in military affairs, but he was extremely haughty and full of himself like a tragic actor, as they say, and it had long been a matter of dispute whether his avarice or his cruelty was the greater. So, with a light-armed auxiliary force composed of Aeruli (Heruli) and Batavians moved up, together with two units (*numeri*) from Moesia, this aforementioned general came to Bononia (Boulogne) in the depths of winter, and having procured vessels and embarked all his troops, he waited for a favourable wind and crossed to Rutupiae (Richborough) opposite. He then proceeded to London so that once he had formed his plans as the situation demanded, he might hasten into battle all the sooner.

Of Lupicinus' activities in Britain nothing is recorded, and any campaign he initiated was evidently cut short by his recall to the continent and subsequent arrest. In this way Julian was seeking to forestall any support he might give to Constantius, with whom Julian was now set on a collision course as a result of being proclaimed Augustus by his troops. Constantius' timely death in 361, however, spared the empire yet another bout of ruinous civil war and left Julian master of the whole empire, but within two years he too had died in allegedly mysterious circumstances while leading a campaign against Persia. With him the dynasty of Constantius came to an end.

NOTES

1 These included not only Constantine and Maxentius, but also Maximian himself, who twice emerged from retirement to resume the rank of Augustus, Licinius, elevated by Galerius at the Conference at Carnuntum in 308, and Maximinus, Galerius' Caesar, who succeeded to the throne on the death of Galerius in 311.

2 The late date of the *Notitia* makes it uncertain how much of the information it contains is relevant to the early fourth century. See Johnson (2), p. 26; Ward (2); Mann.

3 See §260.

4 The text of the *Notitia* reads 1st, though this would seem to be a scribal error, since the 2nd is recorded as being stationed at Great Chesters.

5 A possible conflation of two entries resulting in the erroneous placing of the 1st cohort of Hadrian's Dacians at Castlesteads instead of at Birdoswald (Banna) where their presence is attested; see Rivet and Smith, p. 221.

6 Almost certainly a transposition of the unit's name to its station, which should probably read Uxelodunum (Stanwix).

7 A lacuna unnecessarily inserted by the editor.

8 The order of the *Notitia* suggests we should here find a mention of Mais (Bowness), so that it would seem that somehow the text has become corrupt at this point. Axelodunum = Uxelodunum (Stanwix).

9 For the rank of Count (*Comes*) see Johnson (1), p. 144f; id. (2), p. 26f.

10 On the question of the frequency of the visits see Salway (1), p. 327f; J. Casey.

11 The later association of Constans' visit with the Areani, whose task it was to gather information concerning the tribes beyond the northern frontier of Britain, suggests there may have been hostilities either threatening or begun in the area of Hadrian's wall. See further Salway (1), p. 351ff.

XIII Danger, Decline and Collapse

By 364 the empire was once again divided, this time between Valens in the east and his brother Valentinian in the west. In Britain there were renewed rumblings of pressure from beyond the frontiers.[1]

255. Ammianus Marcellinus (late 4th C. AD) XXVI, 4, 5

At this time, with trumpets sounding for war as if through all the Roman world, the most savage tribes rose up and poured across the nearest frontiers. At one and the same time the Alamanni were plundering Gaul and Raetia, the Sarmatae and Quadri Pannonia; the Picts, Saxons, Scots and Attacotti harassed the Britons with continual calamities . . .

The extent of the attacks in 364 or the means by which the Romans sought to counter them we do not know, but there is no mistaking the desperate straits to which Britain was reduced by the disaster of 367. For virtually the first time the enemy had learned to act in concert and rescuing the situation was to prove an uphill struggle.[2]

256. Ammianus Marcellinus XXVII, 8

Valentinian had set out from Amiens and was hurrying towards Trier when he was overtaken by grave reports indicating that Britain had been plunged into the depths of distress by a conspiracy of the barbarians, that Nectaridus, Count of the coastal district, had been killed, and that the Duke Fullofaudes had been surrounded and captured in an enemy ambush. This news was received with great consternation and Valentinian sent Severus, who at that time was still Count of the household troops, to make good the reverses if chance gave him the desired opportunity. He, however, was recalled shortly afterwards, and Jovinus . . . (lacuna) . . . having set out to the same place was allowed by Valentinian to return quickly[3] with the intention of securing the aid of a powerful army. This he maintained was what the pressing needs demanded. Finally, as a result of the many frightening occurrences reported by constant rumours involving this same island, Theodosius was chosen and instructed to hasten there. He was a man with a very good reputation in military affairs, and having collected a force of young and spirited legionary and auxiliary troops he set off, preceded by an impressive show of confidence. And since, when I was compiling my account of the acts of the Emperor Constans, I set out to the best of my ability the motion of the Ocean's ebb and flow as well as the situation of Britain, I now consider it unnecessary to repeat what has been dealt with once, just as Homer's Ulysses shrinks from repeating his tale to the Phaeacians on account of the excessive difficulty. Suffice to say that at the time in question the Picts were divided into two tribes, the Dicalydones and the Verturiones. These, together with the warlike Attacotti and the Scots, were ranging over a wide area causing much devastation, while the Franks and their neighbours the Saxons ravaged the coast of Gaul with vicious acts of pillage, arson and the murder of all prisoners, wherever they could burst in by land or sea. In order to prevent these happenings, should better luck present an opportunity, that most efficient general made for the furthest point on the earth. On his arrival at the coast of Bononia (Boulogne), which is separated from the tract of land opposite by the narrows of the tidal sea, wont as it is to rise in astonishing surges and then, without any harm to those plying it, to subside until it has all the appearance of a plain, he made a quiet crossing of the Channel and landed at Rutupiae (Richborough), a quiet haven opposite. When the Batavi, Heruli, Jovii and Victores who were following him arrived, all of them units confident in their strength, Theodosius set out and made for London, an ancient city that later generations called Augusta. Dividing his troops into several detachments, he attacked the marauding enemy bands who were roaming about loaded down with the weight of their booty and, quickly routing those who were driving along prisoners and cattle, he wrested from them the plunder that the wretched subjects of Rome had lost. All this he restored to its owners with the exception of a small part, which was paid to his weary troops. Then, in the full flush of success, like someone celebrating an ovation, he entered the city, which up till now had floundered amidst the greatest of hardships, but suddenly had been restored before rescue could even have been hoped for. There he lingered in order to explore safe plans of action, encouraged by his great success to deeds of greater daring, but unsure of the future, since he had learned from the statements of prisoners and the information provided by deserters that this widely scattered enemy mass, made up of various tribes and indescribably savage, could only be overcome by more devious cunning and unexpected attacks. Finally, he issued proclamations, and with a promise of immunity from punishment he called back to their ranks those who had deserted, and many others who were straggling about the countryside on furlough. As a result of this edict very many were induced to return by the offer, and Theodosius, relieved of his anxieties, requested that Civilis, a man of sharp temper but steadfastly just and upright, be sent to him to govern Britain on behalf of the Prefects, and also Dulcitius, a general distinguished for his expertise in military matters.

That part of Theodosius' action against the enemy included naval engagements is suggested by Claudian:

257. Claudian (late 4th C. AD), *Panegyric on the Third Consulship of Honorius* 51–6

And so as to enflame you all the more with a love of battle, he would recount the deeds of your grandfather (the Elder Theodosius), before whom trembled the shores of sun-scorched Libya and Thule, beyond the reach of ships. He it was vanquished the nimble Moors and apt-named Picts; he pursued the Scots with his far-ranging sword; he cleft Hyperborean waves with courageous oars . . .

258. Idem, *Panegyric on the Fourth Consulship of Honorius* 24–33

From here (Spain) came forth your grandfather (the Elder Theodosius), for whom, exultant after his northern battles, Africa wove laurels won from the Massyli. He it was pitched camp amid the frosts of Caledonia, in armour bore the summer heat of Libya, a source of terror to the Moor, conqueror of the British shore, laying waste to North and South alike. What profit (to the Britons) the eternal harshness and cold of their climate, or the uncharted seas? The Orkneys were drenched with slaughter of the Saxons; Thule was warm with Pictish blood, and icy Ireland wept for the heaps of Scottish dead.

cf.

259. Pacatus (late 4th C. AD), *Panegyric on Theodosius* 5, 2

Shall I relate how Britain was brought to her knees by battles on land? In that case the Saxon, exhausted by naval engagements, springs to mind.[4] Shall I speak of the Scots driven back to their own marshes?

Following restoration of the military situation the immediate need was to repair the damage done and prevent a repetition:

260. Ammianus Marcellinus XXVIII, 3

Theodosius, whose reputation as a general was of the highest order, set out from Augusta, previously known as London, in good spirits and accompanied by an army he had assembled with energy and skill. To the troubled and disordered fortunes of the Britons he brought the greatest of assistance, everywhere securing in advance locations suited to ambushing the barbarians, and asking nothing of the rank and file in which he did not actively take the lead. In this way he combined the duties of a hard-working common soldier with the responsibilities of a distinguished general. Once he had routed and put to flight the various tribes which arrogance, fostered by impunity, was inciting to attack Roman property, he completely restored the cities and forts which, though founded to secure a lasting peace, had suffered repeated damage.

While Theodosius was occupied with this there occurred a serious instance of villainy that would have resulted in grave danger had it not been nipped in the bud. A certain Valentinus, a haughty character born in Valeria in Pannonia and brother-in-law to that pernicious Vicar Maximinus who was later Praetorian Prefect, had been exiled to Britain because of a serious crime. Like a dangerous animal he could not bear to be inactive and he stirred himself to acts of wickedness and revolution, nursing an intense feeling of dislike for Theodosius, whom he regarded as the only man capable of blocking his evil designs.

With much consideration of possibilities both open and secret, and with the force of his boundless ambition growing, he attempted to win over exiles and soldiers with promises of rewards for his enterprise as tempting as the moment allowed. The time for putting his plans into effect was already drawing close when Theodosius learned of them through a pre-arranged source and, being a general ever ready to take a bold course of action and resolutely determined to punish what he had discovered, he delivered up Valentinus together with a few of his closest associates to the Duke Dulcitius for the imposition of the death penalty. However, using his military expertise to make projections as to future developments – in this he surpassed all his contemporaries – he forbade the instigation of enquiries into the conspiracy in order to prevent fear from spreading widely and reawakening in the province those disturbances that had been lulled to sleep.

Then, with danger totally removed, since it was common knowledge that none of his undertakings lacked success, he turned to making many necessary reforms. He restored cities and the forts of the garrison, as already mentioned; he protected the frontiers with sentries and guards; he recovered a province which had fallen into the hands of the enemy and so completely restored it to its former state that, by his own account, it had a legally appointed governor, and was thereafter called Valentia[5] by decision of the emperor who, on receipt of this priceless piece of news, felt as great a sense of joy as if he had been celebrating a triumph. In the midst of these outstanding events the Areani, an organisation of men set up in former times and about whom I have given some account in the history of Constans, had gradually fallen into bad habits, for which Theodosius removed them from their stations. They were clearly convicted of having been induced by the receipt or promise of great rewards to betray to the barbarians at various times what was happening on the Roman side. It was in fact their duty to range far and wide over a large area and to inform the Roman commanders of disturbances among the neighbouring tribes.

After dealing with the aforementioned and other similar events in so spectacular a manner, Theodosius was summoned to court and left the provinces dancing for joy, having distinguished himself in a series of salutary victories like Furius Camillus or Cursor Papirius. With good will from every quarter he was escorted to the Channel, and crossing with a gentle wind he reached the Emperor's high command. There he was received with joy and praise and took over from Jovinus, who commanded the cavalry, but who was considered to be lacking in energy.

Probably to the period of Theodosius' restoration belongs the construction of watchtowers along the coast of Yorkshire from Filey to Huntcliff. From the Ravenscar site comes an isolated and semi-literate inscription:

261. *RIB* I 721

Justinianus, commander. Vindicianus master (masbier = magister?) built this tower and fort from ground-level.

A graphic picture of Roman naval operations at this time is presented by Vegetius, writing at the end of the fourth century:

262. *Epitoma Rei Militaris (Abridgement of Military Affairs)* IV, 37

As for size, the smallest galleys have a single bank of oars ... Associated with the larger galleys are scouting skiffs, which have around twenty oars on each side, and which the Britons call Picati (tar-daubed). These are intended to locate and at times intercept the passage of enemy ships and to discover by observation their arrival or plans. However, to prevent these scout vessels being easily visible through the brightness of their appearance, their sails and rigging are dyed sea-green, and even the pitch with which ships are ordinarily daubed is made that colour. The sailors and marines wear sea-green clothing so that as they go about their scouting they may escape detection the more easily not only by night but also by day.

In 372 Valentinian transferred to Britain a king of the Alamanni:

263. Ammianus Marcellinus XXIX, 4, 7

In place of Macrianus Valentinian made Fraomarius king of the Bucinobantes, a tribe of the Alamanni opposite Mainz. A little later, however, because a recent invasion had totally devastated that same district, he transferred him to Britain with the rank of Tribune, and put him in charge of what was then a large and powerful contingent of the Alamanni.

Following the death of Valentinian in 375 the throne of the Western Empire passed to his sons Gratian and Valentinian II, the latter being but 4 years old at the time. Under Gratian, however, relations between the Emperor and the aristocracy and army were to undergo a rapid and profound deterioration leading in 383 to a rebellion that had its origins with Magnus Maximus[6] commanding forces in Britain:

264. *Chronicle of 452,*[7] AD 382

Maximus promptly overcame the Picts and Scots who were engaged in making attacks.

265. Orosius (5th C. AD), *Adversum Paganos* (*Against the Pagans*) VII, 34, 9–10

Maximus, a man vigorous in action, upright, and worthy of imperial honours had he not risen to prominence by breaking his oath of loyalty and an illegal assumption of power, was created emperor by the army in Britain almost against his will. He then crossed to Gaul.

There he treacherously surrounded and killed the emperor Gratian, who was terrified by this sudden attack and was considering crossing into Italy.

266. Zosimus (5th–6th C. AD) IV, 35, 2–6 and 37, 1–3

35 Such was the situation in Thrace. Gratian, however, was surrounded by serious difficulties of a kind that could not easily be endured for long. Following the advice of those courtiers who make a habit of leading emperors astray, he had received certain Alan deserters, enrolled them in his army, rewarded them with generous bounties, and deemed them worthy of responsibility for matters of the greatest importance, while paying his own soldiers scant regard. This engendered in the soldiers a hatred of the Emperor which smouldered away, grew worse, and stirred up in them a desire to rebel – especially in the case of those stationed in Britain, who were steeped more than all others in surliness and anger. In this they were encouraged still further by Maximus, a native of Spain who had served with the Emperor[8] Theodosius in Britain. Peeved because Theodosius was considered worthy of the throne while he himself had not been promoted even to an honorific office, Maximus further roused the soldiers to hatred against the Emperor. They for their part were quick to rebel and proclaim Maximus Emperor. They presented him with the purple robe and diadem, and promptly sailed across Ocean, putting in at the mouths of the Rhine. When the armies in Germany and beyond readily accepted

the nomination, Gratian confronted Maximus in battle . . . (Gratian was then gradually deserted by his troops, who went over to Maximus, and forced to flee towards the Alps and the Danube provinces. Maximus sent his cavalry commander, Andragathius, after him) . . . Andragathius caught Gratian as he was about to cross the bridge at Sigidunum (Belgrade),[9] killed him, and thereby confirmed the rule of Maximus.

37 Such was the end of Gratian's reign. Maximus for his part believed his hold on the throne was secure, and sent an embassy to Theodosius, not begging forgiveness for what he had done to Gratian, but with a somewhat harsh and arrogant message . . . The embassy demanded of Theodosius a truce, concord, and joint action against all enemies of Rome; otherwise he threatened hostility and war. The Emperor Theodosius accepted Maximus as Emperor . . . but he secretly set about preparing for war against him, while employing every manner of flattery and solicitude to beguile him.

267. Gold solidus (*RIC* IX p. 2 no. 2b)

Obverse
D(ominus) N(oster) (Our Lord) Mag(nus) Maximus P(ius) F(elix) Aug(ustus)

Reverse
Victoria Augg (Victory of the two Augusti)

While Maximus' victory over Gratian left him as *de facto* ruler of the western dioceses comprising Britain, Gaul and Spain, in Italy the young Valentinian II continued to maintain the vestiges of legitimate authority, largely as a result of Maximus' reluctance to provoke the intervention of Theodosius in the east:

268. *Chronicle of 452*, AD 383

Fearing Theodosius, the head of the Eastern Empire, Maximus made a treaty with Valentinian.

The existence of Valentinian, however, must have represented in Maximus' eyes an ever-present indictment of his rise to power, and the final obstacle to *de jure* acceptance of his rule. Thus, though it was factors of church administration that provided the pretext for Maximus' invasion of Italy in 387 to secure total control of the west, the true political reasons cannot have been far below the surface:

269. Orosius (5th C. AD), *Adversum Paganos (Against the Pagans)* VII, 34, 10

Maximus drove Gratian's brother, the Emperor Valentinian, out of Italy. Valentinian took refuge in the east, where he was received by Theodosius with fatherly affection and shortly restored to power.

270. *Chronicle of 452*, AD 387

Alleging that the Church was being subjected to intolerable treatment, Maximus found the opportunity to break the pact he had made with Valentinian. Valentinian for his part was afraid of the usurper, who was now threatening his life, and fled to Theodosius for refuge.

271. Sozomenus (5th C. AD), *Ecclesiastical History* VII, 13

In the meantime Maximus gathered a very large army of Britons, neighbouring Gauls, Celts and the tribes thereabouts and entered Italy. His pretext was to prevent any innovation in the national religion and ecclesiastical order. In reality it was to clear himself of the imputation of usurpation.

Faced with Maximus' attack upon what remained of the legitimate Western Empire, Theodosius in the east now had no alternative but to intervene. The final and decisive engagement between the forces of Maximus and Theodosius took place in 388 at Aquileia:

272. Orosius (5th C. AD), *Adversum Paganos (Against the Pagans)* VII, 35, 3–4

At that time Maximus occupied Aquileia, an onlooker at his own victory, while his Count, Andragathius, exercised supreme command of the war. The latter, contrary to expectation, had secured all the entrances to the Alps and the rivers with enormous military forces and a determination that excelled even the valour of his great forces. Then, through the incomprehensible will of God, while he was preparing to catch his enemies off their guard and to overwhelm them with a naval expedition, of his own accord he deserted those same defensive positions he had constructed to block the access routes.

And so, before anyone could realise, not to mention offer any resistance, Theodosius crossed the unguarded Alps and on his unexpected arrival before Aquileia besieged that great and fierce enemy Maximus, who by the terror of his name alone exacted tribute and dues from the savage German tribes, and without recourse to any underhand device, took him prisoner and put him to death.

273. Prosper Tiro (5th C. AD), *Chronicon* 1191 (AD 388)

In the reign of Valentinian and Theodosius the usurper Maximus was seized three miles from Aquileia, deprived of his royal clothing and condemned to death. In the same year his son Victor was killed in Gaul by the Count Arbogast, a Frank by birth.

According to the sixth century writer Gildas, as part of his continental adventure Maximus withdrew a part of Britain's garrison, which never thereafter returned. As a result the provinces became once again subject to the depredations of the Picts and Scots until appeals for help were eventually answered:

274. Gildas[10] (6th C. AD), *De Excidio Britanniae* (*On the Destruction of Britain*) 14–15

14 Thereafter Britain was robbed of all her armed forces, her military supplies, her rulers, cruel as they were, her sturdy youth. They followed in the steps of the usurper mentioned above (Maximus), and never afterwards returned. Totally ignorant of all the usages of war, Britain remained for many years groaning in a state of shock, exposed for the first time to two foreign tribes of extreme cruelty, the Scots from the north-west, the Picts from the north.

15 As a result of their attacks and terrible depredations Britain sent envoys to Rome with letters, making tearful appeals for an armed force to give protection, and promising unwavering and wholehearted submission to Roman rule, if only the enemy could be kept

at a greater distance. Forgetting previous ills, Rome soon prepared a legion, soundly equipped with arms. Crossing over Ocean to Britain in ships it engaged the fierce enemy, and killing a great number drove them all from the place, freeing from imminent slavery a people that had been subjected to such dreadful mangling. The Britons were instructed to build a wall across the island from sea to sea so that when manned it might be a deterrent to keep away the enemy and a means of protection for the people. The wall, however, being built not of stone but of turf, proved useless to the unthinking and leaderless masses.[11]

The death of Valentinian II in suspicious circumstances during 392 led to yet more imperial usurpation in the Western Empire which Theodosius was not able to halt until 394. By the end of January 395, however, he too was dead and the empire divided between his sons, Honorius in the west and Arcadius in the east. Real power throughout the empire, however, lay by now with the general Stilicho, and despite the 'official' attribution of responsibility it is under his aegis that the court poet Claudian mentions new victories at sea and on land in 398:

275. *Against Eutropius* I, 391–3

Then Rome speaks thus: 'Factors near at hand proclaim how great my power is now you (Honorius) are Emperor. With the Saxons subjugated the sea is now more peaceful, with the Picts broken Britain is secure.'

The following year we hear of further strengthening of Britain's position:

276. Claudian, *On the Consulship of Stilicho* (delivered early 400) II, 247–55

Next spoke Britannia, dressed in the skin of some Caledonian beast, her cheeks tattooed, her sea-blue mantle sweeping over her foot-steps like the surge of Ocean: 'I too, when on the point of death at the hands of neighbouring tribes, found in Stilicho protection, when the Scots roused all Ireland and the sea foamed beneath hostile oars. His care ensured I need not fear the missiles of the Scots, nor tremble at the Picts, nor watch on all my shores for Saxons to arrive with every shifting wind.'

Is it with this, as some[12] have suggested, that we should identify
Gildas' description of a second campaign in Britain?

277. *De Excidio Britanniae* (*On the Destruction of Britain*) 16–17

16 The legion (i.e. the one sent after Maximus' fall) was returning
home in triumph and with great joy, when (suddenly), like predatory
wolves driven mad by the extremes of hunger that leap dry-mouthed
into the sheepfold when the shepherd is away, the old enemy burst
over the frontiers, borne along by their oars like wings, by the arms
of their oarsmen, by their sails swelling in the wind. Everything
they slaughtered – whatever lay in their path they cut down like
ripe corn, trampled underfoot, and passed on.

17 So, once more plaintive envoys were sent, their clothes torn, so it
is said, their heads covered in dust. Cowering like frightened chicks
beneath the trusty wings of their parents, they beg the Romans for
help lest their wretched homeland be utterly destroyed, and the
Roman name, which echoed in their ears merely as a word, became
a thing without worth and gnawed at by the insolent taunts of
foreign tribes. The Romans, moved as much as is humanly possible
by the tale of such tragedy, hastened the eagle-like flight of their
cavalry on land and the passage of their sailors at sea, and into
the necks of their enemies they plunged the talons of their sword-
points, talons that at first were unexpected and at length a source
of dread. The slaughter they inflict is like the fall of leaves in
autumn, like a mountain torrent that swollen after storms by
numerous tributaries overflows its riverbed in its noisy course. With
furrowed back and fierce brow it foams wondrously, its waves surging
to the clouds, as the saying goes, waves by which the eyes, though
constantly refreshed by blinking, are dazzled by colliding lines of
eddies, and with a single surge it overwhelms all obstacles in its
path. Thus did our glorious allies quickly put to flight across the
sea such enemy hordes as could escape; for year by year it was
across the sea they piled up booty with no one to resist them.

Again Gildas follows his description of Roman successes with an
account of further wall building:

278. *De Excidio Britanniae* (*On the Destruction of Britain*) 18

The Romans therefore informed our homeland that they could not go on being thus plagued at frequent intervals for expeditions that required so much effort, nor could the marks of Roman power, that great and glorious army, be worn out by land and sea on account of unwarlike and roving bandits. Rather they urge the Britons to stand on their own two feet, to get accustomed to bearing arms, to fight bravely, and in this way protect with all their strength their land, property, wives, children and, what is more important, their lives and liberty. They should not hold out their hands devoid of weapons, ready to be shackled by tribes that were in no way stronger than themselves, but rather hands armed with shields, swords and spears, and ready to kill. So too, in the belief that it would bring some advantage to a people they were to abandon, the Romans built a wall, different from the other, using public and private funds, linking the wretched inhabitants to themselves. They constructed it in their usual fashion: a straight line from sea to sea between cities which happened to have been placed there through fear of the enemy. To the timorous people they gave bold advice and left them manuals on training in the use of arms. They also placed towers overlooking the sea at intervals on the coast to the south where they kept their ships,[13] since there too they feared the savage barbarian beasts. They then bade the Britons farewell, as if intending never to return.

For all the mounting pressures that threatened the boundaries of the continental empire, so long as the central government felt itself able to divert resources to the protection of Britain, the island might continue to look to an effective defence against its foes. By 402, however, the situation had become reversed, and Britain was now a source of troops to defend the empire's heart:

279. Claudian, *Gothic War* 416–18

There also came the legion set to guard the furthest Britons, the legion that curbs the savage Scot and scans the lifeless patterns tattooed on dying Picts.

The immediate reaction of the diocese to the loss of defending forces finds no mention in surviving sources, but by the end of 406 the critical situation on the continent produced within Britain an ostensibly fevered rash of usurpers:[14]

280. Zosimus (5th–6th C. AD) VI, 3, 1

Earlier, when Arcadius was consul for the sixth time along with Probus (AD 406), the Vandals joined forces with the Suebi and Alans, and sweeping over this area devastated the Transalpine tribes.[15] Such was the slaughter they inflicted that they inspired terror even among the forces in Britain, who were then forced through fear the barbarians might advance against them into electing usurpers, that is Marcus, Gratian, and after them Constantine.

281. Orosius (5th C. AD), *Adversum Paganos (Against the Pagans)* VII, 40, 4

While these tribes were rampaging through Gaul, in Britain Gratian, a citizen of the island, was illegally made Emperor and killed. In his place Constantine was elected from the lowest ranks of the military, solely on the basis of the hope engendered by his name, and not because of any valour he had.[16] As soon as he assumed power he crossed to Gaul. There he was frequently tricked by worthless pacts with the barbarians and was the cause of great harm to the state.

282. Zosimus[17] VI, 2–5

2   While Arcadius was still Emperor, and Honorius and Theodosius were consuls for the seventh and second times respectively (AD 407), the soldiers in Britain rebelled, elevated Marcus to the imperial throne, and gave him their obedience as ruler there. However, because he was not in tune with their ways, they put him to death, promoted Gratian and, granting him the purple robe and crown, formed a bodyguard for him as they would an emperor. However, not finding him to their liking either, they deposed him and put him to death after four months, and gave the throne to Constantine. He in turn, after placing Justinian and Neviogastes in command of the Celtic forces, left Britain and crossed the Channel. On his arrival at Bononia (Boulogne), this being the nearest city on the coast and situated in Lower Germany, he remained there for some days, and having won over all the forces as far as the Alps, which form the boundary between Gaul and Italy, he considered his hold on the throne was secure.[18] About this time Stilicho despatched the general Sarus, together with an army, against Constantine, and in an engagement with the general Justinian and

the forces with him Sarus destroyed Justinian and the greater part of his troops. As a result he came into possession of a great store of booty, and being informed that Constantine himself had seized the city of Valentia, which ensured his safety, he set about besieging the place. The remaining general, Neviogastes, entered into talks with Sarus about a pact of friendship and was received by him as a friend, but having exchanged oaths Neviogastes was immediately put to death, since Sarus put no store by the oaths. To the position of general Constantine now appointed Ediovinchus, a Frank by birth, and Gerontius, a native of Britain. Sarus for his part, fearing the experience of these generals in war and their courage, withdrew from Valentia, which he had besieged for seven days. He was, however, sorely pressed by Constantine's generals and it was only with a good deal of effort that he extricated himself . . . (Sarus is forced to use the booty he had earlier seized to ease a way into Italy. Constantine then secures his hold on the Alps) . . .

4 Having thus arranged matters through all of Gaul, Constantine sent Constans, the elder of his sons whom he had invested with the rank of Caesar, into Spain (AD 408). This he did as a result of his desire to gain control of all the tribes there, and thus to increase his domain, and at the same time to eradicate the power of Honorius' kinsfolk there . . . (Constantine in fact feared a twofold attack on him by forces loyal to Honorius: one from Spain, the other from Italy) . . .

5 Having accomplished these objectives in Spain, Constans returned to his father Constantine bringing with him Verenianus and Didymus and leaving there the general Gerontius . . .[19]

283. Zosimus V, 43

At this the usurper Constantine sent eunuchs to Honorius begging pardon for deigning to assume the rank of emperor. He alleged that he had not purposely chosen to do so, but that it was a result of the constraints brought to bear on him by the soldiers. Upon hearing this request and seeing that it was not easy for him to contemplate other wars, with Alaric's barbarians not far away and also his kinsmen being held by the usurper, Honorius gave in to the request and sent Constantine the imperial apparel (AD 409). Honorius' concern for his kinsmen was in fact futile since they had been put to death prior to this embassy.

284. Zosimus VI, 1

And so, with his altogether reasonable requests having been insultingly turned down, Alaric advanced on Rome with all his forces, determined to lay siege to it. At this there came to Honorius an envoy from Constantine, who had usurped power among the Celts, one Jovius, a man outstanding by reason of his education and other virtues. He asked that the peace which had previously been agreed upon be confirmed and at the same time he begged forgiveness for the murder of Didymus and Verenianus, kinsmen of the Emperor Honorius. He alleged by way of excuse that they had been put to death against the wishes of Constantine. Seeing that Honorius was disturbed by this, Jovius said it would be sensible for the emperor, embroiled with the problems of Italy as he was, to give in to Constantine. If he were allowed to return to Constantine and report the situation in Italy, he would soon return with him in person together with all the Celtic, Spanish and British forces to resolve the crisis in Italy and Rome. On these terms Jovius was allowed to depart.

285. Orosius (5th C. AD), *Adversum Paganos (Against the Pagans)* VII, 42, 1–4

In the 1165th year after the foundation of Rome (AD 410) the Emperor Honorius, seeing that no action could be taken against the barbarians with so many usurpers rising up against him, ordered that the usurpers themselves be disposed of as a first move. The supreme command in this war was entrusted to the Count Constantius ... Therefore Count Constantius set out to Gaul with an army, besieged the Emperor Constantine at Arles (the new capital of the Prefecture of the Gauls), took him prisoner, and put him to death (AD 411). At this point ... Constantine's son Constans was killed at Vienne by his Count Gerontius,[20] a man more given to evil than to virtue, who then set up a certain Maximus in Constans' place. Gerontius himself was slain by his own soldiers.

For Britain the continental adventure of Constantine, which at its inception was perhaps regarded as a means of maintaining the island as part of a stable north-west Prefecture, became the event that finally sundered direct Roman rule. Already in 408 came a renewal of Saxon attacks (*Chronicle of 452*, §282 n. 19) and the following year, while Gerontius stirred up revolt against Constantine in Gaul, fresh onslaughts induced the Britons to throw off their allegiance to the usurper:

286. Zosimus VI, 5, 2–3

The barbarians beyond the Rhine, attacking in force, reduced the inhabitants of Britain and some of the Celtic tribes to the point where they were obliged to throw off Roman rule and live independently, no longer subject to Roman laws. The Britons therefore took up arms and, braving the danger on their own behalf, freed their cities from the barbarians threatening them. And all Armorica (Brittany) and the other Gallic provinces followed their example, freed themselves in the same way, expelled their Roman rulers and set up their own governments as far as lay within their power.

That it was Constantine's administration rather than the government of Honorius that Britain repudiated would be given additional weight could we accept the implications of the Emperor's rescript:

287. Zosimus VI, 10, 2

Honorius wrote letters to the cities in Britain bidding them to take precautions on their own behalf.[21]

From this point on Roman rule in Britain ceased forever, and while for a time life undoubtedly continued much as before, the renewal of attacks from outside prompted first a final and unanswered appeal for Roman assistance and then the fateful invitation to the Saxons. Gildas' narrative resumes after the building of the second wall:

288. *De Excidio Britanniae (On the Destruction of Britain)* 19–26

19 And so, as the Romans returned home, the loathsome hordes of Scots and Picts eagerly emerged from the coracles that carried them across the gulf of the sea, like dark swarms of worms that emerge from the narrow crevices of their holes when the sun is high and the weather grows warm. In custom they differed slightly one from another, yet in their single desire for shedding blood they were of one accord, preferring to cover their villainous faces with hair, rather than their private parts and surrounding areas with clothes. Once they learned of the Romans' departure and their refusal to return, more confident than ever, they seized from its inhabitants the whole northern part of the country as far as the wall. To resist them an army was posted on the top of the fortification, an army reluctant to fight, incapable of flight, feckless

through the timorousness of their hearts, an army that day and night languished in senseless idleness. Meanwhile the barbed spears of their naked enemies saw no rest; the wretched citizens were dragged from the walls by them and dashed to the ground. And yet this sentence of untimely death was in fact a blessing for those snatched away by such a fate; for by their sudden end they avoided the wretched torment that hung over their brothers and children. What more can I say? The townships and high wall are abandoned; once again the citizens are put to flight; once again are scattered with less hope of recovery than usual; once again they are pursued by the enemy; once again massacres yet more cruel hasten upon them. The pitiful citizens are torn to pieces by their foes like lambs by butchers. Indeed their lives might be likened to those of wild animals; for they began to keep one another in check by plundering one another of the meagre provisions the wretched citizens possessed as a short-term means of sustenance. Their internal tumults only served in fact to increase their misfortunes from without, since as a consequence of this constant plundering the whole country was being stripped of every bit of food with the exception of the relief that skill in hunting could provide.

20 So again the miserable remnants sent a letter to Agitius,[22] a man of high rank among the Romans, in the following terms: 'To Agitius, Consul for the third time (AD 446) come the groans of the Britons', and a little further on came the complaint 'The barbarians drive us to the sea; the sea drives us back to the barbarians; between these two forms of death we are either slaughtered or drowned'. Yet for all their pleas they got no help. Meanwhile a dread and infamous famine gripped the Britons as they wandered about enfeebled; it forced many of them to surrender to the bloodthirsty brigands without delay in order to get some scrap of food to revive them. Not so others, however; instead they continued the resistance from the mountains themselves, from caves, passes, and dense thickets. Then, placing their trust not in man but in God – as in that saying of Philo: 'When human help ceases, we need the help of God' – for the first time they inflicted serious defeats upon the enemy, who for many years had plundered the land. For a while the insolence of their enemies abated, but not our people's wickedness. The enemy withdrew from our citizens, but they in turn did not draw back from their sins.

21 ... Therefore the shameless Irish robbers returned home, though intending to return shortly, while the Picts in the furthest part of the island then for the first time and for some time thereafter

remained inactive, though they occasionally engaged in forays and plundering raids . . . However, as the devastation settled down, the island began to overflow with such an abundance of riches that no previous period could recall the like, but with these manifold riches came an increase in luxury. 'Reports of such fornication indeed as is not known even among the gentiles.' It was not only this vice that flourished, but all those to which human nature is liable, and especially that which even now overturns every good condition: hatred of truth and those who defend it, love of falsehood and those who contrive it, the adoption of evil instead of good, reverence for wickedness rather than kindness, a desire for darkness rather than the sun . . . (Kings noted for their cruelty are created and deposed only to be replaced by worse examples) . . . If indeed any of them appeared more kindly and to some degree more truthful, against him all would brandish the darts of their hatred without a second thought, as though he wished to subvert Britain . . . And this was the behaviour not only of men of the world but even of the Lord's flock and their pastors, who should have been an example to all the people. In great numbers they wallowed besotted by drunkenness as if soaked in wine, worn out by swelling enmities, contentious disputes, by the grasping talons of envy and a judgment that could not distinguish good from bad . . .

22 Meanwhile God desired to purge his family . . . (reports of fresh attacks by foreign enemies are received) . . . A deadly plague pressed heavily upon the stupid people and within a short span laid low without recourse to the sword so large a number of them that the living could not bury the dead . . . A council is convened to decide the best and safest means of repelling such fierce and frequent attacks and plundering by the aforementioned tribes.

23 Then all the members of the council together with the proud tyrant[23] are blinded; for the protection they find – or rather the means of their homeland's destruction – is to admit into the island, like wolves into the fold, those fierce Saxons – an accursed name – hated as they were by God and men, admit them to repel the northern tribes . . . Then a brood of cubs breaks forth from the lair of the barbaric lioness, borne along in three 'cylae', as they call warships in their language . . . On the orders of that ill-fated tyrant they first fixed their terrible claws in the eastern part of the island as if intent upon fighting for the country, but in fact to attack it. To these the mother lioness, learning her first contingent has prospered, sends another larger load of accomplice dogs . . . Then the barbarians, admitted into the island, succeed in having supplies

given them as if they were soldiers about to undergo great toils on behalf of their worthy hosts – such were their lies . . . They again complain the monthly rations accorded them are not enough, deliberately colouring their case, and declare that unless greater liberality is heaped upon them, they will break their treaty and plunder the whole island. Without delay they follow up their threats with deeds.

24 In just retribution for former crimes there spread from sea to sea a fire heaped up by the hand of the impious easterners. It devastated all the towns and countryside round about, and once alight did not subside until it had burned almost the whole surface of the island, and was licking the western ocean with its savage red tongue . . . Thus were all the settlements thrown to the ground by the frequent battering of the rams, and all the inhabitants along with church leaders, priests, and people laid low as sword points gleamed all around and flames crackled . . .

25 And so, some of the wretched remnants, being caught in the mountains, were slaughtered in heaps; others, worn out by famine, came and surrendered to the enemy to be their slaves forever – if they were not butchered on the spot, something that was the highest boon; others still made for lands across the seas with great lamentation . . . while others, though fearful, held out in their homeland, placing their trust in the high hills, overhanging, steep, and fortified, in the densest forests, and in the sea cliffs, their minds forever in a state of apprehension. After a time the cruel plunderers returned home. To the remnants (of the Britons), given strength by God, flocked the wretched citizens from all directions . . . begging God with one accord . . . that they might not everywhere be utterly exterminated. Under the leadership of Ambrosius Aurelianus, a sober man, who perhaps alone of the Romans had survived the shock of so great a storm, a storm in which his parents, who had surely worn the purple, had perished . . . they recovered their strength and challenged the victorious Saxons to battle. The Lord assented and the victory fell to them.

26 And so, from that time on sometimes our countrymen proved victorious, sometimes the enemy . . . until the year that saw the siege of Mt. Badon, pretty well the last but not the least slaughter inflicted on the villains. It is now 43 years and one month since then, as I know, since it was the year of my birth.[24]

NOTES

1 There is some evidence that the reference to Britain here may have been included simply for oratorical effect; see further Tomlin (2) pp. 473–5.

2 See further Tomlin (1).

3 Text in doubt.

4 The relevance of references associating Theodosius' naval victories over the Saxons with Britain is questioned by Bartholomew (2) p. 173ff., Cotterill p. 229.

5 The location of this province remains very much a matter of dispute. Was it a newly constituted fifth province (Dornier) or the renaming of an already existing unit (Johnson (2), p. 98; cf. Salway (1), p. 411; Hind (1))?

6 See further P.J. Casey (2).

7 On the Chronicle as a source see Muhlberger.

8 Zosimus has evidently conflated the Count Theodosius who rescued Britain from the disaster of 367, with his son of the same name who was appointed to the throne of the Eastern Empire following the defeat and death of Valens in battle against the Goths at Adrianople in 378.

9 Clearly an error of scribal transcription or spelling. Other writers on the subject place Gratian's death at Lugdunum (Lyons):

Prosper Tiro (5th C. AD), *Chronicon* 1180–3 (AD 384)

> In the consulship of Ricimer and Clearchus ... Maximus was made Emperor in Britain as a result of a mutiny of the troops, and soon he crossed from there to Gaul. Gratian was defeated at Paris through the treachery of Merobaudis, his military commander, and fled, but was captured at Lugdunum (Lyons) and killed. Maximus made his son Victor his partner on the throne.

10 On the evidence of Gildas see Lapidge and Dumville; Thompson (2).

11 This addition of wall building to the narrative, presumably attributing to the late fourth century the construction of the Antonine wall, must inevitably bring the validity of Gildas' whole account into question. See, however, Salway (1) p. 405 n. 4, who suggests Gildas may be representing in a garbled form Roman attempts to restore damaged sections of the northern frontier.

12 Miller; Salway (1), p. 420ff.

13 A garbled reference to the Saxon–shore forts?

14 See further Thompson (1).

15 According to Prosper Tiro, *Chronicon* 1230 (AD 406) 'The Vandals and Alans crossed the Rhine and invaded Gaul on December 31st.'

16 Cf. Sozomenus (5th C. AD), *Ecclesiastical History* IX, 11.

> When he (Gratian) too was put to death after no more than four months, they next chose Constantine, thinking that since he bore this name, he would gain firm control of the empire. It was for this reason they appear to have chosen the others too for usurpation.

17 The unsystematic approach of Zosimus to history means the following account is something of a patchwork culled from various parts of his work.

18 A hint of Constantine's success against the barbarians on the continent is given by Zosimus VI, 3, 2: 'In a mighty battle the Romans proved victorious, slaughtering the majority of the barbarians.'

19 That Constantine's hold on Gaul was not without its own troubles is
    suggested by the *Chronicle of 452*, AD 408.

> At that time with the multitude of the enemy gaining the upper hand,
> Roman strength was utterly diminished. Britain was devastated by an
> attack of the Saxons, part of Gaul was laid waste by the Vandals and
> Alans, and what remained was held by the usurper Constantine.

See further Bartholomew (1), Jones and Casey.

20 Relations between the two had in fact deteriorated following Constans'
    delivery of Didymus and Verenianus to his father: Zosimus VI, 5, 2:

> Constans was again despatched to Spain by his father and took with
> him the general Justus. Gerontius became angry at this, and having
> won over the soldiers stationed there he induced the barbarians
> within Celtic lands (Gaul) to revolt against Constantine. Constantine
> was unable to oppose them since the greater part of his army was in
> Spain . . .

21 Rivet and Smith, p. 102 argue that since the remainder of Zosimus' narra-
    tive in this chapter concerns affairs in Italy, the true reading here is more
    likely to be Brettia, i.e. Bruttium. Contrary to the general opinion of
    commentators Thompson (1) p. 310 argues that it was in fact against
    the whole Roman Empire that Britain rebelled, and he sees as the
    instigators of the revolt not the urban population but the peasantry,
    cf. Bartholomew (1).

22 I.e. Aëtius, who from the mid-420s till his death in 454 was the chief
    military force in the west.

23 I.e. Vortigern. On the evidence for his life and career see Ward (1).

24 The final years of Roman Britain are also recorded by Bede, *Historia
    Eclesiastica Gentis Anglorum* (*History of the English Church*) I, 9–16, though so
    closely does he usually follow his sources (Orosius for Maximus to Constan-
    tine III, Gildas 14–25 for the two Roman expeditions and the Saxon
    invasion) that reproduction here would add little to the account. For a
    translation see Baedae, *Opera Historica*, trans. King, Heinemann (1930).
    The sources for the end of Roman Britain are discussed at length by
    Dumville.

Part Three

Religion, Government, Commerce and Society

XIV Religion

For Rome, ruling an empire that was a patchwork of tribes and nations, each worshipping one or, more usually, a diverse range of gods and supernatural powers, mutual tolerance in matters of religion was not only a sensible expedient, but also a natural result of her own practical approach to the divine. As polytheists the Romans did not concern themselves with setting an upper limit upon the number of gods there might be in the world. Where possible they aimed to equate what they found within provinces with what was already familiar to them. At the same time their essentially pragmatic attitude to their own gods could readily be expanded to provide a focus for demonstrations of political loyalty among provincial populations. In only two respects did the practicalities of tolerance break down: the monotheistic systems which refused the simple expression of loyalty contained in sacrifice to Rome's gods, and those systems like druidism whose rituals were deemed to endanger public order and the rule of Roman law.

THE OFFICIAL CULTS[1]

Professions of loyalty by both Roman and native might take many forms. For the army, dedications were frequently centred upon Jupiter himself, either alone or linked to the *Numen* of the Emperor, his guiding spirit or divine power:

289. From Maryport (*RIB* I 815)

To Jupiter, Greatest and Best, and to the divine power of the Emperor, the 1st Cohort of Spaniards set this up.

290. Ibid. (*RIB* I 816)

To Jupiter, Greatest and Best, the 1st Cohort of Spaniards, part-mounted, under the command of the Prefect Lucius Antistius Lupus Verianus, son of Lucius, of the Quirine voting-tribe, from Sicca in Africa (set this up).

291. Ibid. (*RIB* I 817)

To Jupiter, Greatest and Best, the 1st Cohort of Spaniards under the command of the Tribune Gaius Caballius Priscus (set this up).

292. Ibid. (*RIB* I 818)

To Jupiter, Greatest and Best, Gaius Caballius Priscus, Tribune, (set this up).

cf.

293. From Risingham (*RIB* I 1227)

To the divine power of the Emperors, the 4th Cohort of Gauls, part-mounted, made this.

294. From Bath (*RIB* I 152)

This holy place, which was wrecked through insolence, Gaius Severius Emeritus, Centurion in charge of the region, has cleansed afresh and restored to the virtue and divine power of the Emperor.

In other cases altars were erected for the welfare of the Emperor and his family:

295. From Old Carlisle (*RIB* I 897)

To Jupiter, Greatest and Best, for the safety of the Emperor Marcus Antonius Gordianus Pius Felix, the Unconquered Augustus, his wife Sabinia Furia Tranquillina and their whole Divine House, the cavalry squadron called Augusta Gordiana by virtue of its valour, under the command of Aemilius Crispinus, Prefect of cavalry, born in the Province of Africa, from Tusdrus, set this up under the direction of Nonius Philippus, Pro-Praetorian Legate of Augustus, in the consulship of Atticus and Praetextatus.

Alternatively the emphasis might be on the discipline or fortune of the Emperor:

296. From Bewcastle (*RIB* I 990)

To the Discipline of the Emperor.

297. From Carvoran (*RIB* I 1778)

To the Fortune of the Emperor (and) for the welfare of Lucius Aelius Caesar, Titus Flavius Secundus, Prefect of the 1st Cohort of Hamian archers, willingly and deservedly fulfilled his vow because of a vision.

Declarations of loyalty from the native population of Britain on the other hand seem to have had as their focal point not the Capitoline Triad of Jupiter, Juno and Minerva that served in other provinces, or even Rome itself and the Emperor's Spirit, but rather the more immediate expression of Roman power, the Emperor himself, exemplified by the Temple of Claudius at Colchester. Though it is usually argued that the temple was not constructed until after Claudius' death,[2] thus continuing Roman 'official' policy of ascribing divine honours only to deceased emperors, the practice of allowing provincials to venerate a living ruler, which had been adopted by Augustus from earlier eastern customs, was doubtless of value in Britain too:

298. Dio Cassius (2nd–3rd C. AD) LI, 20, 6–8, 29 BC

Meanwhile, in addition to other business he dealt with, Caesar (Augustus) gave permission for sacred precincts to be set up in both Ephesus and Nicea, dedicated to Rome and his father (Julius) Caesar, to whom he had given the title, the Divine Julius. These cities at that time held preeminent positions in Asia and Bithynia respectively. The Romans who lived there he bade pay honour to these two divinities, but he allowed the provincials, whom he styled Greeks, to consecrate precincts to himself, the Asians in Pergamum, the Bithynians in Nicomedia. From such a beginning this practice has also occurred under other emperors, and not only in the Greek provinces but also in the others that are subject to Rome. In the city of Rome itself and the rest of Italy, however, no emperor, no matter how deserving of praise, has dared to do this (i.e. style himself a god). Yet even there divine honours are accorded and shrines set up to emperors who have ruled well, after their demise.

To carry out the necessary rituals of this imperial cult colleges of six priests were established, the *Seviri Augustales*, drawn largely from freedmen, as Lunaris' names declare him to be:

299. From Bordeaux (*JRS*³ 11 (1921) pp. 101–7), AD 237

To the protecting goddess Boudig, Marcus Aurelius Lunaris, Sevir of Augustus in the colonies of York and Lincoln in the Province of Britannia Inferior, (dedicated) this altar which he vowed when he set out from York. He willingly and deservedly pays his vow. (In the consulship of) Perpetuus and Cornelianus.

cf.

300. From York (*RIB* I 678)

Marcus Verecundius Diogenes, Sevir of the colony of York and five-year magistrate (*quinquennalis*), tribesman of the Bituriges Cubi, set this up for himself during his lifetime.

Though designed to foster loyalty, it is clear that the temple of Claudius soon became for the participants of the Boudiccan rebellion a symbol of Roman oppression and economic depredations (Tacitus, *Annals* XIV, 31, §73).

THE NATIVE CULTS

Celtic religion in all its varied manifestations was rooted firmly in the world of nature. For classical writers, however, the fascination that inspired description after description lay not in the gods themselves so much as in those who officiated at the rituals, the Druids. Yet for all the volume of information available on the subject, there is much about the Druids that remains uncertain: their exact relationship to Celtic beliefs, the extent of their religious power in the Roman period and the degree of their connection with anti-Roman sentiment.[4] The earliest extant account is that of Caesar in the middle of the first century BC speaking of the Druids in Gaul:

301. *Gallic War* VI, 13–18

13 Throughout Gaul there are two classes of men who are of some account and are held in esteem. The common people are considered virtually as slaves, never daring to do anything on their own

initiative and never consulted on any matter. Most of them, over-whelmed with debt or heavy taxation or oppressed by the injustices of those more powerful, surrender themselves to the service of nobles, who have the same rights over them as masters do over slaves. Of the two classes mentioned one consists of Druids, the other of Knights. The former officiate at religious ceremonies, supervise public and private sacrifices, and expound on religious questions. Large numbers of young men flock to them for instruc-tion, and regard them with great respect. In fact they hand down decisions on almost all public and private disputes,[5] and if any crime is committed or murder done, or if there is some dispute over inheritance or boundaries, it is they who decide the issue and determine the compensation or penalty. If any individual or tribe does not abide by their decision, they are banned from sacrifices. This is regarded by them as the heaviest possible penalty, and those under such a ban are reckoned to be impious criminals: everyone shuns them, avoids going near them or speaking to them, in case they come to some harm through contact with them. If they seek redress, they are denied justice, and they are refused all honours. Over all the Druids, however, there is one who presides and has supreme authority. On his death, if there is anyone of surpassing merit among those remaining, he succeeds; but if a number of them are of equal standing, the matter is put to the vote among the Druids, and on occasion they even fight over the leadership by force of arms. At a fixed time of the year the Druids hold session at a consecrated spot in the territory of the Carnutes, which is considered to be the centre of all Gaul. To this place come all those who have disputes, and they accept their decrees and deci-sions. It is thought that the druidic system was invented in Britain and then imported into Gaul. There it is that those wishing to make a more detailed study of it generally go to learn.

14 The Druids do not normally take part in war and are not subject to taxation like the rest; they enjoy exemption from military service and immunity to all liabilities. With the attraction of such privi-leges many come to learn of their own volition, or are sent by their parents and relatives. The students reportedly learn a great number of verses by heart, and for this reason many remain under instruc-tion for twenty years. They regard it as contrary to their religious beliefs to commit their teachings to writing, though in almost all other matters such as public and private accounts they use the Greek alphabet. This rule I think was introduced for two reasons: they did not want the teachings to be disseminated among the

masses, nor did they wish their students to rely on the written word and thus pay less attention to the development of their memories. This in fact generally happens to most people: once they have the assistance of written texts, they relax their memories and their application to learning things by heart. A belief they particularly wish to inculcate is that the soul does not perish, but after death passes from one person to another. This they think is the greatest incentive to bravery, if fear of death is thereby minimised. They also engage in much discussion about the stars and their motion, the size of the universe and the earth, the composition of the world, and the strength and power of the immortal gods, all of which they hand on to the young men.

15 The other class consists of the Knights. When war breaks out and they are needed – before Caesar's arrival it was almost a yearly occurrence for the Gauls to be engaged in making raids or repelling them – they all engage in it, and each has a band of vassals and retainers about him in accordance with his birth and wealth. This is the only criterion of dignity and power they recognise.

16 The Gallic nation as a whole is very much devoted to religion. For this reason those affected by more serious diseases or engaged in the dangers of battle either offer or promise to offer human sacrifice, and they employ Druids to act for them in this. They believe in fact that unless one life is given for another, the power of the immortal gods cannot be appeased, and they also have organised sacrifices of the same kind on behalf of the state. Others use enormous figures, the limbs of which, woven out of pliant twigs, they fill with living men. They are then set alight and the men perish, engulfed in the flames. The execution of those caught in the act of theft or brigandage or some other crime is considered more pleasing to the immortal gods, but when there is a shortage of people of this type they resort to executing even those guilty of no offence.

17 They worship Mercury most of all and have very many images of him, regarding him as the inventor of all crafts, their guide on all journeys, and they consider him to be especially important for the acquisition of money in trade. After him they worship Apollo, Mars, Jupiter, and Minerva,[6] about whom they hold much the same ideas as do other races: that Apollo dispels disease, that Minerva teaches the principles of arts and crafts, that Jupiter reigns in heaven, that Mars is Lord of warfare, and it is to him, when they have decided to fight a battle, that they generally promise the booty they look forward to taking. When they are victorious, they sacrifice the

captured animals and assemble their other booty in one spot. One can see large piles of such material at consecrated places in many tribal areas, and it rarely happens that anyone dares, in defiance of religion, either to hide booty in his house or to remove anything once placed in position (on the pile). For such an act is assigned the severest of penalties accompanied by torture.

18 The Gauls declare that they are all descended from Father Dis, and they claim that this is the tradition of the Druids. For this reason they measure all periods of time not by the number of days but of nights . . .

cf.

302. Cicero (mid–1st C. BC), *De Divinatione* I, 90

Not even among barbarians is the practice of divination neglected, since there are Druids in Gaul, one of whom I knew myself, your guest and eulogist Diviciacus the Aeduan. He claimed to have that knowledge of nature which Greeks call 'physiologia', and he used to foretell the future partly by means of augury and partly by conjecture.

In later writers the twin themes of druidic philosophy and human sacrifice continued to fascinate. Again the context is Gaul:

303. Strabo (1st C. BC–1st C. AD) IV, 4, 4–5

Among all the Gauls in general there are three groups of men who are held in special honour: the Bards, the Vates, and the Druids. The Bards are singers and poets, the Vates perform ritual ceremonies and study natural philosophy, while the Druids engage in moral as well as natural philosophy. They are considered to be the most just of men and for this reason they are entrusted with deciding both private and public disputes, so that in earlier times they acted as arbitrators in war and made those on the point of going into battle stop, while cases of murder especially were handed over to them for decision. Whenever there is a large number of such murders, they consider there is also a large crop in store for them from the land. The Druids and others as well say that the soul, like the universe, is immortal, though at some time or other both fire and water will overwhelm them.

In addition to a general openness and high spirits the Gauls are characterised to a large extent by lack of sense, boastfulness, and love of adornment. For they not only wear golden ornaments – torques around their necks and bracelets around their arms and wrists – but those in high positions also wear clothes that have been dyed and shot through with gold. As a result of such volatility of character they appear insufferable when victorious and panic-stricken in defeat. In addition to their witlessness there is also the barbaric and outlandish practice which, to a very large extent, is common to all the northern tribes: that is the fastening of enemy heads to the necks of their horses when they leave the battle, and once they have taken them home nailing the spectacle to their doorposts. Poseidonius[7] at all events says he personally saw this sight in many places and was at first disgusted by it, but later he got used to it and as a result did not give it a second thought. The heads of famous adversaries they used to embalm in cedar-oil and exhibit to their guests; nor did they consider it right to return them for a ransom equal to their weight in gold. However, the Romans put an end to their practice of these customs as well as those concerned with sacrifices and divination that are contrary to our usages. For instance, they would strike a man dedicated for this purpose in the back with a knife and read the future from his death-throes. They would make no sacrifices without the Druids. There are also reports of other kinds of human sacrifice: for example, they used to shoot people to death with arrows, or impale them in their temples, or build an enormous figure out of wood and straw, throw into it cattle, all kinds of wild animals and human beings, and set it all on fire as an offering.

304. Diodorus Siculus (late 1st C. BC) V, 31, 2–5

The Gauls also have composers of songs whom they call Bards. These sing to the accompaniment of instruments like lyres either in praise of people or to deride them. There are also philosophers and theologians called Druids to whom they accord great honour. In addition they make use of soothsayers whom they deem worthy of great respect. These foretell the future by the observation of birds or through the sacrifice of animals, and they hold the masses in subjection to them. Furthermore, when they are involved in consideration of very important affairs, they have a strange and incredible custom: they strike a man dedicated as a victim with a knife in the region over the diaphragm, and when he collapses after the blow, they read the future by his fall, by the convulsions in his limbs, and additionally by the spurting of his blood. It is an ancient and long-standing method of divination in which they have full confidence.

It is also their custom never to make a sacrifice without a 'philosopher'; for they say that thank-offerings should be given to the gods
by means of those who are experts in the nature of the divine, and,
as it were, in communion with it. They also believe it is through
these people that blessings should be sought. Nor is it only in time
of peace that these people, together with the singers of songs, are
given total obedience, but even in time of war, and by friend and
foe alike. Frequently when armies confront one another in line of
battle with swords drawn and spears thrust forward, these men intervene and cause them to stop, just as though they were holding some
wild animal spellbound with their chanting.

305. Lucan (mid-1st C. AD), *Pharsalia* I, 450–8

And you Dryadae (Druids) set aside your arms and sought again
your barbaric rites and the sinister practice of your religion. To you
alone is granted knowledge of the gods and the powers of heaven,
or you alone are ignorant of them. The depths of groves in far-off
forests are your abode, your teaching that the shades of the dead
seek not the silent home of Erebus and the pallid realms of Pluto
deep below: instead the same soul controls a body in another world,
and if what you sing of is true, death is but the mid-point of a long
existence.

306. Pomponius Mela (1st C. AD), *De Chorographia* III, 2, 18–19

The tribes (of Gaul) are arrogant, superstitious and even at times
inhuman, so much so that they believe a human victim is the most
effective and the one most acceptable to the gods. Vestiges of their
savage ways still remain, even if the practices themselves have been
abolished; for though they refrain from outright murder, they nevertheless draw blood when they bring the faithful to the altars.
However, they have their own brand of eloquence and in the Druids
teachers of wisdom. These latter claim to know the size and shape
of the world, the motion of the stars and the heavens, and the will
of the gods. They teach many things to the most noble members
of their race in secret locations, caves or hidden glades, and for a
period of up to twenty years. One of the things they teach has
become common knowledge among the masses, doubtless to make
them braver in war, namely that the soul is eternal and that there
is an afterlife among the shades. For this reason they cremate and

bury with the dead those things that are appropriate to the living. At one time they even put off the transaction of business affairs and the recovery of debts until the next world, and there were some who willingly flung themselves onto the pyres of their kinsfolk as if to live on with them.

307. Valerius Maximus (early 1st C. AD) II, 6, 10

Leaving the town of Massilia (Marseilles) one encounters that ancient usage of the Gauls. It is said that they are in the habit of lending money to be repaid in the next world. The reason for this is they are convinced that the souls of men are immortal. I should call them stupid were it not for the fact that these trouser-wearing folk have exactly the same belief as that held by the Greek Pythagoras.

308. Diodorus Siculus (late 1st C. BC) V, 28, 6

The Pythagorean doctrine prevails among them (the Gauls), namely that the souls of men are immortal and that after a period of years they live again, since the soul enters another body.

309. Diogenes Laertius (3rd C. AD), *Lives of Eminent Philosophers*, Prologue 1

Some say that the study of philosophy had its origins among barbarians. For the Persians had their Magi, the Babylonians or Assyrians the Chaldeans, the Indians their Gymnosophists, and the Celts and Gauls those called Druids or Semnotheoi. This is what Aristotle says in his work *Magicus* and Sotion in the 23rd book of his *Succession*.

310. Ibid. 6

Those who claim that philosophy arose from barbarians explain the systems that operate among each people. They say the Gymnosophists and Druids expounded their philosophy in riddles, bidding people to reverence the gods, do no evil, and practise valour.

311. Ammianus Marcellinus (late 4th C. AD) XV, 9, 4 and 8

4 The Drysidae (Druids) record that part of the population (of Gaul) was in fact indigenous, but that others also were immigrants from islands far away and from regions across the Rhine, people who had been driven from their homes by repeated warfare and by inroads of the raging sea.

8 Throughout these regions the inhabitants gradually became civilised, and the study of praiseworthy skills flourished, a study introduced by the Bards, Euhages (Strabo's Vates) and the Drysidae (Druids). The Bards celebrated the brave deeds of famous men in epic verse to the accompaniment of the sweet strains of the lyre. The Euhages investigated sublime topics, and attempted to lay bare the fundamental laws of nature. The Drysidae were men of greater intellect, bound together into close communities as laid down by Pythagorean teaching. They were inspired by investigations into questions of a secret and lofty nature and, scorning things human, declared the soul to be immortal.

312. Hippolytus (*Pseudo-Origen*) (3rd C. AD), *Philosophumena* or *Omnium Haeresium Refutatio* (*Refutation of All Heresies*) I, 25

Among the Celts the Druids delved deeply into the Pythagorean philosophy, inspired to this pursuit by Zamolxis, a Thracian slave of Pythagoras. Following Pythagoras' death he went there and initiated this philosophy among them. The Celts consider them as prophets and able to read the future because they predict certain events as a result of computations and calculations using Pythagorean techniques. I shall not pass over in silence the methods of this same technique since some people have even presumed to introduce heresies from these people. The Druids also make use of magic.

For details of Druidic 'magic' we must rely on Pliny the Elder writing in the mid-first century AD:

313. *Natural History* XVI, 249–51

249 While on this topic we must not omit the respect paid (to mistletoe) by the Gauls. The Druids – this is what they call their magicians – hold nothing more sacred than mistletoe and the tree on which

it is growing, so long as this is oak. They even choose groves of oak simply for that fact alone, and perform no rites without its foliage. As a result it would seem that they are even called Druids from the Greek word for oak (*drus*). In particular they consider that anything growing on oaks has been sent by heaven and is a sign that the tree has been chosen by the god himself.

250 Mistletoe growing on an oak, however, is a rare find, and when it is found it is gathered with great reverence, above all on the 6th day of the moon (it is the moon that marks out for them the beginning of months and years and cycles of thirty years) because this day is already exercising great influence even though the moon is not half-way through its course. They call it[8] in their language 'all-healing'. Having prepared a sacrifice and banquet beneath the tree with all due ceremony, they bring up two bulls whose horns have been bound for the first time on that occasion.

251 The priest, dressed in a white role, climbs the tree, reaps the mistletoe with a golden sickle, and it is gathered up in a white blanket. They then sacrifice the victims praying that the god makes this gift of theirs propitious for those to whom he has given it. They believe that when taken in liquid form mistletoe imparts fertility to any sterile animal and is an antidote for all poisons. Such is the reverence felt by very many tribes for such worthless matters.

314. Ibid. XXIX, 52–4

52 There is moreover a type of egg held in great esteem by the Gauls but disregarded by the Greeks. Snakes entwined in large numbers make these objects with saliva from their mouths and a secretion from their bodies, employing an ingenious embrace. It is called *anguinum*, snake-egg, (alt. reading, wind-egg). The Druids say that it is thrown into the air by their hissing and should be caught in a blanket before it touches the earth. The catcher should flee away on horseback since the snakes will pursue him until they are prevented from doing so by a river blocking their way. The means of testing such an egg is if it floats against a current of water even when it is set in gold . . .

53 I have indeed seen one of these, the size of a smallish round apple, its shell remarkable for the many gristly cavities like those on the tentacles of an octopus.

54 The Druids praise it greatly as producing success in law-suits and access to kings . . .

315. Ibid. XXIV, 103–4

103 Similar to this plant called Sabina is one called Selago. It is gathered without the use of any iron implement, but using the right hand protruding from the left armhole of the tunic as if the person involved were committing an act of theft. This person should be clad in white, his bare feet washed clean, and an offering of bread and wine made before gathering. It should be carried in a fresh white cloth. The Druids of Gaul teach that its possession wards off all harm and that the smoke of it is good for all eye troubles.

104 The same people mention a plant called Samolus which grows in damp areas. This should be gathered with the left hand by those fasting and be used against diseases of pigs and cattle. The person gathering it should not look at it (alt. look behind him) nor put it down anywhere except in the drinking trough where it is crushed for the animals to drink.

For Rome, however, the apparent 'quaintness' of druidic use of mistletoe and the like could not efface the unacceptable fact of human sacrifice. The reaction was first to restrict and then, as already stated by Strabo IV, 4, 5 and Pomponius Mela III, 2, 18 (§303 and 306) to abolish.

cf.

316. Pliny the Elder, *Natural History* XXX, 13

Magic undoubtedly had a hold on Gaul, even down to living memory; for it was in the reign of Tiberius Caesar that their Druids and that type of soothsayer and healer were abolished. But why mention this about a practice that has crossed Ocean and penetrated to the empty vastnesses of nature? Britain today is mesmerised by it and practises it with so much ceremony that one might think it was she who gave it to the Persians: so unanimous is the world in its acceptance of it, even though its practitioners are quite different from one another, or even ignorant of one another's existence. Nor can one adequately reckon the debt owed to Rome in having put an end to those evil rites in which the greatest act of piety was to murder a man, and to eat his flesh most conducive to good health.

317. Suetonius (2nd C. AD), *Claudius* 25, 5

Claudius totally abolished the dreadful and savage religion of the Druids in Gaul. Under the Emperor Augustus it had merely been forbidden to Roman citizens.

That the Druids themselves continued to exist, however, is suggested by Tacitus' reference to their activities in AD 69:

318. Tacitus (1st–2nd C. AD), *Histories* IV, 54 (after the death of Vitellius)

But nothing inspired the Gauls to believe the end of the empire was at hand so much as the fire on the Capitol. They remembered that Rome had once been captured by the Gauls, but since the abode of Jupiter (the Capitol) had remained untouched, the Roman Empire had survived. Now the Druids with their worthless religion prophesied that heaven had provided a sign of its displeasure in this fatal fire, and it portended control of human affairs would pass to the tribes beyond the Alps.

Despite references to Druidism in Britain by Caesar, *Gallic War* VI, 13 (§301), and Pliny the Elder, *Natural History* XXX, 13 (§316), the first record of contact between Roman and Druid in Britain occurs in Tacitus' description of Paulinus' attack on Anglesey (*Annals* XIV, 30, §73), and it is on this that claims for a druidic role in British resistance to Rome largely depend.

Of the actual gods of Britain few real details survive beyond the name, location and sometimes the sphere of influence. In many cases it is even uncertain whether the god was native to Britain or an import from other Celtic parts of the empire after the conquest:[9]

319. From Carrawburgh (*RIB* I 1534)

To the goddess Covventina, Titus D ... Cosconianus, Prefect of the 1st Batavian Cohort, willingly and deservedly (dedicated this).

320. From Bath (*RIB* I 143)

To the goddess Sulis, for the welfare and safety of Marcus Aufidius Maximus, Centurion of the VI Legion Victrix. Aufidius Eutuches, his freedman, willingly and deservedly fulfilled his vow.

321. Ibid. (*RIB* I 144)

To the goddess Sulis, for the welfare and safety of Aufidius Maximus, Centurion of the VI Legion Victrix, Marcus Aufidius Lemnus, his freedman, willingly and deservedly fulfilled his vow.

322. From Risingham (*RIB* I 1225)

To the god Mogons Cad ... and to the divine power of our Lord Augustus, Marcus G ... Secundinus, seconded for special duty by the Governor (*beneficiarius consularis*), on his first tour of duty at Habitancum, set this up for himself and his own.

cf.

323. From Vindolanda (*RIB* I 1695)

To the goddess Sattada, the assembly of the Textoverdi willingly and deservedly fulfilled its vow.

324. Ibid. (R. Birley pl. 27)

To the gods, the Veteres, Longinus set this up.

325. From Hadrian's wall (*RIB* I 2063)

To the god Maponus and the divine power of the Emperor, Durio and Ramio and Trupo and Lurio, Germans, willingly and deservedly fulfilled their vow.

326. From Hardriding nr. Chesterholm (*RIB* I 1683)

To the god Cocidius, Decimus Caerellius Victor, Prefect of the 2nd Cohort of Nervii, willingly and deservedly fulfilled his vow.

327. From Cirencester (*RIB* I 105)

To the Suleviae,[10] Sulinus, son of Brucetus, willingly and deservedly fulfilled his vow.

cf.

328. From Bath (*RIB* I 151)

To the Suleviae, Sulinus the sculptor, son of Brucetus, willingly and deservedly made this offering.

329. From Colchester (*RIB* I 192)

To the Mother goddesses, the Suleviae, Similis, son of Attus, a tribesman of the Cantii, willingly fulfilled his vow.

That the Mother goddesses also answered a religious need among Roman citizens is shown by a number of dedications to them:

330. From Doncaster (*RIB* I 618)

To the Mother goddesses, Marcus Nantonius Orbiotalus willingly and deservedly fulfilled his vow.

cf.

331. From Newcastle (*RIB* I 1318)

To the Mother goddesses of his homeland across the sea, Aurelius Juvenalis (set up) this offering.

332. From York (*RIB* I 653)

To the Mother goddesses of Africa, Italy and Gaul, Marcus Minucius Audens, soldier of the VI Legion Victrix, pilot of the VI Legion, gladly, willingly and deservedly fulfilled his vow.

333. From Winchester (*RIB* I 88)

To the Mother goddesses of Italy, Germany, Gaul and Britain, Antonius Lucretianus, seconded for special duty by the Governor (*beneficiarius consularis*) restored (this).

334. From Brougham (*RIB* I 773)

To the god Balatucairus, Baculo willingly fulfilled his vow for himself and his family.

cf.

335. From Old Carlisle (*RIB* I 887)

To the holy god Belatucadrus, Aurelius Tasulus, veteran, willingly and deservedly fulfilled his vow.

336. From Carvoran (*RIB* I 1777)

To the goddess Epona P... So... (set this up).

337. From Benwell (*RIB* I 1327)

To the god Antenociticus[11] and the divine power of the Emperors, Aelius Vibius, Centurion of the XX Legion Valeria Victrix, willingly and deservedly fulfilled his vow.

cf.

338. Ibid. (*RIB* I 1329)

To the god Anociticus, Tineius Longus (set this up) having been adorned with the broad stripe (of a senator) and designated Quaestor while serving as Prefect of cavalry by the decrees of our Best and Greatest Emperors, under Ulpius Marcellus, Consular Governor.

INTERPRETATIO ROMANA

Just as Caesar in *Gallic War* VI, 17 (§301) attempted to make the gods of the Gauls more comprehensible to his audience by identifying them with Roman divinities, so in Britain the practice of equating Roman and native or imported provincial gods continues, an additional element in the general process of Romanisation:

339. From Lydney Park (*RIB* I 305)

To the god Mars Nodons, Flavius Blandinus, Drill-instructor (*armatura*), willingly and deservedly fulfilled his vow.

340. From Lancaster (*RIB* I 602)

To the holy god Mars Cocidius, Vibenius Lucius, seconded for special duty by the Governor (*beneficiarius consularis*), willingly and deservedly fulfilled his vow.

cf.

341. From Housesteads (*RIB* I 1578)

To the god Silvanus Cocidius, Quintus Florius Maternus, Prefect of the 1st Cohort of Tungrians, willingly and deservedly fulfilled his vow.

342. From Bowes (*RIB* I 732)

To Vinotonus Silvanus, Julius Secundus, Centurion of the 1st Cohort of Thracians, gladly, willingly and deservedly fulfilled his vow.

343. From Caerwent (*RIB* I 310)

To the god Mars Ocelus, Aelius Augustinus, Deputy-centurion (*optio*), willingly and deservedly fulfilled his vow.

cf.

344. Ibid. (*RIB* I 309)

To the god Mars Lenus[12] or Ocelus Vellaunus, and the divine power of the Emperor, Marcus Nonius Romanus gave this gift from his own resources for his freedom from liability of the college, on August 23rd in the consulship of Glabrio and Homulus (AD 152).

345. From Old Penrith (*RIB* I 918)

To Mars Belatucadrus and the divine power of the Emperors, Julius Augustalis, steward (*actor*) of Julius Lupus, the Prefect, (set this up).

346. From Colchester (*RIB* I 191)

To the god Mars Medocius of the Campeses and the victory of our emperor Alexander[13] Pius Felix, Lossio Veda, grandson (or nephew) of the Caledonian, Vepogenus, set this up as a gift from his own resources.

347. Ibid. (*RIB* I 193)

To the divine power of the Emperors and Mercury Andescocivovcus, Imilico, the freedman of Aesurilinus, gave this marble altar from his own resources.

348. From Bath (*RIB* I 146)

To the goddess Sulis Minerva and the divine power of the Emperors, Gaius Curiatius Saturninus, Centurion of the II Legion Augusta, willingly and deservedly fulfilled his vow for himself and his family.

349. From Corbridge (*RIB* I 1120)

To Apollo Maponus, Quintus Terentius Firmus, son of Quintus, of the Oufentine voting-tribe, from Saena, Camp-Prefect of the VI Legion Victrix Pia Fidelis, gave and dedicated (this).

350. Bronze dish from South Shields (*RIB* II.2 2415.55)

To Apollo Anextiomarus, Marcus A. . . Sab(inus) (dedicated this).

351. From West Coker (*RIB* I 187)

To the god Mars Rigisamus,[14] Iventius Sabinus gladly, willingly and deservedly fulfilled his vow.

352. From Martlesham (*RIB* I 213)

To the god Mars Corotiacus, Simplicia willingly and deservedly set up this offering for herself.

353. From Barkway (*RIB* I 219)

To Mars Toutatis,[15] Tiberius Claudius Primus, freedman of Attius, willingly and deservedly fulfilled his vow.

354. Ibid. (*RIB* I 218)

To the god Mars Alator, Dum. . . Censorinus, son of Gemellus, willingly and deservedly fulfilled his vow.

355. From Housesteads (*RIB* I 1593)

To the god Mars Thincsus and the Two Alaisiagae, Beda and Fimmilena, and the divine power of the Emperor, German tribesmen from Tuihantis[16] willingly and deservedly fulfilled their vow.

cf.

356. Ibid. (*RIB* I 1576)

To the goddesses the Alaisiagae, Baudihillia and Friagabis, and to the divine power of the Emperor, the unit (*numerus*) of Hnaudifridus willingly and deservedly fulfilled its vow.

Here too might be included the Roman habit of personifying districts as divine entities:

357. From York (*RIB* I 643)

To holy Britannia, Publius Nikomedes, freedman of our Emperors (set this up).

358. From South Shields (*RIB* I 1053)

Sacred to the goddess Brigantia. Congenniccus willingly and deservedly fulfilled his vow.

359. From Castlehill (*RIB* I 2195)

To the goddesses of the parade ground (Campestres) and Britannia, Quintus Pisentius Justus, Prefect of the 4th Cohort of Gauls, gladly, willingly and deservedly fulfilled his vow.

360. From near Brampton (*RIB* I 2066)

The vow to the goddess-nymph Brigantia which he made for the welfare and safety of Our Lord the unconquered Emperor Marcus Aurelius Severus Antoninus Pius Felix Augustus (Caracalla) and his whole Divine House, Marcus Cocceius Nigrinus, Procurator of our Emperor and most devoted to his divine power and majesty, has gladly, willingly and deservedly fulfilled.

CURSES

Most dedications, be they addressed to Roman or native divinities, were motivated by feelings of gratitude and the hope of continued favour. That this was not always the case is indicated by the survival of curses, usually inscribed on lead and buried:

361. From Lydney Park (*RIB* I 306)

To the god Nodens. Silvianus has lost a ring. He has dedicated half of it to Nodens. Among those with the name Senicianus, grant no health until he brings it to the temple of Nodens.

The ring found?[17]

362. From Silchester, inscription on a gold ring (*RIB* II.3 2422.14)

Senicianus, live in God.

363. From London (*RIB* I 7)

I curse Tretia Maria and her life and mind and memory and liver and lungs mixed together, and her words, thoughts and memory. May she be unable to speak what is secret nor be able . . . nor . . .

364. Ibid. (*RIB* I 6)

Titus Egnatius Tyrannus is cursed and Publius Cicereius Felix is cursed.

365. From Caerleon (*RIB* I 323)

Lady Nemesis, I give you a cloak and boots. May he who wore them not redeem them except with his life and blood.

366. From Clothall, Hertfordshire (*RIB* I 221)

Tacita, here cursed, is marked as old like gore.

367. From Bath (Tomlin (3) p. 198f.)

I have given to the goddess Sulis the thief who stole my hooded cloak, be he slave or free, man or woman. Let him not redeem this gift except with his blood.

368. Ibid. (Tomlin (3) p. 232f.)

Whether pagan or Christian,[18] whoever it is, whether man or woman, boy or girl, slave or free has stolen from me, Annianus, (son) of Matutina, 6 argentei from my purse, you, lady goddess, exact (them) from him. If through some deceit he has given me (undecipherable) and do not thus give to him but (undecipherable) his blood who has invoked this on me . . .

369. Ibid. (Tomlin (3) p. 114f.)

Docimedis has lost two gloves. (He asks) that (the person) who stole them lose his mind and his eyes in the temple where (she) appoints.

370. Ibid. (Tomlin (3) p. 122f.)

Docilianus, son of Brucerus, to the most holy goddess Sulis. I curse whoever stole my hooded cloak, whether man or woman, slave or free, that the goddess Sulis inflict death on him, and not let him sleep or have children now or in the future until he brings my cloak to the temple of her divinity.

371. Ibid. (Tomlin (3) p. 150f.)

Solinus to the goddess Sulis Minerva. I give to your divinity and majesty my bathing costume and cloak. Do not allow the one who did me wrong sleep or health, whether man or woman, whether slave or free, unless he shows himself and brings the items to your temple [. . .] his children or his [. . .] who [. . .] to him also [. . .] sleep or [. . .] and the rest, unless they bring those items to your temple.

372. From Ratcliffe on Soar, Notts. (*JRS* 53 (1963), pp. 122–4)

To Jupiter, Greatest and Best, is granted that he hound through mind, through memory, through innards, through intestines, through heart, through marrow, through veins, through . . ., whoever it was, whether man or woman who stole the denarii (?) of Canius Dignus, that in his own person he may shortly settle his debt. The god is granted a tenth of the money, when he has repaid it (?).

373. Ibid. (*Britannia* 24 (1993), pp. 310–14)

In the name of Camulorix and Titocuna I have dedicated in the temple of the god the mule/millstone (?) they lost. Whoever stole that mule/millstone, whatever his name, let him pour out his blood to the day he dies. May whoever stole the items involved in the theft die, and whoever stole the (unintelligible), may he too die. Whoever stole it and the (unintelligible) from the house or the pair of bags (?), whoever stole it, may he die by the god.

374. From Uley, Gloucestershire (*Britannia* 19 (1988), pp. 485–7)

Biccus gives to Mercury whatever he has lost (on condition that the thief), whether man or male (sic) may not urinate or defaecate or speak or sleep or wake or (have) well-being or health unless he brings it to the temple of Mercury, nor gain consciousness of (it) unless at my intercession.

375 Ibid. (*Britannia* 20 (1989), pp. 329–30)

To the god Mercury. Docilinus (unintelligible) Varianus and Peregrina and Sabinianus who have brought evil harm to my breast and (unintelligible) I ask you to drive them to the greatest death and grant them neither health nor sleep unless they redeem from you what they have done to me.

376. Ibid. (*Britannia* 23 (1992), pp. 310–11)

Honoratus to the holy god Mercury. I complain to your divine power that I have lost two wheels and four cows and many small items from my house. I would ask the spirit of your divine power not to allow the person who did me wrong health, nor to lie down or sit or drink or eat, be it man or woman, boy or girl, slave or free, unless he brings my belongings to me and is reconciled to me. By my repeated prayers I ask your divine power that my petition make me immediately vindicated by your majesty.

ROMAN IMPORTS

Paralleling the interpretation of native divinities by identifying them with their classical counterparts was an influx of foreign gods from the rest of the empire. Many were major or minor members of the Greco-Roman pantheon, dedications to whom might represent instances of official policy or private piety; others came from the east and brought with them more exotic modes of worship.

I: THE GRECO-ROMAN GODS

377. From Newstead (*RIB* I 2120)

To the god Apollo, Lucius Maximius Gaetulicus, legionary Centurion (set this up).

cf.

378. From Housesteads (*RIB* I 1665)

To the god Apollo, Melonius Senilis, soldier on double pay (*duplicarius*) from Germania Superior, gladly, willingly and deservedly fulfilled the vow he had undertaken.

379. From Newstead (*RIB* I 2122)

To Diana the Queen, on account of a favourable outcome, Gaius Arrius Domitianus, Centurion of the XX Legion Valeria Victrix, gladly, willingly and deservedly fulfilled his vow.

380. From Castlecary (*RIB* I 2149)

To the god Neptune, the 1st Loyal Cohort of Vardulli, Roman Citizens, part-mounted, 1,000-strong under the command of the Prefect Trebius Verus (set this up).

381. Ibid. (*RIB* I 2148)

To the god Mercury, soldiers of the VI Legion Victrix Pia Fidelis, citizens of Italy and Noricum, (set up) this shrine and statuette, gladly, willingly and deservedly fulfilling their vow.

382. From Caernarvon (*RIB* I 429)

To the goddess Minerva, Aurelius Sabinianus, Record-keeper (*actarius*), willingly and deservedly fulfilled his vow.

383. From Maryport (*RIB* I 812)

To the Genius (Spirit) of the place, Fortune the Homebringer, Eternal Rome, and Good Fate, Gaius Cornelius Peregrinus, Tribune of the cohort, Decurion of his home town of Saldae in the province of Mauretania Caesariensis, gladly, willingly and deservedly fulfilled his vow.

cf.

384. From Auchendavy (*RIB* I 2175)

To the Genius (Spirit) of the land of Britain, Marcus Cocceius Firmus, Centurion of the II Legion Augusta (set this up).

385. From Housesteads (*RIB* I 1591)

To the god Mars, Quintus Florius Maternus, Prefect of the 1st Cohort of Tungrians, willingly and deservedly fulfilled his vow.

386. From the Foss Dyke (*RIB* I 274)

To the god Mars and the divine power of the Emperors, the Colasuni, Bruccius and Caratius, gave this at their own expense at a cost of 100 sesterces. Celatus, the coppersmith, made it and gave a pound of copper at the cost of 3 denarii.

387. From Birrens (*RIB* I 2100)

To Mars and the Victory of the Emperor, the Raetian tribesmen serving in the 2nd Cohort of Tungrians commanded by the Prefect Silvius Auspex willingly and deservedly fulfilled their vow.

388. From Stony Stratford (*RIB* I 215)

To the god Jupiter and Vulcan, I, Vassinus, promised six denarii should they bring me, their votary, back safe, and have paid the money in fulfilment of my vow.

389. From Newstead (*RIB* I 2124)

To the god Silvanus, Gaius Arrius Domitianus, Centurion of the XX Legion Valeria Victrix, gladly, willingly and deservedly fulfilled his vow for himself and his family.

cf.

390. From York (*RIB* I 659 restored)

[Sacred to the holy] g[od] Silva[nus]. Lucius Celerinius Vitalis, Adjutant (*cornicularius*) of the IX Legion Hispana, gladly, willingly and deservedly fulfilled his vow. Let this gift form part. I must beware of touching.

391. From Bollihope Common (*RIB* I 1041)

Sacred to Unconquered Silvanus. Gaius Tetius Veturius Micianus, Prefect of the Sebosian squadron, willingly set this up in fulfilment of his vow on account of his capture of an outstandingly fine boar which many before him had been unable to bag.

392. Spoons from Thetford (*RIB* II.2 2420. 11, 12, 14, 15, 17, 20)

(Property) of the god Faunus Andicrose
(Property) of the god Faunus Ausecus
(Property) of the god Faunus Blotugus
(Property) of the god Faunus Cranus
(Property) of the god Faunus Medigenus
(Property) of the god Faunus Narius

393. From Lincoln (*RIB* I 247)

To the goddesses, the Fates, and the divine power of the Emperors, Gaius Antistius Frontinus, Guild-treasurer (*curator*) for the third time, dedicated this altar at his own expense.

394. From Old Carlisle (*RIB* I 890)

To the goddess Bellona, Rufinus, Prefect of the Augustan cavalry squadron, and Latinianus, his son, (set this up).

395. From Maryport (*RIB* I 808)

To Asclepius, Aulus Egnatius Pastor set this up.

396. From South Shields (*RIB* I 1052)

To the god Aesculapius, Publius Viboleius Secundus gave this altar as a gift.

397. From Chester (*JRS* 59 (1969), p. 235)

The doctor Antiochus (honours the) saviours of men pre-eminent among the immortals: Asklepios of the healing hand, Hygeia (and) Panakeia.

398. From York (*RIB* I 644)

To the goddess Fortune, Sosia Juncina (wife of) Quintus Antonius Isauricus, (legionary) Legate of Augustus, (set this up).

399. From Chester (*JRS* 57 (1967), p. 203)

To the goddess Nemesis, Sextius Marcianus (dedicated this) as the result of a vision.

Exhibiting perhaps more than a little imagination is the following:

400. From Catterick (*RIB* I 725)

To the god who invented roads and pathways, Titus Irdas, auxiliary infantryman seconded to the Governor's guard (*singularis consularis*), gladly, willingly and deservedly fulfilled his vow. Quintus Varius Vitalis, seconded for special duty by the Governor (*beneficiarius consularis*), restored this sacred altar in the consulship of Apronianus and Bradua.

cf.

401. From Corbridge (*RIB* I 1142)

Quintus Calpurnius Concessinius, Prefect of cavalry, following the slaughter of a band of Corionototae, fulfilled his vow to the god of most potent power.

II: GERMAN GODS[19]

402. From Birrens (*RIB* I 2108)

To the goddess Viradecthis, (the tribesmen) of the Condrustian district serving in the 2nd Cohort of Tungrians under the Prefect Silvius Auspex (set this up).

403. Ibid. (*RIB* I 2107)

To the goddess Ricagambeda, (the tribesmen) of the district of Vella serving in the 2nd Cohort of Tungrians willingly and deservedly fulfilled their vow.

404. From Lanchester (*RIB* I 1074)

To the goddess Garmangabis and the divine power of our Emperor Gordian for the welfare of the detachment of Suebians of Longovicium, Gordian's own, (the soldiers) deservedly fulfilled their vow.

See also §202, 355, 356, 480–2, 484.

III: THE EASTERN CULTS[20]

Mobility of population among the mercantile classes and as a factor in military life made it inevitable that Britain would be brought into contact with the gods of the east. That some became more than the personal imports of individuals, however, is doubtless due to their offering the convert what was generally absent from the Greco-Roman pantheon: emotional commitment and a sense of belonging.

From Syria came a number of divinities: Jupiter Dolichenus, a Romanised soldier-god who had originally belonged to the Hittites and was particularly popular among officers:

405. From Great Chesters (*RIB* I 1725)

To Jupiter, Greatest and Best, of Doliche, Lucius Maximius Gaetulicus, Centurion of the XX Legion Valeria Victrix, willingly and deservedly fulfilled his vow.

cf.

406. From Corbridge (*RIB* I 1131)

To Eternal Jupiter of Doliche and Caelestis Brigantia and Salus, Gaius Julius Apolinaris, Centurion of the VI Legion, (set this up) at the command of the god.

407. From Piercebridge (*RIB* I 1022)

To Jupiter, Greatest and Best, of Dolyche, Julius Valentinus, Centurion from Germania Superior, gladly, willingly and deservedly set this up at the command of the god for himself and his family in the second consulship of Praesens and Extricatus (AD 217).

Similarly Astarte and Melkaart:

408. From Corbridge (*RIB* I 1124)

You see me, an altar of Astarte. Pulcher set me up.

409. Ibid. (*RIB* I 1129)

To Heracles of Tyre (Melkaart), the priestess Diodora (set this up).

In the reign of Septimius Severus (AD 193–211) the Libyan origins of the Emperor, and his Syrian-born wife, Julia Domna, were to become the subject of religious allegory:

410. From Carvoran (*RIB* I 1791)

The Virgin in her heavenly place rides upon the lion, bearer of corn, inventor of law, founder of cities, by whose gift it is our good fortune to know the gods; therefore she is Mother of the gods,[21] Peace, Virtue, Ceres, the Syrian goddess, weighing life and laws in her balance. Syria has sent the constellation seen in the heavens to Libya to be worshipped. From this we have all learned. Thus, led by thy godhead, Marcus Caecilius Donatianus has understood, serving as Tribune in the post of Prefect by the Emperor's gift.

cf.

411. Ibid. (*RIB* I 1792 restored)

To the Syrian goddess, under Calpurnius Agricola, Pro-Praetorian Legate of Augustus, Lic[in]ius [C]lem[ens, Prefect] of the 1st [Co]hort of Ha[mians], (set this up).

From Egypt came Isis and Osiris, the latter in his Greco-Roman guise of Serapis:

412. From London, a graffito on a jug (*RIB* II.8 2503.127)

In London, at the shrine of Isis.

413. Ibid. (*Britannia* 7 (1976), p. 378f.)

For the honour of the Divine House, His Excellency Marcus Martianius Pulcher, Pro-Praetorian Legate of the Augusti, ordered the restoration of the temple of Isis [. . .] which had collapsed through age.

414. From York (*RIB* I 658)

To the holy god Serapis, this temple was built from ground-level by Claudius Hieronymianus, Legate of the VI Legion Victrix.

Of all the pagan eastern cults, however, the most significant was that of Mithras,[22] originally an element in Persian Zoroastrianism, which offered its devotees an escape from darkness into light, but demanded in return life-long commitment and discipline, hence its appeal to the military. As a god of light Mithras was frequently equated with the sun:

415. From Housesteads (*RIB* I 1599)

To the Unconquered Sun Mytras (Mithras), Lord of Ages, Litorius Pacatianus, seconded for special duty by the Governor (*beneficiarius consularis*), willingly and deservedly fulfilled his vow for himself and his family.

cf.

416. Ibid. (*RIB* I 1600)

To the Unconquered Sun Mitras, Lord of Ages, Publicius Proculinus, Centurion, willingly and deservedly fulfilled his vow for himself and Proculus, his son, in the consulship of our Lords Gallus and Volusianus.

In other cases the equation with the sun is omitted:

417. From Carrawburgh (*RIB* I 1545)

Sacred to the Unconquered god Mithras, Aulus Cluentius Habitus, Prefect of the 1st Cohort of Batavians, of the Ultinian voting-tribe, from Colonia Septimia Aurelia Larinum, willingly and deservedly fulfilled his vow.

cf.

418. Ibid. (*RIB* I 1546)

To the Unconquered god Mitras, Marcus Simplicius Simplex, Prefect, willingly and deservedly fulfilled his vow.

419. Ibid. (*RIB* I 1544)

To the Unconquered Mithras, Lucius Antonius Proculus, Prefect of the 1st Cohort of Batavians, Antoninus' own, willingly and deservedly fulfilled his vow.

420. From Rudchester (*RIB* I 1395)

To the Unconquered god Mytras, Publius Aelius Titullus, Prefect, gladly, willingly and deservedly fulfilled his vow.

Alternatively, we find dedications to the sun god in contexts that are clearly Mithraic, or associations of Mithras with other gods:

421. From Rudchester (*RIB* I 1396)

To the Unconquered Sun, Tiberius Claudius Decimus Cornelius Antonius, Prefect, restored this temple.

422. Ibid. (*RIB* I 1397 restored)

To the Sun-god Apollo, Unconquered [Mithras], Aponius Rogatianus [. . .

423. From High Rochester (*RIB* I 1272)

Sacred to the Unconquered god and the Sun-companion for the welfare and safety of the Emperor Caesar Marcus Aurelius Antoninus Pius Felix Augustus. Lucius Caecilius Optatus, Tribune of the

1st Cohort of Vardulli together with his fellow-devotees (raised this), built from ground level, as an offering to the god.

As the central element in the religion, and the one most frequently represented, was Mithras' sacrifice of the cosmic bull, from whose blood stemmed all animal and vegetable life. Since, however, Mithraism was essentially a dualistic cult, there was an evil counterpart in Arimanes:

424. From York (*RIB* I 641 restored)

Volusenus Iren[aeus gave] this as a gift to Arimanes, [willingly and deservedly fulfilling] his vow.

Inevitably the salvationist aspects of Mithraism brought it into competition with the other major eastern saviour-cult, Christianity.[23] The earliest evidence for the religion in Britain comes in a fleeting reference from Tertullian writing *c.* AD 200:

425. *Against the Jews* 7, 4

. . . places in Britain inaccessible to the Romans, but which have submitted to Christ.

Not until after Constantine's edict of toleration in AD 313, however, does evidence of an organised church begin to emerge:

426. *Acts of the Council of Arles* AD 314

Eborius, bishop of the city of York in the province of Britain, Restitutus, bishop of the city of London in the above-mentioned province, Adelphius, bishop of the city Colonia Londenensium,[24] also Sacerdus, presbyter, and Arminius, deacon.

427. Athanasius (4th C. AD), *Letter to the Emperor Jovian* 2

This article of faith was agreed upon by those Fathers (of the Church) meeting in Nicaea (AD 325), and all the Churches everywhere voted for it: those in Spain and Britain and Gaul . . . and those Churches in the East with the exception of the few that hold Arian opinions.

428. Athanasius, *Apologia Contra Arianos* (*Defence Against the Arians*) 1

(The matter was decided) for the third time at the great synod assembled at Sardica (AD 343) by the orders of those Emperors most beloved of God, Constantius and Constans, at which our adversaries were overthrown. To the judgements on our side were given the votes of more than 300 bishops from the provinces of Egypt, Libya . . . and Britain.

429. Sulpicius Severus (5th C. AD), *Historia Sacra* II, 41, AD 360

The Council was therefore commanded to assemble at Arminium (Rimini), a city in Italy, and the Prefect Taurus was instructed not to dismiss those assembled before they agreed on a single doctrine. He was in fact promised the consulship if he brought the matter to a successful conclusion. And so state officials were sent through Illyria, Italy, Africa, Spain, and Gaul, and somewhat over 400 western bishops gathered at Arminium by invitation or compulsion. The emperor had given instructions that they all be given food and board, but this seemed improper to our representatives from Aquitania, and to those from Gaul and Britain. They refused the treasury grants and preferred to live at their own expense. Only three from Britain made use of public funds through lack of private means, and they refused a collection offered by the others, thinking it more holy to be a burden to the treasury than to individuals.

Within Britain itself evidence for Christianity at the time comes largely through the use of the Chi-Rho monogram, ☧, as a decorative device and the occurrence of Christian formulas:

430. Pewter ingots from the Thames (*RIB* II.1 2406. 1–10)

Either: (Product of) Syagrius, Hope in God, ☧
Or: Syagrius A ☧ W

431. Silver bowls from Chesterton (*RIB* II.2 2414.1–2)

1 A ☧ W Innocentia and Viventia gave this.
2 A ☧ W I prostrate myself and honour your holy sanctuary, O Lord.
Publianus

432. Bone plaque from York (*RIB* II.3 2441.11)

Hail, sister, live in God.

cf. From Richborough (*RIB* II.3 2422.70)

Justin, live in God.

Here too may be included the Cirencester word-square (itself a palindrome) which was once regarded as containing a secret reference to Christianity, though such an origin has now been seriously questioned.[25]

433. Cirencester word-square (*RIB* II.4 2447.20)

ROTAS	=	Arepo, the Sower, holds the wheels with
OPERA		care (or as his work).
TENET		
AREPO		
SATOR		

=

```
                              P
                              A
              A               T               O
                              E
                              R
                    PATERNOSTER
                              O
                              S
              A               T               O
                              E
                              R
```

cf. Manchester (*RIB* II.6 2494.98)

ROTAS
OPERA
TENE[T

Recent finds of letters, however, begin to reveal more personal concerns and the problems caused by heresy:

434. Letter from Bath (*ZPE*[26] 100 (1994), pp. 93–108)

Obverse: Vinisius to Nigra: [The grace] of our Lord Jesus Christ to thine. (Your) husband's faults Vinisia has related to Vilius' Similis. [. . .] with all your strength [. . .]. Unless in just conflicts [. . .].

Reverse: The enemy of Christ has sent Biliconus from Viriconium (Wroxeter) in order that you may take him in the sheepfold, although a dog of Arius. Pray to Christ for light. XPS Apulicus carries these sheets.

That Britain, like the rest of the empire, suffered from the periodic outbursts of persecution against the Christians is shown by the martyrdom of St Alban, variously dated to the reigns of Septimius Severus,[27] Decius or Valerian,[28] or Diocletian.[29] The earliest reference occurs *c.* 470:

435. Constantius, *De Vita Germani* (*The Life of Germanus*) 16

With the damnable heresy curbed and its authors refuted and with the minds of all restored to calm by the purity of the faith, the priests sought out the blessed martyr Alban, intending to give thanks to God through the saint . . .

cf.

436. Gildas (6th C. AD), *De Excidio Britanniae* (*On the Destruction of Britain*) 10–11

10 By God's own free gift in the above-mentioned time of persecution, as we conjecture, (i.e. the reign of Diocletian), and lest Britain be totally plunged into the thick gloom of black night, He kindled for us the brilliant lamps of the holy martyrs . . . I mean St Alban of Verulamium, together with Aaron and Julius, citizens of the City of the Legion (Caerleon) . . .

11 The first of these, through love, hid a confessor who was being pursued by his persecutors and on the very point of being arrested, thus imitating Christ who laid down his life for his sheep. First he hid him in his house and then, exchanging clothes with him, willingly exposed himself to the danger of persecution in the garments of the above-mentioned brother . . .

437. Bede (8th C. AD), *Historia Ecclesiastica Gentis Anglorum* (*History of the English Church*) I, 7

This Alban, who was as yet a pagan, received into his house as a guest a certain priest fleeing from persecution at the time when the commands of the heathen emperors were raging against the

Christians. Seeing that this man applied himself night and day to constant prayer and vigils, and influenced by God's grace, he began to imitate his example of faith and piety. Gradually he was taught by the man's salutary encouragement, and relinquishing the darkness of idolatry became a whole-hearted Christian. While the aforementioned priest was being entertained in his house for some days, news reached the ears of the impious prince that one of Christ's confessors, for whom the role of martyr had not yet been assigned, was lying low in the house of Alban. As a result he straight away ordered soldiers to make a careful search for him. When they came to the martyr's cottage, St Alban soon showed himself to the soldiers in place of his guest and mentor, dressed in the man's clothes, the hooded cloak that he wore, and was led off to the judge in bonds. It happened that at the time Alban was brought to him the judge was offering sacrifices to the pagan gods at the altars. When he saw Alban, he became enflamed with anger at the fact that Alban had ventured to offer himself of his own free will to the soldiers in place of the guest he had harboured, and thus to expose himself to danger. He ordered him to be dragged to the images of the gods before which he stood and said: 'Since you preferred to conceal that profane rebel rather than surrender him to the soldiers so that he might pay the penalty he deserves for his blasphemy and contempt of the gods, you will suffer the penalty for which he was due if you attempt to reject the rites of our religion.' But St Alban, who had voluntarily given himself up to the persecutors as a Christian, was not in the least afraid of the prince's threats. Rather, being girded with the armour of spiritual warfare, he openly declared he would not obey his commands. Then the judge said: 'Of what house and stock are you?' Alban replied: 'What business is it of yours of what lineage I am born? If on the other hand you desire to hear the truth of my religion, know that I am now a Christian and devote myself to Christian service.' The judge said: 'I seek your name, so tell me it without delay.' The other replied: 'The name given me by my parents is Alban, and I revere and ever worship the true living God who created all things.' Then, filled with anger, the judge said: 'If you wish to enjoy the blessings of a long life, do not refuse to offer sacrifice to the great gods.' Alban replied: 'These sacrifices which you offer to the pagan gods can neither help their recipients nor fulfil the wishes and desires of those praying. Rather, whoever offers sacrifice to these images shall receive as his reward the eternal punishment of Hell.' When the judge heard this, he was roused to great fury and ordered the holy confessor of God to be beaten by the torturers in the belief that since words had failed, he could weaken the constancy of his heart with the lash. Though afflicted by most cruel torture, Alban bore it with patience and even with joy for God's sake, and when the judge realised that he could not be overcome by torture or enticed from the rites of the Christian religion, he ordered him to be beheaded.

As he was being led to his death, Alban came to a river which separated the town from the place of his execution by its very swift course. There he saw a large crowd of people, both men and women of all ages and social class, who were clearly drawn by divine impulse to follow the blessed confessor and martyr. They filled the bridge over the river to such an extent that they could scarcely all get over before nightfall. Indeed since almost all had gone forth, the judge was left in the city without any attendants. So, St Alban, in whose mind was a burning desire to come quickly to his martyrdom, approached the torrent, and raising his eyes to heaven, he saw the bed of the river instantly dry up and the water withdraw and make a path for his steps. When the executioner himself saw this along with others, he hastened to meet Alban when he came to the place appointed for his execution, doubtless urged on in this by divine impulse. Casting away the sword he held ready drawn, he threw himself at his feet and earnestly desired that he himself be thought worthy of being executed either with the martyr he was ordered to slay or in his place ... (Alban climbs a hill and causes a stream to appear) ... So it was that the brave martyr, there decapitated, received the crown of life which God promised to those who love him, but the man who set his unholy hands upon that pious neck was not allowed to rejoice over the death; for his eyes fell to the ground along with the head of the blessed martyr. Beheaded too at that time was the soldier who previously had been impelled by the will of Heaven to refuse to strike the holy confessor of God ... Then the judge, daunted by such great and unprecedented heavenly miracles, soon ordered a halt to the persecution. He was beginning in fact to pay honour to the slaughter of saints, through which he previously believed he could force them to give up their allegiance to the Christian faith. The blessed Alban suffered on the 22nd of June near the city of Verulamium ... At that time there also suffered Aaron and Julius, citizens of Caerleon, and many others both men and women in various places ...

At a later date, the closing years of Roman influence saw both a renewal of sanctity in Patrick:

438. Patrick, *Confessio* 1

I, Patrick, a sinner, the lowest and the least of all the faithful, the most contemptible of many, had as my father Calpornius, a deacon and son of the presbyter Potitus who lived in the village of Bannavem Taburniae. He had a small estate nearby and there I was taken prisoner. I was then about 16. I was ignorant of the true God, and was led off into captivity in Ireland along with so many thousands of people.

and in Pelagianism the rise of a heresy that was not perhaps without political overtones at a time when self-help might mean survival:[30]

439. Prosper Tiro (5th C. AD), *Chronicon* 1248–52

In the consulship of the illustrious Lucian ... At this time (AD 413) the Briton Pelagius put out the doctrine against the Grace[31] of Christ that bears his name, assisted by Coelestius and Julian, and drew many into his error, declaring that each man was directed to righteousness of his own choice and received as much grace as he deserved, since Adam's sin harmed him alone: it did not also bind those that came after him. As a result it was possible for those who so wished to be free from all sin; all children were born as innocent as the first man before the fall, nor should they be baptised in order to lay aside (original) sin but to be honoured with the sacrament of adoption (into the Church).

440. Ibid. 1299–1301

In the consulship of Florentius and Dionysius (AD 429) ... the Pelagian Agricola, son of the Pelagian bishop Severianus, corrupted the Church in Britain by the introduction of his doctrine.

Unable to refute the arguments of the heresy, the Catholic church in Britain appealed to the bishops of Gaul:

441. Constantius (5th C. AD), *De Vita Germani* (*The Life of Germanus*) 12–27

12 At the same time (AD 429) an embassy sent from Britain made it known to the bishops in Gaul that the Pelagian heresy had taken hold of the people far and wide in their land, and that they should send help to the Catholic faith as soon as possible. For this reason

a large assembly was summoned, and by a unanimous decision they solicited with their prayers those two brilliant lights of religion, Germanus and Lupus, both apostolic priests ... (They cross to Britain despite adverse weather conditions and bolster up the Catholic faith) ...

14 ... The authors of the evil doctrine maintained a low profile and like malign spirits groaned at the loss of people who escaped their clutches. Finally, after much thought they deigned to enter the lists. Forth they came, gleaming with their riches, brilliantly clothed, and surrounded by much flattery. They preferred to submit to the hazard of public debate rather than to incur the ignominy of silence among the people they had subverted, lest they seem to have damned themselves by keeping quiet. A truly vast multitude of people was invited, along with their wives and children, and assembled there. The people were present as observers and judges while the opposing sides presented vastly differing appearances: on one side divine authority, on the other human presumption; on one side faith, on the other heresy; on one side Pelagius as teacher, on the other Christ. The blessed priests first gave their opponents the opportunity to state their case; this took up much time to no purpose and filled the ears with nought but empty words. Then the venerable bishops poured forth torrents of their eloquence along with thunderings from the apostles and evangelists. Their own speech was interspersed with scriptural passages and they followed their own weighty declarations with written testimony. Vanity stood convicted; heresy refuted ... (Germanus cures the blind daughter of a man said to exercise the 'power of a Tribune'. They then go to the shrine of St Alban).

16 ... The priests sought out the blessed martyr Alban, intending to give thanks to God through the saint ... (Germanus is hurt in a fall, and while he is resting in a house the buildings in the vicinity catch fire. However, while the flames consume all around, the building containing Germanus is untouched. Following this, Germanus cures many sick people and is eventually himself cured by miraculous means) ...

17 In the meantime, the Picts and Saxons joined forces and made war on the Britons, whom the same need had brought together into the camp, and since in their fear the Britons judged themselves not quite equal to the enemy, they sought the help of the holy bishops. They for their part hastened their promised coming and instilled such a feeling of security and confidence that one would have thought a great army had arrived. And so it was that with these

apostolic leaders there was Christ militant in the camp. The forty days of Lent were also at hand, which the presence of the priests made all the more holy in as much as the people, taught by daily preaching, eagerly flocked to receive the grace of baptism. For most of the army sought the water of salvation ... With the festival of Easter over, the greater part of the army, fresh from their baptism, prepared to take up their arms and get ready for war. Germanus declared himself their leader in battle, picked out those lightly armed, scouted the surrounding countryside and noticed a valley, surrounded by lofty mountains, in that quarter where he expected the arrival of the enemy. Here he assembled his new army with himself as its leader.

18 Soon there came upon them the fierce host of the enemy, which those lying in ambush saw approaching. Then suddenly Germanus, the standard-bearer, exhorted and commanded all his men to repeat his words together in a loud voice, and with the enemy in their negligence confident that their arrival was unexpected, the priests three times cried out 'Alleluia'. All replied in unison, and the close confines of the mountains re-echoed the cry they raised. The enemy forces were struck with terror and fear that both the rocks around them and the very vault of heaven threatened to overwhelm them. They scarce believed the swiftness of their feet sufficient (to escape) the terror hurled upon them. They fled in all directions, cast aside their weapons, were glad to have saved their unprotected bodies from the danger ... (Germanus and Lupus return to the continent) ...

25 In the meantime (*c.* AD 446) it was reported from Britain that once again the perversity of Pelagianism was spreading through the agency of a few people. Once more the entreaties of all the priests are conveyed to that most blessed man, that he defend the cause of God which earlier he had championed. Speedily he agreed to their request since he delighted in exertion and gladly devoted himself to Christ ... Together with Severus, a bishop of singular holiness, he put to sea led only by the inspiration of Christ. The elements conspire to produce a smooth crossing ... (Their arrival is followed by a miracle of healing which confirms the Britons' belief in Catholic doctrine) ...

27 ... He then turned to preach to the people about repentance for their transgressions, and by universal assent the authors of that enormity, condemned to be banished from the island, were brought to the priests for conveyance into the depths of the continent, so that the land might have the pleasure of being rid of them, and they the profit of their repentance.[32]

NOTES

1 See further Henig, pp. 68–94.
2 See Henig, p. 69f. On the imperial cult in Britain see Fishwick.
3 *Journal of Roman Studies.*
4 See further Salway (1), p. 676ff; Henig, pp. 19–24, 206–7; Chadwick.
5 The overtones of political power that Caesar gives here are stated more forcibly by Dio Chrysostom (1st–2nd C. AD), *Discourse* XLIX, 8.

> Without them (the Druids) kings could do nothing nor make any plans, with the result that it was they in fact who ruled, and the kings were their servants and ministered to their will . . .

cf. Strabo IV, 4, 4, §303; Diodorus Siculus V, 31, 2–5, §304.
6 Clearly an instance of Caesar 'Romanising' his information.
7 Geographer of the second–first century BC.
8 Opinion is divided as to whether Pliny here refers to the moon itself or more specifically to the sixth day of its course.
9 See further Ross; Norman; Salway (1), p. 666.
10 Apparently of Gallic origin.
11 The fact that Antenociticus/Anociticus is found only at Benwell suggests he was either a very localised native divinity like Coventina or imported by the auxiliary unit stationed there.
12 Lenus had a major sanctuary at Trier.
13 Alexander Severus AD 222–35.
14 Originally from Aquitaine.
15 From north-east Gaul.
16 Cf. §202.
17 On the identification see Haverfield, *Victoria County History, Hants* I, p. 283; Goodchild, *Antiquity* 27 (1953), pp. 100–2; Toynbee, *Journal of the British Archaeological Association* 16 (1953), p. 19.
18 Cf. from Aylesford, Kent (*Britannia* 17 (1986), p. 428 no. 2), which may have Christian connotations.

> A gift to the gods by which Butu has perished and the items which [. . .] neither health nor safety unless and until in the house of God . . .

19 Distinction between German and Celtic is at times difficult, though the following are probable enough.
20 See Harris and Harris.
21 I.e. Cybele from Asia Minor. Evidence of the worship of Cybele comes from inscriptions by Dendrophori, branch-bearers who were associated with her worship: a funerary urn from Dunstable, Beds. (*Britannia* 11 (1980) 406–7): 'Regillinus presented the urn of the Dendrophori of Verulamium.'
22 See Henig, pp. 97–109; Walters; Vermaseren.
23 On Christianity in Britain see Barley and Hanson.
24 Evidently corrupt: Lindinensium? (Lincoln), Legionensium? (Caerleon). See Rivet and Smith, p. 49f.
25 See Clark, p. 21f., *Britannia* 10 (1979), p. 353 n. 70.
26 *Zeitschrift für Papyrologie und Epigraphik.*
27 Morris, cf. Johnson (2), p. 32; Salway (1), p. 720; Frere (1), p. 321.
28 Thomas, p. 48.

29 Salway (1), p. 721 argues against setting the event in the reign of Diocletian on the grounds that actual control of Britain lay in the hands of Constantius Caesar, who merely closed the churches:

Eusebius (4th C, AD), *Historia Ecclesiastica (History of the Church)* VIII, 13, 13

> Constantius took no part in the war against us (Christians), but kept the devout under his rule free from harm and harsh treatment, nor did he destroy the church buildings or take any other fresh measures against us.

cf.

Lactantius (4th C. AD), *De Mortibus Persecutorum (On the Deaths of the Persecutors)* 15

> For lest he appear to disagree with the instructions of his superiors, Constantius allowed the assemblies to be destroyed, that is their walls, which could be rebuilt, but the true temple of God, which lies in men, he kept unharmed.

30 See Brown, Myers, Wood, p. 260f.
31 In other contexts *gratia* (grace) could be a dirty word, implying political patronage and therefore corruption.
32 The account of Germanus' visits to Britain is repeated almost verbatim by Bede I, 17–21.

XV Government, Commerce and Society

GOVERNMENT

Following the conquest of south-east Britain, brought about by the concentrated efforts of the legions and their associated auxiliary troops, came the need to extend, garrison and administer what had been gained. Overall control of the new province lay with the governor, but at a local level government was delegated to a variety of institutions as soon as was practicable.[1] As an early and temporary expedient friendly tribes were allowed internal autonomy under a client king, thus freeing Roman troops for deployment along the frontier or in areas that had offered resistance. The most famous was Cogidubnus,[2] who represents the system at its most successful:

442. Tacitus, *Agricola* 14

> Certain tribal areas were given to King Cogidubnus – he in fact remained totally loyal down to our times – in accordance with the Roman People's old and long-standing policy of making even kings their agents in enslaving peoples.

Less harmonious on the other hand were Rome's relations with the kingdom of the Iceni, where on two occasions riding roughshod over agreements and native sensibilities caused major problems for the Romans (Tacitus, *Annals* XII, 31, §70, *Annals* XIV, 31, §73). Another instance of the system's failure is probably Cartimandua of the Brigantes (Tacitus, *Annals* XII, 40, §71, *Histories* III, 45, §95).

With time tribal areas were converted into *civitates peregrinae*, non-citizen cantons:

443. From Wroxeter (*RIB* I 288 restored)

For the Emperor Ca[esar] Trajan H[a]drian Augustus, son of the deified Trajan, conqueror of Parthia, grandson of the dei[fied N]erva, Pontif[ex] Maximus (High Priest) in the fourteenth year of his holding Tribunician Power (AD 130), [thrice Consul, Father of his Country], the *Civitas* of the Cornovii (set this up).

Each had its own local capital, usually with the urban status of vicus[3] or village, the smallest unit of local administration, as is the case with Petuaria, ostensibly the capital of the Parisi of East Yorkshire:

444. *RIB* I 707 (restored)

For the honour of the Divine House of the Emperor Caesar Titus Aelius H[adri]anus Antoninus A[ugustus Pius], Father of his Country, [thrice] Consul, and the Divine Power of the E[mperors], Marcus Ulpius Januarius, Aedile[4] of the *Vicus* of Petu[aria] (Brough-on-Humber), [gave] this stage at his own expense.

In other cases the term *vicus* was used simply to designate a small town that had grown up around a military site:

445. From Chesterholm (*RIB* I 1700)

For the Divine House and the Power of the Emperors the villagers (*vicani*) of Vindolanda (set up) this sacred offering to Vulcan under the direction of [. . .] willingly and deservedly fulfilling their vow.

446. From Old Carlisle (*RIB* I 899)

To Jupiter, Greatest and Best, and to Vulcan, for the welfare of Our Lord Marcus Antonius Gordianus Pius Felix Augustus, the leaders of the villagers (*vikani*) dedicated this from money contributed by the villagers.

So far as the scant remaining evidence indicates, administration in the *civitates* tended to mirror that found in the more important urban settlements, the colonies, and in the municipium of Verulamium (St Albans). Here power was vested in the *Ordo*, a local senate, composed of decurions:[5]

447. From York (*RIB* I 674)

To the spirits of the departed (and) of Flavius Bellator, *Decurion* of the colony of York. He lived for 29 years [. . .] months.

448. From Lincoln (*RIB* I 250a)

To the spirits of the departed. Volusia Faustina, a citizen of Lincoln, lived 26 years, 1 month, 26 days. Aurelius Senecio, *Decurion*, set this up to his well-deserving wife.[6]

cf. the inscription from Caerwent, capital of the Silures:

449. *RIB* I 311 (restored)

To [Tiberius Claudius] Paulinus, Legate of the II Legion Augusta, Proconsul of the province of (Gallia) Narbonensis, the Emperor's Pro-Praetorian Legate of the province of (Gallia) Lugdunensis, by decree of the *Ordo* the *civitas* of the Silures (set this up).

450. From Old Penrith (*RIB* I 933)

To the spirits of the departed (and) Flavius Martius, Senator[7] in the *civitas* of the Carvetii, of Quaestorian rank, who lived for 45 years. Martiola, his daughter and heiress, had this set up.

Acting as executive officers of the *Ordo* were two *Duoviri Iuridicundo*:

451. *RIB* II.5 2487.1

Commonwealth of the people of Gloucester: The Duoviri Perpetuus and Aprilis.

RIB II.5 2487.2
Commonwealth of the people of Gloucester: The Duoviri Optatus and Saturninus.

RIB II.5 2487.3
Commonwealth of the people of Gloucester: The Duovir Publius Aelius Finitus.

RIB II.5 2488.1
Commonwealth of the people of Gloucester: The (Duoviri) quin-quennales[8] Iul(ius) Flor(us) and Cor(nelius) Sim(. . .)

While administration within the *civitates* remained strictly limited to local affairs, expressions of wider non-citizen concern could be voiced, if only in very restricted areas, through the delegates sent to the Provincial Council:

452. From London (*RIB* I 5 restored)

To the divine power of C[aesar Augustus], the prov[ince of] Brita[in][9] (set this up).

453. Ibid. (*RIB* I 21)

To the spirits of the departed (and) of Claudia Martina aged 19, Anencletus, provincial slave, (set this up), for his most dutiful wife. Here she lies.

THE ECONOMY OF BRITAIN

Trade between Britain and the continent was already an established fact long before the first contacts with Rome (Strabo IV, 4, 1, §21), but pre-eminent among the exports mentioned by writers in the early period (cf. Strabo IV, 5, 2, §14) was Cornish tin:[10]

454. Diodorus Siculus (late 1st C. BC) V, 22

However, I shall give a detailed account of the customs in Britain and the other particular usages when I come to Caesar's expedition to Britain. For the time being I shall deal with the tin produced there. Those inhabitants of Britain around the promontory called Belerium (Land's End) are particularly hospitable and civilised in their way of life as a result of their dealings with foreign merchants. They it is who produce the tin, working the ground that bears it in an ingenious manner. This is stony and contains seams of earth in which they mine the ore and refine it by smelting. They hammer it into the shape of knucklebones and transport it to an island that lies off Britain called Ictis (St Michael's Mount?); for at low tide the space between is left high and dry and they transport the tin here in large quantities by means of wagons. A strange thing occurs around the nearby islands between Britain and Europe, for at high tide the causeways between them and the mainland are covered and they seem to be islands, but at low tide the sea recedes and leaves a large area high and dry so that they look like peninsulas.

There (Ictis) merchants buy the tin from the natives and transport it to Galatia (Gaul). Finally, making their way on foot through Galatia for around 30 days, they bring their merchandise on horseback to the mouth of the river Rhone.

The prospect of economic gain indeed was doubtless a factor in the invasions of both Caesar and Claudius. In Caesar's case Britain must have held out the prospect of an escape from the chronic debts his political ambitions created, though in the event Britain proved a disappointment, as Cicero ironically mentioned (§30).

cf.

455. Plutarch (1st–2nd C. AD) *Caesar* 23.3

In many battles Caesar defeated the enemy rather than benefited his own men, since there was nothing worth taking from the natives, whose living standard was low.

By Claudius' day on the other hand the economic potential was better known, and within six years of invasion exploitation of mineral resources was well under way, especially of lead, the ore of which often contained an element of silver:

456. Lead ingot[11] from the Mendips, Somerset (*RIB* II.1 2404.1)

Tiberius Claudius Caesar Augustus, Pontifex Maximus (High Priest), in the ninth year of his holding Tribunician Power (AD 49), sixteen times saluted Imperator, from Britain.

In frontier areas military involvement is well attested:

457. Lead ingot from Blagdon, Somerset (*RIB* II.1 2404.2)

British (lead) II Augusta. V(eranius) and P(ompeius) (consuls AD 49)

cf.

458. Lead ingot found at St Valéry sur Somme, France (*RIB* II.1 2404.24)

(Property of) Nero Augustus. British (lead). The II Legion (made this).

With time, however, civilian prospectors begin to make their appearance:

459. Lead ingot from Bossington, near Stockbridge, Hants. (*RIB* II.1 2404.3) AD 60

(Property of) Nero Augustus, Consul from January 1st for the fourth time. British (lead).
From July 1st Pontifex Maximus (High Priest), Consul.
From the silver works. (Product of) Gaius Nipius Ascanius XXX.

Ascanius' name also appears on an ingot from Carmel in Flintshire, suggesting wide-ranging commercial interests:

460. *RIB* II.1 2404.38

(Product) of Gaius Nipius Ascanius.[12]

By the reign of Vespasian on the other hand (AD 69–79) the Flintshire field was clearly under imperial control:

461. From Chester (*RIB* II.1 2404.31) AD 74

The Emperor Vespasian Augustus, Consul for the fifth time, and Titus, Imperator, Consul for the third time.
Deceangl(ian lead).

cf.

462. Lead ingot from Hints Common, Staffs. (*RIB* II.1 2404.34) AD 76

The Emperor Vespasian, Consul for the seventh time, and Titus, Imperator, Consul for the fifth time.
Deceang(lian lead).

Evidence from Gloucestershire, though, shows continuing civilian activity and an early reference to a mining company:

463. Lead ingot from Syde, Glos.
(*RIB* II.1 2404.13) AD 79

(Property of) the Emperor Vespasian Augustus, Consul for the ninth time, Brit(ish lead) from the silver works.
(Product of) the company at Nove[. . .

As new areas were opened up for exploitation production clearly began to over-reach itself and in the 70s we hear of the need to limit production:

464. Pliny the Elder (1st C. AD), *Natural History* XXXIV, 164

Lead is used for pipes and sheets. In Spain and throughout the whole of Gaul it is extracted with considerable effort; in Britain, however, it is so abundant within the upper layers of the earth that there is a law forbidding its production beyond a certain amount.

Following Agricola's annexation of Brigantia Roman exploitation once more increased, spurred on by the building programmes that followed conquest:

465. Lead ingot from Heyshaw Moor nr. Pateley Bridge, Yorks. (*RIB* II.1 2404.61–2) AD 81

The Emperor Caesar Domitian Augustus, Consul for the seventh time.
Bri]g(antian lead).

The Derbyshire field in particular seems to have been very active, with private developers prominent:

466. From Matlock Bank (*RIB* II.1 2404.40)

(Product) of Lucius Aruconius Verecundus. From the mine at Lutudarum.

467. From Yeaveley (*RIB* II.1 2404.59–60)

(Product) of the company at Lutudarum. Brit(ish lead). From the silver works.

468. From Tansley Moor (*RIB* II.1 2404.51)

(Product) of Publius Rubrius Abascantus. From the mine at Lutudarum.

469. From Matlock Moor (*RIB* II.1 2404.41)

Ti(berius) Cl(audius) Tr(iferna). (From the mine at) Lutudarum. Br(itish lead). From the silver works.

Restoration of Triferna's name suggests identifying him with a contractor also operating in the Mendips:

470. *RIB* II.1 2404.7

(Property of) the Emperor Vespasian Augustus.
Brit(ish lead). From [the silver works V]EB
LXV Ti(berius) Cl(audius) Trif(erna).

471. *RIB* II.1 2404.9[13]

(Property of) the Emperor Vespasian Augustus. LRA[D]
Brit(ish lead). From the silver works VEB
Ti(berius) Cl(audius) Trif(erna)
LXIIX
[Ti(berius) Cl(audius)] Trifer(na)

The products of Lutudarum are also found over a wide area:

472. From Pulborough, Sussex (*RIB* II.1 2404.42)

(Product of) Ti(berius) Cl(audius) Tr(iferna). (From the mine at) Lutudarum. Br(itish lead). From the silver works.

473. From Hexgrove Park, Notts., S. Cave, E. Yorks., Brough-on-Humber (*RIB* II.1 2404. 46, 47, 48–50)

(Product) of G(aius) Jul(ius) Protus. Brit(ish lead) from Lutudarum. From the silver works.

474. From Belby, nr. Howden, Broomfleet, Brough-on-Humber, Ellerker, E. Yorks., Caves Inn, Warks. (RIB II.1 2404. 53, 54, 55, 57, 58)

(Product of) the Company at Lutudarum. Br(itish lead). From the silver works.

In contrast, ingots cast with datable inscriptions show lead being produced under imperial supervision from the reign of Hadrian (AD 117–38) to Septimius Severus (AD 196–211):

475. From Wirksworth, Derbyshire (*RIB* II.1 2404.39)

(Property) of the Emperor Caesar Hadrian Augustus. From the mine at Lutudarum.

476. From Bristol (*RIB* II.1 2404.17)

(Property) of the Emperor Caesar A[nto]ninus Augustus Pius, Father of his Country.

477. From Sassenay, France (*RIB* II.1 2404.72a)

[Property of the Emperor Casesar Lucius Septimius Severus Pertinax] Augustus, Conqueror of Parthia and Adiabene.
DL P L(egion) VI[14] CVC [. . .] VICVC

Associated finds with illegible ingots suggest indeed that production continued into the reign of Constantius II (AD 337–61) and beyond (from Towcester *RIB* II.1 2404.67).

While the evidence of ingots shows that companies were operating in areas of metal extraction, it is also clear that the establishment of Roman-style guilds to supervise production was taking place from an early date:

478. From Chichester (*RIB* I 91 restored)

To Neptune and Minerva this temple (is dedicated) for the safety of the Divine House on the authority of Tiberius Claudius Cogidubnus, [Gr]eat Ki[ng] in Britain,[15] by the guild (*collegium*) of smiths and its members from their own resources, [Clem]ens son of Pudentinus presenting the site.

cf.

479. From Silchester (*RIB* I 70 restored)

... without contr]ibutions from their own resources gave this [gif]t, [entrust]ed to him, by the gui[ld] (*collegium*) of [pere]gr[i]ni [dwelling] at Calleva (Silchester).

International trade too between Britain and the continent is shown by dedications made by merchants (as Marcus Aurelius Lunaris and Marcus Verecundius Diogenes §299, 300 probably were).

cf.:

480. From E. Scheldt (*L'Année Epigraphique* 1975 p. 168 no. 651)

To the goddess Nehalennia, Placidus, son of Viducius,[16] a citizen of Velocasium and trader with Britain, willingly and deservedly fulfilled his vow.

481. From Germania Inferior (*L'Année Epigraphique* 1973 p. 105 no. 370)

To the goddess Nehalennia, Marcus Secundinus Silvanus, trader in chalk with Britain, willingly and deservedly fulfilled his vow.

482. From Ganuenta, E. Scheldt (Bogaers (2) p. 19)

To the goddess Nehalennia, Gaius Aurelius Verus, trader with Britain, willingly and deservedly (dedicated this altar) on account of his vow.

483. From Cologne (*CIL* XIII 8164a)

To Apollo, Gaius Aurelius Verus of the Claudian voting tribe, trader with Britain, *moritex*(?), gave this as a gift, the site being presented by a decree of the decurions.

484. From Ganuenta, E. Scheldt (Bogaers (2) p. 17)

To the goddess Nehalennia, Publius Arisenius Marius, freedman of Publius Arisenius V[. . .]hius, trader with Britain, willingly and deservedly [fulfilled his vow] for her good protection of his wares.

Nor was lead and its associated silver the only mineral that was mined. Exploitation of tin continued apace in order to make pewter by mixing it with lead (§430), and bronze by mixing it with copper:

485. Copper ingot from Aberffraw, Anglesey (*RIB* II.1 2403.3)[17]

(Product of) the partners Nat. . . Sol. . ., resident in Rome.

Coal too, though of limited use in industry, was evidently deemed worthy of mention:

486. Solinus (3rd C. AD), *Collectanea Rerum Memorabilium (The Collection of Curiosities)* 22, 10

In Britain are many great rivers, and warm springs adorned with sumptuous splendour for the use of mortals. Minerva is patron goddess of these and in her temple the eternal flames never whiten into ash, but rather, when the fire dies away, it turns into rocky round masses.

The other major resource Rome was not slow to exploit was Britain's agricultural wealth, which figures in descriptions of the island even before the Claudian conquest (§8, 11, 12, 14). The very fact of occupation brought an immediate spur to production in order to feed the garrison and other official personnel through the *annona*, the grain tax, and with taxation came openings for corruption:

487. Tacitus (1st–2nd C. AD), *Agricola* 19

Agricola made the collection of the corn tax (*annona*) and tribute less onerous by spreading the burden fairly, and by cutting out schemes aimed at private gain, which proved a greater source of resentment than the tribute itself. For instance, the natives were forced to go through the farce of sitting outside locked granaries and actually buy grain, thereby discharging their obligations by the payment of money. Alternatively, out-of-the-way routes and distant districts were stipulated, so that tribal areas made their deliveries to remote and inaccessible stations even though there were winter quarters close at hand.[18] As a result, an obligation that should have been easy for all was turned into a source of profit for a few.

Britain's continuing importance as a producer of grain throughout its Roman occupation is well illustrated in fact by the loss felt at the usurpation by Carausius (§210) and the efforts of Julian to ensure supplies for the Rhine garrison (§249–53).

As well as grain, early writers on Britain also make reference to the island's abundance in livestock:

488. Pomponius Mela (1st C. AD), *De Chorographia* III, 6, 50

(Britain is) huge and fertile with those things that benefit cattle rather than men.

From sheep came wool good enough to make its finished products worth particular mention on inscriptions:

489. From Thorigny, France (*CIL* XIII, 3162)

I would like you to accept ... a British bed-spread.

and as part of Diocletian's edict on prices:

490. Edictum Diocletiani XIX, 28, 29, 48

British coverlet, 1st form: 5,000 denarii
British coverlet, 2nd form: 4,000 denarii
British hooded cloak: 6,000 denarii

Other products recorded include dogs, already known in the period between Caesar and Claudius from Strabo (§14)

cf.

491. Grattius (early 1st C. AD), *Cynegeticon* 174–81

But what if you reach the straits of the Morini washed by a fluctuating sea, and choose to pass among the Britons? How great then is your trade, how far (your profit) beyond your outlay! If you haven't set your mind on looks and deceptive beauty – this is the one thing British pups lack – then, when hard work comes and bravery must be shown and impetuous Mars calls in dire crisis, you would not admire the famed Molossians as much.

492. Oppian (early 3rd C. AD), *Cynegetica* I, 468–80

There is a strong breed of hunting dog, small in size but no less worthy of great praise. These the wild tribes of Britons with their tattooed backs rear and call by the name of Agassian. Their size is like that of worthless and greedy domestic table dogs: squat, emaciated, shaggy, dull of eye, but endowed with feet armed with powerful claws and a mouth sharp with close-set venomous tearing teeth. It is by virtue of its nose, however, that the Agassian is most exalted, and for tracking it is the best there is; for it is very adept at discovering the tracks of things that walk upon the ground, and skilled too at marking the airborne scent.

493. Nemesianus (3rd C. AD), *Cynegetica* 225f

Britain sends us swift hounds, adapted to hunting in our world.

494. Claudian, *On the Consulship of Stilicho* (delivered early 400) III, 301

British dogs that can break the necks of great bulls.

beer:

495. Dioscorides (1st C. AD), *De Medica Materia* (*On Medicine*) II, 88

And (there is the drink) called *curmi*, prepared from barley, which people often use as a drink instead of wine, but it causes headaches and bad humours and is harmful to the nerves. Such drinks are also prepared from wheat as in Spain and Britain in the west.

pearls:

496. Suetonius (2nd C. AD), *Julius* 47

Caesar invaded Britain in the hope of finding pearls.

cf. Tacitus (1st–2nd C. AD), *Agricola* 12 (§15)

497. Pliny the Elder (1st C. AD), *Natural History* IX, 116

It is clear that small pearls of a discoloured appearance are produced in Britain, since the deified Julius wanted it to be known that the breastplate he dedicated to Venus Genetrix in her temple was made of British pearls.

498. Aelian (2nd–3rd C. AD), *On the Characteristics of Animals* XV, 8

Pearls occur also in the western ocean where the island of Britain is, though they have a more golden appearance and a duller and darker sheen.

499. Ammianus Marcellinus (late 4th C. AD) XXIII, 6, 88

It is well known that this type of gem (pearls) occurs and is gathered even in the recesses of the British sea, though they are of lesser quality.

jet:

500. Solinus (3rd C. AD), *Collectanea Rerum Memorabilium* 22, 19

. . . there is there a very large supply of that excellent rock, jet. If you wish to know what it looks like: it has the appearance of a black jewel; if its nature you seek: it burns with water and is extinguished with oil; if its power: when warmed by rubbing, it holds onto things in contact with it, like amber.

SOCIETY

Without doubt the best documented evidence we have for the inhabitants of Roman Britain consists of the discharge certificates (diplomas) awarding citizenship to auxiliary troops on their retirement from service, inscriptions recording the careers of more highly placed officers and officials, and the correspondence and documents of individuals that have come to light in recent years, especially at Vindolanda on the Stanegate.

Diplomas:

501. From Malpas, Cheshire (*RIB* II.1 2401.1) AD 103

[The Emperor Caesar] Nerva Trajan [Aug]us[tu]s, conqueror of Germany and Dacia, son of the deified Nerva, Pontifex Maximus (High Priest), in the seventh year of his holding Tribunician Power, four times saluted Imperator, Father of his Country, five times Consul, to the cavalry and infantry who are serving in the four squadrons and eleven cohorts called: 1st Thracian, 1st Pannonian Tampiana, Sebosius' Gauls, Vettonian Spaniards, Roman citizens; 1st Spanish, 1st Vangiones 1,000-strong, 1st Alpine, 1st Morini, 1st Cugerni, 1st Baetasii, 1st Tungrians 1,000-strong, 2nd Thracians, 3rd Bracari, 3rd Lingones, 4th Dalmatians, who are in Britain under Lucius Neratius Marcellus, and have served for 25 or more years each and whose names are appended, has granted citizenship for themselves, their children and posterity, together with the right of legal marriage with the wives they had when citizenship was granted, or, if they were unmarried, those they have subsequently married, so long as it is only one.

January 19th, in the second consulship of Manius Laberius Maximus and Quintus Glitius Atilius Agricola.

(Copy) for the Decurion (troop-leader) Reburrus, son of Severus, from Spain, in the 1st Squadron of Pannonians Tampiana commanded by Gaius Valerius Celsus.

Copied from and compared with the bronze tablet affixed in Rome to the wall behind the temple of the deified Augustus near (the statue of) Minerva.

(Witnesses)

Quintus Pompeius Homerus	Gaius Papius Eusebes
Titus Flavius Secundus	Publius Caulus Vitalis
Gaius Vettienus Modestus	Publius Atinius Hedonicus

Tiberius Claudius Menander

502. From Wroxeter (*RIB* II.1 2401.8) AD 135

[The Emperor Caesar] Trajan [Hadrian Augustus, son of the deified Trajan, conqueror of Parthia], grandson of the [deified] Nerva, [Pontifex Maximus] (High Priest) in the 19th year [of his holding Tribunician Power], thrice Consul, Father of his Country, [to the cavalry and infantry who have served in ... squadrons and] 31 [cohorts] called: [...] Augustus' Gauls [...], the Petriana squadron 1,000-strong, 1st Asturians, [...] Tungrians, [...], 1st Vardulli 1,000-strong, 1st & 2nd [...] 1,000-strong, 1st Hamians, 1st & 2nd

Dalmatians, [. . .], 1st Baetasii, 1st Batavians [. . .], 3rd, 4th & 6th Nervii, [. . .], 5th Gauls and 7th Thracians who [are in Britain under Mummius] Sisenna, [have served] for 25 [or more years] and have been honourably [discharged], and whose names are appended, has granted citizenship for themselves, their children and posterity, together with the right of legal marriage with the wives they had when citizenship was granted, or, if they were unmarried, those they have subsequently married, so long as it is only one. April 14th in the consulship of Lucius Tutilius Pontianus and Publius Calpurnius Atilianus.

(Copy for [Ma]nsuetus, son of Lucius, of the Treveri, ex-infantryman of the 2nd cohort of Dalmatians commanded by Julius Maximus, from Rome.

Copied and compared with the bronze tablet affixed in Rome to the wall behind the temple of the deified Augustus near (the statue of) Minerva.

503. From Sydenham, Kent (*RIB* II.1 2401.2)

The Emperor Caesar Nerva Trajan Augustus, conqueror of Germany and Dacia, son of the deified Nerva, Pontifex Maximus (High Priest) in the 9th year of his holding Tribunician Power, four times saluted Imperator, five times Consul, Father [of his Country], to the cavalry and infantry who are serving in 2 squadrons and 11 cohorts called: 1st Tungrians and the Classiana squadron, Roman citizens; 1st Celteberians, 1st Spanish, 1st Lingones, 1st Loyal Vardulli, 1st Frisians, 1st Nervii, 2nd Vascones, Roman Citizens, 2nd [Lingo]nes, [2nd A]sturians, [2nd] Pannonians, [. . . Dal]matians [who are] in Britain [. . .] and who have [served for] 25 [or more years] and whose [names are appended, has granted citizenship] for themselves, their children [and posterity], together with the right of legal marriage [with the wives] they had [when the citizenship was granted, or, if] they were unmarried, [those they have subsequently married] so long as [it is only one . . .]

The discovery of such diplomas in Britain shows that their recipients, though originally from elsewhere in the empire, chose to settle in Britain, the country they had served in. By the same process we find diplomas awarded to British auxiliaries who chose to settle in continental provinces:

504. From Dacia (Burn 71), AD 106

The Emperor Caesar Nerva Trajan Augustus, conqueror of Germany and Dacia, son of the deified Nerva, Pontifex Maximus (High Priest), in the fourteenth year (AD 110: wrong) of his holding Tribunician Power, six times saluted Imperator, five times Consul, Father of his Country, has granted Roman citizenship before completion of their service to the infantry and cavalry serving in the 1st Cohort of Britons, 1,000-strong, Trajan's own, awarded the *torquis*, loyal and true, Roman Citizens, which is in Dacia under Decimus Terentius Scaurianus, and whose names are appended, for loyal and true service in the Dacian campaign.

August 11th at Darnithithis in the consulship of Lucius Minicius Natalis and Quintus Silvanus Granianus.

To Infantryman Marcus Ulpius Novantico, son of Adcobrovatus, from Leicester.

505. From Mehadia, Dacia (*L'Année Epigraphique* 1980 p. 202, no. 760) AD 154

[The Emperor Caesar] Titus Aelius [Hadrianus Ant]oninus Augustus Pius, son of the [deified Had]rian, [grandson] of the deified Trajan, [conqueror of Parthia], great-grandson of the [deified Ner]va, Pontifex [Maximus] (High Priest), [with Tribunician Power ...], twice saluted Imperator, 4 times Consul, Father of his Country, ... 27th of September in the consulship of Sextus Calpurnius Agricola and Tiberius Claudius Julianus ... (has granted) to the Briton Ivonercus, son of Molax, infantryman of the 1st Ulpian Cohort of Britons 1,000-strong, under Lucius Nonius Bassus ...

506. From Pannonia (*CIL* XVI, 49), AD 105

...]with the wives they then had when citizenship was granted, or, if they were unmarried, those they have subsequently married, so long as it is only one.

January 12th, in the second consulship of Tiberius Julius Candidus Marius Celsus and Gaius Antius Julius Quadratus.

To Infantryman Lucco, son of Trennus, of the Dobunni, in the 1st British Cohort 1,000-strong, Roman Citizens, under the command of Quintus Caecilius Redditus, and to Tutela, daughter of Breucus, his wife, Azalian,[19] and to Similis his son,

and to Lucca his daughter,
and to Pacata his daughter.

In other cases it is clear that the individual involved, though discharged from service in Britain, chose to return home:

507. From A-Szöny, Hungary (*CIL* XVI, 69), AD 122

The Emperor Caesar Trajan Hadrian Augustus, son of the deified Trajan, conqueror of Parthia, grandson of the deified Nerva, Pontifex Maximus (High Priest), in the 6th year of his holding Tribunician Power, thrice Consul, Proconsul, to the cavalry and infantry who have served in the thirteen cavalry squadrons and thirty-seven cohorts which are called: 1st Pannonian Sabiniana, 1st Pannonian Tampiana, 1st Spanish Asturians, 1st Tungrians, 2nd Asturians, Picentius' Gauls, Classicus' Gauls and Thracians, Roman Citizens, Petreius' Gauls 1,000-strong, Roman Citizens, Sebosius' Gauls, Vettonian Spaniards, Roman Citizens, Agrippa's Miniata (squadron), Augustus' Gauls, Augustus' Vocontii, Roman Citizens; 1st Nerva's Germans 1,000-strong, Roman Citizens, 1st Celtiberians, 1st Thracians, 1st Africans, Roman Citizens, 1st Lingones, 1st Loyal Vardulli 1,000-strong, Roman Citizens, 1st Frisians, 1st Vangiones 1,000-strong, 1st Hamian archers, 1st Dalmatians, 1st Aquitanians, 1st Ulpius Trajan's Cugerni, Roman Citizens, 1st Morini, 1st Menapians, 1st Sunuci, 1st Baetasii, 1st Batavians, 1st Tungrians, 1st Spanish, 2nd Gauls, 2nd Vascones, Roman Citzens, 2nd Thracians, 2nd Lingones, 2nd Asturians, 2nd Dalmatians, 2nd Nervii, 3rd Nervii, 3rd Bracari, 3rd Lingones, 4th Gauls, (4th Lingones), 4th Breuci, 4th Dalmatians, 5th Raetians, 5th Gauls, 6th Nervii, and 7th Thracians who are in Britain under Aulus Platorius Nepos, and, having served for 25 years, have received honourable discharge from Pompeius Falco and whose names are appended, has granted citizenship for themselves, their children and posterity, the right of legal marriage with the wives they then had when citizenship was granted, or, if they were unmarried, those they have subsequently married, so long as it is only one.

July 17th, in the consulship of Tiberius Julius Capito and Lucius Vitrasius Flamininus.

(Copy) for Gemellus, son of Breucus, Pannonian formerly on pay-and-a-half (*sesquiplicarius*) in the 1st Pannonian Tampiana under the command of Fabius Sabinus.

Copied and compared with the bronze tablet affixed to the wall behind the temple of the deified Augustus near (the statue of) Minerva at Rome.

(Witnesses)

Tiberius Claudius Menander	Aulus Fulvius Justus
Tiberius Julius Urbanus	Lucius Pullius Daphnus
Lucius Nonius Victor	Quintus Lollius Festus
Lucius Pullius Ant . . .	

Career inscriptions:

For many high-ranking Romans it is clear that Britain was but a stage in their careers:

508. From Nomentum, Italy (*CIL* XIV, 3955)

Gnaeus Munatius Aurelius Bassus, son of Marcus, of the Palatine voting-tribe, Procurator of Augustus, Prefect of Engineers, Prefect of the 3rd Cohort of archers, Prefect again of the 2nd Cohort of Asturians, Census Officer for Roman citizens at the colony of Victory at Colchester in Britain, Curator of the Nomentum road, Patron of this same town, Priest for life, Aedile with magisterial power, Dictator[20] four times.

509. From Camerini, Italy (*ILS* 2735)

To Marcus Maenius Agrippa Lucius Tusidius Campester, son of Gaius, of the Cornelian voting-tribe, host of the deified Hadrian, father of the senator, Prefect of the 2nd Flavian Cohort of Britons part-mounted, chosen by the deified Hadrian and sent on the expedition to Britain, Tribune of the 1st Cohort of Spaniards part-mounted, Prefect of the mailed squadron of Gauls and Pannonians, Augustus' Procurator of the British fleet, Procurator of Britain, Knight on the Establishment, patron of this town, the villagers of Censorglacium having gained through the favour of his mediation and by the kindness of our Greatest and Best Emperor Antoninus Augustus Pius those privileges in which they are permanently confirmed (set this up) on ground given by decree of the Decurions.

510. From Lambaesis, Africa (*JRS* 2 (1912), p. 22)

To the spirits of the departed. Tiberius Flavius Virilis, Centurion of the II Legion Augusta, Centurion of the XX Legion Valeria Victrix, Centurion of the VI Legion Victrix, Centurion of the XX Legion Valeria Victrix, Centurion of the III Legion Augusta, Centurion of the III Legion Parthica, Severus' own, commanding the 2nd Century of Hastati of Cohort 9, lived 70 years, served 45. Lollia

Bodicca, his wife, and Flavius Victor and Victorinus, his sons and heirs, had this made at a cost of 1,200 sesterces.

Correspondence:

While diplomas and inscriptions present their information in the stylised language of official documents, the chance survival of actual hand-written material from individuals stationed at Vindolanda on the northern frontier presents us with the unique opportunity to glimpse day-to-day life at the fort in the period AD 90–120: its military strength, the supplies it needed, the concerns of its personnel and their families, the dealings of its soldiers, slaves and civilians. The writing tablets that have been recovered are not the wax-filled frames one might expect (though these do occur on the site) but thin leaves of wood, (mostly birch, alder and oak) about the size of a postcard, written on with ink.[21] Though their preservation is remarkable, due entirely to the airless conditions that quickly established themselves on the rubbish heaps that were their final resting place, the texts they carry are often either fragmentary or barely legible. Painstaking restoration, however, does allow a reconstruction of the information they hold:

511. An inventory of military personnel present in a mil-liary infantry cohort (Bowman and Thomas 154) AD 92–7

18th of May. Complement of the 1st [Co]hort of Tungrians under the Prefect Julius Verecundus: 752, including 6 centurions.

Of these, absentees:	
Governor's guards:	46
At the office of Ferox at Coria:	337, including 2(?) centurions
At London:	1(?) centurion
[. . .]	6, including 1 centurion
[. . .]	9, including 1 centurion
[. . .]	11
[. . .]	1
	45
Total absentees:	456, including 5 centurions
Remainder present:	296, including 1 centurion
Of these:	
Sick:	15
Wounded:	6
With eye trouble:	[10]
Total:	31
Remainder, fit for duty:	[2]65, including [. . .

512. Military reports[22] (Bowman and Thomas 164)

The northern Britons [. . .] There are great numbers of cavalry. The cavalry do not use swords, nor do the wretched Britons mount to hurl their javelins.

513. Bowman and Thomas 76 AD 97–103

15th of April. Report of the 9th Cohort of Batavians. Everyone who ought to be at his post is there and will see to the baggage. The *optiones* and *curatores*[23] submitted the report. The *optio* Arcuittius from the century of Crescens delivered it.

514. Requests for furlough (Bowman and Thomas 175)

I, Messicus, ask you my lord[24] that you consider [me a worthy person] to whom you may grant leave at Coria (Corbridge).

515. Bowman and Thomas 168

. . .] of the century of Felicio. [I ask you my lor]d Cerialis that you consider me a worthy person [to who]m you might grant [lea]ve.

Cerialis, commander of the fort at some time in the period AD 97–103 and to whom the soldier from the century of Felicio addressed his request, lies at the heart of a rich collection of documents on a wide range of subjects:

516. A request to Cerialis for advancement (Bowman and Thomas 250)

. . .]ius Karus to [hi]s Ceri[alis], g[reetings] . . . Brigionus has requested me, sir, to recommend him to you. I ask, therefore, sir, that you consent to support any request he has made to you. I ask that you see fit to recommend him to Annius Equester, centurion in charge of the region, at Luguvalium [. . .] I shall be indebted [to you] . . . I hope that you are prospering and in good health. (2nd hand) Farewell brother.[25]
To Cerialis, Prefect.

517. Cerialis seeks influential friends in order to advance his own prospects[26] (Bowman and Thomas 225)

. . .] to his Crispinus. Since Grattius Crispinus is returning [. . .] and [. . .] I have gladly taken this opportunity, sir,[27] of greeting you, you who are my lord and whom it is my special wish to be in good health and in possession of his every hope. For you have always deserved this of me right up to your present [. . .]. In reliance upon this [. . .] you first [. . .] the most noble [. . .] Marcellus, my Governor. Therefore [. . .] the opportunity now of [. . .] of your friends, through his presence, of whom I know you have very many, [thanks to] him. Fulfil whatever I expect of you, however you wish, and [. . .] so furnish me with friends that through your kindness I can enjoy a pleasant period of military service. I write this to you from Vindolanda [. . .] winter quarters.

518. Cerialis receives good-luck wishes from his friends (Bowman and Thomas 248)

Niger and Brocchus to their Cerialis, greetings. It is our hope, brother, that what you are about to do will be successful. It will indeed be so since it is both in accord with our desire to make this prayer on your behalf, and you yourself are most worthy. You will meet our Governor quite soon for sure. (2nd hand) We hope, lord and brother, that you are well and prospering.
To [Fl]av[ius] Cerialis [. . .] of Cohort . . .

519. Letters forwarded to Cerialis (Bowman and Thomas 263)

. . .]to his Cerialis [. . .] and the letters which you had received from Equester, Centurion of the 3rd Cohort of Batavians [. . .]. 28th February (or 30th April)[28] [. . .] lady [. . .]
To Flavius Cerialis, Prefect of the 9th Cohort of Batavians from Vitalis the Decurion.[29]

520. Cerialis helps out with clothing
(Bowman and Thomas 255)

Cl]odius Super to his Cerialis, greetings. I was glad that our friend Valentinus duly approved the clothing on his return from Gaul. I greet you through him and ask you to send the things I need for my boys (slaves?), i.e. 6 cloaks, [. . .] other cloaks, 7 [. . .], [6?] tu[nics] which you are well aware I cannot properly obtain here since we are [. . .] for their transfer. (2nd hand) May you fare well, my dearest lord and brother, and . . .
To Flavius Cerialis, Prefect, from [C]l[o]dius Super, Centurion.

521. Cerialis himself asks for hunting nets[30]
(Bowman and Thomas 233)

a) gruel (or lettuces)
pork-crackling
pig's trotters

b) Flavius Cerialis to his Brocchus, greetings. If you love me, brother, I ask you to send me hunting nets(?).

The friendship between Cerialis and Brocchus extended to their wives also. Two letters of a social nature survive written by Brocchus' wife Claudia Severa to Cerialis' wife Sulpicia Lepidina:

522. Bowman and Thomas 291

(1st hand) Claudia Severa to [her] Lepidina [gr]e[eti]ngs. On the 11th of September, sister, I warmly invite you to come to us for the day celebrating my birthday. You will make [the day] more enjoyable for me by your arrival, if [you come?]. Give my greetings to your Cerialis. My own Aelius and my little son send their greetings. (2nd hand) I shall expect you sister. Farewell, sister, my dearest soul, as I hope to prosper, and hail.
(1st hand) To Sulpicia Lepidina (wife of) Cerialis. From Severa.

523. Bowman and Thomas 292

. . .] greetings. As I told you, sister, and promised that I would ask Brocchus and come to you, I did ask him and he replied that it was perfectly open to me, together with [. . .] to come to you however I can, since there are certain essential matters that [. . .]. You will

receive my letters and as a result know what I am going to do
[. . .]. I was [. . .] and shall remain at Briga. Give your Cerialis my
greetings. (2nd hand) Farewell, sister, my dearest and most longed-
for soul. (1st hand) To Sulpicia Lepidina (wife of) Cerialis. From
Severa (wife of) B[rocchus].

Since forts were major centres of consumption in terms of foodstuffs
and equipment, it comes as no surprise that lists of such commodities
also survive. In some cases it is clear that the items referred to were
for use by the whole fort, in other cases by the commander and his
entourage with their accounts maintained by their household slaves:

524. Civilian contractors supplying the army in the period AD 104–20 (Bowman and Thomas 180)

Account of wheat me[asured out from what
I myself have put into the barrel:
to myself, for bread [. . .
to Macrinus, *modii*[31] 7
to Felicius Victor on the order of Spectatus
modii provided, 26
in three sacks, to father,[32] *modii* 19
to Macrinus, *modii* 13
to the oxherds at the wood, *modii* 8
likewise to Amabilis at the shrine, *modii* 3
. . .] September, to Crescens
on the order of [Firmus?], *modii* 3
likewise [. . .
to Macr[inus], *modii* 15(?)
likewise to Ma[. . .], *modii* 3+[33]
to father [. . .], *modii* 2
26th September
to Lu[. . .], the [*Ben*]*eficiar*[*ius*],[34] *modii* 6
to Felicius Victor, *modii* 15
for plaited loaves, to you, *modii* 2
to Crescens, *modii* 9
to the legionary soldiers
on the order of Firmus, *modii* 11+
to Candidus, *modii* [. . .
to you, in a sack [. . .
to you, [. . .
to Lucco, in charge of the pigs [. . .

to Primus, (slave?) of Lucius [. . .
to you [. . .
to Lucco for his own use [. . .
likewise that which I have sent (?) [. . .
in [. . .
to father, in charge of the oxen [. . .
likewise, within the measure [. . .
15 pounds yield 15+ pounds [. . .
total, *modii* [. . .
likewise to myself, for bread, *modii* [. . .
total of wheat, *modii* 320½

On the reverse side of the accounts in §524 is the draft of a complaint addressed in all probability to the provincial governor concerning violent treatment at the hands of army personnel and the failure to gain redress through the normal channels. Significantly, the writing on both sides of the tablet is identical:

525. Bowman and Thomas 344

. . .] all the more [. . .] goods [. . .] or pour them away. As an honest man I beg your majesty not to allow me, an innocent man, to be beaten with rods and, sir, [. . .] I was unable to complain to the Prefect because he was detained by ill-health. I have complained to the *Beneficiarius* [. . . Cen]turions of his unit. I beg your mercy not to allow me, someone from overseas and an innocent man about whose good faith you may enquire, to have been beaten with rods until the blood flowed as if I had committed some crime.

The same person again was responsible for a list of monies received and amounts still outstanding:

526. Bowman and Thomas 181

. . . C]andidus:	2(?) denarii
For timbers bought:	7(?) denarii
Tunic:	3(?) denarii
From Tetricus:	[. . .]
From Primus:	2½(?) denarii
From Alio the vet.:	10+ denarii
From Vitalis, the bath-attendant:	3(?) denarii
Total:	34½ denarii

The remainder owe:

Ingenuus:	7 denarii
Acranius:	3 denarii
Vardullian horsemen:	7 denarii
Companion of Tagmatis, the flag-bearer:	3 denarii
Total:	20 denarii

Another letter, which sheds considerable light on commodity-dealing, seems to involve characters already mentioned in §524:

527. Bowman and Thomas 343

Octavius to his brother Candidus, greetings. 100 lbs of sinew from Marinus I will settle up. From the time you wrote to me on this matter he has made no mention of it to me. I have written to you many times that I have bought nearly 5000 *modii* of grain still in its ears and on this account I need money. Unless you send me some – at least 500 denarii – the result will be that I shall lose what I put down as a deposit – about 300 denarii[35] – and shall be embarrassed. For this reason I am asking you – send me some money as soon as possible. The hides that you write about are at Catterick – write that they be given to me as well as the wagon you mention in your letter, and write to me what is with the wagon. I would have already been for them except I did not wish to injure the draught animals while the roads are bad. See Tertius about the 8½ denarii he received from Fatalis. He has not credited them to my account. Rest assured that I have completed the 170 hides and have 119 *modii* of threshed cereal. Be sure to send me money so that I can have ears of grain on the threshing floor. I have already threshed all that I had. An associate of our friend Frontus has been here. He was wanting me to hand the hides over to him and was ready to pay cash. I told him I would give him the hides by the 1st of March. He decided he would come on January 13th, but he didn't turn up, nor did he bother to secure them since he had hides. If he had given the money I would have handed them over to him. I hear Frontinius Julius has for sale at a high price the leather goods he got from here at 5 denarii apiece. Greet Spectatus I[. . .] and [. . .] Firmus. I have received letters from Gleuco. Farewell. Vindolanda.

While at least some of the persons mentioned in the passage above are likely to have been military personnel, the following letter is clearly a transaction between civilians, even if the goods they deal in show they were suppliers to the military:

528. Bowman and Thomas 309

Metto to his Advectus very many greetings. I have sent you wooden items by means of Saco:
hubs, 34 in number
axles for carts, 38 in number
among them an axle turned on the lathe, 1 in number
spokes, 300 in number
boards for a bed, 26 in number
seats, 8 in number
knots?, 2 in number
shelves, 20 in number
. . .], 29 in number
benches?, 6 in number
I have sent you goat-skins, 6 in number
(2nd hand) [I hope] you are well, brother.

In contrast to the large scale of supplies for the fort, other accounts are on a more domestic level, perhaps connected with the headquarters, and certainly recorded by slaves. They date from the period AD 97–103, and the mention of 'lords' in the final line and Briga (cf. §523) suggests the writer was a slave belonging to Cerialis:

529. Bowman and Thomas 190

. . .] for the festival [. . .] denarii
. . .] for the festival [. . .] denarii
. . .] for the festival [. . .
19th of June
of barley, [. . .
of beer, [. . .
20th of June
of barley, *modii* 4
of beer, *modii* 2
[21st of Ju]ne of barley [. . .
. . .] to the granary
. . .]
. . .] *modii* 2
22nd of June
of barley, *modii* 5½

Allatus?, of [Ma]ssic wine [. . .
23rd of June
of barley, *modii* 5½
of wine, *modius* 1, *sextarii*[36] 14
of beer, *modii* 3
24th of June
of barley, *modii* 6+
of beer, *modii* 3, *sextarii* [. . .
of wine, *modius* 1, *sextarii* 12
of sour wine, *sextarii* 2
through Privatus
of fish sauce, *sextarii* 1½
through Privatus
of grease, *sextarii* 10 as a loan (?)
to the lord for alms
through Privatus
of wine, *modius* 1 for the festival
of the goddess
of wine, *sextarii* 12
through Privatus
25th of June
of barley, *sextarii* 11½ (?)
the lords [have] rem[ained] at Briga

That officers and their families enjoyed a high standard of living is
suggested by the following, which probably came from the *Praetorium*:

530. Bowman and Thomas 191

. . .] denarii, [. . .], spices [. . .], roe-deer [. . .], salt [. . .], young pork
[. . .], ham [. . .], in [. . .], wheat [. . .], venison [. . .], in [. . .], for
preserving [. . .], roe-deer [. . .]. Total, denarii [. . .]. (2nd hand)
Total, denarii 20+. (1st hand) cereal [. . .], denarii [. . .]

Since slaves were given the task of maintaining accounts, it is not
surprising to find contacts at this level between households:

531. Bowman and Thomas 301

Severus to his Candidus greetings. As regards the . . . for the Saturnalia[37] I ask you, brother, to see to them at a price of 4 or 6 asses[38]
and radishes to the value of not less than half a denarius.
Farewell brother.

To Candidus, (slave of) Genialis the Prefect, from Severus, slave of
[. . .

cf.

532. Bowman and Thomas 302

. . .] bruised beans: 2 *modii*, 20 chickens, a hundred apples – if you
can find nice ones – a hundred or two hundred eggs – if they are
for sale there at a reasonable price [. . .] 8 *sextarii* of fish-sauce
[. . .] a *modius* of olives.
To [. . .] of Verecundus.

In other cases the accounts and letters that survive show what are
perhaps more personal aspects of life: details for instance of a return
journey from Vindolanda to York (?):

533. Bowman and Thomas 185

. . .] for wine:	½ denarius
July (8th–14th)[39]	[at Isurium] (Aldborough, Yorks.)
for wine	¼ denarius
July (9th–14th)	
for wine	¼ denarius
July (10th–14th)	
[6 lines]	
. . .]	8
for wine	¼ denarius
of barley	1 *modius*, ½ denarius 1 as
wagon axles	
two for a carriage	3½ denarii
salt and fodder	1 denarius
At Isurium (Aldborough) for	
wine	¼ denarius
At Cataractonium (Catterick,	
Yorks.) for lodgings	½ denarius
for wine	¼ denarius
at Vinovia (Binchester) for	
vests (?)	¼ denarius
of wheat[	
This makes	78¾ denarii
Grand total	94¾ denarii

A letter between auxiliary soldiers:

534. Bowman and Thomas 310

Chrauttius to Veldeius his brother and old messmate, very many greetings, and I ask you, my brother Veldeius – I am surprised that you have not written anything back to me for such a long time – if you have heard anything from our elders[40] or . . . in what unit he is, and to give him my personal greetings and Virilis too, the veterinary doctor. Ask him if you can send through one of our friends the shears he promised me in exchange. And I ask you, brother Virilis, to give my greetings to our sister Thuttena and to Velbuteius. Write back to us [. . .] he is. I hope you are enjoying the best of fortune. Farewell. London. To Veldedeius,[41] groom of the governor, from his brother Chrauttius.

cf.

535. Bowman and Thomas 311

Solemnis to his brother Paris[42] very many greetings. I want you to know that I am in good health, as I hope you are in turn, you most neglectful man, who have sent me not so much as a single letter. But I think that I am behaving in a more considerate manner in writing to you [. . .] to you brother, [. . .] my old mate. Pass on my greetings to Diligens and Cogitatus and Corinthus, and I ask that you send me the names [. . .
To Paris [. . .] of the 3rd [Coh]ort of Batavians, from Solemnis.

A request for clothing:

536. Bowman and Thomas 346

. . .] to you [. . .] pairs of socks from Sattua, two pairs of sandals and underpants, two pairs of sandals [. . .] Greet [. . .]ndes, Elpis, Iu[. . . , . . .]enus, Tetricus and all the messmates with whom I hope you live in the greatest good fortune.

A reference to oysters:

537. Bowman and Thomas 299

. . .] which is the main reason for my letter: that you are steadfast. A friend sent me 50 oysters from Cordonovi, so that all the more speedily [. . .
To Lucius, Decurion.

From elsewhere in Britain comes a variety of material allowing us to glimpse through often transient references the interests and concerns of the province's inhabitants, their enthusiasms, loves, business worries, and advertising.

538. A letter from London (*RIB* II.4 2443.7)

Rufus, son of Callisunus, (sends) greetings to Epillicus and all his associates. I believe you know I am very well. If you have made the list, please send it. Make sure you do everything carefully so that you squeeze every last penny from that girl.

539. From Leicester, a fragment of pottery (*RIB* II.7 2501.586)

Verecunda the actress, Lucius the gladiator.

Inscriptions on rings:

540. From Castell Collen, Powys (*RIB* II.3 2422.19)

Sweet Love.

541. From Bedford (*RIB* II.3 2422.5)

Long life to Eusebius.

542. From Wroxeter (*RIB* II.3 2422.47)

Love (me). I love (you).

543. From London (*RIB* II.3 2422.75)

Give me life.

544. From Chesters (*RIB* II.3 2422.80)

Who will separate mine and yours while life lasts?

Inscriptions on tiles:

545. From Binchester (*RIB* II.5 2491.146)

Armea has taught me to say 'thank you, but no' to all others.

546. From London (*RIB* II.5 2491.147)

Austalis has been wandering about by himself every day for 13 days.

547. On a box flue-tile from Leicester (*RIB* II.5 2491.3)

Primus has made 60 of these.

548. From Silchester (*RIB* II.5 2491.1)

Clementinus made this box flue-tile.

549. A bath-house *pila*[43] brick from Wiggonhold, W. Sussex (*RIB* II.5 2491.2)

20 pila-bricks, 4 voussoir (arch) flue-tiles, 560 box flue-tiles.

550. A brick from Silchester (*RIB* II.5 2491.159)

Enough.

551. A building stone from Norton nr. Malton, Yorks. (*RIB* I 712)

Good luck to the Genius (spirit) of the place. Use this goldsmith's shop to your good fortune, young slave.

Advertising:

552. Painted inscription on an amphora from Southwark (*RIB* II.6 2492.24)

Lucius Tettius Africanus' excellent fish-sauce from Antipolis (Antibes, France).

Oculists' stamps: four sided small stone slabs used for impressing the details of the remedy onto the material itself:

553. From Sandy, Bedfordshire (*RIB* II.4 2446.2)

a) Gaius Valerius Amandus' vinegar ointment for running eyes.
b) Gaius Valerius Amandus' drops for cloudy vision.

c) Gaius Valerius Valentinus' celandine ointment after an attack of inflammation of the eyes.
d) Gaius Valerius Valentinus' mixture for clearing the vision.

554. From Kenchester, Herefordshire (*RIB* II.4 2446.3)

a) Titus Vindacius Ariovistus' nard ointment.
b) Titus Vindacius Ariovistus' green ointment.
c) Titus Vindacius Ariovistus' infallible ointment.
d) Titus Vindacius Ariovistus' frankincense ointment.

555. Ibid. (*RIB* II.4 2446.21)

a) Aurelius Polychronius' 2-stone ointment after (an attack of inflammation of the eyes).
b) Polychronius' copper oxide ointment.
c) Aurelius Polychronius' swan-white ointment for attacks (of inflammation of the eyes).
d) Polychronius' gall ointment.

556. From Cirencester (*RIB* II.4 2446.4)

a) Atticus' frankincense ointment with egg, for all pains.
b) Atticus' mild ointment for all pains after an attack of inflammation of the eyes.
c) Atticus' poppy ointment for all pains.
d) Atticus' quince ointment for soreness (of the eyes).

557. From Lydney Park, Glos. (*RIB* II.4 2446.9)

a) Julius Jucundus' ointment as drops.
b) Julius Jucundus' quince-oil ointment.
c) Julius Jucundus' ointment for application with a small sponge.

558. From St Albans (*RIB* II.4 2446.11)

a) Lucius Julius Juvenis' anti-irritant balsam.
b) [Lucius Julius Juvenis'] myrrh ointment, twice a day with egg after an attack of inflammation of the eyes.
c) Flavius Secundus' ointment for white scars.

559. From London (*RIB* II.4 2446.27)[44]

a) Gaius Silvius Tetricus' misy ointment for infections and scars.
b) Gaius Silvius Tetricus' ointment for attacks of inflammation of the eyes.
c) Gaius Silvius Tetricus' fragrant ointment for soreness of the eyes.
d) Gaius Silvius Tetricus' biprosopum for at[tacks of inflammation of the eyes].

For the most part, however, the ordinary soldier or civilian of Britain only gained a lasting memorial at death. Here it is we learn of length of service, the span of life, and the love between husband and wife, parents and offspring, master and servant:

The army:

560. A very old soldier from Caerleon (*RIB* I 363)

To the spirits of the departed. Julius Valens, veteran of the II Legion Augusta, lived 100 years. Julia Secundina, his wife, and Julius Martinus, his son, had this made.

561. An armourer from Bath (*RIB* I 156)

Julius Vitalis, Armourer (*fabriciensis*) of the XX Legion Valeria Victrix, with 9 years' service, aged 29, a Belgian, buried at the expense of the Guild of armourers. Here he lies.

562. A medical officer from Housesteads (*RIB* I 1618)

To the spirits of the departed (and) to Anicius Ingenuus, Medical officer (*medicus ordinarius*) serving in the 1st Cohort of Tungrians. He lived 25 years.

563. A Brigantian serving at Mumrills (*RIB* I 2142)

To the spirits of the departed. Nectovelius, son of Vindex, aged 29, with 9 years' service, a Brigantian, served in the 2nd Thracian Cohort.

564. A soldier of the VI Victrix from London (*RIB* I 11)

To the spirits of the departed. Flavius Agricola, soldier of the VI Legion Victrix lived 42 years 10 days. Albia Faustina had this made for her peerless husband.

565. A standard-bearer from York (*RIB* I 673)

Lucius Duccius Rufinus, son of Lucius, of the Voltinian voting-tribe, from Vienne, Standard-bearer (*signifer*) of the IX Legion, aged 28, lies here.

566. From Lincoln (*RIB* I 257)

Gaius Valerius, son of Gaius, of the Maecian voting-tribe, soldier of the IX Legion, Standard-bearer of the century of Hospes, aged 35, with 14 years' service, stipulated in his will that this be set up. Here he lies.

567. From Chester (*RIB* I 525)

To the spirits of the departed (and) of Decimus Capienius Urbicus of the Voltinian voting-tribe, from Vienne, Standard-bearer with 24 years' service, aged 44. His heir had this made.

568. A soldier from Bath (*RIB* I 157)

Gaius Murrius Modestus, son of Gaius, of the Arniensian voting-tribe, from Forum Julii (Fréjus), soldier of the II Legion Adiutrix Pia Fidelis, [in the century] of Julius Secundus, aged 25, with [. . .] years' service, lies here.

569. Ibid. (*RIB* I 158)

To the spirits of the departed. Marcus Valerius Latinus, son of Marcus, citizen of Equestris, soldier of the XX Legion, aged 35, with 20 years' service, lies buried here.

570. A soldier from Lincoln (*RIB* I 256)

Lucius Sempronius Flavinus, soldier of the IX Legion, in the century of Babudius Severus, with 7 years' service, aged 30, a Spaniard of the Galerian voting-tribe, from Clunia.

571. From Caerleon (*RIB* I 360)

To the spirits of the departed. Julius Julianus, a soldier of the II Legion Augusta, with 18 years' service, aged 40, lies here. His wife Amanda had this set up.

572. An *emeritus* (veteran) from Templebrough (*RIB* I 620)

To the spirits of the departed (and) to Crotus, son of Vindex, *emeritus* of the 4th Cohort of Gauls, aged 40. Flavia Peregrina, his most devoted wife, made this monument and set up this inscription to her most devoted husband.

573. A soldier from Wroxeter (*RIB* I 292 restored)

[Titus F]laminius, son of Titus, of the Pollian voting-tribe, from Fa[. . .], aged 45, with 22 years' service, soldier of the XIV Legion Gemina. I served as a soldier and here I am. Read [this] and be happy, more or less. The gods prohibit you from the wine-grape and water when you enter Tartarus. Live honourably while your star grants you time for life.

574. A camp-prefect from Chester (*RIB* I 490 restored)

To the spirits of the departed. Marcus Aurelius Alexander, Camp-Prefect (*praefectus castrorum*) of the XX Legion [Valeria Victrix], a Syrian from Os[roene, li]ved 72 years . . .

575. An *optio* from Chester (*RIB* I 492)

To the spirits of the departed. Caecilius Avitus from Emerita Augusta, Deputy-centurion (*optio*) of the XX Legion Valeria Victrix, with 15 years' service, aged 34. His heir had this made.

576. Ibid. (*RIB* I 544)

. . .] a Deputy-centurion (*optio*) in the century of Lucilius Ingenuus, awaiting promotion, who died by shipwreck. (Here) he lies.

577. A centurion from York (*RIB* I 675)

To the spirits of the departed (and) of Titus Flavius Flavinus, Centurion of the VI Legion. His heir, Gaius Classicius Aprilis, ordered this to be made before his death.

578. An auxiliary standard-bearer from Corbridge (*RIB* I 1172)

To the spirits of the departed. Flavinus, trooper of the *Ala* (squadron) Petriana, Standard-bearer in the troop of Candidus, aged 25 with 7 years' service, lies here.

579. A *cornicularius* from Great Chesters (*RIB* I 1742)

To the spirits of the departed (and) to Aelius Mercurialis, Adjutant (*cornicularius*), his sister Vacia made this.

580. An armament-keeper from Castlesteads (*RIB* I 2003)

To the spirits of the departed (and) of Gemellus, Armament-keeper (*custos armorum*). His heir, the Centurion Flavius Hilario, had this made.

581. Two soldiers from Ambleside (*JRS* 53 (1963), p. 160)

To the good gods and the departed. Flavius Fuscinus, reservist lived 60 years.
To the good gods and the departed. Flavius Romanus, Record-keeper (*actarius*) lived 35 years and was killed in camp by enemy action.

The family:

582. From York (*RIB* I 690)

To the spirits of the departed (and) of Simplicia Florentina, most innocent soul, who lived ten months, Felicius Simplex, her father, (a soldier) in the VI Legion Victrix, (set this up).

583. Ibid. (*RIB* I 685)

To the spirits of the departed (and) of Flavia Augustina who lived 39 years, 7 months, 11 days, her son Saenius Augustinus who lived 1 year, 3 days, [. . .] (a daughter?) who lived 1 year, 9 months, 5 days. Gaius Aeresius Saenus, veteran of the VI Legion Victrix, had this set up for his beloved wife and himself.

584. Ibid. (*RIB* I 684)

To the spirits of the departed. Corellia Optata, aged 13. You secret spirits who inhabit the Acherusian realm of Pluto, and whom the meagre ashes and shade, the mere semblance of a body, seek after the brief light of life, I, the father of an innocent daughter, the victim of unfair hope, pitiably bewail this her final end. Quintus Corellius Fortis, her father, had this set up.

585. Ibid. (*RIB* I 677)

To the memory of Valerius Theodorianus from Nomentum. He lived 35 years, 6 months. His mother and heir, Emilia Theodora, had this set up.

586. Ibid. (*RIB* I 686)

To the spirits of the departed (and) of Julia Brica, aged 31, and Sempronia Martina, aged 6. Sempronius Martinus had this set up.

587. Ibid. (*RIB* I 687)

To Julia Fortunata from Sardinia. (She was) a loyal wife to her husband, Verecundius Diogenes.

588. Ibid. (*RIB* I 688)

To the spirits of the departed (and) of Julia Velva who lived a most dutiful life for 50 years. Her heir, Aurelius Mercurialis, had this made in his lifetime for himself and his family.

589. Ibid. (*RIB* I 695)

To the spirits of the departed (and) of Eglecta, aged 30, who lies here beside her son Crescens, aged 3. Antonius Stephanus had this set up for his wife.

590. From Bath (*RIB* I 155)

To the spirits of the departed. Gaius Calpurnius Receptus, Priest of the goddess Sulis, lived 75 years. Calpurnia Trifosa, his freed-woman and wife, had this made.

591. Ibid. (*RIB* I 164)

To the spirits of the departed (and) of Successa Petronia, who lived 3 years, 4 months, 9 days. Ve [. . .] omulus and Victoria Sabina set this up for their dearest daughter.

592. From Lincoln (*RIB* I 251)

To the spirits of the departed. Flavius Helius, a Greek by birth, lived 40 years. Flavia Ingenua set this up for her husband.

593. Ibid. (*RIB* I 252)

To the spirits of the departed (and) of Gaius Julius Calenus of the Galerian voting-tribe, from Lyons, veteran of the VI Legion Victrix Pia Fidelis. Julia Sempronia, his daughter, (set this up).

594. From Caerleon (*RIB* I 357)

To the spirits of the departed. Titus Flavius Candidus from Ulpia Traiana, soldier of the II Legion Augusta, with 7 years' service, aged 27. His brother had this set up.

595. Ibid. (*RIB* I 359)

To the spirits of the departed (and) of Gaius Julius Decuminus, veteran of the II Legion Augusta, aged 45. His wife had this made.

596. Ibid. (*RIB* I 369)

To the spirits of the departed. Tadia Vallaunius lived 65 years and Tadius Exuperatus, her son, lived 37 years, having died on the German expedition. Tadia Exuperata, her devoted daughter, set this up for her mother and brother beside her father's tomb.

597. Ibid. (*RIB* I 373)

To the spirits of the departed and the memory of Julia Secundina, his devoted mother, who lived 75 years, Gaius Julius Martinus, her son, had this made.[45]

598. Ibid. (*RIB* I 375)

To the spirits of the departed. Julia Veneria, aged 32. Julius Alesander, her devoted husband, and Julius Belicianus, her son, had this monument made.

599. From Chester (*RIB* I 594)

Hid beneath this earth is she who once was Aelia Matrona and lived for 28 years, 2 months, 8 days, together with Marcus Julius Maximus her son who lived 6 years, 3 months, 20 days, and Campania Dubitata her mother who lived for 50 years. Julius Maximus, soldier seconded to the Governor's guard (*singularis consularis*) from the squadron of Sarmatians, her husband, set up this memorial to his incomparable wife, to his son who was most devoted to his father, and to his most steadfast mother-in-law.

600. Ibid. (*RIB* I 537)

To the spirits of the departed (and) to Lucius Festinius Probus, his son who lived 2 years, 29 days, his father, Lucius Sempronius Probianus, had this made.

601. Ibid. (*RIB* I 558)

To the spirits of the departed (and) of Flavius Callimorphus who lived 42 years and of Serapion who lived 3 years 6 months. Thesaeus had this made for brother and son.

602. From Old Penrith (*RIB* I 931)

To the spirits of the departed. Aurelius lived 11 years. Avo, his most devoted father, set this up as much for himself as for his son.

603. Ibid. (*RIB* I 932)

To the spirits of the departed (and) of Marcus Cocceius Nonnus, aged 6. Here he lies.

604. Ibid. (*RIB* I 937)

To the spirits of the departed (and) of Ylas, his dearest foster-child aged 13, Claudius Severus, military Tribune, (set this up).

605. From Carlisle (*RIB* I 955)

To the spirits of the departed. Flavius Antigonus Papias, a citizen of Greece, lived 60 years more or less and returned to the Fates his soul, which he had on loan that long. Septimia Do[. . .] (set this up).

606. From South Shields (*RIB* I 1065)

To the spirits of the departed (and) to Regina, his freedwoman and wife, a Catuvellaunian by race, aged 30, Barates of Palmyra (set this up).

607. From Chesters (*RIB* I 1482)

Sacred to the spirits of the departed (and) of Fabia Honorata. Fabius Honoratus, Tribune of the 1st Cohort of Vangiones and Aurelia Eglectiane made this for their most sweet daughter.

608. Ibid. (*RIB* I 1483)

To the spirits of the departed (and) to his sister Ursa, his wife Julia, and his son Canio, Lurio the German (set this up).

609. From Risingham (*RIB* I 1250)

Sacred to the spirits of the departed (and) to Aurelia Lepulla, his most devoted mother, Dionysius Fortunatus, her son, (set this up). May the earth lie light upon thee.

610. From Carvoran (*RIB* I 1828)

To the spirits of the departed (and) to Aurelia Aia, daughter of Titus, from Salonae, Aurelius Marcus of the Century of Obsequens (set this up) for his most holy wife who lived 33 years without any stain.

611. From Birdoswald (*RIB* I 1919)

To the spirits of the departed (and) of Aurelius Concordius, who lived 1 year 5 days, the son of the Tribune Aurelius Julianus.

612. From Wroxeter (*RIB* I 295)

To the spirits of the departed. Placida aged 55. (Set up) on the instructions of her husband of 30 years.
To the spirits of the departed. Deucsus aged 15. (Set up) on the instructions of his brother.

Master and servant, patron and client:

613. From York (*RIB* I 683)

To the spirits of the departed (and) of Aelia Severa, honourable woman, formerly wife of Caecilius Rufus. She lived 27 years, 9 months, 4 days. Caecilius Musicus, his freedman, set this up.

614. From Chester (*RIB* I 560)

To the spirits of the departed. Atilianus and Antiatilianus aged 10, Protus aged 12. Pompeius Optatus, their master, had this made.

615. Ibid. (*RIB* I 559)

To the spirits of the departed (and) to Etacontius his well-deserving freedman, Gaius Asurius Fortis, his patron, set this up.

616. From South Shields (*RIB* I 1064 restored)

To the spirits of the departed (and) of Victor, a Moor by race, aged 20, freedman of Numerianus, trooper in the 1st squadron of Asturians, who most devotedly co[nduc]ted (him to his grave).

617. From High Rochester (*RIB* I 1290)

To the spirits of the departed (and) of Felicio, a freedman, who lived 20 years.

618. From Halton Chesters (*RIB* I 1436)

To the spirits of the departed (and) [. . .] of Hardalio. The guild of his fellow slaves set this up to one who deserved well.

NOTES

1 Frere (1) p. 181ff.; Salway (1) p. 535ff.
2 Cf. §478.
3 Frere (1) p. 197.
4 Responsible for the maintenance of public buildings, streets and drainage.
5 Frere (1) p. 249f.; Salway (1) p. 575ff.; Liversidge p. 26ff.
6 The right-hand section of this tombstone was doubtless intended for the inscription of Senecio, but at some stage was usurped: 'To the spirits of the departed. Claudius Catiotus lived 60 years.'
7 The abbreviations used in the inscription are open to various interpretation. Thus, *Sen.* has been taken as *Senator* = decurion, if the office is a civilian one, or 4th C. non-commissioned officer if the context is military, or *Senior*, the third element in Flavius Martius' name. Similarly, the C has been variously interpreted as *Civitas* or *Cohort*. See further Salway (2) p. 246f.
8 Every fifth year (hence quinquennales) the Duoviri were given the task of filling vacant seats in the Ordo and revising tax registers; cf. §300, Frere (1) p. 195.
9 Presumably represented by the Council, cf. Frere (1) p. 196f.; Salway (1) p. 532f.
10 I omit here consideration of the Cassiterides, the Tin Isles, which have sometimes been identified with the Scillies, but are better located off northwest Spain. See further Rivet and Smith p. 43; Hawkes.
11 The usual description of the oblong piece of lead recorded by Leland but subsequently lost. Whittick, however, regards it as a commemorative lead plaque which does not guarantee lead production in the Mendips in AD 49.
12 Cf. Webster.
13 Cf. *RIB* II.1 2404.10: (Property) of the Emperor Vespasian Augustus. British lead. [From the s]ilver works. VEB. (Property) of the Emperor. Ti(berius) C[laudius Triferna].
14 A British provenance comes from interpretation of LVI as the British legion VI Valeria Victrix, cf. LEG XX also on an ingot from Sassenay (*RIB* II.1 2404.72b).
15 The restoration of Bogaers (1) for the original restoration 'King and Legate of Augustus in Britain'. For the career of Cogidubnus see Barrett (1); A.R. Birley (4) p. 208ff.; Cunliffe (1) p. 21ff., 54f.
16 Cf. From York (*Britannia* 8 (1977), 430–1): . . .] and the Spirit of the place [and the divine power of the Au]gusti, Lucius Viducius [. . . Pla]cidus who has his home at Velocasium (Rouen), [. . .t]rader, [gave] this arch and shrine [. . . in the consulship] of Gratus and [Seleucus] (AD 221).
17 Cf. bun-shaped ingots from Parys mountain, Anglesey (*RIB* II.1 2403.1,2) inscribed: Jul(ius) Es . . .
18 See Ogilvie and Richmond p. 215f.
19 i.e. from W. Hungary.
20 Title of the annual magistrate in some Italian towns.
21 See further Bowman pp. 13–19. For similar tablets cf. §152.
22. These appear to be routine reports of inspection. Bowman and Thomas record up to 27 instances from Vindolanda.

23 The *optio* was a deputy centurion, the *curator* either a rank in units with cavalry or someone with a specific function.

24 Evidently the standard mode of address from an ordinary soldier to the commander of his cohort.

25 Use of the term 'brother' indicates equality of rank rather than a blood relationship, i.e. that Karus, like Cerialis, commands a cohort of auxiliaries.

26 Comparison of handwriting shows that the letter comes from Cerialis.

27 Use of the term, lit. 'my lord', suggests that Crispinus is of superior rank to Cerialis and evidently well enough placed to recommend the Prefect to the governor, who must be Lucius Neratius Marcellus, present in Britain in AD 103.

28 The uncertainty is caused by the incomplete text, i.e. 'the day before the 1st of Ma[rch] or Ma[y]'.

29 Commander of a troop of cavalry.

30 The letter is evidently only a draft, written on a tablet also used for a list of household goods probably compiled by one of Cerialis' servants.

31 The *modius*, a measure for corn and other bulky materials, is estimated as sufficient to supply the daily energy requirements of seven soldiers.

32 The references 'to myself' (1.3), 'to you' (1.25f., 29), and 'to father' (1.7, 33) suggest to Bowman and Thomas a firm of contractors consisting of two brothers and their father.

33 The use of + indicates that damage to the text may mask an originally larger number.

34 Soldier seconded to special duties.

35 Since this was a year's pay for a soldier at the time, the quantities involved are clearly large-scale.

36 The *sextarius* was *c.* 1 pint, or one sixteenth of a *modius* dry measure.

37 The Saturnalia was the main midwinter festival, during which masters and slaves exchanged roles for a time.

38 The as was a sixteenth of a denarius.

39 The loss of the number involved in the date prevents certainty as to the exact date.

40 lit. 'parents' but Bowman and Thomas suggest that since Veldeius and Chrauttius are not related, since their names have different ethnic origins, such words as 'brother' and 'sister' and 'parent' are being used in a more generalised sense.

41 This is probably the more correct form of the name, with Veldeius as a shortened version.

42 Absolute certainty as to whether the names belong to soldiers or their slaves cannot be ascertained.

43 Used to support the hypocaust.

44 Cf. *Britannia* 21 (1990) 275–83.

45 Cf. §560.

Bibliography

GENERAL

Frere S. (1) *Britannia, A History of Roman Britain*, 3rd edn (London, 1987)
Liversidge J. *Britain in the Roman Empire* (London, 1968)
Ordnance Survey Historical Map & Guide of Hadrian's Wall (Southampton, 1989)
Ordnance Survey Historical Map & Guide of Roman Britain (Southampton, 1991)
Salway P. (1) *Roman Britain* (Oxford, 1981)
Todd M. *Roman Britain 55 BC–AD 400* (London, 1981)

SPECIFIC

Barley M.W. and Hanson R.P.C. *Christianity in Britain, 300–700* (Leicester, 1968)
Barrett A.A. (1) 'The Career of Tiberius Claudius Cogidubnus', *Britannia* 10 (1979), pp. 227–42
—— (2) 'Chronological Errors in Dio's Account of the Claudian Invasion', *Britannia* 11 (1980), pp. 31–3
—— (3) 'Claudius' British Victory Arch', *Britannia* 22 (1991), pp. 1–19
Bartholomew P. (1) 'Fifth-Century Facts', *Britannia* 13 (1982), pp. 261–70
—— (2) 'Fourth-Century Saxons', *Britannia* 15 (1984), pp. 169–85
Birley A. *The People of Roman Britain* (London, 1979)
Birley A.R. (1) 'Virius Lupus', *Archaeologia Aeliana* 50 (1972), pp. 179-89
—— (2) 'Petillius Cerialis and the Conquest of Brigantia', *Britannia* 4 (1973), pp. 179–90
—— (3) 'Roman Frontiers and Roman Frontier Policy: Some Reflections on Roman Imperialism', *Transactions of the Architectural and Archaeological Society of Durham and Northumberland* 3 (1974), pp. 13–25
—— (4) *The Fasti of Roman Britain* (Oxford, 1981)
Birley E. (1) *Roman Britain and the Roman Army* (Kendal, 1961)
—— (2) 'The Adherence of Britain to Vespasian', *Britannia* 9 (1978), pp. 243–5
Birley R. *Vindolanda, a Frontier Post on Hadrian's Wall* (London, 1977)
Bogaers J.E. (1) 'King Cogidubnus in Chichester: Another Reading of R.I.B. 91', *Britannia* 10 (1979), pp. 243–54
—— (2) 'Foreign Affairs' in *Rome and her Northern Provinces*, B. Hartley and J. Wacher (eds.) (Sutton, 1983), pp. 13–32
Boon G.C. 'Potters, Oculists and Eye Troubles', *Britannia* 14 (1983), pp. 1–12

Bowman A.K. *Life and Letters on the Roman Frontier* (London, 1994)

Bowman A.K. and Thomas J.D. *The Vindolanda Writing Tablets (Tabulae Vindolandenses II)* (London, 1994)

Brassington M. 'Ulpius Marcellus', *Britannia* 11 (1980), pp. 314–15

Braund D. 'Observations on Cartimandua', *Britannia* 15 (1984), pp. 1–6

Breeze D.J. and Dobson B. 'Hadrian's Wall: Some Problems', *Britannia* 3 (1972), pp. 182–208

Brown P. 'Pelagius and His Supporters: Aims and Environment', *Journal of Theological Studies* 19 (1968), pp. 93–114

Burn A.R. *The Romans in Britain: An Anthology of Inscriptions*, 2nd edn (Blackwell, 1969)

Casey J. 'Constantine the Great in Britain – The Evidence of the Coinage of the London Mint, AD 312–314', in *Collectanea Londiniensia: Studies in London Archaeology and History Presented to Ralph Merrifield*, J. Bird *et al.* (eds.) (London, 1978), pp. 181–93

Casey P.J. (1) 'Carausius and Allectus – Rulers in Gaul?', *Britannia* 8 (1977), pp. 283–301

—— (2) 'Magnus Maximus in Britain' in 'The End of Roman Britain', *British Archaeological Reports* 71 (1979), pp. 66–79

Chadwick N.K. *The Druids* (Cardiff, 1966)

Clark F. *The Rise of Christianity* (Open University A291, Units 13–16, 1974)

Corpus Inscriptionum Latinarum (Berlin, 1871–)

Cotterill J. 'Saxon Raiding and the Role of the Late Roman Coastal Forts of Britain', *Britannia* 24 (1993), pp. 227–39

Cunliffe B. (1) *The Regni* (London, 1973)

—— (2) *The Temple of Sulis Minerva at Bath, Volume 2, The Finds from the Sacred Spring* (Oxford, 1988)

Davies R.W. 'Some Troop Movements to Roman Britain', *Klio* 60 (1978), pp. 363–93

Dornier A. (1) 'The Reorganisation of the North-Western Frontier of Britain in AD 369: Ammianus Marcellinus and the "Notitia Dignitatum"' in *Roman Frontier Studies 1969*, E. Birley, B. Dobson and M. Jarrett (eds.) (Cardiff, 1974), pp. 102–5

—— (2) 'The Province of Valentia', *Britannia* 13 (1982), pp. 253–60

Dumville D.N. 'Sub-Roman Britain: History and Legend', *History* 62 (1977), pp. 173–92

Eichholz D.E. 'How Long Did Vespasian Serve in Britain?', *Britannia* 3 (1972), pp. 149–63

Fishwick D. (1) 'The Imperial Cult in Roman Britain', *Phoenix* 15 (1961), pp. 159–73, 213–29

—— (2) 'The Imperial "Numen" in Roman Britain', *JRS* 59 (1969), pp. 76–91

Frere S. (2) '*RIB* 1322', *Britannia* 17 (1986), p. 329

Graham A.J. 'The Division of Britain', *JRS* 56 (1966), pp. 92–107

Grueber H.A. *Roman Medallions in the British Museum* (London, 1874)

Hanson W.S. *Agricola and the Conquest of the North* (London, 1987)

Hanson W.S. and Campbell D.B. 'The Brigantes: From Clientage to Conquest', *Britannia* 17 (1986), pp. 73–89

Harris E. and Harris J.R. *The Oriental Cults in Roman Britain* (Leiden, 1965)

Hassall M. 'The Date of the Rebuilding of Hadrian's Turf Wall in Stone', *Britannia* 15 (1984), pp. 242–4

Hawkes C.F.C. *Pytheas: Europe and the Greek Explorers*, 8th J.L. Myres Memorial Lecture (Oxford, 1977)

Henig M. *Religion in Roman Britain* (London, 1984)

Hind J.G.F. (1) 'The British "Provinces" of Valentia and Orcades', *Historia* 24 (1975), pp. 101–11

—— (2) 'The "Genounian" Part of Britain', *Britannia* 8 (1977), pp. 229–34

Inscriptiones Latinae Selectae, ed. Dessau, H. (Berlin, 1892–1914)

Jarrett M.G. 'An Unnecessary War', *Britannia* 7 (1976), pp. 145–51

Johnson S. (1) *The Roman Forts of the Saxon Shore* (London, 1976)

—— (2) *Later Roman Britain* (London, 1980)

Jones M.E. and Casey P.J. 'The Celtic Chronicle Restored: A Chronology for the Anglo-Saxon Invasions and the End of Roman Britain', *Britannia* 19 (1988), pp. 367–97

Kenworthy J. (ed.) 'Agricola's Campaigns in Scotland', *Scottish Archaeological Forum* 12 (Edinburgh, 1981)

Lapidge M. and Dumville D. (eds.) *Gildas: New Approaches* (Woodbridge, 1984)

Mann J.C. 'What Was the Notitia Dignitatum For?', in *Aspects of the Notitia Dignitatum*, R. Goodburn and P. Bartholomew (eds.) (Oxford, 1976), pp. 1–9

Marcovich M. 'Sator Arepo', *Zeitschrift für Papyrologie und Epigraphik* 50 (1983), pp. 155–71

Maxwell I.S. (1) 'The Location of Ictis', *Journal of the Royal Institution of Cornwall* 5 (1972), pp. 293–319

—— (2) 'Two Inscribed Roman Stones and Architectural Fragments from Scotland', *Proceedings of the Society of Antiquaries of Scotland* 113 (1983), pp. 379–90

Merrifield R. *London, City of the Romans* (London, 1983)

Miller M. 'Stilicho's Pictish War', *Britannia* 6 (1975), pp. 141–5

Morris J. 'The Date of St. Alban', *Hertfordshire Archaeology* 1 (1968), pp. 1–8

Muhlberger S. 'The Gallic Chronicle of 452 and its Authority for British Events', *Britannia* 14 (1983), pp. 23–33

Myers J.N.L. Review of E.A. Thompson, *Saint Germanus of Auxerre and the End of Roman Britain* (Woodbridge, 1984), *Britannia* 17 (1986), pp. 458–60

Nash D. 'Reconstructing Poseidonius's Celtic Ethnography, Some Considerations', *Britannia* 7 (1976), pp. 111–26

Norman A.F. 'Religion in Roman York' in *Soldier and Civilian in Roman Yorkshire*, R.M. Butler (ed.) (Leicester, 1971), pp. 143–54

Ogilvie R.M. and Richmond I. *Cornelii Taciti de Vita Agricolae* (Oxford, 1967)

Phillips E.J. 'The Gravestone of M. Favonius Facilis at Colchester', *Britannia* 6 (1975), pp. 102–5

Rankov N.B. 'M. Oclatinus Adventus in Britain', *Britannia* 18 (1987), pp. 243–9

Rivet A.L.F. and Smith C. *The Place Names of Roman Britain* (London, 1979)

Roman Imperial Coins (London, 1926–94)

Roman Inscriptions of Britain, Vol. I: *Inscriptions on Stone*, Collingwood R.G. and Wright R.P. (Oxford, 1965)

—— Vol. II: *Instrumentum Domesticum*, Frere S.S., Roxan M., Tomlin R.S.O. and Hassall M.W.C. (Stroud, 1990–5)

Ross A. *Pagan Celtic Britain* (London, 1967)

Salway P. (2) *The Frontier People of Roman Britain* (Cambridge, 1965)

Shackleton Bailey D.R. *Cicero's Letters to Atticus* (Cambridge, 1965–70)

—— *Cicero: Epistulae ad Familiares (Letters to his Friends)* (Cambridge, 1977)

Shiel N. 'The Episode of Carausius and Allectus', *British Archaeological Reports* 40 (1977)

Speidel M.P. 'The Chattan War, the Brigantian Revolt and the Loss of the Antonine Wall', *Britannia* 18 (1987), pp. 233–7

Stevens C.E. (1) 'Britain Between the Invasions (BC 54–AD 43), A Study in Ancient Diplomacy' in *Aspects of Archaeology in Britain and Beyond*, W.F. Grimes (ed.) (London, 1951), pp. 332–44

—— (2) 'The Will of Q. Veranius', *Classical Review* 1 (1951), pp. 4–7

Syme R. *Tacitus* (Oxford, 1958)

Thomas C. *Christianity in Roman Britain to AD 500* (London, 1981)

Thompson E.A. (1) 'Britain AD 406–10', *Britannia* 8 (1977), pp. 303–18

—— (2) 'Gildas and the History of Britain', *Britannia* 10 (1979), pp. 203–26

Tomlin R.S.O. (1) 'The Date of the "Barbarian Conspiracy"', *Britannia* 5 (1974), pp. 303–9

—— (2) 'Ammianus Marcellinus 26, 4.5–6', *Classical Quarterly* 29 (1979), pp. 470–8

—— (3) 'The Curse Tablets' in Cunliffe, B. *The Temple of Sulis Minerva at Bath, Volume 2, The Finds from the Sacred Spring* (Oxford, 1988)

—— (4) 'Vinisius to Nigra: Evidence from Oxford of Christianity in Roman Britain', *Zeitschrift für Papyrologie und Epigraphik* 100 (1994), pp. 93–108

Van Arsdell R.D. *Celtic Coinage of Britain* (London, 1989)

Vermaseren M.J. *Mithras, the Secret God* (London, 1963)

Wacher J. *The Towns of Roman Britain* (London, 1974)

Walters V.J. *The Cult of Mithras in the Roman Provinces of Gaul* (Leiden, 1974)

Ward J.H. (1) 'Vortigern and the End of Roman Britain', *Britannia* 3 (1972), pp. 277–89

—— (2) 'The British Sections of the Notitia Dignitatum: An Alternative Interpretation', *Britannia* 4 (1973), pp. 253–63

Webster G. 'The Lead-Mining Industry in North Wales in Roman Times', *Flintshire Historical Society* 13 (1952–3), pp. 5–33

Whittick G.C. 'The Earliest Roman Lead-Mining on Mendip and in North Wales: A Reappraisal', *Britannia* 13 (1982), pp. 113–23

Wilkes J.J. '*RIB* 1322: A Note', *Zeitschrift für Papyrologie und Epigraphik* 59 (1985), pp. 291–6

Wood I. 'The Fall of the Western Empire and the End of Roman Britain', *Britannia* 18 (1987), pp. 251–62

Wright R.P. 'Carpow and Caracalla', *Britannia* 5 (1974), pp. 289–92

Index of Literary Sources

Index of Inscriptions

General Index

Prominent figures are indexed under the names by which they are usually known, others under their gentile names.

Printed in the United Kingdom
by Lightning Source UK Ltd.
112538UKS00001B/64-90

Roman Britain

A sourcebook

Second edition

WITHDRAWN